"THE TRUTH, JACK. LET US HAVE IT BETWEEN US."

"Do you feel nothing at all when you see me?" Gwendolyn asked.

"I only wish I knew myself," he said, still gazing at her. "I tell myself it's simply your beauty—you are very beautiful, after all." He shrugged lightly and looked away. "Perhaps that's all it is."

"No," Gwendolyn said, "something so superficial would only make you smile and flirt, as other men do, as I'm sure you do when you meet an attractive female. And just as I do when I meet a handsome man. Do you believe in fate, my lord?"

Jack looked at her again, with an expression of consternation. "Miss Wells, I hope I misunderstand you."

Gwendolyn laughed. "I'm sure you do not. But if you have, let me make myself clear. I believe in fate. And you're mine."

Dell Books by Mary Spencer

Dark Wager

Lady's Wager

Mary Spencer

❧

Lady's Wager

A Dell Book

Published by
Dell Publishing
a division of
Bantam Doubleday Dell Publishing Group, Inc.
1540 Broadway
New York, New York 10036

ISBN: 0-440-22492-6

Printed in the United States of America

Published simultaneously in Canada

November 1998

10 9 8 7 6 5 4 3 2 1

OPM

When I first met June Perkins I was eaten alive with envy because she was beautiful, outgoing, and a genuinely warm and loving person. (Everything I wasn't!) Now, nearly thirteen years (and six babies, innumerable episodes of *All My Children,* and many trips to Taco Lita) later, I look at June and feel only admiration—because she is beautiful, outgoing, and a genuinely warm and loving person. I'm so very honored to call her my friend.

I've said it before, June, but it bears repeating: If there were only more people like you around, this world would be a far, far better place to live. To you this book is dedicated, with love and gratitude for so many years of fun and friendship. The next trip to Taco Lita is on me!

Prologue

*H*is search was almost over.

Jack Sommerton forced a measure of calm upon himself as his carriage progressed slowly down the dark and cobbled street. Leaning back against the cushioned seat, he gazed out the window and attempted to concentrate on the never-ceasing fall of rain. He'd waited so long to find the woman; he'd not let himself be overcome by nerves at this last moment. He had learned the benefit of patience in such matters as these.

Nineteen years, he thought ruefully. Nineteen long, frustrating years. He'd been ten when he'd first heard the rumors, although perhaps he'd already known, with a childish instinct, that everything was not as he'd been told. He'd been trying to discover the truth ever since. Now, at last, he was closing in upon it.

The carriage pulled to a stop before a dark, narrow alleyway that was swamped by sewage running in small rivers down the street. A footman jumped from his rooftop perch and held the door open, inviting his master into the night's wet misery. Jack pushed his pistol more securely beneath the folds of his greatcoat and pulled his hat firmly upon his head before alighting. Rain misted his face at once, but he had no care for it. A tall man moved toward him.

"M'lord."

"Victor," Jack replied. "I apologize for leaving you to wait so long in the rain. I was unable to get away before now. Are you certain this is the woman we're looking for?"

Victor nodded, causing water to run off the brim of his hat. "She's the one, m'lord. I can't say that she'll talk to ye. Doesn't want to, leastwise."

"I understand. Take me to her."

Victor turned and headed down the dark alleyway, and Jack followed behind, stopping only once to kick away a large rat that had scurried beneath his foot.

It wasn't far to the small, smoke-filled tavern. When they entered the crowded dwelling, all noise rapidly died away, and Jack found himself the object of every eye. It didn't disturb him. He was always stared at when he visited such places. Few members of the ton made their way into such filthy dens if they could avoid doing so. Jack had always rather enjoyed them. The thought distressed him no small end. It was proof, he had decided long ago, that his origins were vastly different from those all of society allowed they were.

A soft murmuring started after a few silent moments passed. He caught the whisper of his title—*Rexley*—on the lips of a few and again was not disturbed. He was well-known among these people, despite the fact that he'd never visited this particular hovel before. He was well-known in nearly all of London's darker, seedier districts.

"This way, m'lord." Victor nodded toward the dwelling's farthest corner. "I paid the keeper to make sure she stayed."

The crowd made room for Jack as he followed behind his minion, almost as if they didn't wish to so much as brush against his elegant evening clothes. He was used to this too, although it had not always been so. It had taken some few years to gain enough respect among such hardened citizens to keep from having his pockets skillfully picked and his finery molested by curious hands.

It was impossible to see more than a few feet through the dwelling's thick smoke, but as they neared the darkened corner the huddled figure became clearer. She was, he knew—if she was the right woman—only in her mid-forties, but she looked far older. Her hair was gray and stringy, her face wrinkled beyond her years, and her body thin and stooped. She was hunched beneath a woolen shawl bearing so many holes that it seemed unlikely to keep her warm. In her hands was a mug of ale, at which she was staring with lowered eyes.

"Annie?" Victor touched the woman's shoulder. " 'E's 'ere. T' Earl of Rexley. I've brought 'im, just as I said."

Slowly she looked up, her gaze traveling from the bottom of Jack's black, multicaped cloak until she reached his face. She stared at him for a wide-eyed moment, then attempted to rise out of her chair.

"Now, don't take fright," Victor said with rough reassurance, pressing her back down. " 'E ain't goin' to 'arm ye."

"Indeed not," Jack said gently. "I only wish to speak with you, Annie. May I sit?" He nodded toward a nearby chair.

Looking as frightened as a trapped rabbit, she made a silent motion of assent, and Jack pulled the chair near and sat down in it.

"You've nothing to fear," Jack assured her. "I merely seek information that I believe you possess. Your name is Annie Grey, is it not?"

She gave a curt, nervous nod.

"And you assisted a midwife by the name of Margaret Bidwell some years ago?"

"Old Meggie," she whispered. "Aye."

"Did you assist her in a particular birth twenty-nine years ago when a young prostitute named Lara came to her for help?"

"I—I don't 'member. Can't think that far back."

"I realize you were but a girl at the time," Jack said carefully, "but I would appreciate it if you would try to recall whatever you can. It would have been in the month of October. Lara had been new to the area and worked the streets for only a few months before giving birth to the child. She died shortly thereafter, and no one knew where she had come from or who her people were."

"Oh," the woman's dark eyes lit with remembrance, "I do 'member such a gel. Pretty and young, wi' fine manners. She weren't like t' other 'ores. Nice gel, she was." She was shaking her head. "Shouldn't've been on the streets, that one. Never said much to anyone. Kept to 'erself. Popular wiv the gents till she got too far along."

Jack sat forward slightly. "When her time came due, she sent for Old Meggie?"

"Oh, aye, they all did, them 'ores. Knew Old Meggie'd do right by 'em."

"And did you assist her in this particular birthing?"

She became thoughtful, lifting a dirty finger to her chin. "I can't 'member . . . seems like . . . seems like I did. I 'member the baby. A fine boy, as pretty a baby as ever I seen. Didn't cry 'ardly atall, 'nd took to 'is mama real 'ungry like, though she was near too weak t' feed 'im. She was . . . dark-'aired, I 'member, but that baby was fair as the day."

Jack's heart was pounding furiously in his ears, and he drew in a slow, quiet breath. He had never been so close as this before. It almost seemed impossible that he should be nearing the truth at last.

"How long was it before Lara died? Who took care of the baby?"

" 'Twas only a day or two afore she went. Never got out of 'er bed again after the babe was born. Knew she was goin', she did, 'nd 'eld on to that child long as she could, cryin' awful 'ard when Mrs. Toby took 'im away."

"Mrs. Toby?"

The woman nodded. "She ran the boardin'ouse where most of them 'ores lived."

"Where was it? The boardinghouse?"

She smiled, showing gaps of teeth. "Oh, y' won't find it now. Burnt to the ground years ago."

"What did Mrs. Toby do with Lara's baby?"

"Kept 'im till a fine gent came 'nd took 'im away. 'Twas 'is pa, I s'pose. They was both fair alike."

Jack's throat tightened with a familiar pain. "The fair gentleman. Did you see him? His face? Or hear his name? Did he . . . perhaps look somewhat like me?"

Her eyes widened again and she stared him full in the face. "I didn't see 'im close like, m'lord. Say," she said with a measure of wariness, "y' wasn't that baby, was ye?" Her gaze moved over his fine clothing, from top to toe and back up to his face again. "But ye couldn't be. Ye wouldn't *want* to be."

"His name," Jack pressed. "I'll pay you well if you can but remember."

She shook her head. "I only just saw 'im from a window, m'lord. 'E came in 'is fine carriage, just afore Lara died, 'nd then took that pretty baby away wiv 'im when she'd passed on."

"Was there a crest on the carriage? Anything at all that you can remember?"

"No, m'lord. Old Annie couldn't think back that well if y' gave me the 'ole royal treasure. Mrs. Toby, now, she might be able to tell ye."

"She's still alive?" Jack asked with disbelief.

"Oh, aye. Well 'nd alive, but in a bad sort o' business nowadays, or so I 'ears." She shook her head and frowned. "Ye'd do better to stay clear of 'er, m'lord. She was t' keep quiet 'bout that baby. We all of us tried to get 'er to tell us 'oo that fine gent was, but 'er mouth was closed tight. She'd signed a paper, y' see, right and proper, 'nd couldn't go against it. But she might tell ye now, if ye was to pay 'er well enough."

Disappointment surged through him, hot and sharp. So close. He was so close. And yet as far away as ever.

"Do you know where Mrs. Toby might be found, Annie?"

She was thoughtful again.

"Queen's Crossing," she said at last. "That's what I 'ear, best as I can 'member. Surely Victor 'ere could find out fer ye."

"Thank you, Annie." Jack pulled a small leather pouch from beneath his greatcoat and pushed it into one of her hands. "I should like to repay you beyond this small measure," he said. "I have an estate in Somerset with several small cottages. You may have one of them for your own, if you wish, and comfort for the remainder of your life. I should be glad to make certain of that in exchange for the great service you have done me this night."

A stain of color crept across the wrinkled cheeks, and she grinned up at him. "Oh, no, m'lord. 'Tain't needful that ye should do such as that for me. I've 'eard of ye and 'ow ye take folks in, 'specially 'ores 'nd the like. But I'm 'appy as I am, m'lord, 'nd wouldn't like it nowhere else. I do thank ye for the offer."

"I'm the one who is thankful," he told her. "And will continue to be so. You know how to get in touch with me if you should ever need me, Annie. Only send word through Victor, and I'll come.'' He leaned over and squeezed her hand briefly, then turned to leave.

"M'lord.'' She stopped him. He turned. The purse, he saw, was clutched tightly in her fingers. "Y' was a fine baby, m'lord. Finest I ever saw. Yer mama cried 'er 'eart out when she 'ad to let go of ye, it grieved 'er that much.''

He stared at her for a long moment.

"Thank you, Annie,'' he murmured at last. "Thank you.''

He left as he had come, walking slowly out of the silent tavern and into the chilling rain, letting the darkness swallow him.

Chapter One

The storm had been raging for only three days, but to Gwendolyn Wells it seemed far longer.

"It should have been christened something altogether different," she muttered as she slowly trod up the stairs from the *Fair Weather*'s lower decks toward the cabin she shared with her father. "The *Heaving Multitudes* would be far more appropriate." A large swell stopped her progress momentarily. Gwendolyn leaned against the passageway until the wooden boards beneath her feet regained a less daunting slope, then she continued on her way until she reached the cabin door.

In one hand she carried a bucket, which she set down the moment she crossed the cabin threshold. In the other she carried several wet cloths.

"There's my angel of mercy," said Professor Wells, glancing up from the table at which he worked with imperturbable ease. "How are our fellow passengers faring, my dear?"

Gwendolyn wiped her heated face with one of the rags and then threw it with the rest of them into the bucket. "Mrs. Blaylock has given me permission to toss her overboard and put her out of misery, and Mrs. Geoffrey has promised to put me in her will if I'll send her in afterward."

Professor Wells's eyebrows rose. "My, my. I had no idea that doing one's Christian duty could be so profitable. Will you need help hefting them over your shoulder?"

Ignoring this, Gwendolyn crossed the small cabin and collapsed into a chair. "Mrs. Sutcliff is going to give birth any day now, I fear, and she's already so very weak. I do wish Doctor Hallam weren't ill. You'd think a ship's doctor would have a constitution as stout as Uncle Hadley's side-yard whiskey."

"What with the captain being so likewise affected," Professor Wells commented, "I shouldn't think Doctor Hallam has anything to be ashamed of. It does seem rather strange that the crew of a ship should be so indisposed to bad weather. Oh, and speaking of the crew, Mr. Hanbury stopped by earlier to ask after you. Sopping wet, he was— from climbing the rigging, I imagine—and a fortunate thing it was too, else I'd have had to invite him in." He sighed. "I fear he's fallen beneath your spell, dear. As have most of the rest of the crew. I was rather relieved when Captain Joseph became ill, else I believe I should have had the distinct displeasure of receiving his offer."

"Poor Papa," Gwendolyn said with a weary smile. "I know how vexing it is for you."

"I shouldn't have minded if it had been only one or two requests for your hand, my dear, but it began to grow rather wearisome after the first dozen. I do wish you'd make an effort to discourage some of these gentlemen, Gwennie. Or at least accept one of them."

"I will," she said reassuringly. "When I've found the right one. I'll say yes even if he hasn't asked me anything."

"But, my dear, you've already had half the men in Boston throwing themselves at your feet. My head aches just thinking of all those fellows who insisted upon seeing us off on our voyage. What a morose lot they were, begging you not to go. I very nearly lost my breakfast. I'm beginning to think the man doesn't exist who you'll have."

Gwendolyn closed her eyes and wished she might take a short nap. But she'd promised Mrs. Sutcliff that she would return within the hour. If she could but keep the younger woman calm, the birth of the child might possibly be delayed long enough for this storm to finally pass and for Mrs. Sutcliff to regain some of her strength.

"He exists, Papa, and I shall know him at once, just as I've told you many times before."

"Ah, yes. You'll simply look into his eyes and know."

She ignored the slightly sarcastic tone of her father's voice. Her beliefs about how she would find her future mate *did* sound rather foolish, and yet Gwendolyn knew it would be just as she said. She would recognize her man at once when she finally met him. It would happen as immediately as she recognized every man who *wasn't* the right one.

"It won't take more than a moment and I'll be sure. And there will be much more to it than simply gazing into his eyes. Perhaps I shall also have to hear his voice."

"I see," said Professor Wells. "And when do you think you might happen upon this gentleman? Sometime in the near future, may I dare to hope? You are nearing your twenty-fourth birthday, after all, Gwennie, and not growing any younger."

"Oh, Papa," she said, yawning, "I don't know. I only know that he exists and that I shall have to continue to search him out until I've found him."

"Well, when you do at last run this fellow down to earth, dear, I hope you'll let me know at once. I shall be exceedingly relieved."

She laughed. "You'll be the very first to know, Papa.

I'll simply point him out and say, 'Him.' And that will be that.''

"It will, will it?'' the professor said skeptically. "Somehow I rather doubt it. Nothing with you has ever been so simple, Gwennie, my love. And in the meantime I must necessarily continue turning away the droves of admirers you apparently can't cease drawing.''

Still keeping her eyes closed, she smiled. "I shall do everything in my power to discourage the male population of England, I promise. But perhaps it won't be necessary. Cousin Lad says I haven't anything to worry about, as most of the worthy gentlemen in England don't wish to have much to do with Americans. Except for Lord Severn, of course. Lad said in his last letter that the viscount can barely contain his eagerness to make your acquaintance.''

"Ah, yes, Viscount Severn,'' the professor said. "I'm quite looking forward to chatting with a fellow chemist again, especially after such a tedious voyage. And I've heard remarkable things about that young man. I'm terribly pleased Lad was able to arrange a meeting.''

"As is Lord Severn. Lad wrote that the man nearly fainted at the idea of being introduced to you. Your fame has preceded you all the way to Europe, Papa. Even the Royal Academy is anxious to have you lecture.'' She opened her eyes and smiled at him. "I'm very proud of you.''

Professor Wells flushed slightly, but maintained his resigned expression. "It's a great honor to be allowed to speak before the Academy. I only hope they'll not take umbrage at my being an American.''

"Pish! I know very well you don't give a care for any such foolish notions, despite what Lad says about British sentiment toward the United States. The war has been over for well over four years now.''

"But there are still hard feelings on both sides. Who is

that particular gentleman Lad keeps writing about? The one who dislikes Americans so much? He warned us to be prepared for a rather difficult case with the fellow if we should ever meet him. Do you recall?''

''Rexley,'' Gwendolyn said. ''The Earl of Rexley. His younger brother died during the war and he's hated Americans ever since. Lad says he's an insufferable snob and very aware of his consequence, but somehow they've become friends. I can scarce imagine it. Lad never used to abide such people. I do hope he hasn't changed overmuch since becoming the grand and glorious Earl of Kerlain. I remember how he hated leaving the States in order to claim his title. He swore he'd return before long, but now he seems ready to remain in England for the rest of his days.''

''That's what happens when a woman becomes involved,'' her father said practically. ''Lad fell in love and everything else changed. You'd do best to remember that before picking out your man, dearest.''

''Indeed,'' said Gwendolyn, ''I shall.''

Another swell nearly lifted both Gwendolyn and her father out of their chairs. Her father slammed his arms down on the papers he'd been working on just in time to keep them from sliding to the floor, and Gwendolyn gripped her chair with both hands.

A moment later, when the ship had subsided again, Gwendolyn laughed. ''It's really rather fun, once you become used to it. Rather like galloping a fine steed.''

''I shall make certain to remind you of that if we happen to sink,'' her father told her, and she laughed again.

Rising from her chair, she bent and kissed his whiskery cheek. ''I must leave you to your chemistry again, Papa, and return below. I promised Mrs. Sutcliff I'd be back shortly.''

''You mustn't weary yourself,'' he said, looking at her

closely. "Gwennie, when was the last time you had any sleep? You look terribly pale."

"I'm fine," she assured him, laying one of her hands over his and squeezing. "Perfectly fine, Papa. I don't want you worrying about anything. Certainly not about me."

He sighed. "I'm afraid that's impossible, my dear. I worry over you constantly."

"I know," she said with sympathy. "Especially because I haven't a husband to do so in your place. But I promise, Papa, that I shall do my best to find the man who may relieve the burden from your shoulders. And I shall behave myself perfectly in London. I give you my solemn vow, you'll have nothing at all to worry over."

Chapter Two

❧❧❧

"You seemed to like that quite well, my lord." The young woman giggled and pressed a little closer. "Didn't you, now?"

With a sigh of great contentment, Jack curled an arm about the girl's ample waist and then closed his eyes.

"Wonderful, Georgie. As always." He yawned, feeling blissfully relaxed and comfortable. "Absolutely wonderful."

"I know what you'll like now," Georgie whispered near his ear, and Jack smiled.

"You're going to kill me, sweetheart. I've got to rest a bit."

"Oh, not for what I've got in mind." Her lips and tongue tickled the skin beneath his ear, while one of her clever hands sneaked beneath the blankets, stroking his thigh. "You just lie there and let Georgie take good care of you."

Jack willingly let her have her way, feeling his exhausted body miraculously coming back to life. Georgie was a delightful girl. One of his favorites, although he had many. He couldn't imagine anything more pleasant than lying in her comfortable bed and letting her take advantage of him.

"Georgie," he groaned as her tousled red head disappeared beneath the blankets, following the path her hand had already traveled. "You lovely, wicked girl."

A loud knock fell on the door, and Jack groaned again, although this time with displeasure. Georgie abruptly sat up and the blankets slid down to the foot of the bed.

"What's that?" she asked in a frightened tone, staring at the door as if she expected a constable to come barging in.

Another loud knock.

"Go away!" Jack shouted. "I've paid for her for the rest of the afternoon."

A matronly voice answered from the other side of the door. "I'm sorry, m'lord," said Mrs. May, the madam of the house, "but there's a gentleman here asking for you. He's quite insistent."

"Damnation," Jack muttered under his breath. He stretched out a hand and patted Georgie's bare knee reassuringly. To Mrs. May he said, "Whoever he is, send him off. I don't wish to be disturbed by anyone. Is that quite clear?" He couldn't imagine any of his particular acquaintances tracking him down here, despite the fact that they knew he frequented the place. Wulf and Lucky certainly wouldn't do so, and Kerlain, to his knowledge, had never been known to frequent *any* such den of iniquity, unless there was some form of gambling to be had.

"He claims to be Viscount Severn, m'lord," said Mrs. May, beginning to sound rather desperate. "And, truth to tell, I'm afraid he may tear my house apart. My other girls are becoming quite nervous. He's a big brute, m'lord, and very insistent to see you. Please come and calm him, sir. I beg you."

"Gad." Jack sat up and began looking for his clothes. He'd kill Wulf for interrupting him. The lackwit. If he'd frightened a woman as formidable as Mrs. May, the idiot must have worked himself into one of his vaporish states.

Ten minutes later he opened the door to Mrs. May's private parlor and found his friend nervously pacing in a circle before the fire, nibbling on the nails of one hand. Jack could certainly understand why Mrs. May had been concerned for the safety of her home. Wulffrith Lane, Viscount Severn, was more like a massive mountain that had sprouted arms and legs than an ordinary man. Worse, he was composed mostly of solid muscle. If the fellow hadn't been possessed of an equally impressive brain, which nonetheless seemed incapable of thinking logically unless it was involved in the calculation of numbers or chemicals, he might have been England's most notorious fighter. But fighting was one of Wulf's weakest points. Not that he couldn't wreak havoc when he was in a rage, but he was always terribly messy about it. It was rarely necessary for him to put himself to such trouble, however. One look at Wulf was generally enough to frighten off the most troublesome pests.

"What the devil's the matter with you?" Jack demanded sharply. "Didn't you realize I was occupied?"

Wulf started at the sound of his voice, and his face filled with relief.

"Jack, thank God." He wrapped his meaty hands together as if he'd start pleading. "Thank God. I've been looking for you everywhere. I don't know what I would have done if I hadn't found you."

"What have you done now?" Jack asked, well used to clearing up the difficulties Wulf got himself into. Those who were exceedingly brilliant, Jack had discovered, were often as helpless as babes when it came to living among more-normal persons.

"Nothing, I swear it!" Wulf said earnestly, wringing his hands. "But you've got to help me, Jack. Kerlain's taken ill. He's . . . he's *bedridden*."

Jack stared at him. "You came to Mrs. May's house

and interrupted my afternoon to tell me that Kerlain is *ill*? Wulf''—he sighed and rubbed at an ache that was developing between his eyes—"Kerlain had better be on his *deathbed*, or I vow I'll have you committed to an asylum.''

"But you don't understand," Wulf said miserably. "I would have gone to Lucky if he'd been in Town, but he ain't, and you're the only one who can help. It's Professor Wells. *Professor Wells*, Jack. His ship is arriving today. This very afternoon. And Kerlain ain't going to be able to meet him.''

"Ah," Jack said with understanding. "Professor Wells.'' Wulf had talked of little else for the past four months, ever since Kerlain had announced that he'd arranged for the famous chemist to travel to London for a visit with the Royal Society. Wulf worshiped Professor Wells almost as much as he did his mentor, Viscount Hemstead. "I see. But what does that have to do with me?''

"Well, I . . . Jack, I need you to meet him with me and help to get him and his daughter settled over at the Clarendon, since Kerlain can't do it. There ain't anyone else. Lucky's out at Pearwood, I told you.''

Jack knew it wouldn't do any good to suggest that Wulf might attempt to meet Wells and his daughter by himself. With Wulf's typical bumbling, they'd never make it out of the docks. Not that Jack particularly cared. After all, Wells and his daughter were Americans. He would have preferred it altogether if they'd never made the journey to England in the first place.

"What about Hemstead?" he suggested. "Surely he'd be the better choice.''

Misery creased Wulf's craggy face. His shaggy black hair waved back and forth as he shook his head. "He's right in the middle of a hydrogen experiment. I begged him to come, but he couldn't leave off at just this moment. You know how important sequence and timing are in chemistry.''

Jack didn't know and didn't particularly care. He sighed again. Loudly.

''What about Robby then? He'd do it. And only think what an impression it would make on Professor Wells and his chit to have the Earl of Manning welcome them to England's fair shores.''

Wulf groaned. ''He and Lady Manning are out at Pearwood with Lucky, seeing the new baby. Won't be home for another two days.''

''By gad, that's right,'' Jack muttered, surprised that he hadn't remembered. He usually kept good track of the Earl of Manning's whereabouts.

''Then I suppose it must be me,'' Jack said, resigned to his fate.

''Thank you,'' Wulf said with open relief. ''Thank you, Jack. You're the best friend a man could ever have.''

''Yes,'' said Jack dryly. ''I only hope you remember that next time I require a favor of you. And Kerlain had best be truly ill. If this is one of his games—''

''It's not,'' Wulf vowed earnestly. ''I promise, he's sick as can be. Saw him with my own eyes. Never saw a fellow so poorly before, and it ain't even from drink.''

''Kerlain has gulled you before, my friend,'' Jack told him, casting a longing glance toward the ceiling, above which Georgie waited for his return. ''Come along, then. I'd best get you out of here before either your fiancée or your mistress discovers that you were in Mrs. May's house in the middle of the day. Bella would have your head, and Yvette would make you a bullock. I don't suppose you thought to bring your carriage? No? Then we'll have to return to Brannard to fetch mine.''

* * *

The *Fair Weather* docked in London on the very day it was supposed to, which, given the storm it had weathered mid-Atlantic, was nothing short of miraculous.

"I hope Lad hasn't been waiting long," Gwendolyn remarked as she tied her bonnet more securely beneath her chin. "Although it appears to be a pleasant day, at least. I had rather expected rain, from what we've heard of London."

"I only hope the boy is here," Professor Wells said from where he was carefully tucking away the notes he'd been making on his latest study. "I shouldn't like to have to traverse London's unfamiliar streets without aid."

"Never fear, Papa. Your sense of direction may be dismal, but I'll not let any harm come to you. Do you think this outfit suitable? I don't want to embarrass Lad if the fashions in the States differ too greatly from those in England."

"My dear," said her father, glancing at her, "it won't matter in the least. You'll drive every man who sees you straight to insanity regardless, and that is what Lad will find disconcerting. It's been six years or longer since the boy last saw you. I doubt he'll be prepared for the change."

"Papa, how you exaggerate," Gwendolyn told him, suppressing a sigh. He made her sound like Helen of Troy, or, worse, Medusa. She knew very well that her looks were pleasing, but she was far from being a spellbinding enchantress. Her mirror showed that very plainly. Reddish-gold hair, blue eyes, and a face that seemed perfectly ordinary. If men found something in all that to make themselves behave as fools, there was little she could do to stop them.

"I only wish I were," said the professor. "Are you ready, dear? The other passengers are already disembarking."

"In a moment," Gwendolyn said. "I've only this last trunk to finish packing. You go ahead and find Lad, Papa. I'll join you shortly."

"Very well." He picked up the bag that contained his precious notes. "I'll send one of the men down to collect the trunk. Don't keep us waiting, Gwennie."

She applied herself dutifully to her task the moment her father left the cabin, stopping only once or twice to make certain she hadn't forgotten anything and, more importantly, that her father hadn't left behind any of his scribblings. Nothing could prove more upsetting to any scientist, Gwendolyn knew, than losing such seemingly insignificant scraps.

She had just finished going through the drawers of the small desk her father had used during their journey when a brief knock fell on the door.

"Come in," she called out, and Mr. Hanbury's handsome, rugged face appeared around the door.

"Miss Wells, I hope I haven't intruded?"

"No, of course not," she assured him cheerfully, bending to look under the desk. "My trunk is ready now. I'm terribly sorry for the delay. It's one of my greatest failings, I fear. Being late."

"I can't imagine you having any faults, Miss Wells," he said, and she thought he sounded rather odd.

"Then your imagination has failed you, kind sir. Papa says I'll drive him to an early grave and then be late attending the funeral." She laughed, finally straightening. "Which is probably true enough, given that I—" The words died away as she caught sight of his expression. It was one with which she was quite familiar, and she gave a silent, inward groan. "Mr. Hanbury," she began, but he was already moving toward her.

"Miss Wells, please let me speak," he said in an earnest tone that made her heart sink. She wished, fully, that she hadn't sent Papa away. "I've tried to stop the feelings that have been growing for you in my heart—"

Oh, dear, she thought. It was worse than she'd imagined. She already felt like laughing.

"—but it's impossible. I realize I'm merely a first mate on the ship and that you could have any man you wished for, but if there's any chance at all that you might consider my suit, I should be the happiest man on God's earth."

She had to bite the inside of her lip, harshly, before she could speak in an even tone.

"Mr. Hanbury, you're very kind," she said as gently as she could, "and you've been so good to both my father and me during the voyage, but I'm afraid that I can't—"

"Oh, I realize that!" he said, moving so quickly that she couldn't avoid him before he took hold of her hands. "I know of the difficulties in a match for us. Your father, for one, and the difference in our social standings. But where there is love, nothing is impossible." He kissed her hands fervently.

"Mr. Hanbury! Please don't!"

Her attempts to free herself only succeeded in inflaming him further. The next thing Gwendolyn knew, she was wrapped tightly in the man's arms.

"I love you!" he declared hotly, crushing the breath out of her. "If you but say the word, I'll battle any foe to keep you!"

"Mr. Hanbury, the only word I wish to say is *no*! Please release me at once!"

He didn't seem to hear her.

"No man could ever love you as dearly as I do, Miss Wells," he vowed. "I shall cherish you forever, and even longer."

"If you don't kill me with mindless drivel first," she managed, gasping for air. "Mr. Hanbury, I beg you. Let me go!"

He appeared disinclined to do so and began to drop heavy, passionate kisses on the side of her face, loosening her bonnet and sickening her even further. Gwendolyn remained calm, however. She'd been in such unfortunate situations before and knew of any number of effective methods for handling them. She had just made a small, tight fist and pulled her arm back in order to put one of them to use when she heard someone speak in a distinct, clipped British accent.

"I beg your pardon."

Mr. Hanbury froze and began to turn his head, and the next moment he was physically lifted off the floor. Relieved, Gwendolyn stepped back. She briefly saw a tall, muscular, fair-headed gentleman standing behind Mr. Hanbury, gripping him by the shirt and hefting him up as if he were nothing but a child.

"I believe the lady has made herself perfectly clear," the gentleman continued, ignoring Mr. Hanbury's inarticulate struggles. "She wishes to be left alone. You will be so good as to do so now and in the future."

"This is a . . . private matter!" Mr. Hanbury choked out, swinging an arm in a useless attempt to strike his captor. "Put me down!"

"It's not very pleasant when you're the one held hostage, is it?" the other man said, and lightly tossed Mr. Hanbury across the room, where he landed against a wall. "I would attempt to explain this matter to you more fully, sir, save that I'm loath to waste my time on an ignorant and savage cretin. Leave now, before I lose my temper."

Something in the man's tone must have convinced Mr. Hanbury to obey, for the first mate promptly stood, dusted himself off, made a swift bow to Gwendolyn, and left.

The blond gentleman waited until the door had closed before turning to face her. He was a shockingly beautiful man—the sort who could fill a woman with envy and admiration all at once. His hair was so fair it seemed tinged with white, a color against which his blue eyes stood out starkly. His face was aristocratic, finely boned, and yet thoroughly, undeniably masculine. His clothing, cut of the most elegant cloth and in the latest stare of fashion, covered a physique that was not only muscular and fit but also perfectly proportioned. He stared down at Gwendolyn from his superior height with a look of disdain, as if he was displeased by the mere sight of her.

Perhaps it was because she wasn't used to being frowned at by men, or perhaps it was the memory of what had just passed with Mr. Hanbury, but for some odd reason Gwendolyn met that cold, disapproving gaze head on and began to laugh. She couldn't stop. And the more she laughed, the funnier everything seemed. She doubled over with it, laughing as if she'd never cease, and at last sat down on the edge of her bed.

"Oh!" she said, giggling, wiping at tears that rolled down her cheeks. "Oh, forgive me. I shouldn't laugh at poor Mr. Hanbury. I'm s-sorry." She looked up at him, striving mightily to contain her mirth, and found that he was still frowning, more fiercely than ever. At the sight of it, she started to laugh again. "But d-didn't you hear him?" she asked. "The th-things he said!"

"I'm glad you found it so amusing," the gentleman said dryly.

" 'I'll b-battle any foe to k-keep you!' " she managed. " 'I shall cherish you forever, and even . . . *even l-longer!*' Oh!" She fell back on the bed. "Oh, my sides hurt!"

The handsome gentleman stood silently, gazing down at her until Gwendolyn at last began to calm. She grinned at him like a drunken idiot.

"Don't you find it the least bit amusing?" she asked.

No, Jack thought. He didn't find it amusing. Or her, for

that matter. There wasn't anything even remotely humorous about the situation. In fact, quite the opposite. He was not only unamused, he was utterly terrified.

She was the most beautiful woman he'd ever seen. If he'd attempted to conjure up such a female in his dreams, that fictional female still would have fallen short of the reality of this one. She lay before him, her bonnet come loose and her red-blond hair partly fallen out of its arrangement. Her dress was caught beneath her, pulling the fabric tight against her shapely figure, and she was gazing up at him with a smiling mouth that looked exceedingly kissable and sparkling blue eyes that looked fully inviting. It was almost more than any reasonable man could be expected to take. He wanted nothing more than to tear his clothing off and join her on the bed.

Jack had never been enslaved by women, except perhaps by those in the demimonde. But such fancy ladybirds were different. He loved them all in a general sense, never with any lasting or particular favoritism. Other women— the marriageable kind—had attempted for years to capture his heart, or at the very least his attention, and had always failed. Even the most beautiful and charming among them had done little more than garner his mild appreciation. But this woman—she frightened him to his very core. He had a fleeting notion that if she ever laughed at any love words he spoke to her as she was laughing at the fool who'd been here earlier, he'd want to throw himself in the Thames and never surface.

She sat up at last, still grinning like a silly child, and began to straighten her hair and bonnet.

"Dear me, I am sorry," she apologized once more. "How very foolish. And it truly is unkind of me to make fun of Mr. Hanbury. He appeared to be in earnest and I shouldn't wish to hurt his feelings, despite the unpleasantness of his declarations. Thank you for rescuing me." She stood and took a moment to smooth down her skirts before extending one gloved hand. "I'm Gwendolyn Wells."

Jack stared at her hand for a moment before accepting it in his own. She was dainty and feminine, even in the tiny bones of her fingers. He wanted to turn about and flee.

"I'm Rexley," he said, and watched her eyes widen with recognition.

"Rexley?" she repeated, and pulled her hand away. "The Earl of Rexley?"

"Yes." He felt distinctly uneasy. Kerlain must have written of him to his relatives in America, and he could only just imagine what had been said. He and Kerlain were friends, but a wariness yet existed between them. Kerlain disliked the English almost as much as Jack disliked Americans. "I'm sorry to inform you that the Earl of Kerlain has taken ill. I've come in his place to welcome you to England."

Concern filled her lovely features, and Jack felt an unwelcome urge to take hold of her hand again.

"Lad is ill? Is it serious?"

"Not at all. A mild complaint, merely. He'll most likely be well before a week is out. I should be honored to escort you and Professor Wells to your hotel in Kerlain's stead and see that you're settled."

"How very kind," she said with open gratitude, and Jack's heart began to ache again. She was a dangerous woman, this one. He would avoid her like the plague the moment he got her into the Clarendon. "My father went out ahead of me. . . ."

"Viscount Severn and I met him earlier. I left them on the dock and came in search of you. We had waited a quarter of an hour and became concerned."

"Was it that long? I do apologize. Of course I'm so glad that you came to look, else I might never have realized. But I'm sure I would have eventually. Realized, I mean."

"Realized?" he asked, bewildered.

"Yes" was all she said. The smile she gave him made his toes curl in his boots.

God almighty, he thought. A dangerous woman in every way. He had a strong urge to cross himself.

"It's such a relief to finally meet you," she said more softly. "After all this time. It seems as if it's been forever. I was beginning to think our paths would never cross."

"Pardon me?" What on earth was the woman talking about? For how long had Kerlain been writing to her about him? He'd only known the fellow for two years.

She sighed lightly. "Shouldn't we be going?"

He made arrangements for her trunk to be carried down to his waiting carriage, then escorted Miss Wells to the dock, where her father and Wulf were deeply involved in a discussion of physics. Wulf, when introduced to Miss Wells, didn't appear to be at all affected by the woman's uncommon beauty. But Jack wasn't overly surprised. Wulf wasn't like other men when it came to women. He was deeply in love with his fiancée, Bella, and, except for his mistress, didn't have the least interest in other females. Expressing his delight at the acquaintance, Wulf took Miss Wells's dainty hand in his enormous paw and vigorously shook until Jack told him to stop. The next moment he and Professor Wells went back to their discussion.

Jack reluctantly turned his attention to Miss Wells. "You must be weary from your long journey. We shall have you safely at your hotel as soon as possible." At his signal, the footman opened the carriage door, and Jack offered Miss Wells his hand to assist her climbing in.

Gwendolyn smiled at him and said, "Thank you, my lord. Would you allow me a private word with my father first, please? There's something important I must tell him.''

Lord Rexley's hand dropped and he nodded. "If you can take his attention away from science."

She was glad that he understood just how difficult a task that was. His own experiences with Lord Severn had probably taught him well.

She touched her father's sleeve and leaned closer to him.

"Papa," she whispered. "I promised you'd be the first to know. Him."

Even science couldn't hold him in the face of such a pronouncement. Professor Wells straightened and stared at his daughter.

"Him?"

"Yes." She nodded. "Him."

He looked past Lord Severn, who was blissfully still talking about physics, to where the Earl of Rexley was overseeing the loading of Gwendolyn's trunk. *"Him?"* he asked incredulously.

"Yes." Gwendolyn followed her father's gaze. "Him."

"But, my dear, you've only just met him. You've only just set foot in England. The man's done nothing but scowl at you."

"Nonetheless," she said. "Him."

Professor Wells knew better than to debate the issue with his daughter when her eyes held that particular gleam. She had clearly set her heart upon the Earl of Rexley, and if he was the man she wanted, she would have him.

"Very well," he said. "If you're quite certain."

"I'm certain," she said, gazing at the man in question as if he were the most magnificent creature on earth. "Quite, quite certain."

"But what if he doesn't want you, my dear?"

Her smile grew feline. "I shall make him."

"Gwennie," he said in a warning tone. "I don't want you doing anything untoward."

She looked at him with surprise. "Me, Papa? How could you think it?"

"Easily."

"I'll behave myself," she promised. "You'll have nothing to worry about. My lord?" she addressed Lord Rexley, who turned and frowned at her. "We're ready now." Holding out her hand, she let him help her into the carriage.

Chapter Three

⚶

He had attempted to sit opposite her in the coach, but somehow she ended up beside him while Wulf squashed his massive frame into a corner of the opposite seat in an effort to make enough room for Professor Wells. The two chemists continued their discussion—Jack gave up trying to understand what it was about—while Gwendolyn Wells leaned forward to look out her window. The movement tightened the cloth of her dress more closely about her breasts, and Jack was irritated with himself for not pulling his gaze away more quickly than he did.

"Such a lovely day," she said, speaking in a light but firm tone that she had clearly learned would carry over the intense chattering of scientific discourse. Jack had learned the same trick himself during his many years of acquaintance with Viscount Severn. Geniuses, he'd found, had an unfortunate tendency to forget the existence of other beings, who, if they didn't wish to be ignored, had to find ways of making themselves known. "We encountered the most awful storm while we were at sea." She turned back to him and smiled. "I was afraid London would be wet and miserable as well."

"I'm sure it will be," he replied dauntingly, having not the slightest wish to encourage a longer stay on the part of the Wellses. "Soon. March and April can be quite unpredictable."

"It's the same in the States, I'm afraid," she said with a sigh. "But, even so, Boston is usually lovely this time of year."

He didn't want to talk about the United States, where his only brother had died in a war that had been too senseless to believe. It had been as much the fault of Britain's politicians as anything else, but he found it impossible to forgive the former colonies or their citizens. David had died on that foreign ground, at the hands of an American, for a hopeless, fruitless cause.

"Then you'll wish to return to it soon," he remarked more bitingly than he'd wanted, and again felt aggravated. He'd been taught from his cradle how to behave well, even in unwanted situations. One attractive American female wasn't going to be the undoing of that. It might be easier, of course, if she wouldn't smile at him in such an engaging way. And if the scent of her perfume, light and floral, didn't tease the senses in such an arousing manner. It occurred to him briefly that he'd always thought Americans were an unwashed, uncouth lot. Obviously he'd been mistaken. Most women finished a long ocean voyage smelling of stale sweat and must. Gwendolyn Wells walked off a ship—after being confined upon it for more than a month—smelling like a bouquet of fresh lilies.

"I had thought so too," she agreed pleasantly, "but I can't really say now. Everything has changed."

"Changed?"

Her smile softened, and she leaned closer. Jack minutely pressed farther away. "Yes, of course," she said. "I don't expect you to understand, certainly. After all, we've only just met."

He stared at her with incomprehension, wondering if she might be slightly mad. She spared him the necessity of having to think up some reply by abruptly changing the subject.

"Do you stay in London most of the year, Lord Rexley? Or are you one of these aristocrats we hear of in the States who divides his time hither and yon? I do hope you'll remain in Town for the time being. I should so like the opportunity of getting to know you better. My father and I both, I should say."

For pity's sake! Jack thought. The brazen chit had been on English soil for only an hour and she was already flirting. With him, of all people. She was probably used to men falling at her feet with but the least bat of an eyelash, but if she thought he was the sort of man who'd readily fall for her ample charms, she would soon learn differently.

"Miss Wells," he began, prepared to deliver a cutting, albeit perfectly polite, rebuff.

She wouldn't let him finish.

"Oh, dear. I've misspoken already, haven't I? I can see it by the look on your face." Her grin was thoroughly unrepentant. "Lad warned me that the English aren't used to such forthright American speech, but I do hope you'll forgive me. A day such as this doesn't occur often. Once in a lifetime, really." She gave a happy sigh and sat back. "Tomorrow I'll behave with perfect respectability, I vow. Will you be so good as to take us to visit Lad, my lord, before installing us at our hotel? I should like to see him and make certain of his health."

Americans, Jack had long ago decided, were useless at making conventional polite discourse. He'd spent enough time with Kerlain to become used to a conversation traveling in several different directions in as many minutes.

"I think it might be best if we went directly to the Clarendon, Miss Wells," he told her, hoping she'd not argue the point. It was beyond hoping that she'd realize a young woman, even chaperoned by a parent, should not visit a gentleman's rooms. If Kerlain had had the decency to rent a suitable town house and hire attendant servants, it would be a wholly different matter. In fact, if that had been the case, Jack would have been escorting Professor Wells and his daughter to that fictional establishment rather than to a mere hotel. But Kerlain was notoriously tightfisted with the fortune he'd spent the past three years amassing, and he rented only three small, unremarkable rooms for himself and his lone manservant in a barely respectable part of town. It was well enough for his male friends to visit him there—Jack, himself, had spent several happy evenings in Kerlain's parlor getting pleasantly drunk and losing money—but quite another for a gently bred young female to do so. Certainly not if she wished to maintain her reputation. "I believe Lord Kerlain would wish you and Professor Wells to be made comfortable until he regains his health within a day or two. I would be glad to convey any message to him this afternoon, however, that you might wish to send."

"But surely we must go to him ourselves?" she protested, and reached across the swaying carriage to touch her father's knee. "Don't you agree, Papa? We must go to see Lad at once, mustn't we? Before the hotel? It's been so many years, I'm sure he'd be surprised if we were to delay our greetings."

Professor Wells blinked at her for an uncomprehending moment, clearly pulling his facile brain away from science. "Yes, of course, dear," he said. He looked at Jack. "I should like to see my nephew as soon as may be. Is it possible, Lord Rexley?"

Wulf's eyes widened in shock, and he looked fully embarrassed. "Oh, no, Professor. You don't want to go to Kerlain's lodgings. And you can't take Miss Wells there."

"Can I not?" Professor Wells appeared to be surprised

at this. "Surely it's allowed. He's my nephew, after all, and Gwendolyn's cousin."

"But it's not . . . it's just not *done*, sir," Wulf said, floundering. He looked to Jack for help.

"Such nonsense," said Miss Wells with a laugh. "If we can't go to visit our own relative—a sick man, at that—then we're doomed before we've even begun. Isn't that right, Papa?"

Jack silently concurred, but said instead, "I believe Lord Kerlain would prefer to put off your long-anticipated reunion another day or so, Professor, until he has regained his strength and can greet you in a more appropriate setting."

"Yes," Wulf agreed, nodding his dark, shaggy head. "Yes, that's right. It ain't fitting to take a young lady to such lodgings. Kerlain will want to do the thing proper at the Clarendon, when he's well."

"I have no care for what Lad's lodgings may be like," Miss Wells retorted, slanting an amused glance in Jack's direction. He had the feeling that she was used to getting her way. "And I'm sure Papa doesn't either. Take us to him, if you please, Lord Rexley."

"Jack," Wulf said in a worried tone, but the next moment Professor Wells took up their scientific discussion from where it had left off, and Wulf reluctantly gave his attention to it.

Jack held Gwendolyn Wells's gaze for a long, quiet moment, then leaned forward to tap on the roof of the carriage and give his coachman new directions. Sitting back, he saw that his female companion was purely pleased.

"Thank you," she murmured before turning her attention out the window once more.

Americans, he thought with a rueful shake of his head. If this was how Professor Wells and his daughter meant to go on, then London would be on its head before another month was out. She was certainly going to cause a sensation, no matter how oddly she behaved. He could envision the tides of men who would be swarming around her at balls and parties. But that was Kerlain's worry, not his.

The thought of Kerlain's reaction when his American relatives showed up so unexpectedly at his door made Jack smile. What an uncomfortable situation it would be. He could almost feel sorry for his scalawag friend. Almost. His smile widened. Perhaps it would be worth a little scandal to see the usually unflappable Earl of Kerlain caught in a bit of a tight spot. Especially if he wasn't truly ill, which Jack had good reason to believe was the case. Yes, indeed, he thought as he settled more comfortably against the cushioned seat. Perhaps a visit from his American relatives was just the cure that poor Kerlain needed, and Jack, despite his earlier misgivings, would be the friend to deliver it.

The Earl of Kerlain, however, proved to be a better actor—or liar, in Jack's opinion—than Jack had expected. He emerged from his private chamber in what was clearly a hastily donned bed jacket, looking for all the world as if he had dragged himself from his deathbed but had done so gladly for the chance to embrace his beloved relatives once more. It was masterfully done, Jack had to admit. If he hadn't known Kerlain quite so well, he might have fallen for the act himself. Everyone else present in the shabby parlor certainly did, except for Kerlain's dubious manservant, Lloyd, who looked upon the affecting spectacle with an expression set somewhere between exasperation and long-suffering.

Jack sat in a corner of the room, content to watch and listen as Miss Wells and her father fussed over their supposedly ailing relative, trying to convince him that a physician should be fetched at once. Kerlain's efforts to gently rebuff the suggestion only added to the facade of illness and succeeded in wrenching more pity than before from the others. Even Wulf, Lord bless his naive soul, was racked with concern. He hovered over Kerlain when he wasn't pacing about the room, emphatically agreeing with everything that Professor Wells and his daughter insisted upon to facilitate the earl's recovery. Kerlain took it all in like a glutton, feeding upon their concern while at the same time managing to allay their fears. From time to time he glanced at Jack with a twinkle of amusement, a master, as always, of his surroundings.

"You should be ashamed of yourself," Jack told him an hour later, having returned to the earl's lodgings after at last depositing Miss Wells and her father at their hotel. "I've never seen such an affecting performance in my life."

"Really?" Kerlain asked the question with a grin, gazing at his reflection in a mirror as he tied a freshly starched cravat about his neck. "Could I give Edmund Kean a run, do you think? And, more importantly, would there be any profit in it?" He made a tutting sound. "Come now, Rexley. I was truly ill. How can you doubt it?"

"Easily," Jack muttered.

Kerlain went on as if Jack hadn't spoken. "My amazing recovery has simply been sped by the arrival of my dear uncle and cousin." He glanced at his companion in the mirror. "The shock of how sweet little Gwennie's turned out must have done the trick. Quite a looker, wouldn't you say?"

"Gad," Jack muttered wearily. "And to think I once held you among the cleverest of my acquaintances. This is too shabby, even for you, Lad."

"Not that I expect you to come out and admit that any

American, even a female, is exceptional," Kerlain told him affably, "but she *is* stunning."

"And to pretend to being ill just to throw her in my path. Really, Lad." His tone made Jack's feelings on the subject clear. "You haven't suddenly begun to mistake me for Wulf, I pray?"

His cravat perfect, Kerlain at last turned and met Jack eye to eye. "She'll have London at her feet in a month," he predicted. "Less. Every man in Town will be her devoted slave."

"And he interrupted me, I'll have you know, at Mrs. May's," Jack told him tautly. "While I was fully occupied. I should wring your bloody American neck."

Kerlain waved the words away with a motion of his hand as he began searching through his closet for a coat. "You spend far too much time—and money—at that establishment. Wasting your life away in such a fruitless pursuit of pleasure when you should be looking to find yourself a suitable wife and set up your nursery. Did I tell you that Gwennie loves children? Dotes on them. Always has."

With a groan, Jack rubbed at the ache between his eyes. "Lad, you damned rogue. What have you wagered now? That I'd set sight on your cousin and wed her before the season is out? I vow, between you and Wulf I'll be driven mad. I do wish Lucky would come back to Town and keep the two of you in line."

Kerlain's smile was angelic. "Jack, for pity's sake, how can you believe I'd do such a thing? You've made it clear that you don't wish to be made a part of my wagering, and I've given you my word. I'm merely making polite conversation."

"About your cousin," Jack noted dryly.

"Mmmm, yes." Kerlain was momentarily distracted as he pulled on a silver waistcoat, fitting it about his muscular frame. It was a well-made garment, Jack noted, just as all of Kerlain's clothes were. The man might live like one of the genteel poor, but in every other respect he presented himself as the nobleman that he had become. Not that Kerlain wanted to dress in such finery. He complained constantly about what he considered to be British society's foolish devotion to fashion. At the same time he realized the importance of carefully following that same fashion if he wished to continue being invited into society's hallowed halls. "But we have to talk about something, don't we? It might as well be my beautiful cousin. And she is beautiful, regardless of how you may try to deny it."

"I don't deny it."

"Of course you don't. You'd be a liar if you did, and insulting, and then I'd have to challenge you to a duel, as British honor demands. In America I'd simply beat you senseless. She's stunningly lovely." Kerlain slipped one arm into an elegant, tight-fitting black coat, grimacing as if the task were distasteful. Jack watched with bemusement. He couldn't remember the last time he'd had to dress himself, what with his valet always about to do the chore. But Kerlain found the idea of spending money on a decent valet to be ridiculous, especially when he could dress himself. Lloyd, whom Jack was certain had formerly been employed as a common street thief, was no good at such things. Not that it mattered. Kerlain always managed to look perfectly presentable and was one of London's most sought-after guests. Women thronged around him as thickly as Jack suspected men would throng around Gwendolyn Wells. "Of course, she's better bred than I am," Kerlain said.

Jack uttered a laugh. "That's not hard to manage, I'm sure. Most of London's street sweepers are better bred than you are."

Kerlain grinned at him. "True enough. But I'm serious.

There's nothing shady on that side of the family. Her mother was from one of Boston's best clans. Ancient money, all that. You noticed her accent? Uncle Philip is from Tennessee, like all the best Americans, but Gwennie's all Boston.''

"I had noticed that she doesn't possess your ability to butcher the King's English," Jack said. "On the other hand, there is that rather flat, nasal sound. Why must you colonials always sound as if you're holding your noses when you speak?''

"It's something to set us apart from that aggravating noise you royalists over here make when you try to talk," Kerlain returned pleasantly. "Is it any wonder we wanted our independence? Did they seem pleased with the hotel? Gwennie and Uncle Philip? I appreciate you getting them settled.''

"You made damned sure I'd be the one to do so.'' He was as angry as ever. He hated being managed, especially by Kerlain, who managed anyone and everyone so damned easily. "It was a waste of time, both mine and yours. Your cousin, lovely though she may be, is safe from my attentions. You know it as well as I do, so why try to make the impossible happen? You only risk incurring my everlasting wrath and her humiliation. You can't need funds that badly. For all that you live like a pauper, I know very well you've made yourself more than wealthy off the fortunes of others in the past three years.''

Kerlain gave a slight shrug. "I haven't harmed anyone with my wagering, so far as I know. In fact, you must admit, I've played matchmaker to a great many successful unions thus far, Lucky's among them. If I've enjoyed some personal gain from my efforts, I fail to see what's wrong with that.''

"Damn you, Lad!'' Jack's fist slammed down on the

table between them. "I won't be a party in your gaming. *Won't* be. Understand it."

"Calm yourself, my friend." Kerlain moved to pour each of them a glass of wine. "I haven't wagered on your being wed to Gwennie. I give you my word of honor on that."

"Then why in God's name this spectacular ruse?" Jack demanded. "You purposefully threw her in my path."

"Or perhaps I threw you in hers," Kerlain murmured before sipping from his glass. "Come, take it." He held Jack's glass out until it was accepted. "It isn't poison, for pity's sake. I apologize for the trouble. I admit that I thought perhaps you and Gwennie might take to each other, but I've clearly been wrong. I often am when it comes to you." He offered the other man a smile. "But if you dislike the girl, you must certainly have nothing to do with her. I'll do what I must to keep her out of your way."

"Do that."

"I will." Kerlain lifted a hand. "Promise it. Well." He let out a breath. "First things first, I suppose. I must find Gwennie a maid, since she didn't think to bring one along on the voyage. Can't think why she didn't. Things are different in the States, but not *that* different. Quite a shock to have her showing up here at my lodgings, even with Uncle Philip along." He glanced at Jack. "That was your idea, I suppose?"

"Hardly." Jack shook his head. "I tried to dissuade the girl, but she insisted, and her father along with her. You'll certainly have your hands full if that's how she means to go on. But don't worry about the maid. I've already lent her a suitable one from my own staff. Lydia should already be installed at the Clarendon by now."

"Did you?" Kerlain arched an eyebrow. "That was good of you, Jack."

Jack drained his drink and set the glass down with finality. "Don't read any more into it than there is," he warned. "A simple kindness to a dim-witted female is all it was."

Kerlain chuckled. "You've always been a fool for women. They'll be your downfall. Heaven knows they've been mine." This last he finished with a sigh.

Jack shrugged. "She had to have a maid. I couldn't have a woman who looks like your cousin wandering about London all alone, wreaking havoc, could I?"

"Certainly not," said Kerlain. "I'm grateful to you for the service. Have you plans for the evening already? I'm off to Whitleby's for an early supper and some convivial company. Come and join us."

Jack eyed him with a measured look. "Whitleby, eh? Going to fleece him next, are you? Does your luck never run out, Kerlain?"

"Oh, yes," Kerlain replied. "Long ago, in fact, it ran out completely. But gambling doesn't have to do with luck. It's a cold-blooded sport comprised of wits rather than brawn. For me it's simply a means to an end."

"You're filthy rich," Jack said more softly, "yet you live like a pauper and gamble each night as if it were your last. Do you enjoy the sport that greatly?"

Kerlain's handsome features tightened into a rare, unhappy expression. "I despise gambling. You have no idea how much."

"Then why do it? You can't want for more funds than you already possess."

"I don't care about the money, no. But it must be had, and I must get it as I can. Gambling seems preferable to outright thievery, and about as safe as investing."

Jack shook his head. "One day I'll find out the mystery of you, Lad Walker. I swear it."

"I'm sorry to put you to the trouble, Jack. Truly. But I suppose it can't be helped. You're too curious for your own good, although it must have come in handy when you were spying for Wellington. But I'm not shaking in my boots yet. You've too many mysteries of your own to solve before you tackle any of mine, don't you? Perhaps I'll be the one to find you out first.'' He slanted a friendly, probing look at Jack. ''Tell me, have you heard from Lucky of late? I hear that Robby and Lady Manning have gone to Pearwood to look at the latest addition.''

''I've not had word from him in over a week.'' Jack didn't let himself react to the hidden meaning in Kerlain's words. Rumors had been flowing behind his back for too many years to bother him much now. There wasn't a member of the ton who hadn't either noticed or made sly mention of the strong resemblance between himself and the Earl of Manning. Kerlain had done it a number of times, but Jack accepted that as fair play. He'd certainly probed openly enough into Kerlain's secrets and odd behaviors. ''He and Clara are well, I'm sure, as is my godson and the newly arrived Miss Katharine. Lucky takes well to having children. Quite the contented family man, he is. I shouldn't be surprised if we didn't see them back in London for some time.''

''Mmmm,'' Kerlain intoned thoughtfully. ''I'm glad for him. He's a fortunate man in his good lady wife. He and Robby both. We should all find such happiness, eh?''

There had been a time when Jack never would have associated the word *happiness* with Lucien Bryland, who had been his closest friend since their days together at Oxford. Viscount Callan had been, before his marriage to Lady Clara Harkhams, filled with distrust for the fairer sex in general and for Lady Clara in particular. He'd been so certain that she would betray their marriage vows that he'd decided well before the wedding to put her away at his country estate after only six months of marriage. The Earl of Kerlain had wagered that at the end of six months,

Lucky would still be at his wife's side—and willingly so. It had been badly done, in Jack's opinion. He'd been furious at his friend for taking the wager so blindly, for sending Lady Clara's innocent name all over London as the object of such an ignoble bet. But, despite the troubles that had arisen, all had turned out well. Lucky and Clara had found a rare happiness together, and Kerlain had come away from the betting ten thousand pounds the richer. It had been the first such bet, but by no means the last. In the past two years Kerlain had played the dual roles of matchmaker and bettor to many of fashionable society's most notorious bachelors—and each time he'd come away the winner.

In Jack's opinion, Kerlain was a rogue and a con, no more, no less, who possessed the uncanny ability to twist his victims pliably to his most charming will, and despite the unlikely friendship that had sprung up between them, Jack didn't trust the American in the least. He refused to become Kerlain's next intended victim, even when presented with a woman so exactly beautiful and alluring as Miss Gwendolyn Wells.

"Join us tonight," Kerlain cajoled pleasantly. "Whitleby and his particulars are decent enough fellows, but I'd be glad to have a friend in my corner." He grinned. "To prop me up when the waters get choppy. Lend moral support, that sort of thing."

Jack couldn't hold back a bark of laughter. "I've known you for two years, Lad, and have yet to encounter one frailty that requires support of any kind. Gad, it's usually the other way 'round. Your victims come away from the gaming table scorched to the bone. No, I'll leave Whitleby and his companions to your gentle ministrations. I've more important tasks to attend to this night."

"Ah." Kerlain nodded knowingly. "More ramblings in and about London's rookeries, is it? You're either the bravest man I know or the stupidest. One of these dark nights you'll find yourself in more trouble than you can handle in those alleys you so love to haunt. What is it this time? Another whore in trouble? Or one of your precious spies to rescue? Or, perhaps, one of your mysteries to solve?''

Jack sighed. It was no use trying to feign ignorance with Kerlain. The man had his nose in everyone's business, private or otherwise.

"There is, as it happens, a young woman—"

"I knew it!"

"—who I wish to find before her master does. She's had a baby—"

"Oh, gad."

"—which he wants to sell before putting her back to work. I intend to make certain that doesn't happen. She's been on the run for two months, but I believe I've discovered her whereabouts at last."

Kerlain's handsome face grew taut with anger.

"Such charming people you know, Jack. Want any help?"

Jack smiled. "No. Not tonight. You need to stay alive to provide your cousin and uncle escort during their time in England. I shudder to think that such a responsibility might fall to my shoulders if anything should happen to you. Wulf would insist, you know. I'd appreciate it if you'd not mention my whereabouts to anyone who may ask."

"Of course not. I never do."

"Yes." Jack took up his gloves. "Thank you. I'll be on my way, then. Enjoy fleecing Whitleby."

"I shall." Kerlain moved to escort his guest to the door. "Perhaps I'll meet you in the park tomorrow morning? I fancy an early ride."

"Perhaps."

"Otherwise I can't say when we shall next meet. I'll be busy taking Gwennie and Uncle Philip about. Lady Jersey was so kind as to provide vouchers to Almack's. And then there are a number of invitations for the weeks to come. Balls, parties, dinners, musical evenings. It makes me weary just thinking of it. Surprising, really, how eager the ton is to entertain my relatives."

"I don't know why it should be." Jack set his hat upon his head and began to pull on his gloves. "Your uncle is a famous man, and Americans are generally interesting to put on display."

Kerlain laughed. "I suppose that's true. I shall have to warn Gwennie and Uncle Philip that they're about to be paraded about Town like rare animals from the zoo. Not that they'll care so very much. Gwennie's never given notice to the proprieties, and Uncle Philip is too distracted to mind."

"You'll have your hands full, just as I said," Jack told him. "But better you than me."

He left, and Kerlain stood by the door, listening as his manservant escorted the Earl of Rexley down the stairs and out to the street. Strolling to the window, he gazed to where his friend stood on the pavement, setting his hat more firmly about his head before climbing into his waiting carriage. In another moment the carriage was set into motion, ambling leisurely down the street.

"We shall see who has his hands full, my friend," Kerlain murmured as he watched it go. He smiled. "We shall see."

Chapter Four

❧

The day was beautiful, and the prospect of seeing London under blue and sunny skies too compelling to be denied. Gwendolyn, gazing out the window of the parlor that she shared with her father at the Clarendon, made her decision. "We shall go out," she stated, glancing at the young woman whom Lord Rexley had sent to serve as her maid.

Lydia, being a sensible, well-trained servant, gaped at her new mistress. It had been impressed upon her by Lord Rexley that Miss Wells was an American and therefore bound to be somewhat less civilized than a real lady, but even so she was shocked. "But, my lady," she said carefully, "would it not be best to wait until Professor Wells returns? I had understood he was to arrange for a proper carriage to convey you about Town."

"Carriage?" Gwendolyn smiled at the girl. "I only wish to take a short walk, my dear. We shall leave the shopping for tomorrow. Although I am eager to acquaint myself with the latest fashions—especially if we're to go out in society—today I only wish to have some idea of the city itself. Bond Street," she said decisively, clapping her hands together and sitting on the window seat. "That's not too far a distance, is it? We shall go there and decide which shops we shall attack on the morrow and have our battle plan quite ready. We always hear of the Bond Street fashions in America, but to actually be there . . . it almost seems impossible!''

Lydia returned her mistress's wide smile with an uncertain one of her own. If they only meant to walk, perhaps it would not be so unremarkable, although the accompaniment of a footman would lend the outing more decorum. As it was, Lydia was afraid they would draw a good deal of notice. Miss Wells was remarkably beautiful, and her wardrobe quite fine already. Dressed as she was, in a pretty day dress of blue and white, she was going to fetch attention, especially from men. Lydia wasn't certain that she was up to the demands of playing guardian to such a vivid and stunning lady, and she wished, heartily, that Lord Rexley had sent another maid in her stead.

''Shall I arrange with the hotel for a footman to attend us, miss?'' Lydia asked hopefully.

Gwendolyn met this suggestion with a laugh. ''I hardly think we need go to that extreme. We shall do very well on our own. Go and make yourself ready, Lydia, and then come back and help me with my hat and cloak. We'll spend an hour or two out-of-doors in this delightful weather and return with an appetite for our tea.''

Lydia seemed dubious about such prospects but dutifully left the room to do as she was bid. Gwendolyn, with a sigh, turned back to the window to look out at busy Piccadilly.

She was unhappy with herself, with her father and her cousin, and, most of all, with the Earl of Rexley. Her father's crimes were understandable, she supposed. He'd abandoned her that morning almost as soon as Viscount Severn had arrived with his proposal of a visit to Lord Hemstead, a chemist with whom her father had shared a long and enlightening correspondence and most especially wished to meet. Lad's sins were equally pardonable. He had arrived shortly after her father and Viscount Severn left, looking amazingly well for a man who'd been so ill the day before. He'd been in a great rush, explaining with profuse apologies that he must leave Town for a day or two in order to attend to important matters that had suddenly, unexpectedly, arisen. But he would be back as soon as he possibly could, he promised, in order to escort her about Town and to the various events to which she and her father had been invited. Gwendolyn had been stunned at the pile of elegant requests he had set before her. Parties? Balls? Dinners? Dances? Lad had seemingly accepted invitations for them to dozens of gatherings. And Almack's! She'd never dreamed that she would find herself crossing those hallowed assembly doors, but Lad had it all arranged. It was all very exciting, and yet, once Lad had taken his leave, Gwendolyn had settled down to the gloomy thought of having to spend the next few days alone, in her hotel room, with only Lydia for company.

And then there was the Earl of Rexley.

She'd lain awake the whole night long and told herself that it was impossible, after waiting so many years to find the man she could love, that she should have fallen for *him*. It couldn't he helped, she supposed, for she only had to think of his name to know that her heart had at last found its mate, but he was so . . . problematic. She'd never wanted to live in England. But would he, an earl, consider living in the United States? And he certainly didn't look anything like what she'd thought he would. She'd always imagined that the man for her would be dark-haired and dangerous-looking, perhaps bearing a scar or a wound from the war. She had never considered that he might, instead, look like the sort of fellow who's blue blood ran with centuries of aristocrats and nobility in it. But that, like the man himself, couldn't be changed. He was The One—she knew that as surely as she drew breath—and Gwendolyn resigned herself to the fact.

Now all that remained was the actual getting of him. That Lord Rexley had not yet recognized her as his perfect mate didn't particularly bother her. The truth would dawn on him eventually if she simply put herself in his way often enough. It was impossible that it wouldn't happen, and all that remained was for her to be patient. She was good at waiting. She'd waited for him, after all, for a great many years, and now that she'd found him she could wait a while longer.

"Are you certain you wish to go out, miss?" Lydia asked when she returned, bearing Gwendolyn's bonnet and cape. "It may become chilly in an hour or so."

Gwendolyn took the cape and set it about her shoulders. "If it does, we shall simply return to the hotel. But even if it is for a quarter of an hour, we'll go out. I'll be half-mad in a day or two from sitting indoors, which is something I never did in Boston, even in the worst weather. Be of good cheer, Lydia." She lifted the pretty beribboned bonnet from her maid's fingers and gave her a look of confidence. "We'll come to no mischief, I promise you. My father will kill me if we do."

But mischief, as Gwendolyn had discovered on numerous previous occasions, seemed determined to follow her regardless how she might try to evade it.

Bond Street was even more delightful than Gwendolyn had imagined it. Charming, bustling shops and a variety of businesses lined the street, and she took note of the lending libraries with special interest. It was a busy avenue, crowded with people of every kind, from fashionably dressed matrons in gleaming black carriages to young dandies who strutted like peacocks. Gwendolyn drew her usual amount of attention from the males she passed, but she ignored it as politely as possible and managed with deft and well-seasoned skill to ward off any man who attempted to catch her eye. Lydia, she could tell, was greatly relieved.

They made their way to Burlington Arcade, which Gwendolyn thought enchanting, and from there found their way back to Piccadilly. Gwendolyn knew that they were not far from Almack's, and she talked a hesitant Lydia into taking her there. She wanted just to see what the famous assembly looked like. Somehow she had expected that it would look like a grand theater but was severely disappointed to find that it was truly quite ordinary in appearance.

"Well," she said with a sigh, gazing at Almack's unprepossessing front, "I suppose we should return to the hotel. It will be time for tea shortly, and you must be growing famished." She smiled at Lydia. "I hope I've not worn your feet down to the bone, my dear."

"Oh, no, miss." Lydia made something of a curtsy. "You mustn't worry about me. It's my duty." This last she said somewhat confidentially, as if Gwendolyn, being an American, must have the services of a maid explained to her.

With a laugh, Gwendolyn started moving west toward a street that she hoped would lead them directly to their hotel. Behind her, Lydia gave a loud cough.

"Miss?"

Gwendolyn turned to find that her maid hadn't moved an inch.

"That's Saint James, miss." The girl nodded nervously toward the street ahead.

"Is it?" The name was familiar, although Gwendolyn couldn't quite remember why.

"Yes, miss."

Gwendolyn gazed at her expectantly, but Lydia obviously believed that this was all that needed to be said.

Gwendolyn turned to look at St. James.

"Does it not lead back to Piccadilly?"

"Oh, yes, miss, it does."

"And, unless I'm quite mistaken, the Clarendon should be nearly across from us once we reach the end of Saint James?"

"Yes, miss."

"Then let's be on our way."

Once again she started walking, and once again Lydia coughed, although this time with more desperate insistence.

"Miss!"

Gwendolyn patiently turned back to her.

"Yes, Lydia?"

Lydia looked fully despairing. Her hands were held tightly together in front of her bosom. "It's Saint James, miss," she repeated, wringing her hands in a pleading gesture. "Shouldn't we be going back this way? To Duke Street?" She looked hopefully back toward the street that they had earlier taken.

"It would only make for a longer walk," Gwendolyn said. "I can't see the sense in it. And I know your feet are sore, Lydia."

Lydia's gaze went past Gwendolyn to rest on Saint James ahead. "Not *that* sore, miss."

"Now you're being foolish," Gwendolyn chided. But an idea occurred to her. "Is there some law against walking on Saint James? Pedestrians aren't allowed?"

Lydia woefully shook her head. "No, miss. It isn't that. But Lord Rexley will be quite angry if he—"

"Lord Rexley," Gwendolyn interrupted, "hasn't anything to say in the matter. Come along, Lydia."

"Yes, miss." The maid sounded as if Gwendolyn were taking her to her own execution.

Moments later Gwendolyn suddenly remembered why

Saint James sounded so familiar. It was the street where so many famous men's clubs were located, and the remembrance filled her with delight.

"Why, how marvelous!" she declared, looking up and down the avenue and clasping her gloved hands together. "I've long wondered what these famous bow windows should look like. Boodles, and Brooks!" She glanced back at Lydia, who looked wretched. "Even in America we hear of them and of all the fine gentlemen who belong to such clubs. I shall be able to boast of seeing them to my friends. Now, which is White's? Point me in the direction, Lydia."

Obediently, Lydia pointed out the popular club and dutifully followed behind as Gwendolyn made her way.

"Here it is!" Gwendolyn stopped directly in front of the famous bow window where the elegant Mr. Brummel and Lord Alvanley had formed their exclusive "bow-window set." "Isn't it wonderful, Lydia?"

Lydia, in reply, groaned.

Gwendolyn stood admiring it for a full minute or more before noticing that there were several men standing on the other side of the window, admiring her in return. And not only admiring, but some of them openly leering. She blinked to make certain that she saw what she did—dozens of males crowding each other to have a look at her, all of them grinning openly and eyeing her with disturbing appreciation.

"Heavens," she murmured, realizing suddenly what she must look like standing on the pavement, looking so directly into a gentlemen's club. "One would think they'd never before seen a woman passing by."

To this, Lydia groaned again.

Gwendolyn, as a parting gesture, leveled her most cold-eyed stare at the men assembled in the window, but just when she would have walked away there was a great commotion inside the club. The men in front of the window were roughly jostled away, and a familiar face pushed to the fore. Gwendolyn, seeing him, smiled in spite of herself. And then, despite the furious expression on Lord Rexley's handsome face as he glared back at her, she lifted her hand and waved. Another man, as fair and handsome as Lord Rexley, had pushed his way through to stand beside him, and he smiled widely and laughed. He nodded at Gwendolyn, and she found herself smiling and nodding in turn. Lord Rexley's expression grew even more foreboding, and Gwendolyn blushed to see his lips moving just enough to utter what were clearly a few angry remarks.

"Perhaps, Lydia, we should leave," she said, realizing that retreat, at this point, was most assuredly the wisest course. "I should like very much to see what the rest of the street possesses."

She'd gotten scarcely a dozen steps away when she heard the doors to White's opening and Lord Rexley's booted feet closing in behind her.

"Miss Wells." He spoke curtly, with barely controlled anger. His footsteps, as he neared her, sounded purposeful and loud on the pavement. But Gwendolyn knew how to handle an irate man. She fixed a pleasant smile on her face before turning about and spoke in a tone that never failed to charm.

"Why, Lord Rexley. What a pleasant coincidence to meet you again so soon."

He had clearly left the club in haste: His hat was not yet on his head, and he was pulling his second glove forcefully onto his hand.

"Lydia," he addressed the maid, who stared at him wide-eyed, "I believe I told you to keep her out of trouble."

"I tried, my lord, but she—"

"Never mind. Miss Wells," he said, his blue eyes glittering at her in an unsettling manner, "you will do me the favor of taking my arm." It was not a request but a command. He shoved his hat on his head and stiffly held his elbow out at her. "I will escort you back to your hotel. *Now*, if you please."

Her smile fixed firmly in place, Gwendolyn remained calm. Her beloved was angry, for she'd somehow misstepped—already. That was plain enough. But she'd spent so many years managing the masculine sex that there was little left to bother her. Instead, she took in his appearance. He was a marvelous figure, dressed in tight-fitting buff pantaloons, an elegant waistcoat of gold-embroidered maroon, and a dark-blue coat. She found him wonderful to look at, even when he was irate.

"Dear me," she said. "I seem to have made mischief, and only one day in London. And after I promised Papa that I'd be good. I do apologize."

Lord Rexley's handsome countenance began to redden. He tilted his elbow toward her a bit further.

"Miss Wells," he began, the words sounding like a growl in his throat.

"May I ask what it is that I've done?" she asked innocently. "I fear I don't know. In the United States women are allowed to walk freely on the streets, albeit at their own risk. It comes of being a democratic society, you know."

"They are allowed the same freedoms here," he stated curtly. "But *not* on Saint James."

She looked about her. "No? I can't understand why. It seems to be a perfectly acceptable area of town."

"It is an area where ladies do not parade themselves unless they wish to be taken for something rather less refined." His meaning was clear.

Despite her every attempt to keep from doing so, Gwendolyn felt her eyes widening with surprise.

"Because there are so many gentlemen's clubs here? Why—I confess that I find such a stricture ridiculous. To be taken for a light-skirts simply because one walks—"

"Miss Wells!"

"It's true!" she insisted.

"Take my arm." He bit each word out. "Now."

She noted his tone and dutifully took his arm. She had never been so stiffly escorted in her life. Lydia fell into step behind them as Lord Rexley began leading Gwendolyn back in the direction of the Clarendon. As they neared White's, where the bow window was yet crowded with interested gazes, Lord Rexley muttered, "Don't look at them. Just keep walking."

"But, my lord, this is so perfectly ridicu—"

"I shall discuss the merits of a refined civilization with you later, Miss Wells. For now you'll do as I say."

She made a *hmphing* sound but did as she was bid. It wouldn't do to let him think her implacable.

"Hold there a moment, Jack."

Lord Rexley stopped just a few steps beyond the bow window. Gwendolyn glanced at him and saw the look of complete misery on his countenance.

"Oh, gad," he muttered.

She pressed his arm and he shook his head, as if the matter were hopeless. The next moment he was turning her about again.

"Robby," he said as the gentleman who'd stood beside him in the window strolled up to them. "This is hardly the time—"

"Nonsense, my boy. There never was a better one." He was a handsome man, Gwendolyn saw, and nearly a picture of Lord Rexley. Indeed, although he was somewhat older, they were so similar as to almost be two versions of the same man. "I believe I have the pleasure of greeting Miss Wells of America?" He smiled charmingly at Gwendolyn and possessed himself of her hand, bending over it in the grand, elegant style of an earlier era.

"Yes," Lord Rexley told him, in a tone that was as dire as if he were warning the other man of imminent danger. "Miss Wells, may I make known to you the Earl of Manning? My lord, this is Miss Wells."

Gwendolyn had expected to be introduced to one of Lord Rexley's relatives. His uncle, perhaps, or his father—even a much older brother. But the formality of the introduction told her that there was no relationship between the two men save that of friendship. Aside from that, Lad had written to her about Lord Manning, and what she did know about him was that he was one of the most powerful, influential men in England. That knowledge, combined with the amazing likeness between the two earls, set her off balance. She stammered, with little of her usual grace, "M-my lord," and managed a curtsy.

Lord Manning smiled at her and maintained his gentle grip on her hand.

"Miss Wells, how pleased I am to make your acquaintance. Lord Kerlain has told me so much of you. We've awaited the arrival of your father and yourself lo these many months. Tell me, how do you find London thus far?"

"*Robby,*" said Lord Rexley, his voice tight. He gestured toward White's bow-window, still crowded with avid onlookers.

"My dear boy, relax," the Earl of Manning admonished gently. "The more you object, the more they'll talk." He gave Lord Rexley a friendly, meaningful look, then deftly pulled Gwendolyn out of the other man's grasp and settled her on his own arm. "My godson is high-strung, I fear. A condition we must learn to bear and forgive.''

His godson? she thought. There might yet be some relation between them. A distant cousin, perhaps? It was not unheard of for older cousins to be named as godparents, and there must be some explanation for the striking resemblance between them.

''Indeed, my lord,'' she murmured.

Lord Manning was even more elegantly dressed than her beloved, and just as handsome; no small feat, that. With unequaled grace he moved her gently toward Piccadilly. ''I've had my carriage called for and would be delighted if you would consent to return to Manning House in order to meet Lady Manning and take tea with us. My wife has been as eager as I to make your acquaintance. Do say you'll come, I beg, despite the inexcusable suddenness of the invitation. My good lady wife will never forgive me if I don't bring you to meet her, after having been so fortunate myself. It would only take your father's presence, as well, to make our happiness complete.''

Gwendolyn was utterly charmed; she recognized a fellow master in the art of manipulation at once, and liked him.

''I should be honored, my lord. My father will be disappointed to have missed such a treat.''

''A matter we shall rectify as soon as may be!'' his lordship declared grandly. ''And that I promise. Oh, dear.'' His pleasant expression suddenly froze, and he pulled Gwendolyn to a stop. ''How unfortunate.''

Another gentleman was approaching them from the opposite direction, his footsteps slowing and his eyes narrowing at the sight of both Lord Manning and Lord Rexley. When his gaze came to rest upon Gwendolyn, however, his dark, handsome countenance filled with immediate admiration.

"Grand," Lord Rexley muttered. "Just what we need to top the day off properly."

"Behave yourself, Jack," Lord Manning murmured. "We can hardly ignore the man." He raised his voice in happy greeting as the newcomer drew closer. "Walsh! What a delightful coincidence. How does the day find you?"

He was somewhat shorter than both Lord Manning and the Earl of Rexley, but elegant in his dress and manner. He smiled pleasantly at Gwendolyn and touched the brim of his hat in salute to her.

"Manning," he replied without looking at him. "Rexley." This was said in a less friendly tone. "The day finds me well, I thank you." He kept smiling at Gwendolyn, clearly waiting for an introduction.

"If you're on your way to White's," Lord Rexley said, "don't let us stop you, Walsh."

"I'm sure there's no hurry," Lord Manning said, glancing briefly at his godson. "My lord, allow me to introduce to you Miss Gwendolyn Wells of the United States. Her father is the famous American chemist, Professor Philip Wells, who has traveled to England to lecture at the Royal Academy. Miss Wells, I make known to you Viscount Walsh."

"Miss Wells," Lord Walsh murmured, accepting the gloved hand she offered and lifting it to his lips. "I'm delighted."

Gwendolyn endured the foolishness of the moment, the look in his eyes and the overlong press of his lips against her fingers, just as she'd endured it hundreds of times before.

"Thank you, my lord. I'm likewise pleased to make your acquaintance."

"May it be hoped that you will grace our fair country with your beauty for any length of time?"

"Indeed it may," she replied, while beside her Lord Rexley made a choking sound. "My father intends to pursue a course of scientific experimentation in concert with the Academy for several months. Our plan is to remain throughout the summer."

"We are fortunate, then," Lord Walsh said. "I hope I may have the honor of seeing and speaking to you in the future. Often."

"Ah, here's my carriage, at last," Lord Manning said brightly. "We must be on our way, Walsh. Good day to you."

"Good day, Manning," Lord Walsh replied, then murmured caressingly, "and to you, Miss Wells." He turned last to Lord Rexley, who gave him such an unpleasant look that he said nothing. The two men held unsmiling gazes for a tense moment, and then Lord Walsh bowed to Gwendolyn and continued on his way.

Gwendolyn found herself being handed into an elegant, open barouche. Lydia demurely took the place beside her. Lord Manning, standing on the pavement beside a mulish Lord Rexley, motioned the other man toward the carriage. "In with you, Jack," he said in an affable but definite tone.

Lord Rexley didn't move but stood glaring after Lord Walsh's retreating figure. Lord Manning, with great patience, prodded him again. "Jack."

Lord Rexley finally put his foot upon the step and lifted himself into the seat. As he settled himself he looked at Gwendolyn and stated, simply, "Stay away from Walsh."

"Jack, Jack," Lord Manning chided, taking his own seat. "You'll be frightening the poor girl."

"He seemed a nice gentleman," Gwendolyn said as the carriage started into motion, "although he reminded me somewhat of Mr. Hanbury." She looked at Lord Rexley.

"You remember him, I'm sure, my lord. And how witty he was with the turn of a phrase?"

A ghost of a smile crept across Lord Rexley's lips, and then he shook his head and sighed. "Yes. But Walsh isn't Mr. Hanbury, Miss Wells. You tell her, Robby."

The older man appeared to be distinctly uncomfortable at this request.

"I suppose it might be best to keep a distance from Lord Walsh if at all possible, Miss Wells. He's not a bad fellow, exactly, just . . . rather devious."

"Devious?"

"He's a crook," Lord Rexley stated, crossing his arms over his chest. "And a whoremonger. Makes all his money peddling flesh."

"Good God, Jack," Lord Manning uttered, shocked, "control that unruly tongue of yours. By gad, you're worse than Lucky. Miss Wells, I do apologize."

"There's no need, my lord," she assured him. "I'm not easily shocked, I promise you. The United States is possessed of the same vices that are to be had here in England, and Boston is no exception."

"I'm sure that's true, although a gentleman would never speak thus in a lady's presence." He glared pointedly at Lord Rexley, who looked away. "As to Lord Walsh, I'm sure you'll run into him from time to time, but it might be wisest to discourage his interest. Word has it he's looking for a wife, and I can't think your father would want that sort of fellow courting you."

Gwendolyn laughed. "My lord, how truly you speak. He doesn't want *any* fellows courting me."

"Smart man," Lord Rexley muttered, causing his god-father to scowl at him again.

Manning House was a magnificent place, clearly one of London's finer—and older—dwellings. When she complimented Lord Manning on it as he handed her down from the carriage, he gave her a smile of complete affection.

"My child, how very kind of you," he said warmly, handing Lydia down as well before turning to gaze at the tall and elegant building. "I must admit to being rather overfond of it. I'd be pleased to give you a tour of its finer aspects after tea, if you like, although I doubt Lady Manning will be willing to release you from her company." Setting her hand over his arm, he began to escort her to the door. Lord Rexley and Lydia followed behind. "My good lady has been feeling somewhat lacking in company of late, I fear. Ten months ago she was generous enough to present me with not one, but two fine sons. It was indeed a blessed event," he replied when she murmured delighted congratulations, "but she has been tied to the little beasts ever since."

"What he means to say," Lord Rexley explained as a footman opened the doors, "is that Lady Manning refuses to hand them over to their nurse."

"Quite understandable," Gwendolyn said approvingly.

"We did enjoy a recent visit to my nephew and his wife in the country, which my lady considered a high treat," Lord Manning said conversationally as he gave his hat and gloves to his butler. "We only returned this morning, by fortunate coincidence." The smile he gave Gwendolyn was beatific. "Else I'd not have had the pleasure of making your acquaintance this afternoon. Hemmet," he addressed the butler, "this is Miss Lydia, one of Lord Rexley's staff. Please take her to the kitchen and make certain that Cook takes good care of her." He extended his arm to Gwendolyn. "I'll escort Miss Wells and Lord Rexley up to the nursery."

It was somewhat novel to take tea in a nursery, but Gwendolyn found the experience to be delightful. Lady Manning, rising from where she had been seated on the floor playing with her young sons, greeted the intrusion with a wide smile and genuine pleasure.

"The boys are wonderful, of course," she said, having given the charge of one chubby blond infant to his father and the other to Lord Rexley, "but I do miss being able to get about Town and visit as I used to do. Not that my lord isn't very good to help me, but I daren't leave them alone with him too long, else there would be very little left of the furniture. He spoils them shamelessly and hasn't the heart to stop them from doing what they please."

"Unfair, my love," said his lordship, not seeming to mind that his son was chewing upon his previously perfect cravat, having first pulled it free of its intricate folds. "They've only just begun to walk and have done very little damage since, although I admit that it was a pity about the vase. But Faron couldn't have known it was Chinese and invaluable, could he?"

"Indeed not," said Lord Rexley, smiling at his young charge as he bounced him up and down to the response of ecstatic gurgles, "any more than Master Samuel could have known that a string of his mother's pearls can't be endlessly pulled at without breaking. Did you ever find them all, by the way?"

"You see what I mean?" Lady Manning said with a sigh. "I suppose I should let Nurse take care of them more, as she wishes to do, but somehow I can't bring myself to do so. Whenever I plan an outing they have this way of looking at me when I come to kiss them good-bye that makes me feel horribly guilty." She smiled at Gwendolyn. "But that's typical of men, isn't it? Whether they're young or old. We must simply accept it."

Gwendolyn couldn't suppress her laughter. "Wisely said. But they're such beautiful babies that I can't imagine you'd want to leave them for long. How very fortunate you are, ma'am."

Lady Manning gave her a look of affection. "Now, here is someone I like, my lord. And quite sensible too. You did very well in bringing her home to tea." She cast a grin at her husband. "I'm tempted to send you men off together—all of you—and keep Miss Wells to myself for an hour or so, or at least until she tires of hearing me brag about the children. I haven't even begun to tell you about my daughter Sarah yet, Miss Wells. She stayed behind at Pearwood to help my niece with the baby, else you would have already met her."

"I should be delighted to hear more about all of your children," Gwendolyn assured her.

"Heavens, I believe I shall keep you here forever!" Lady Manning declared with a laugh, leading Gwendolyn toward a group of chairs that had clearly been added to the nursery for the use of adults.

The hour that passed was exceedingly pleasant. Lord and Lady Manning, Gwendolyn discovered, weren't at all like the stuffy aristocracy she had on occasion met in the United States and which she had equally dreaded meeting in England. They were warm and open and didn't seem to mind in the least when she stepped wrong during their conversation, as Gwendolyn was afraid she did rather often. Lord Rexley, who had taken his seat with the child yet in his arms, was another matter. He seemed not to want to look at her—whenever she glanced at him his gaze dropped to the angelic toddler who'd fallen asleep in his arms or even to some distant piece of furniture, rather than on herself—but always the focus of his eyes ended upon her, willingly or not. She found it difficult, too, to keep from gazing at him every spare moment. And to see him with a blond, blue-eyed child who bore such a marked resemblance to him only made matters worse. She couldn't help but think that one day he would hold their own child in his arms thus and would look just as he did at that moment.

She felt as if she were surrounded by blond, angelic beings. A whole family of them. Lady Manning was as fair as her husband and children and utterly beautiful as well as charming. Before their hour together was done she had insisted that Gwendolyn call her Anna and that they plan a day of shopping together soon to hunt for the latest fashions.

"For if I don't snatch a few hours to tend to the matter, I'll not only become crazed from being with the children all day, but I shall also look a dowd, and that is a combination too awful to contemplate."

"As if you could ever look such a thing," his lordship said gallantly, lifting his wife's hand to kiss it. Master Faron had long since fallen asleep, comfortably splayed across his father's expensively clothed, though somewhat drooled upon, chest. "In a sack you'd be stunning. But I agree that you must have a day free of the children in order to buy whatever you wish and take Miss Wells about Town to lend her your excellent aid. She'll be as lost as in a fog without some idea of where to purchase the many articles women find so necessary."

Gwendolyn expressed her ardent agreement, and a day was agreed upon.

"I'd best return Miss Wells to her hotel," Lord Rexley said after this. "Professor Wells may have returned and will be wondering where his daughter is."

Lord Manning began to rise with his sleeping child in his arms. "Quite right, my boy," he said. "But as I'm the one who carried Miss Wells off, I shall do the returning."

"No," Lord Rexley stated in a definite manner, rising from his own chair to transfer the unsuspecting infant in his arms to his mother's care. "There's no need for you to do so, Robby, when I shall be more than glad to convey

Miss Wells while on my own way home. Lend me your carriage," he said, reaching down to take Gwendolyn's hand and pull her to her feet, "and I'll have it returned to you shortly."

Half an hour later Lord and Lady Manning stood by the nursery window. Having just put their children into their beds, they looked down at the pavement as Lord Rexley handed Miss Wells into the waiting carriage.

"Now, what do you make of that, my dear?" the earl asked his wife.

She slid a hand over the arm he held about her waist. "I think it quite amazing. And certainly more than time that Jack found a woman to interest him." Before he could make a fitting comment she added, "A *respectable* woman, I should have said. Heaven knows he's plenty of interest in the other sort. Miss Wells would do for him quite well, I think."

His lordship chuckled and gave her a squeeze. "I agree entirely, my love. I quite like her. And an American too. Completely unexpected, but perhaps just what he needs." He grew more serious. "He's been so hard since David and his parents died. Miss Wells may help him get beyond that."

"I think she may," Lady Manning murmured. "She may help him get beyond a great many troubles. Dear Jack," she said, sighing. "I do wish you'd tell him the truth, Robert. All these years, and he's never known."

"I should like nothing better than to have the matter out in the open," Lord Manning said. "But I promised his parents I would say nothing unless Jack asked it of me. I've dropped a hint a time or two, but he's never approached me on the subject, at least not since he was a boy. And you know how he is, love. He can't be made to do anything."

She smiled. ''Rather like you in that regard, my dear. Clearly an inherited quality.''

''Perhaps,'' he admitted somewhat wistfully. ''Indeed, I'm sure it must be.''

Chapter Five

The ride from Manning House to the Clarendon was completed, on Jack's part, in near silence. Miss Gwendolyn Wells, however, contented herself with chatting amicably on any number of conversational topics, never daunted by his stiff one- and two-syllable replies. Lydia, wiser than she, noted his mood and sat quietly throughout the short journey.

He didn't know why he should be spurred to aggravation on account of Gwendolyn Wells. The fact that he was only served to annoy him further. He'd known the woman for only two days, and on each of them she'd managed to become embroiled in a predicament. He could understand a female who looked like she did being importuned by men, whether she encouraged such attentions or not. But to be seen walking down Saint James in the middle of the afternoon was beyond belief. Nothing could have been more disastrous to her reputation, and Jack silently cursed the Earl of Kerlain for being so negligent in keeping his cousin from such a foolish misstep.

With a weary sigh, Jack briefly closed his eyes and told himself that he was being both irrational and unfair. Miss Wells couldn't have known that Saint James was London's unspoken—and inviolate—sanctuary for men and that the only kinds of women who dared walk its length were those who wanted the intimate company of those same men. She couldn't have known how the sight of her through White's bow window would cause a near-riot in that select club or have imagined the ribald comments that the presence of such a beauty would elicit from the club's patrons. She certainly never could have realized that waving to him as she had—*waving*, for pity's sake, as if she were a giddy schoolgirl—would start a rampant flame of rumors spreading through London, not only about herself, but him, as well. And perhaps even about Walsh, since that fool had just about drooled all over her within full view of the club's yet-crowded window. Jack's only consolation in that quarter was that she'd evidently found the man to be as insipid as he did. Her comment comparing him to that lovesick sailor Hanbury had been—well, he had to admit it—slightly amusing.

He didn't know why he should care so much about what happened to her. Perhaps it was because he was so tired. That surely must be the reason. He'd spent the night in a fruitless search for Nancy Randall and her child, and the frustration had kept him from finding any rest even after he'd returned to Brannard. He was afraid for the girl, more afraid for the child. If her pimp found her before Jack did, she'd be fortunate to come out of the meeting alive. The child, if it was healthy, would be sold to one of the houses where youngsters were fostered for the sole purpose of making money. He or she would be made into a whore by the age of five, dead of disease and ill-use before twelve. The knowledge filled him with a grim rage. He had to find Nancy and her child before another week was out. He should be searching for them even now, yet it was impossible to carry out such tasks in the light of day. In daylight he must be the Earl of Rexley. Ever proper, aristocratic. And doing nothing better than keeping dim-witted, pestilential females like Miss Wells out of trouble.

He opened his eyes and looked at her, taking in her vivid coloring, her beauty, the pretty, feminine manner in which she chattered and smiled. If he wasn't careful he'd find himself falling for the woman. God forbid. She'd certainly entranced Robby and Anna within but a few minutes of meeting them. He wasn't going to think about how Walsh had reacted to her. Not that he could blame any of them. She was not only beautiful but also charming and quick-witted and possessed of a kindly sense of humor— an attractive female all the way around. And if he was wise he'd drop her off at the Clarendon and make a run for his very life.

But when they reached the hotel Jack found himself handing the women out and escorting them to their rooms. Lydia, admirable creature that she was, judiciously disappeared.

"Shall I send for tea?" Gwendolyn asked, pulling off her gloves.

"Not on my account, thank you." He removed his hat and set it on a small table near the door. "I will remain only for a few moments. I have no doubt that in the United States it is quite unexceptional for young women to remain with gentlemen in a room unaccompanied, but here, I assure you, it is not an accepted practice." He cringed inwardly at the tone of his voice, at how pompous and toplofty he sounded.

She appeared to be, more than anything else, amused. The gaze she set on him was laced with a smile.

"Do you mean to say that I'm in some danger from merely being alone with you, my lord? Shall I take up the fire poker now, do you think, in order to save myself from your lecherous advances?"

It seemed impossible, but Jack could have sworn that he felt himself blushing. His skin grew heated, at any rate.

"Miss Wells," he said coldly. "Let me assure you that

of any man in England, you are in the least danger from
me. I would advise you to take note of that and remember
it. My intention in remaining now is only to impart what I
believe is, for you, sound advice."

"Advice?" she repeated, taking a seat near the fire.
"Goodness, that sounds terribly dire. I think, rather, that
I'm in for a scold. Please don't trouble yourself, Lord
Rexley. Papa will be more than dutiful in taking me to
task once he discovers that I've trespassed upon one of
London's more-hallowed traditions. That is what I've
done, is it not?"

"Miss Wells, I don't believe you understand the extent
to which your reputation may suffer from such a blatant
disregard of form. I only wish to advise you to apply to
your cousin, Lord Kerlain, to guide you in such matters as
this. I'm sure that you would not wish to find yourself
unaware of what is not acceptable here?"

"Oh, certainly not," she replied affably. "But I fear
Lad hasn't any better respect for British conventions than
I do. Does it not seem to you, my lord, that barring
women from traversing a perfectly acceptable avenue such
as Saint James is a trifle foolish?"

"Not in the least. The fact that you misunderstand the
matter only serves to underscore the importance of your
becoming better educated in our ways. However, it is more
fitting that your cousin should guide you. I only wished
to—"

"Advise me," she put in with that same hint of amusement. "Yes, I know. My father has for many years longed
to do the same, but I am clearly the most stupid of creatures, for it never does any good. But I do appreciate your
efforts, my lord, regardless of how it may seem otherwise,
and only wish I were a better pupil. However, I do promise
to *try* to do better." She pressed her hands together in an
earnest manner. "If I only had someone wiser to gude me,

I believe I should have better success in keeping from trouble." She looked at him expectantly.

Jack was more than proof against such obvious bait. "Your father and cousin must surely be adequate to such a task."

She laughed with a delight so clear and unaffected that it made him shiver in unwanted response. "Do you think so?"

Well, no, he didn't, but he wasn't going to admit it, and he certainly wasn't going to offer himself up as her guardian, no matter how charming he found her, especially when she was smiling at him as she was now.

"If not, then you must do as you see fit."

"I suppose I must," she said. "Although I don't doubt it will land me on the wrong footing again. It's a pity I can't command your aid, Lord Rexley." She looked at him in an openly teasing manner. "What with your vast knowledge of what's acceptable."

It took Jack a moment to realize that she was mocking him. Mocking *him*—the Earl of Rexley. He might have told himself in that same moment that he admired her for it, for not treating him as if he were made of some precious substance and fawning over him as other ladies were given to do. He might have reminded himself, as well, that there were any number of people who teased him in just such a manner—Robby and Lucky, to name two. But he didn't do so. Instead, he let himself be angry. And anger, which had served him well during the war in the way of making him fight in battles, now served to make him foolish. He had lectured her on proper behavior, yet now he forgot everything he knew about the subject. Even as he opened his mouth to speak, he knew he would later regret the words.

"I have no doubt, Miss Wells, that you mean to be clever and thereby irresistibly captivating. I also have no doubt that you're used to such tactics working with any number of other men, but, unfortunately, you're out of your depths with me. Flattering as your efforts are, I warn you that I have no desire to gain a wife, or a mistress if that was your intent''—her eyes widened at this—''and I likewise have no interest in setting up a flirtation. I would appreciate your bearing this in mind in future.''

There was a silence when he finished speaking, and Jack couldn't decide who was more shocked by what he'd just said—himself or Miss Wells. She paled when he would have expected her to flush, and she quietly contemplated him when he would have thought she'd fly into a rage or tears and rise up to slap him soundly across the face. It was what any other woman of his acquaintance probably would have done. But Gwendolyn Wells merely drew in a long, deep breath, steadied herself, and replied, ''I'm almost tempted, sir, to put such a challenge to the test.''

Damn her! he thought furiously. Why couldn't she weep and throw things and make him feel badly enough to apologize? Instead, she only goaded him further.

''I wouldn't were I you,'' he suggested tightly. ''I have no desire to humiliate you in public, ma'am.''

She gazed at him with an expression that was close to pity. ''And I wouldn't wish you to do so either,'' she said gently. ''It's not a memory I should ever wish to burden you with.''

Gad, he thought. Women. There were times when he couldn't fathom why he liked the lot of them so much.

He had to leave, he decided, before he did or said something even more foolish than he already had. He never should have come. Never should have tried to warn her into behaving properly. When she'd waved at him at White's he should have waved back and let his friends think whatever they damned well pleased.

"It's clearly of no use trying to reason with you, Miss Wells," he heard himself saying as he gathered up his hat and gloves. "I shall take the matter up with your cousin."

"Oh, but Lad is out of town," she said, rising from her chair and moving toward him. "It's really all his fault that I was out alone, you see. I had no one to take me in hand."

That stilled him. "Out of town?" He stared at her. "Kerlain has gone out of town only the day after his relatives arrived? The damned fellow was supposed to be on his deathbed yesterday!"

"Yes, well, it did seem very odd to me as well," she told him. "But he must have recovered rather quickly, and he did tell me that the matter calling him away is urgent."

"When does he intend to return?"

"Shortly. As soon as may be, in a day or two. In the meantime, I have only my own self for company, and that, as you know," she said with a smile, "can be quite trying."

"What of your father, then? Surely he could have taken you about?"

She shrugged lightly. "My father went off with Lord Severn—you know how scientists are." Stopping before him, she said, "I simply wished to take some fresh air and had no notion of what trouble walking down Saint James would cause. Surely, my lord, you can't fault me for what was only a matter of ignorance?"

He couldn't, of course, but he didn't say so. Instead, he jammed his hat on his head and glared at her.

She stepped nearer, until he could smell the faint perfume of lilacs that rose from the heat of her skin.

"I will do better, I promise," she said. "And despite whatever unfortunate behavior I may have displayed and my equally unfortunate remarks, I truly am grateful for your kind intention in striving to correct my misunderstanding. And so sorry for having caused you to put your-self out. You have been very good to get me out of scrapes two days running. You must think me quite a troublemonger, but I generally avoid adversity for much longer stretches of time. Forgive me, I pray.''

He felt a perfect dolt beneath her charming grace. He stood there with his hat on his head and hardly knew what to say.

"Of course,'' he mumbled at last. "And I . . . pray your pardon for what I said earlier . . . if I have caused any offense. It was unforgivable to speak as I did.''

She laughed and waved his words away with a flut-tering movement of one delicate, feminine hand. "You were quite right, my lord. I'm a shameless flirt, I fear, and deserved every word. Can we not cry friends? If I promise not to attempt to be clever and''—she grinned—"capti-vating?''

That, he thought, would be impossible. She was the most captivating woman he'd ever met. And too clever for her own good. And his.

She held her hand out as if to shake his and seal the bargain, but Jack found that he couldn't bring himself to touch her. Instead, he bowed stiffly and said, "I should be delighted to claim friendship with you, Miss Wells. Now, if you'll pardon me, I must take my leave.''

He walked out the door without taking the time to put his gloves on and stood in the hallway, once the door had closed, trying to gather his wits. He felt slightly breath-less, as if he'd just had a narrow escape, and in his mind's eye he could see her still standing before him, beautiful and smiling, her dainty hand held out toward his. The vi-sion disturbed him deeply, as she disturbed him. In her presence he felt as if fate were pressing in all about him, and he wanted only to make it stop.

He made his way home, not delaying even to speak to

those acquaintances who hailed him. Brannard loomed like a safe haven as he neared it, and when his butler, Barton, opened the door, it was with relief that Jack crossed the threshold.

His servants began assailing him at once.

"May I take your hat, Lord Rexley?"

He handed it with an automatic motion into the girl's outstretched hands. "Thank you, Pru."

"Your gloves, Lord Rexley?"

"Here you are, Grace."

"A fire has been started in the library, my lord."

"Very good, Lucy."

"Shall I bring you some brandy, sir?"

"Yes, Lizabeth, that would be fine."

He spent a great deal of time in his library, and it was where he went now to find solace and comfort. To think. The fire, as Lucy had promised, welcomed and warmed him. Lizabeth brought him a decanter of his favorite brandy, then discreetly and quietly took her leave. Jack sat in his most comfortable chair to contemplate, as he often did, the portraits that hung prominently above the mantel on the room's southern wall. The visages that smiled down at him had at once a calming and unsettling effect. They were not the faces of physically beautiful people. His father had been a small man; Jack had towered over him by the age of fifteen. Small and slender, his once-dark hair had been fringed with gray early in life and the top of his head was balding slightly. He had been a gentle man, a scholarly man, quiet and affectionate and much loved by the many friends who claimed him. His mother had been small too, a dainty and birdlike creature, sometimes silly and girlish, usually animated with smiles and laughter, always full of love and consideration for others. He hadn't looked in the least like either one of them. Not in the least.

He had loved his parents deeply. Miles and Dorothy

Sommerton, the Earl and Countess of Rexley, were the two people he'd cared most about in his life, next to his only sibling, his younger brother, David. He knew few families among the ton who were truly happy, or who even abided one another, but his had been one of the fortunate few. They had been happy, almost sinfully so, had enjoyed being together as much as possible. There had been no one he had admired or wanted to emulate as much as his parents, and no one he'd wanted more to please. How easy a thing that had been, to please them, he thought now with a familiar tightening ache in his chest. How readily they had given both their love and their approval.

He carried David's portrait in his watch and took it out now to look at it. His brother had been a handsome young man, a taller version of their father, always smiling and carefree. He had possessed everything that Jack had known he'd lacked. He'd been charming, and easygoing, and kindly natured. And legitimate.

Jack knew that much was true, because he'd witnessed his parents' surprise and happiness at the knowledge of the coming child, had seen his mother grow large with the babe, and had been brought in to see his younger brother directly after he'd been born.

He had loved David from the moment he'd set sight on him. It seemed strange to Jack now that it should have been so, when David might have so easily taken everything away from him, even his parents' love. He had been, if what Jack suspected was true, the rightful heir to the earldom. But Jack had never been made to feel that his brother's birth was anything but what it was—the coming of a much-wanted second child into a close and loving family. In truth, it had been all the more impressed upon him that he was the eldest and, as the heir to the title, responsible for his younger brother. It was not a duty that he had taken lightly, but one in the end, that he had been unable to keep.

He had loved David. Even when they were children there had been none of the fighting or squabbling that was usual with siblings. David had been too gentle a soul for that; Jack had felt only the instinct to protect him, take care of him, make certain that he was happy and content.

When David had turned eighteen, Jack had let him come to London to stay with him, and he had taken him proudly about Town to introduce him to his friends and to women and to all the usual vices that young men enjoy. Not that he hadn't kept a close eye on him every moment, for he had, and it had nettled David to be so well protected by his older brother, though he'd been, as always, good-natured about it. And David, kind soul that he was, had done his best to be entertained. In the end, however, he'd gone back to the country, back to his studies and his greenhouses, back to the quiet life that both he and their parents enjoyed. There had never been, for him, the rest-lessness, the questioning, that had always possessed Jack. He had been a true Sommerton, calm and content. The only rash decision he'd made had been in joining the army at the age of twenty, and he'd done that—so he'd written his elder brother—only because Jack was serving with Wellington in the Peninsula and it seemed unfair to him that he should be doing nothing better for England than finishing his education. By the time Jack had received David's letter, it had been too late to stop him. He would never forget the feeling of shock and despair that had come over him when he'd read his brother's words. It had marked the beginning of a journey for him—a journey filled with losses, ending in loneliness. First David, and then his parents. And then an aloneness beyond anything he'd imagined.

He felt a fraud, living at Brannard, bearing the title of

Rexley. It should have been David, always should have been David, and never him, who was so inferior, who held so much darkness within. He was like some shabby beggar come to sit in the Earl of Rexley's chair, and all he could do, day to day, was keep up the pretense. And yet there were times when he felt confused, when the skin of aristocracy was so comfortable that he began to think that perhaps he simply had it all wrong. Perhaps he truly *was* Jack Sommerton, the legitimate child of Miles and Dorothy. Perhaps he was only different because he'd inherited his coloring and self from some distant relative—some very long-past, distant grandparent.

He had to discover the truth, one way or another. He couldn't think beyond that, to what would happen when he finally knew. He *wouldn't* think of it, of losing all that he was, all that he had, of becoming, suddenly and irrevocably, nothing more than the bastard son of a whore, fathered by an aristocrat who'd never cared to so much as admit to being his sire.

But that, he thought, was unfair to Robby. The man had been his friend as well as his godparent; he'd certainly kept Jack out of trouble more than once. And acknowledging bastard children who were begotten by whores wasn't done among the ton, not unless one had a spouse who would give that same child a name and never say otherwise. He supposed if Robby truly was his father that he'd done as much for him as he possibly could while keeping within the accepted social confines. When his parents had died two months apart from each other, so shortly after David's death, Robby had been there, taking care of funeral arrangements, keeping the world at bay, giving Jack the time and privacy he needed to grieve. It was a gift Jack had not been able to forget.

And yet, despite what he owed the Earl of Manning in friendship, he needed the truth. And when he at last held proof in his hands Jack wouldn't hesitate to confront him. Regardless of what it would cost them both.

Tonight he would go out searching again. Tonight and tomorrow night and the night after that. Sometimes he thought it would never end. The lead to Queen's Crossing had come to naught, just as he'd suspected it would. He'd run across too many dead ends in his search to be surprised.

"God," he murmured, and lowered his gaze to the fire. His fingers tightened about the glass before he lifted it and drank. He was tired, and that was all. Tired to his very bones. He wanted to go to bed and sleep for an eternity. Better yet, he wanted to go to Mrs. May's house and fall asleep in the arms of a soft, warm woman. Just to sleep—since he felt too weary to do much else—while listening to her chatter in good English accents, and not in the flat, nasal American tones that had filled his dreams the night before.

"Damn," he muttered, standing and draining his glass. He would go out in search of Nancy Randall whether he was tired or not, if only to keep Gwendolyn Wells out of his brain. He'd never let a woman cut up his peace before and wasn't about to start now. He'd keep away from her from now on, would avoid her like the very plague. He would see her on occasion at various events, he had no doubt—there was hardly any way in which he could avoid that—but she'd not see him crossing her threshold again for any reason. He'd leave her to Kerlain's precarious care, which was just as it should be, and just as it *would* be.

He sealed this resolve with a firm, silent nod and, feeling perfectly secure in his determinations, set his glass aside and strode from the room to prepare for the coming night.

Chapter Six

❦

The Earl of Rexley called upon Gwendolyn first thing in the morning. She was surprised, for when he'd left her the previous afternoon she'd not expected to see him again so soon. Indeed, she'd thought she'd have to wait until they met at some ball or assembly before she'd have another chance to exchange words with him and continue in her task of making him see the light. But there he was, bright and early, and being introduced into the parlor by Lydia.

He didn't come alone. The young woman he brought with him entered the room with her bespectacled eyes nervously cast down and her gloved hands folded as if she were trying to keep them from trembling. She was a beautiful girl, from what Gwendolyn could see of her, with blond tendrils escaping from beneath her bonnet, which framed a heart-shape face, and possessed of a stunning figure that made Gwendolyn suffer a pang of jealousy.

"Miss Wells," said the Earl of Rexley, "I hope I find you well this morning? Forgive the early call, I pray, but I wished to introduce you to a particular friend. Miss Christabella Howell."

He said the last three words just in time, for Gwendolyn had begun to think that the woman was his betrothed or of some romantic import to him, and as that clearly wouldn't do, she'd been about to do something quite, quite foolish. Like tear the interloper's hair out or push her out the window. But Miss Christabella Howell was a name most familiar to her. Her cousin had written often of the girl who was betrothed to Viscount Severn and who Lad himself greatly admired.

"Why, Miss Howell, what a pleasure. You are Lord Hemstead's daughter, are you not?" She moved toward her guest with an outstretched hand. "Lad has written of you so often, I feel as I already know you."

Miss Howell's startling blue eyes flew up to Gwendolyn's face. The spectacles did nothing to hide her pure English beauty. "He has? Written of me? Oh, my."

"But only the most glowing reports, I promise," Gwendolyn assured her quickly, bemused by this response. "And to tell me of your betrothal to Lord Severn, whom he wished to make better known to Papa before we came to England."

Understanding filled the girl's lovely face. "Oh! I see! How very kind of him."

Gwendolyn indicated a nearby table laden with trays. "Would you like a cup of tea? Or coffee? I vow we cannot go without our coffee, even in England, and it is amazingly well done here." She began to lead her guests toward the sitting area.

"Yes, thank you," Miss Howell said, losing some of her nervousness. "Wulf drinks a great deal of coffee during the day, especially while he's working in the laboratory. It makes him quite shaky at times." She adjusted the spectacles that were perched on her tiny nose. "I've tried everything I can think of to make him stop, but he never shows an inclination to listen to me."

Gwendolyn laughed. "Papa drinks several pots every day while working at his desk and could most likely never give up the habit. Please be seated, Miss Howell." She smiled at Lord Rexley and motioned him toward a chair.

"And you, my lord. I'm sure Papa will come in soon. He's had something of a belated start this morning, as Lord Severn refused to bring him home until late last evening. They dined at White's with your father, I believe, Miss Howell. He shall be so delighted that Lord Rexley has brought you to visit."

She poured tea for Miss Howell and herself and coffee for Lord Rexley.

"Thank you," replied Miss Howell, accepting her cup. "Papa was ecstatic when he returned home last night. He so enjoyed meeting Professor Wells. They are to prepare some hydrogen demonstrations together for the enlightenment of the scientists at the Academy when Professor Wells gives his speech. And Wulf is to assist. He is so very excited, as you might imagine."

Gwendolyn slanted a grin in Lord Rexley's direction. "Yes, I might. I do hope they'll not blow up the Royal Academy, however, between the three of them." Lord Rexley shared her humor at the idea, she saw. He actually looked amused. "Would it be blamed on Papa's being an American, do you think, my lord?" Gwendolyn asked innocently. "As an act of espionage?"

The smile on his face vanished. He set his coffee cup aside.

"I've brought Bella to you, Miss Wells," he stated, coming to the point of his visit, "so that she might lend you her aid."

"Have you?" she asked. "How very kind. And quite proper too, I'm sure, as you are such an authority on these things." She should have resisted teasing him, she supposed, especially as it made him look so irate, but she could hardly forbear after he'd made such a fuss the day before. "And how is it that you're to aid me, Miss Howell? I don't wish to be a burden to you."

Miss Howell, clearly a timid creature, blushed to the

roots of her hair and nervously adjusted her spectacles again. "I-I hardly know, Miss Wells. Jack—that is, Lord Rexley—has only said that—"

"Bella is to show you about London," Lord Rexley announced curtly. "That is what you wished, is it not, Miss Wells? Someone to guide you about town?"

"Why, yes, of course," Gwendolyn replied at once, giving him credit for such a clever evasion. She'd hoped his natural sense of gallantry, combined with their unalterable destiny, would lead him to offer his own escort. But she was pleased that he'd felt enough of a concern to bring Miss Howell to her. It was certainly more than Lad had thought to do, and him her own cousin. "I am most grateful, to both of you. But I should never want to imposition you, Miss Howell. Although I confess myself much in need of guidance while in England, you must tell me if such a plan is abhorrent to you in any way. I don't wish to put you out."

"Oh, no!" Miss Howell said, still flushed with embarrassment. "I would deem it an honor, Miss Wells, to act as your guide and companion. Indeed, I can think of nothing I should like better."

Gwendolyn gave her a warm smile. "Very fine. We shall do famously, and I will be forever in your debt. And in Lord Rexley's, of course." She turned the smile on him. "Thank you, my lord."

The door opened and her father sailed in, yet settling his coat about him. "Good morning!" he said in greeting. "I apologize for being so long. Good morning, Lord Rexley. How good it is to see you again. I must give you my thanks in rescuing my Gwennie yesterday afternoon. She told me the full of it, and I find myself in your debt and also in Lord and Lady Manning's."

Lord Rexley, who had stood at Professor Wells's arrival, accepted the man's hand when it was offered. "Sir, not at all. I was more than pleased to lend Miss Wells my aid, and my godfather, Lord Manning, was delighted to make her acquaintance. Both he and his lady have waited with some anticipation these many months for your arrival in London and considered it a great boon to be able to entertain your daughter before any others could lay claim to doing so. They hope to make your acquaintance as well, quite soon.''

''I should be pleased to do so,'' Professor Wells declared heartily. ''Please introduce me to this young lady who waits so patiently. Do I understand that I have the honor of meeting Miss Howell?''

The introductions were made, and, much to Gwendolyn's amazement, her father and Miss Howell soon fell into scientific discussion. The girl was of a far more disciplined mind than her own and was clearly as well studied in chemistry as were her father and fiancé.

After a few minutes of being excluded from the conversation, Lord Rexley appeared to find something behind Gwendolyn interesting.

''I never should have expected to find such a fine instrument in a hotel,'' he said, and stood. ''Miss Wells, I believe this clock upon the mantel to be of some antiquity. Will you examine it with me to give your opinion?''

Gwendolyn hadn't the least knowledge of clocks or their antiquity, but she obediently followed him toward the fire, stood next to him—away from her father and Miss Howell, who were oblivious to any changes in the room— and pretended to look at the clock.

''Yes, I do believe I was right,'' the Earl of Rexley said loudly, although he was ignored by the two people who remained seated. ''What do you think, Miss Wells?'' In a lower voice, for her ears alone, he said, ''I would appreciate it if you'd be kind to Bella.''

Gwendolyn was surprised by this. ''But of course. Why

should I not be?'' More loudly she added, ''It *is* a fine clock, my lord.''

''She's a gentle soul and very sweet-natured,'' he told her. ''But very easily . . . bewildered, save in matters of scientific discourse. Then, as you can see, she very nearly matches Viscount Severn.''

''She does remind me of him somewhat, yes,'' said Gwendolyn, slicing a careful glance at that young lady. ''Not,'' she added, ''in the physical sense. They've been betrothed for quite a long time, have they not? Lad wrote me something of it.''

''He's nothing to say on the matter,'' the earl said more tightly. ''And if you value your cousin's skin, you'd best keep him away from Bella while she's in your company. Wulf likes Kerlain well enough, but he's violently jealous where Bella is concerned. And Kerlain, far beyond my understanding, has never seen fit to keep his interest in the girl to himself.''

''*Lad*?'' Gwendolyn repeated. ''An interest in Miss Howell? But surely not. You mistake the matter, sir.''

''I do not,'' Lord Rexley replied. ''He has openly sought Bella out at every opportunity that has presented itself and has made his preference for her above any other female clear. He and Wulf have even, on occasion, come to blows over the matter. The only thing that's kept Wulf from killing your cousin outright is Kerlain's association with your father. Wulf didn't wish to ruin his chances of meeting the esteemed Professor Wells.''

''You are mistaken,'' she repeated firmly. ''My lord, I'm telling you the truth. And there is no need to roll your eyes as if I were ready for an asylum. Lad has admitted in his letters to me that he holds Miss Howell in esteem and affection, but his feelings are not in the least indecorous. He merely thinks of her as a—how can I put it?'' She searched for the right words. ''As a kindred spirit.''

"Lower your voice, if you please." He set his hands behind his back and inspected the clock minutely. "A kindred spirit, indeed. I can't think where you've formed such a notion, as if a man like Kerlain could possibly have anything in common with a virtuous young female like Bella." He continued speaking even when she opened her mouth to protest. "You've never seen the way he looks at her, Miss Wells. It is not the look that one gives a kindred spirit. Being a man, I believe I know the difference."

She was hard put not to laugh out loud. "And being a woman, sir, I believe I know the difference as well. You may be certain that I do."

His head turned slowly and he looked at her, first full in the face, then down the length of her body and back up again, a visual exploration that was openly assessing and at the same time licentious. Gwendolyn felt as if she'd been suddenly shoved into a hot oven. "Of that," he said deliberately, "I have no doubt. But you've not yet had the pleasure of watching your cousin when Bella is before him. He foams at the mouth. It's indecent. One can hardly blame Wulf for becoming so violent over the matter."

Gwendolyn was truly shocked. "My lord, I vow, I simply cannot believe it. There is clearly a great deal you do not know about Lad, for if you did you should never believe what you do of him."

He looked at her then, with a sharpness that set her instantly on edge. "If there is something you might tell me that would shed light on his behavior, then do so." He looked as if he were an eagle in search of prey, but his voice was as gentle and inviting as a warm breeze. "Otherwise, I must continue to believe what I see."

She gazed at him warily. "Lad must tell you. I cannot do so."

His eyes moved back to the clock. "I see." His tone was clipped.

"But you *do* mistake the matter," she told him. "If you knew the full of it, you would understand. He cares for Miss Howell as a friend, and nothing more. Anything else would be quite impossible."

"Regardless of what you may think or believe," he said, "I must yet insist that you do what you can to keep Kerlain away from Bella. Quite apart from Wulf's objections, Bella herself finds his attentions unsettling, and it would be sorry repayment for her kindness to you if she were to be forced into his company."

Gwendolyn stiffened beneath the implied insult.

"Sir," she said, turning to face him, "I would never *force* an acquaintance into the company of anyone with whom he or she did not wish to be. However, I would likewise never cut my own cousin for such little reason as you have given me. If you fear so much for Miss Howell's well-being, then I can only wonder that you have allowed an acquaintance to be made between us, much less initiated one."

"Hush!" he commanded. "Look at the clock." Then in a louder voice said, "There's no need to become so excited, Miss Wells. It doesn't appear to be so valuable as I had first thought."

"Oh, I am relieved, my lord," she replied in an equally loud tone. "I won't regard the expense, then, if I ever break it"—she lowered her voice—"by bashing it on your head. Now, if you will excuse me—"

He gripped her elbow to keep her from leaving.

"No. You have no cause for anger. You mistake me completely. I meant you no offense."

"Not to me, perhaps, but my cousin!"

He glanced at her with a look that was unfathomable. "No, nor Lad." It was the first time she'd heard him speak her cousin's Christian name. "I claim him among my closest friends and would do nothing less than speak the truth of him—or what I know to be the truth of him. Were he here, he would not deny that he has but himself to blame for my concerns regarding himself and Bella. He has purposefully set out to cause trouble between her and Wulf, and that is a fact. Why he does it, I cannot say, but you may ask him whether I speak falsely.''

''You may be certain that I will.''

''Good.'' He released her. ''Do I have your word that you'll keep Bella from him?''

Gwendolyn stared up at him, torn between anger and mystification. At last she said, ''I shall not arrange to meet with him while I am with Miss Howell. That, I promise. If we should meet him while we are out, I will not in any way avoid him.''

He was thoughtful for a moment, then nodded. ''It is enough. I trust you'll do all you can to keep Bella out of trouble.''

She laughed. ''My lord, I hardly know what to make of you. Have you brought Miss Howell to me for safekeeping? I had thought she was supposed to keep *me* out of trouble.''

He grinned. ''That too. Or should I say, most especially?'' His manner was suddenly genuine and warm.

He was a devil, she thought with a wry smile, and would give her a lifetime of bemusement and joy. How quickly his moods changed! And how determined he was to keep her at arm's length. Though perhaps not just her, but the world in general. Even with his godfather, Lord Manning, he'd been careful and closed. She had only seen glimpses, such as now, of the man behind the elegance and formality. But she had time to discover more, she thought with satisfaction. All the time in the world.

She found herself gazing at his lips and wondering how long it would be before he kissed her. And what it would feel like when he did. She'd been kissed three times in her life—kisses that she'd allowed, as numerous ardent suitors had attempted to apply their lips to hers without permission and had quickly found themselves much the worse for it—and each had been different and pleasant. She had no doubt, however, that kissing Jack Sommerton would be something far beyond any of those undertakings. And not just because he was The One. He simply looked as if he'd be quite good at doing whatever he set his mind to.

He took note of her regard and stiffened. His lips, which she yet contemplated, pressed into a straight line and his face once more took on the mask of distant but perfect civility. Gwendolyn smiled.

"You are kind, Lord Rexley, to think of my well-being. Or, rather, of keeping me out of trouble. I cannot think why you should bother youself on my account, but I am grateful."

He held himself coldly now, the utterly cold and proper Earl of Rexley, as he had been before. But before he could make whatever cutting reply had surely been forming upon those delightful-looking lips, there was a scratch at the parlor door, and then Lydia was entering and announcing the arrival of Viscount Severn.

The viscount entered the room in a great, clumsy rush of movement and speech, a quantity of papers clutched in one hand.

"Professor Wells," he said without a greeting, without even stopping to see who else was in the room. "I've spent the whole night going over the calculations we discussed yesterday and believe I've come up with a new proposal that you'll find most intriguing."

Professor Wells and Miss Howell both stood, but to Gwendolyn's surprise, the burly viscount excitedly pushed straight past his fiancée without so much as a word and instead began to show the papers he held to the professor. Much to Gwendolyn's shame, her father eagerly took the papers and began to examine them without uttering a word to bring Miss Howell to Lord Severn's notice. The two men began talking at once, rapidly and with great excitement, until Lord Rexley loudly cleared his throat and said, "Wulf," in a manner that drew the attention of the entire room.

"Oh, Jack!" Viscount Severn greeted happily. "You here? Wonderful, wonderful. Pleasant surprise, of course. Hope you're well."

With that he returned his attention to the professor. Miss Howell, Gwendolyn noticed, stood where she was, looking at her fiancé with silent longing. She said nothing, only waited to be noticed. Gwendolyn had never seen anything so pathetic. She kept waiting for the girl to say something, but nothing came. If it had been her, Viscount Severn would already be groveling apologetically on the carpet.

"Wulf." This time Lord Rexley's voice was filled with distinct displeasure. It had an amazing effect on the bull-like Lord Severn, who instantly stood fully upright and gave the earl his complete attention.

"Yes, Jack?" he said meekly.

"You've forgotten yourself. There are ladies present."

Lord Severn was momentarily bewildered by this statement. He stared at his friend—Gwendolyn could almost see his oversize brain turning over the idea of women being present and what that fact importuned—and then, as if for the first time, he turned his befuddled and concerned gaze on Gwendolyn.

"Oh, ma'am," he said, as if he were a naughty, errant, and very contrite schoolboy. "Beg pardon. Didn't see you. Terribly sorry. Good morning, Miss Wells."

Having made this declaration, he looked to the earl for approval.

Lord Rexley nodded slightly, then gestured in Miss

Howell's direction. The viscount turned and saw his fiancée, who smiled at him. He seemed utterly surprised to find her standing not three feet away from him.

"Bella, what the devil are you doing here? Thought you was home helping your father with equations this morning. You haven't left him to copy them all out himself, have you?"

The censure in his voice had an immediate effect on Miss Howell. She looked thoroughly ashamed of herself. "Oh, I came only because Jack—Lord Rexley—was so good as to invite me out, and Papa said he could make do for an hour or two. I shall be home this afternoon before he goes into the laboratory, I promise."

"I should think so!" Lord Severn stated severely. To Professor Wells he said, "You know how it is, sir, to have to write equations out yourself. Most vexing to the thought process."

Gwendolyn didn't doubt that her father would agree. He had several assistants at home who wrote down everything for him. Gwendolyn had long since declared she would no longer do so.

Nudging Lord Rexley, she leaned to whisper, "How long have they been betrothed?"

Lord Rexley sighed before replying, "Eight years. Since Bella was seventeen."

Merciful heavens! Gwendolyn straightened with indignation. She'd considered herself long on the shelf at twenty-four, but Miss Howell must feel positively ancient at twenty-five. Eight years! And Viscount Severn clearly none the better for it.

"Lord Severn!" she said briskly, moving toward Miss Howell. "As I understand that you intend to escort my father to Lord Hemstead's home shortly, I beg that you will inform him that his daughter will *not* be home before he goes into the laboratory. She will be out shopping with me until quite late this afternoon.''

''I will?'' Miss Howell asked.

''Yes, indeed. I doubt we'll return in time for you to be of any use to these gentlemen at all.''

''But—'' Lord Severn began.

''You shall simply have to write out the equations yourselves, my lord,'' Gwendolyn stated. ''Papa has beautiful handwriting, I assure you, odd as that may seem in a scientist. It's actually readable. You won't mind writing your own work out as you did on the ship, will you, Papa?''

She couldn't tell who was more flustered—her father or Lord Severn.

''Of course not,'' her father said after a moment's confused hesitation. He glanced from Gwendolyn to Lord Rexley to Lord Severn to Miss Howell, whose pained expression clearly made his decision. ''Of course not, Miss Howell,'' he said more warmly, moving to take that young woman's hand and pat it. ''You mustn't worry over the matter in the least. We shall do perfectly well without you.''

''But, sir!'' Lord Severn protested.

''Nonsense, my lord,'' said the professor. ''Miss Howell shouldn't have to spend her days locked away in a laboratory with a lot of fusty chemists. A young lady needs entertainments, after all. Gwendolyn gave up assisting me years ago.''

''But Bella likes to assist,'' his lordship insisted. ''Don't you, Bella?''

Miss Howell began to look guilty again. ''Oh, yes. I do. And I shouldn't wish to be the cause of any discomfort, if you feel that you truly need me.''

''There,'' said Viscount Severn approvingly. ''You're a good girl, Bella. Always have been.''

Gwendolyn's hands curled into fists. She was ready to

declare war. The oversize clodpate of a viscount made Miss Howell sound like a well-behaved dog. She wanted to break his great big nose.

"Wulf," Lord Rexley interposed. It amazed Gwendolyn to see how much effect that single word, issued from Lord Rexley's mouth, could have on his friend. Viscount Severn attended immediately.

"Of course," he began obediently, "if you'd *like* a day away from the laboratory, Bella—"

"She would," Gwendolyn said tartly. "And as I am much in need of Miss Howell's assistance, that is the end of the matter."

The viscount gave in with good grace, until a few moments later when he and Professor Wells were about to take their leave. As he shook Gwendolyn's hand, he said in a low tone, "Say, you're not going to be having Kerlain for an escort today, are you, Miss Wells? I don't like to have him around Bella. Not that Lad ain't a grand fellow, mind you, when he's on his own, but . . . I just don't like him around Bella. Can't keep his eyes in his head. Or his hands to himself, if you know what I mean." His craggy features screwed up in distaste. "Always kissing her fingers and telling her how nice she looks and that sort of thing. Enough to turn a fellow's stomach, you know. Bella's too sensible for it, of course, but I don't like to see another man slobbering all over her. Not the thing, y' see, even from a man's friends. Not the thing at all."

Gwendolyn stared at him. The man was a completely insensate brute. She wouldn't blame Miss Howell if she did come to prefer Lad to such an indelicate clump. Clearly she never received such fine attention from her own fiancé.

"My cousin is not promised to attend us today, my lord. Indeed, he is not even in town. Please make yourself easy on the matter."

Lord Severn looked thoroughly relieved. He squeezed Gwendolyn's hand in heartfelt thanks with such strength that she could actually hear her bones cracking. It was all she could do to keep from shaking her abused limb to alleviate the pain when he released her.

"You'll be shopping along Bond Street, I suppose?" Lord Rexley asked after the viscount and Professor Wells had taken their leave. He was pulling on his gloves and smiling warmly at Miss Howell.

"It is entirely up to Miss Wells," that young woman said. She was clearly excited at having a day all to herself. Gwendolyn noticed that a glow had come into her face that chased away her timid appearance and left her looking quite fetching.

Lord Rexley turned his gaze upon Gwendolyn, his eyes narrowing as he did so. "And you, Miss Wells? Today you have Miss Howell to lend you company, and shortly hereafter Lady Manning shall do likewise. You have some specific idea of where you wish to go?"

"No," Gwendolyn replied lazily. "But we shall do very well, my lord, never fear. I shall run Miss Howell ragged before the day is out and spend enough money to make my father feel faint. Lad has arranged a great many gatherings for us to attend, and I mean to look good at each of them. Three nights from now at Almack's, as an example. I shouldn't wish to appear too . . . colonial, would I? Only imagine how distressing that should be." He answered her beaming mien with a glare. "Do you wish to lend us your escort today, my lord? To make certain of us?" She infused pure innocence into the words.

His mouth thinned again into a straight line—a stubborn expression that Gwendolyn found perfectly endearing.

"God forbid," he muttered, then mastered himself in order to say more reassuringly to Miss Howell, "I fear

I've too many matters to attend to this afternoon in order to accompany you, but I do leave you my coach and servants. You must make certain that Miss Wells makes use of them, Bella. Otherwise, I fear she will lead the both of you far afield. Be quite firm with her if you must, and never forget,'' he commanded, putting his hat upon his head, ''that she's a savage American.''

Chapter Seven

✧✦✧

*A*lmack's was just as unprepossessing inside as it was outside, Gwendolyn discovered to her great disappointment. Lady Manning, who with Lord Manning had escorted her to the assembly, had warned her not to expect too much, but she certainly hadn't expected so *little*. Even at home the balls and parties she'd attended were far more elegant and grand. Gwendolyn could hardly understand why Almack's had gained such an awe-inspiring reputation. The actual assembly rooms were plain and small, the food and drink quite ordinary, and the dancing reserved. She was afraid that she would have a disappointingly dull report to give her particular friends when, and if, she at last returned to the United States. If they'd considered their own gatherings dull, they would be quite reassured that the Almack's of which they had all dreamed made Boston parties seem wonderful by comparison.

"This is the worst of making a come-out," Lady Manning told her confidingly as they stood fanning themselves and waiting for the dancing to resume. "Once you've made your bow to Almack's, you need never come again, although it's always wise to return at least once or twice. It's an honor to be invited, of course, and something of a necessity if you want to be fully accepted by the ton, but otherwise it's a dead bore."

"But why is it of such import?" Gwendolyn asked. "It hardly seems grand enough to make any difference."

"Now, that, my dear, you must not mistake," Lady Manning warned. "Every young lady who wishes to be invited to ton gatherings must first be invited to Almack's, and although that's the only fact that makes it such an important event, it is a very real one. To be cut by Almack's is to be cut in general. It's positively idiotic, I know, but it can't be helped. Young ladies seek the approval of Almack's the way mothers dream of their daughters marrying into the aristocracy. It isn't necessarily better to marry a royal duke, but as there are so few of them it seems somehow more desirable. It's an achievement to brag of, at any rate."

"Much like securing an invitation to Almack's," Gwendolyn said with a laugh. "I'm grateful that you accompanied me, else I certainly would have stepped wrong. Although it was very bad of my cousin to ask you to do so when he had promised to bring me himself. But I should have been rather at a loss even with his company, I fear."

"Nonsense," said her ladyship. "You've taken perfectly well, just as I knew you should. There isn't a man in the room who hasn't asked to dance with you. And those who haven't secured a dance on your card are filled with envy for the lucky fellows who have. You remind me quite of your cousin, Kerlain, when he first came to London." Lady Anna smiled at the memory. "Such a handsome rogue he was. He couldn't walk about a room like this without being swarmed by hordes of young ladies and their mamas. I've never seen such a fuss over a man, and an impoverished American at that. I have the feeling the case will be much the same with you, my dear."

"Oh, that," Gwendolyn said with a light shrug. "Men don't particularly bother me. I've grown quite used to such foolishness, tiresome as it is. But I'm afraid that I can't seem to stop making a nuisance of myself. It never used to be so bad in Boston—at least, I don't think I was quite so troublesome. But here in London I can't seem to do anything but step wrong. Two days ago, when I was out shopping with Bella, I unwittingly caused the most dreadful carriage accident—''

"Quite understandable," murmured Lady Anna, "considering the way men look at you, my dear. See there, across the room?" She pointed with her fan. "Sir Howard has just walked straight into Lady Farthington and spilled his punch down her dress because he couldn't keep his eyes from you."

Gwendolyn watched the spectacle of Sir Howard desperately making his apologies to Lady Farthington and gave a shake of her head. "As to that, I suppose you may have the right of it, for men will be the most foolish of creatures and any number of them had difficulty keeping their cattle under control even in Boston, but there is no accounting for what happened yesterday in the park. I don't suppose"—she looked hopefully at Lady Anna—"that you've *not* heard of it yet?"

"What? The commotion with Lord Astley's dog, do you mean?" At Gwendolyn's groan Lady Anna went on more kindly. "You mustn't despair over that, my dear. People have so little of real interest to talk about, and you are new to town. I'm sure the gossips will leave you in peace after a few weeks. And, really, everyone knows what a fool Astley is over his dogs. The creatures are spoiled and terribly ill-behaved. There was no fault in your mistaking the matter."

"Indeed, I never meant any harm," Gwendolyn insisted. "I only wished to *pet* the beast. It seemed to be a perfectly nice creature, and we've always had dogs at home. And in truth I don't fault the dog as much as I do Lord Astley. It was *his* behavior that upset the animal so much, and then he made no effort to handle the beast when it began to bark and jump about and overset all those horses.''

"Ah," Lady Anna said with a nod. "I had heard there were horses involved and a number of carriages as well. Something of a wild fracas, I was told."

"It was simply an unfortunate coincidence," Gwendolyn told her. "Several gentlemen had stopped to pay their respects to Miss Howell and myself, many of them on horseback. They became rather agitated by the dog's behavior—the horses, I mean, not the gentlemen—and one in particular became excited. When I think of it now, it's a wonder that no one was trampled. As it was, I feared the constable was going to arrest me, especially as Lord Astley was so insistent that I'd harmed his foolish dog."

"It's a fortunate thing that Jack happened to be so close at hand, then," Lady Anna said.

"Yes, I suppose it was," Gwendolyn replied. "Although he didn't have to become quite so aggravated. I know how it must have appeared, especially as he'd already seen me out of two previous difficulties—and I *am* grateful for the trouble he took—but I'm certain that I could have handled the matter well enough without his aid. And there were any number of other gentlemen present who offered to intercede on my behalf as well. Lord Rexley needn't have bothered at all."

"Was he very angry, my dear?" Lady Anna asked kindly.

Gwendolyn fanned herself more agitatedly. "Well, yes, he was. Which was quite unjust. I'm sure I can't be the most troublesome female he's ever encountered, despite his insistences. It is something of a problem, I admit. I had hoped to give him a rather better impression on our next encounter." She snapped her fan shut. "Do you know, I

can't decide what to make of Viscount Severn." She motioned to where Lord Severn was hovering protectively
over Christabella Howell, just as if he expected some harm
to come to her at any moment. He'd been singularly attentive to his fiancée since arriving at Almack's, dancing
with her, fetching her glasses of lemonade, and generally
keeping every other man at bay. "The last I saw of him,
he was treating Miss Howell as if she were a naughty
child. Tonight he acts as if she's a goddess."

Lady Anna chuckled. "Dear Wulf. He's something of a
mystery to all of us, but most especially to Bella, I fear.
He loves the girl, there's no denying that, and he's usually
extremely attentive to her, just as he is now. I think he
must realize how quickly she'd be snapped up by another
if he were ever to lose her. But there is his science, and it
tends to get in the way of everything else, including his
devotion to her. But I don't need to explain how that is to
you, as you've had your father for an example. I often
think, however, that if he would simply wed the girl the
situation would sort itself out."

"I imagine it would," Gwendolyn concurred. "My
mother used to tell me what a dreadful roustabout my father was before she took him in hand and married him. He
learned rather quickly never to ignore her in favor of
chemistry. Thank you, my lord," she added when Lord
Manning suddenly appeared to hand first her, then his
wife, a glass of lemonade. "How very kind. I was dying
of thirst after so much dancing."

Lord Manning made an elegant bow. "I am your humble servant, Miss Wells, and yours, of course, my love."
He set an arm about his wife's slender waist. "I apologize
for the delay. A dozen men and more stopped me to inquire about the heavenly creature in my chaperonage. I
was obliged to repeat your name and specifics in detail.

I'm afraid you'll receive any number of visits in the morning."

"I am sorry, sir," Gwendolyn said with genuine remorse. "I'm sure it was most tiresome for you. My father never ceases to complain of being so frequently bothered."

"Not at all," he said with a smile. "I've never been so popular. Quite a boon to my ego, it is."

"Lord Walsh appears to be particularly interested," his wife noted. "But you mustn't dance with him again, Gwendolyn, no matter how charmingly he may ask."

Gwendolyn hadn't particularly wanted to dance with him the first time, but she didn't say so aloud. Instead, she replied, "There is only the next waltz free, but I'm determined to rest my feet. It's been a month or more since I've danced so much."

"Stand firm to your resolve, my girl," Lord Manning murmured near her ear, "for here comes Walsh, ready to snatch you up again."

He was right. Lord Walsh was approaching them with a particular gleam in his eye, and Gwendolyn inwardly sighed with resignation.

"Lady Anna," he greeted, coming to a stop before them. "Miss Wells. Manning. Are you enjoying the evening?"

"Very much," Lady Anna said, fanning herself, "although it's too hot in these stuffy rooms, as usual."

"Alas, there is no garden in which to cool oneself with a stroll," the viscount replied. "Would you care to move nearer one of these open windows, Miss Wells? I should be glad to lend you my escort."

"No, I thank you, my lord. I'm content here."

"I was hoping that perhaps you'd not yet promised the next waltz, although I can't imagine that being so. Still, I thought I might take my chances, as dancing the minuet with you was such a delight.''

He was worse than Mr. Hanbury, Gwendolyn thought irreverently. At least the first mate hadn't been dripping with such sickly sweetness.

"You're terribly kind, Lord Walsh," she replied politely, "but I fear I must refuse. I've decided to sit this next dance out and rest. It's my feet." She stuck one slippered foot out slightly from beneath her gown. "They're quite large, you see, and somehow wear out more easily. Probably because there's so much more of them than there should be."

It was supposed to be a joke. A very poor one, she admitted, but a jest all the same. She looked up, smiling at the man, and he only stared back with incomprehension. Which made her laugh. She had no notion what it looked like from across the room to a certain newcomer who stood at the entrance to the room, watching her. To the Earl of Rexley it appeared that Gwendolyn Wells was not only flirting with Viscount Walsh, who was turned away from him, but was also smiling up at the damned fellow and even laughing with him.

Lord Manning, who was striving not to chuckle out loud at the befuddled look on Walsh's face as he gazed at Gwendolyn's wiggling foot, glanced toward the commotion stirring in Almack's entryway and fell still at what he saw there.

"In all my days"—he set a hand over his heart in a dramatic gesture—"I should never have expected to see Jack Sommerton entering these hallowed chambers. Anna, my love, tell me I'm not seeing a mere vision. Why, the boy swore to me long ago that nothing could make him attend Almack's. I shan't even repeat the fulsomeness of his oath, for it's quite too tart for delicate ears. What on earth has brought him here tonight?"

"And in such fine form," Lady Anna remarked.

Gwendolyn turned to look at the sight that held Lord and Lady Manning captive and found that Lord Rexley was, indeed, standing at Almack's open entryway. He was a sight to make anyone stare, beautiful in a dark blue coat and knee breeches, his white waistcoat intricately embroidered with silver thread. She'd never seen a man so stunningly handsome or so utterly at home with his own beauty, as if he took it all for granted. His hair was softer in candlelight, more golden than white, with a subtle glow and sheen. His eyes were darker too, closer to midnight blue than mere blue. His every aspect, in fact, had lost any angelic mien. He was simply a beautiful man, and Gwendolyn stared.

Lord Rexley stared back. Or rather frowned, but she was used to that. The next moment he was heading in her direction, although when he arrived he gave his attention to Lord and Lady Manning.

Lord Walsh, seeing him come, said, "I believe I'll take myself off and find some refreshment." He made a swift bow and departed, ignoring Lord Rexley just as Lord Rexley ignored him.

"Lady Anna," the earl said, making a grave bow. "Robby." At last he turned to Gwendolyn. "Miss Wells. I hope I find you in good health this evening?" The tartness of his tone seemed to indicate otherwise, but Gwendolyn smiled and nodded.

"Indeed you do," said Lord Manning, "except for giving us such a delightful shock. I nearly fainted at the sight of you, my boy, and only think what such a spectacle would have done to my consequence. I never should have lived it down in the Lords. Now, don't say anything more." He held up a staying hand when his godson tried to speak. "Go and make your bow to our hostesses and try to keep from letting *their* shock go to your head. Go on with you now." With the same hand he waved Lord Rexley toward the place where Lady Jersey and Mrs. Drummond-Burrell were standing, looking at him behind fluttering fans that little concealed their astonishment at his presence. "And when you've finished there come back and waltz with Miss Wells," Lord Manning said as Lord Rexley obediently walked away. The words made the younger man turn back.

"Damn it, Robby—"

"Mind your language, my boy," Lord Manning reprimanded. "You're not at Mawdry's, after all."

"I'm sure Lord Rexley doesn't wish to dance, my lord," Gwendolyn said quickly. "And I've just now told Lord Walsh that I shall sit the next waltz out. What would he think to see me on the dance floor?"

"Only that your feet have been rested enough," replied his lordship. "I do beg this favor of you, Miss Wells. If Jack has at last found the fortitude to attend Almack's, he must dance. Do you not agree, Anna, my love?"

"Indeed, Jack must certainly dance," Lady Anna agreed pleasantly, fanning herself in a languid motion. "And Miss Wells should accompany him. I'm sure she will be so kind as to do so."

"There you have it." Lord Manning gave a single nod. "Go and make your bow, Jack, and be quick about it. The music will be starting again shortly."

And so Gwendolyn found herself a few minutes later being turned about Almack's dance floor in the arms of the Earl of Rexley.

He didn't make any attempt at polite conversation, but launched out with, "What in blazes were you doing flirting with Walsh? I told you to stay away from him."

Her eyes widened. "My lord, you are not, may I remind you, my father. Even if you were, I should speak to whomever I please. And I was *not* flirting with him."

"You were smiling at him. Laughing with him. And I'll wager you danced with him as well."

"Only a minuet." She shrugged lightly. "I could hardly tell him no when he asked. It would have been rude beyond measure, and despite the fact that I find him rather dull, he's done me no personal harm."

He made a grumbling sound but said nothing, and they danced in a strained silence.

"What a pleasant coincidence," she remarked after a few moments, "that we should both make our first appearance at Almack's on the same night."

"The gossips will have a grand time over the fact," he replied curtly. "I could wring Robby's neck."

"I'm sorry if you find dancing with me so unpleasant a chore," Gwendolyn told him. "For my part, I find you a very good partner."

He looked down at her, and his grip on her hand tightened. Holding her gaze, he at last expelled a taut breath.

"I find you an excellent partner, Gwendolyn Wells. I wish to God that I did not, but I suppose I should have to be a complete block to do otherwise. You're a very beautiful woman. I don't deny the fact. And I don't know why that should make you smile," he said with an irate edge. "It's nothing more than the truth, and you know it well enough."

"Do I? I'm sorry if you find my appearance so distressing."

"For pity's sake! Stop apologizing."

"Very well," she said pleasantly. "Although I *was* going to make the attempt one last time to express my earnest regret for what happened yesterday. You were so disinclined to listen to me when you escorted me back to the Clarendon. But if you don't wish for me to tell you how sorry I am over Lord Astley's stupid dog, then I shan't. Shall we try to make normal conversation instead?''

He shook his head slightly. "How you chatter," he said more softly. "I don't seem to know where you'll end up after you've started."

The words had the oddest effect on Gwendolyn, as if they were love words rather than a simple statement. The hand he held against the small of her back felt hot suddenly.

"A normal conversation," she reminded him, striving to maintain her perfectly civil composure. "I'll begin. Let me see. I know. What brought you to Almack's tonight?"

"I came to dance with Bella."

"With Miss Howell?"

"Yes, with Miss Howell. Wulf won't let her dance with anyone but himself, myself, Lord Manning, and Viscount Callan. Being as that's the case, I often attend the same functions as Bella does so that she can have the opportunity to dance with someone who doesn't tower over her quite so much as Wulf does."

"That's very kind of you."

He looked at her more closely. "You don't believe me?"

"I never said so."

"You think I came because of you? Because you're so beautiful and so desirable and therefore I must, like every other man, seek you out?"

"Not at all," she replied sincerely. "The notion is ridiculous."

"I'm glad you think so. Because I find it equally ridiculous." All the same, the hand on her back pressed her closer. His fingertips curled slightly against her spine, causing her to arch against him in a manner that made Gwendolyn draw in a rapid breath.

"My lord, I believe we were going to attempt a normal

conversation? I don't wish to argue with you yet again. Yesterday was quite enough for me.''

"Ah, yes. Yesterday.'' He pulled her into a turn more swiftly than she'd expected, and Gwendolyn felt, for a shocking moment, the press of his loins against her stomach. She swallowed hard at the sensation and wondered if he was purposefully trying to unsettle her. Because if he was, it was working all too well. His tone, however, remained steady and unaffected. "I've heard of little else than what occurred in Hyde Park with Lord Astley and his blasted dog. I've waited the day long to hear of what debacle you've mired yourself in today, but have thus far been disappointed. What did you do? Lock yourself in a closet to stay out of trouble?''

"Not at all,'' she replied, beginning to lose her patience. "I spent the day wandering alone about Piccadilly and Bond Street, accosting strange men and yodeling at the top of my lungs. London has been too shocked to speak of it yet, but I'm certain it will be in all the papers by the morrow.''

He glared at her. "By God, you're the most aggravating and impossible female I've ever in my life had the misfortune to—''

"Yes, I know,'' she threw back angrily, tugging at his hand. "You've already told me more times than I can count. Let me go.'' She strove to break out of his grip. "I find that I no longer wish to dance.''

He held on to her more tightly. "Be quiet!'' he commanded in a hushed tone. "Everyone is watching. If you create a scene here I'll . . . damn it, Gwendolyn, I vow I'll take you over my knee. Will you behave?''

"I am not one of Lord Astley's dogs, my lord,'' she informed him heatedly. "I believe I deserve an apology.''

He gaped at her. "For *what*?''

Gwendolyn would have kicked the ignorant beast in the

ankle if he'd slowed down their dancing enough to have allowed it. "I'll give you five seconds to think on the matter, my lord," she told him, "and if at the end of that time you've not yet thought of what is clearly obvious, I shall scream at the top of my lungs."

"You wouldn't."

"I will," she warned. "I never lie, as you will eventually learn."

His eyes narrowed, and he nearly waited out the five seconds before saying, "Miss Wells, I apologize sincerely if I have in any way been offensive in referring to your . . . unfortunate capacity for causing mischief at every turn."

It wasn't much, but it was probably all she'd get out of the man.

"And so," he went on. "A normal conversation. Little though you may credit it, I am probably the most capable man in London at carrying on such trivialities."

At this she raised her eyebrows. "Are you?"

"Indeed. I have had years of practice. So. How do you find the weather, Miss Wells?"

"Why did you come here?" she asked again, fully serious now.

"Myself, I find it a bit chilly, despite the sunny afternoons." He pulled her into another deft turn, and again their bodies brushed intimately. "I believe it may rain tomorrow."

"Jack." His hands tightened on her at the sound of his Christian name. "The truth. Let us have it between us. Do you feel nothing at all when you see me?"

An unpleasant sneer pressed his lips. "Miss Wells, you almost invite insult. Do you truly wish to know what I feel when I see you?"

"Yes," she murmured. "I want to know."

He held her gaze steadily, and the sneer slowly died

away. They danced for a full minute without regard for the other couples around them, and when he drew her slightly nearer she made no resistance, despite how she knew it must look to the interest focused upon them. She searched his eyes to see what lay behind the veils there but saw only a deep, abiding distrust . . . and perhaps even fear.

"I only wish I knew myself," he finally said, still gazing at her. "I tell myself it's simply your beauty—you are very beautiful, after all." He shrugged lightly and looked away. "Perhaps that's all it is."

"No," she said, "something so superficial would only make you smile and flirt, as other men do, as I'm sure you do when you meet an attractive female. And just as I do when I meet a handsome man. Do you believe in fate, my lord?"

He looked at her again, with an expression of consternation. "Miss Wells, I hope I misunderstand you."

She laughed. "I'm sure you do not. But if you have, let me make myself clear. I believe in fate. And you're mine."

He blinked at her, plainly stunned by this.

"I am *not*."

"Yes," she said gently, "I'm afraid you are. I knew it the moment I set sight on you. In the cabin on the *Fair Weather,* do you remember?"

He abruptly brought the dance to an end and, taking her arm, stiffly guided her through the other couples and off the dance floor. It was impossible at Almack's to find a quiet corner in which to speak privately. He took her to a small couch instead and nearly shoved her onto it.

"When does Kerlain return to town?" he demanded. Nearby, a small group of elderly matrons edged discreetly closer.

"Lad?" Gwendolyn asked. "I had expected him today, but he was delayed yet again. He sent a message to Lord and Lady Manning, asking them to escort me to Almack's in his place—''

"I *know* that much," he said impatiently, and set a hand to his forehead in exasperation. "Damn you, you've made me addlepated with your ridiculous notions. I am not your fate, do you understand me? Get the idea out of your mind. Completely. Damn!" He suddenly seemed to realize just how loudly he was speaking and that the matrons nearby had heard every word. He gave the women a withering glare that had them hiding behind their fans as they quickly moved away. He looked back at Gwendolyn. "Very fine," he told her angrily. "Now it's going to be all over London, you pestilential female. Will you stop smiling at me in that foolish manner?"

"I don't know why I should. I doubt the grand Earl of Rexley loses his composure very often, and I believe I should take advantage of it while I may. Won't you sit down, Jack dear? You're causing a scene. In Almack's. People are beginning to stare."

"When is Kerlain returning?" he demanded in a lowered tone. He looked as if he might shortly start to tear his hair out by its blond roots.

"By tomorrow," she replied simply. "Unless, of course, he's delayed again." At his murderous expression she added quickly, "I'm sure he'll not be."

"When he comes to see you," he said, leaning closer, "which he will most likely do before I'm able to bring him to ground, tell him that he'd best present himself to Brannard before nightfall or I'll have his head on a platter. And if you receive another missive from your wretched cousin, be so good as to notify me. At once. I'll take matters into my own hands then. And one more thing, Miss Wells."

"Yes, my lord?"

"I shall grant you a favor and forget what you've said

tonight, and I advise that you do the same. I hope you understand what I say?''

Gwendolyn sighed. "Perfectly, my lord. As does half of Almack's. I believe you'll have a difficult time sleeping tonight, thinking of everything you've said. But do remember that I hold none of it against you." She leaned forward on the couch, tilting her face upward to look at him confidingly. "And if anyone should ask what this was all about, I shall simply tell them that you're suffering the ague and therefore not your usual perfect self."

He straightened away from her and drew in a long, slow breath. When he had exhaled it, and after some of the redness had left his face, he said, "You must be mad, Miss Wells. I can hardly think of any other reason for such . . . bizarre behavior. Knowing Kerlain, it must run in your family. It was a favor I was granting, just as I told you." He smiled unpleasantly. "Better women than you have tried to force me to the altar. I bid you good night, Miss Wells." He made an elegant bow for the benefit of all those who watched, then turned on his heel and purposefully walked away.

Chapter Eight

❧

*A*lmack's, Jack thought with distaste as he stood on the pavement outside that establishment, waiting for his carriage to arrive. He never should have come to the place. He'd spent years avoiding it, knowing full well that the establishment served only one purpose for eligible bachelors, and that was to trap them into marrying one of the equally eligible females who were regularly paraded there for inspection. He wasn't even quite certain, exactly, how it was that he'd come to be there in the first place. He'd set out from Brannard with every intention of whiling away a few hours at his favorite gaming hell before meeting with several of his men in order to pursue a lead he'd received that regarded, curiously enough, the whereabouts of both Nancy Randall and Mrs. Toby. Somehow, between his home and Mawdry's, he'd given his coachman the instruction to stop at Almack's. It had been a foolhardy idea. He hadn't even known if he'd be allowed beyond the assembly's hallowed doors, since he held no invitation.

He'd given himself any number of excuses for making the uncharacteristic visit. Bella would be there, he knew, because Robby had mentioned the fact to him earlier in the day, and as Wulf was as loath to attend Almack's as Jack himself, it seemed plausible that she might be in want of a dancing partner. Of course, she'd been to Almack's before and he'd never felt compelled to attend, but he suddenly hated to think of sweet, shy Bella standing alone, a wallflower, while Gwendolyn Wells spent the evening fighting off a bevy of would-be dancing partners.

And Robby and Anna would surely be in need of him, Jack equally assured himself, although this excuse was rather more vague than the others. He had the notion that they'd require rescuing from whatever trouble Gwendolyn Wells was certain to get into—but this, when he thought of it now, was inane. Robby wasn't in his dotage, after all, and a more capable man at handling trouble Jack had yet to meet. As to that, Lady Anna wasn't a shrinking violet either. If Gwendolyn Wells somehow managed to burn Almack's to the ground, Lady Anna probably wouldn't do so much as blink an eye.

For whatever reason—although not, he assured himself, because of Miss Wells—Jack had found himself at Almack's, half-praying that he'd be turned away by the doorman. Instead, he'd been readily admitted, and what had followed made him feel like banging his head against Almack's brick exterior. He had steeled himself against Gwendolyn Wells, had prepared to do nothing more than make her a polite bow and then ignore her for the remainder of the evening. It had to be done, he told himself, not only for his own peace of mind, but to protect both their reputations. London was talking, just as he had expected, and that had to be put to an end. Especially after what had happened the day before in Hyde Park with Lord Astley and his dog. It had been mere coincidence that he'd been riding through the park at the same time that Miss Pestilence Wells had been wreaking her usual havoc, but coupled with the incidence on St. James, his coming to her aid was enough to create plenty of gossip.

And so he had repeated silently, as his name was announced, that he would make his bow to Miss Wells and to Robby and Lady Anna, and he would dance with Bella and then sit with her for a while. He would even be pleasant to Almack's patronesses and drink a glass of lemonade and pretend to enjoy it. Then he would make his good-byes and leave. And he would do it all without showing the least interest or partiality to Gwendolyn Wells. The gossips would have nothing more to feast upon in *that* direction.

But it hadn't happened that way at all. In fact, now that Jack thought of it, nothing that he'd intended had come to pass. He paced a few steps in one direction and set a hand to his forehead, shaking his head slightly at the remembrance of what he'd felt when he'd set sight on her.

He was inured to beauty, just as she'd said. And equally inured to females dressed in alluring finery. But there was something about seeing *her* in a ball gown that made his head spin. The worst part was that he couldn't particularly recall what the actual dress had looked like. It was just her, with her red-gold hair swept up in a simple design, and the soft white skin of her bare neck and shoulders exposed by the gown's low neckline, and her lively face lit up in a smile—which she had been directing at Lord Walsh.

What in the name of heaven was the foolish woman thinking of? To so openly flirt with a devil like Walsh could only invite trouble. He'd warned her about the man. *Robby* had warned her, and Robby rarely troubled himself to warn anyone about anything.

It hadn't precisely been the idea of rescuing her from yet another folly that had driven him in her direction. It had been something far more unsettling. For a moment, seeing that smile lifted toward another man, Jack had felt for the first time in his life a decided need to commit murder. Where the feeling had come from he had no notion. That it had been unfounded, ridiculous, and unwelcome was without doubt. Thank heavens he'd mastered himself into some semblance of order by the time he'd reached her side, else he'd have more to regret than dancing with her and causing the kind of disgusting, possessive scene that always had him laughing behind his hand at other men.

Possessive? he thought. Now, where had that come from? He wasn't possessive over Gwendolyn Wells. He hardly even knew the woman, and what he did know was that she was a scheming, troublemaking female.

Her fate indeed. He snorted at the idea. What kind of nonsense was that? It sounded like something out of one of those sappy romantic novels that were so popular among young ladies. He wasn't her fate, or anyone else's, thank God. Which was just as well, for she'd be far from well served by ending up with someone like him—a man who didn't even know what or who he truly was.

Lifting his head toward the dark sky, he gazed at the stars and the swift-moving clouds that first hid and then revealed them. Of course, it wouldn't be much better for him, being married to someone like her, troublesome and American as she was. But there would be her beauty to provide some measure of compensation, and that wit and humor that he had previously admired. He could almost envision what it would be like. Almost—

"Yer lordship?"

He recognized the voice and felt an immediate hardening within. Whatever fancies he'd been leisurely entertaining vanished. He looked about to see who was watching him. A footman stood nearby, waiting to assist Almack's patrons in and out of carriages, a number of which were presently arriving, including his own, Jack saw. He stepped back into the shadows, meeting the questioning glance of his coachman as he did so. The coachman, well trained, took note and drew the team of horses to a stop somewhat farther away from Almack's than might be expected.

"Victor," Jack greeted the man softly. "You have what I want?"

Victor nodded and held out a crumpled piece of paper. "Wrote it down, in case you're wantin' me to go in wiv the boys. Left Babbit wiv 'em."

"No, I want you with me," Jack told him. In the small moonlight he squinted at the note, then crushed it in his fist. "Very well. Take me to him. Babbit knows what to do if you don't arrive?"

"Aye, m'lord."

"You have the weapons?"

"Aye. Everything's just as you wished it, m'lord."

"Let's be on our way, then."

Jack pushed the note into an inner pocket, never realizing that it missed its mark and fell to the ground instead.

But Gwendolyn, having just exited Almack's with Lord and Lady Manning, saw it fall. Her gaze had been immediately drawn to the sound of Lord Rexley's voice and then had become riveted to the sight of him standing in close conversation with a man who looked as if he'd just broken out of Newgate. She had no time to contemplate the strangeness of the moment; almost at once Lord Rexley and his companion turned and made their way toward a waiting carriage.

"Where are you going, my dear?" Lord Manning asked. He was in the midst of arranging his wife's cloak more warmly about her shoulders and appeared not to have seen his godson in company with the other man.

"A moment, please, my lord," she called back, hurrying to the place where the note lay on the pavement. She picked it up just as Lord Rexley's carriage moved past her, and as she stood she could see through the window, beyond the glare of the swinging carriage lantern, the briefest glimpse of Jack Sommerton taking from the strange man what very much looked to be a pistol. He didn't see her at all.

"Gwendolyn?" Lady Manning called.

"Yes, ma'am," Gwendolyn replied obediently. She quickly pulled the note apart and tried to read what was scrawled there. *Ware* was written on top, and beneath it, she squinted to see, was what appeared to be *St. Bart's 2.*

"I'm coming!"

Stuffing the note into a pocket inside her cloak, she hurried toward Lord and Lady Manning and their waiting carriage.

St. Balthasar—or St. Bart's, as it was called by those who lived there—was one of London's meanest rookeries and, at two o'clock in the morning, one of its darkest. Soot-covered dwellings were piled one on top of the other, so poorly built that they leaned precariously on the edge of collapse, and so tall that the dank alleyways they created were never touched by the light of either sun or moon. Rivers of sewage ran freely beneath makeshift bridges of unmortared brick and board, and the constant damp and lack of light encouraged a slick, dripping film of slime to grow on every surface.

Unpleasant business was conducted during all hours in St. Bart's stench-ridden alleyways, but the most unpleasant was left for these late—or rather, early—hours. It was now that the rats who inhabited the rookery returned from their nightly ventures, bringing with them whatever they had stolen or killed for. Here and now they could make a profit on their labors, for here was where a buyer could always be found, and now was the time when they did their buying. Crooks from all over London came to St. Bart's to sell their harvest of goods; buyers came to purchase those goods for far less than they would have to pay otherwise. It was, for all involved, a very agreeable way to do business, and for one man in particular—Moses Ware—it was even more so.

Jack made his way with great care into the center of the rookery, walking slowly and steadily, careful to keep his features blank of any emotion. From the shadows he could feel the faces that watched his progress, seeing those same faces only when the occasional bonfire made it possible. He was accompanied by his two best men, Victor and Babbit, whose reputations had made this meeting possible and whose presence was the only reason Jack had been allowed to stray this far into St. Bart's. He was fully aware that without his certain alliances, he'd be a dead man by now. His own reputation among the lower classes wasn't enough to do him any good here, and his nobility and wealth gave no protection. The authorities never went into St. Bart's. Murder was not investigated here and seldom even discovered. Bodies were stripped of goods and clothes and then shoved naked into the rivers of oozing sewage to become part of the filth that defined the place.

For all its sins, St. Bart's provided one necessary service for the citizens of London's underworld. It was sanctuary. The one safe refuge in all of the city where thieves and prostitutes might hide from vengeful bosses and pimps—if they could first make their way safely inside and put themselves into the keeping of the man who ruled it. Because out of all the kings who ran the myriad rookeries in London, the one who ran St. Bart's was by far the most fearsome.

Moses Ware.

Jack had heard the name and the stories of violence and crime that were associated with it for years, but he'd never before entered the man's lair in order to meet him. In fact, he'd avoided St. Bart's almost as devoutly as had London's remaining crime kings. Moses Ware wasn't the kind of man one sought if one could avoid it. But Jack couldn't avoid it any longer. Nancy Randall and her baby were here, and Jack had come to bring them out.

The alleyways were mazelike, running in no particular pattern, growing darker and danker as Jack and his men made their way farther along. It was almost like traveling to a different country, Jack thought as they neared a particularly large bonfire where several men awaited them—a country that bore a striking resemblance to Hades.

"That's far enow," a rough voice stated. A man matching the voice, dark-haired and dark-eyed, stepped forward. "Yer Rexley?"

Jack nodded. "Aye."

The black eyes traveled past him. "Victor, it's been a long time."

"So it 'as, Fin."

"Di'n't think you was still alive, goin' off to war as ye did. A bleedin' 'ero now, is it? 'Nd you too, Babbit. Never thought to see a thievin' murderer like you take the King's shillin'."

" 'Twas that or 'ang, Fin Drogin. But I don't have t' tell you that, do I?" John Babbit's voice was quiet, measured. Jack was aware of a bitter undercurrent beneath the words.

"Is Moses Ware ready to receive us?" he asked. He didn't want the encounter to become more complicated than it already was. He only wanted to get Nancy and her baby out of St. Bart's and safely on their way to his estate in Somerset.

Fin Drogin gave him a long, silent look. The half dozen men standing behind him moved restlessly.

"Aye. Come along. We've been ready this long while."

They were led to a place not far away, across another bridge, where an open tavern shone with light made all the brighter for the deep darkness inside the maze, and where the boisterous sounds of voices and laughter died away as Jack and his men appeared. There was almost a cheerfulness to the place, reeking as it was with the strong smells of greasy foods and liquor—a refuge of warmth and comfort in the midst of the filth that made up St. Bart's.

Jack surveyed the tavern in a low sweep. It was three-sided—barely—with most of one precariously sagging wall being shored up by a few thick timbers. A ragtag assortment of men filled the room, sitting at tables or leaning against the long wooden board that served as a bar, all of them looking at the newcomers. In the back of the tavern, hidden partly by darkness and partly by smoke, was a particularly large table, and behind it, surrounded by more of his men as well as a few women, sat the man whom Jack instinctively knew was Moses Ware. He looked too confident to be anyone else.

"Mind yer manners," Fin Drogin muttered as he led the way. Jack followed, winding his way through the clutter of tables and chairs. Behind him, he heard the reassuring footsteps of his men. Fin Drogin stopped at the large table. "This is 'im," he said, shrugging toward Jack.

Moses Ware nodded slowly, his gaze assessing Jack from top to toe. He didn't rise from the chair in which he sat, his arm resting indolently about the waist of an attractive woman who was perched on his lap, but Jack could tell that he was a big man. Big like Wulf was big, and apparently just as muscular. Black hair curled over his forehead, and equally black eyes steadily held Jack's gaze. Intelligent eyes, Jack noted. But then the man who ran St. Bart's wouldn't be a fool by any stretch.

"You're Rexley?" Moses Ware asked.

"Yes."

"Handsome devil, ain't he, Mosey?" the woman on the lap murmured, smiling. "Lookit them fine clothes."

Moses Ware shoved her to her feet. "Shut yer gob, Ellie, or I'll shut it meself. Go and fetch 'is lordship a pint." To Jack, he said, "Will you sit?"

"It's not necessary," Jack replied. "I'd like to conclude our business as quickly as possible. You have the girl?"

"I 'ave 'er," Moses Ware said. "And 'er brat. She come to me fer safekeepin', 'nd I give 'er m' word I'd not let Rickard find 'er. She's t' work fer me now, y' understand? We 'ave an agreement." He sat back in his chair, his expression blank. "A pretty gel, is Nan Randall. The kind wot makes a man plenty money afore she's done up. Nice, 'ealthy gel, she is. Rickard thought so. You do too. Seems like there's plenty of buyers for sweet little Nan. Makes me wonder if she ain't worth more than I'd first figured."

"I want her *and* the child," Jack told him. "What's your price, Ware?"

Ellie had returned with a mug of ale, which she set on the table in front of Jack. " 'Ere you are, m'lord." She smiled at him widely, revealing perfect white teeth, a rarity among common street whores. She was a remarkably beautiful woman and knew it. Moses Ware stretched out a hand and grasped her about the waist again, pulling her close while keeping his eyes on Jack.

"My price?" he repeated thoughtfully. "Mebbe I should be the one askin' you that question, my lord the earl. 'Ow much you willin' to do so as to add Nan and her babe to yer collection? Eh? You got so many 'ores 'nd suchlike in yer keepin' that the loss of one pretty gel like Nan ain't goin' to make a difference. Mebbe yer willin' to pay to get 'em, but mebbe you ain't willin' to pay what it is that I want."

"Money isn't a problem," Jack told him.

Moses Ware stared at him. "Money ain't what I want."

"I had a feeling it wasn't." Jack wished, heartily, that he had his pistol with him. They'd been searched before they'd been allowed to enter St. Bart's and all their weapons taken.

Moses Ware lifted a hand and snapped his fingers. A curtain behind the bar was lifted and a frightened young girl holding a baby was brought out. She looked younger than her sixteen years and much thinner than when Jack had last seen her. The child she held so protectively against her chest seemed an impossibly tiny bundle.

"Oh, my lord!" She was stopped when she tried to go to Jack, but Moses Ware said, "Let 'er," and she was released. Tears streamed down her pretty face as she walked unsteadily to Jack's side, gazing up at him pleadingly. "I din't want you to come. 'E'll kill you if 'e finds out."

"Nancy." Jack touched her arm reassuringly, fully relieved to simply find her alive. "You should have come to me long ago. I would have had you safe even before the child was born."

"Rickard will kill you!" she said again, clutching the child so tightly that it made a sound of protest. " 'Nd me too. Oh, I wish you 'adn't come. Ware's goin' to take care of me."

"But what about your child?" Jack asked. "You can't want him, or her, in the midst of all this?" He made a motion with his hand in the general direction of the tavern and everything beyond.

"Ah, now, there's wot it is," said Moses Ware. " 'E wants that child, just as I told ye, Nan. 'E wants that baby and 'e wants to know where to find Mrs. Toby 'nd all the little babies she takes care of. Ain't that so, m'lord?"

"Mrs. Toby is an entirely different matter." Jack turned to face him. "And will require an entirely different price, I presume. Let us finish first with what we have at hand. Nancy and the child are coming with me. What do you want in exchange?''

Ware leaned forward to pick up a tankard of ale. ''Nan stays 'ere 'nd pays her debt t' me. You take the child. Got enough bastards to feed as it is.''

Jack shook his head. ''Nancy and her baby are coming with me. Tonight. And I don't have enough patience to play games. Tell me what you want.''

Moses Ware smiled. ''What I want, I got to 'ave Nan fer. It's Rickard I'm after. 'E'll come fer 'er. Wants 'er, just as you do. 'Nd 'e wants that baby to give to Mrs. Toby too. Little girl babies sell fast 'nd easy, 'nd Nan's baby girl is sweet as new cream.''

''Please,'' Nancy said desperately, pressing both herself and the child against Jack's arm. ''Please take her!'' Her voice was thick with tears. ''Take my baby safe away, I beg ye!''

''I'm taking the *both* of you from here,'' Jack promised her.

Moses Ware slammed his tankard on the table. ''Not unless you give me Rickard!''

''How do you want him?'' Jack asked. ''Delivered to you personally? Or strung up at Newgate?'' He slapped the palm of his hand down on Ware's table, making a greater noise than the man had done. ''You tell me, Ware, what you want, and I'll damned well give it to you! But no more games. Understand it.''

''Fine,'' said Ware. ''Very fine, m'lord. You want the gel and 'er brat, then you bring me Rickard. 'Ere. To Saint Bart's. I want 'im alone. No one else. 'Nd then you get Nan. No trouble.''

''*And* Mrs. Toby?''

''And Mrs. Toby,'' Ware said with a nod. ''You bring me Rickard and you'll find out what you want t' know. Even who it is she works for.'' He gestured with a single finger toward Nancy Randall and her child. "Take the babe tonight as proof of m' word."

Jack stood silent for a long moment, thinking the matter over. That he could deliver Rickard, a much lesser crime lord than Ware, was probable. Already he could envision a dozen different ways to accomplish the deed. But could he then trust Ware, in turn, to deliver Nancy and the information about Mrs. Toby? Or should he attempt to wrest her and the babe free from St. Bart's tonight? Which would prove the least difficult, and the most promising? It was a ticklish decision, and he found himself wavering.

But then the decision was taken out of his hands. A sudden commotion started up at the entrance to the tavern, and all eyes were drawn to it. Moses Ware stood and Jack turned, the better to see what was the cause.

"Sweet livin' days," Ware murmured in amazement.

"Oh, my God," Jack said with stunned disbelief.

"Dear me," said Gwendolyn Wells, who was forcibly escorted toward them at the hands of two of Ware's men. She stopped before Jack and gave him a look filled with apology. "I'm dreadfully sorry," she said, her hands fluttering nervously. "I came to make certain that you weren't in any trouble, but I seem to have . . . stepped wrong again."

Chapter Nine

❧

"God's feet," Moses Ware said in amazement. "Wot 'ave we now? A very gift from 'eaven."

Jack snorted. "Far from it. If you only knew." He could hardly think of what to do or say; it seemed impossible that anything worse could have happened. Gwendolyn Wells stood not a foot away from him, smiling hopefully, nervously tenting and untenting her glove-encased fingers.

"My," she said after a moment's silence—a silence brought on by her stunning presence. "I-I had no idea what sort of place this was when I told the cab driver where I wished to go. He tried to talk me out of it, you see, but I just couldn't quite believe . . . well, I'm sure you can imagine my surprise." She smiled brightly and cast a nervous glance at Moses Ware.

No, Jack thought, it couldn't possibly be worse. She was too beautiful to be let go of, dressed even as she was in a demure gown and cloak that were a full contrast to the elegant clothes she'd worn earlier at Almack's. Despite the simpleness of her dress, Jack doubted that anyone present had ever seen a more expensively clad woman step a foot inside St. Bart's. But it wouldn't have mattered if she'd worn a nun's costume. Moses Ware would never let such a beauty slip out of his grasp. Everyone in the room—man, child, and woman alike—was gaping at Gwendolyn Wells as if she were an apparition who'd flapped into the tavern on a pair of wings. Although that wasn't quite true. Victor and Babbit, standing just behind her, were giving her quite another sort of look—one that Jack imagined matched his own current expression. She'd ruined everything, and now he didn't know how he or his men were going to get themselves, let alone Gwendolyn Wells and Nancy Randall, out of St. Bart's alive. He shot Victor and Babbit a look of apology, and they grimly shook their heads.

"I'm sorry to have intruded," she went on, chattering in her usual manner, "but I do have a very good explanation. I found a note you'd dropped, you see, and—"

"Note?" Ware asked, looking to Jack with raised eyebrows.

"About our meeting," Jack explained, his gaze held on Gwendolyn's face. With a sigh he said, "When and where. Nothing more."

"This yer lady, then?" Ware's voice was filled with admiration.

"Yes," both Jack and Gwendolyn said in the same breath. "And I'm going to beat her thoroughly when I get her home, never fear," Jack added with complete sincerity.

"Now, no need to be in a takin'," Moses Ware said kindly. "Nice little bit, she is. Very nice. Never seen such a fine lady in all my days, and that's God's truth. And a brave soul, she is, comin' 'ere to see to yer safety, m'lord. Introduce us, properlike, if't please ye."

Jack drew in a slow breath and at last pulled his gaze from Gwendolyn's pale face. The way Moses Ware was looking at her didn't bode well. The man was just about slobbering with desire. That his request for an introduction had been more of a command wasn't lost on Jack either. Moses Ware wanted Gwendolyn and had probably already decided to have her. It was understandable, of course, especially if he believed her to be nothing more than an expensive ladybird.

"Certainly," he said slowly, thinking carefully upon what to say. "Miss Gwendolyn Wells, I have the honor of presenting to you Mister Moses Ware. Mister Ware, this is Miss Wells, of the United States. She is my . . . fiancée."

Jack wasn't certain who was more surprised by this pronouncement, Moses Ware or Gwendolyn Wells. She, at least, recovered more quickly.

"How do you do, Mr. Ware?" she chirruped brightly, stepping forward to reach her dainty hand across the table to where Ware yet stood. She looked impossibly clean and neat compared to the brutish man; Jack had to grit his teeth to keep from grabbing her and pulling her back. "I'm terribly pleased. And I do apologize for the intrusion. I simply didn't know what to think when I saw that note and saw my betrothed going off with—well, with that gentleman there." She waved her other hand at Victor. "I'm afraid I don't know his name, but you can imagine my surprise and bewilderment." Moses Ware continued to gaze at her as if he'd never seen anything so amazing in his life, and he let her shake and then drop his hand without response. Gwendolyn took a few steps backward toward Jack, until she bumped into him. "And then to be brought here, to this place—oh, but I've already told you that the cabbie didn't want to bring me. Which I can perfectly understand. Now, that is. At the time I—"

"Gwen, darling," Jack said tightly, setting his hand about her waist and squeezing. "That's enough."

"Yes. Yes, I'm sure it is, Jack, dear. Quite, quite enough. And if you're finished with your business, which I do hope is the case, I should be very glad to leave. It is rather late, after all, and—oh—I've left the cabbie waiting. I'm sure he's starting to wonder just where on earth I've—"

"Yer goin' to marry 'er?" Moses Ware asked, laughing. "I ken see why," he said, his appreciative gaze moving up and down the length of Gwendolyn's form, and then back up again, "but if 'twere me I'd keep 'er gagged night 'nd day, 'specially when yer 'preciatin' 'er"—he chuckled—"*finer* qualities." He laughed at this as if it were a grand joke, and nearly everyone else in the tavern joined him.

"Gad," Jack muttered under his breath, taking the opportunity to cast a searching glance about. He almost didn't see Victor jerking his head slightly toward the opening of the tavern, and even when he did he wasn't certain what it was that the other man meant. But there was little time to think on the matter. He had to make a decision.

"Miss Wells's interference, unfortunate as it is, changes nothing, Ware. You want Rickard, I'll deliver him. Tomorrow. My word of honor on it. Nancy and the baby come with us." He took Nancy's elbow, ready to lead her out, and felt her deep trembling. In her arms, the baby squirmed and began to fuss.

"Wait," Ware said, holding up one hand. A circle of men took a step inward, closing the space between Jack and their master, cutting off any path of escape. "We'll make us a bargain. You want Nan and the babe. Take 'em wiv you, then. But yer lady stays 'ere wiv me."

"*What?*" Gwendolyn cried.

"I'll take good care of 'er," Ware promised with a slow smile. "Mebbe I ken teach 'er 'ow to keep quiet, 'specially when a man don't want a woman's prate to distract 'im. Eh?"

Jack felt a dark chill sweep over him at the words. It

was a sensation such as he'd never known before and gave rise to an equally unknown anger.

"No," he stated flatly.

" 'Nd if you don't bring Rickard, then I'll keep 'er. Make good use of 'er. I could make a fortune off a bit like that, once I've broke 'er in and taught 'er a few tricks."

"Tricks!" Gwendolyn said heatedly. "I am not a dog, Mister Ware."

"Shut up, Gwen," Jack said.

"I want 'er dress," Ellie put in, only to be cuffed by Ware.

"You keep yer yap shut too, Ellie."

Ellie defiantly shoved him. "I want 'er dress, ye great bastard!" she shouted at the top of her lungs. "You ken 'ave 'er, but I get the dress!"

"You most certainly do not!" Gwendolyn said with great affront. "I am not remaining here, and I am not giving anyone my dress."

"Yes, you are, m' fine lady," Ware said, nodding at his men, who moved even closer.

"My lady comes with me," Jack said. "I won't leave without her."

The two men stared at each other in silence until Jack suddenly moved.

"You want the dress?" he asked. "You can have it." He started unlacing Gwendolyn's cloak with terse, jerking motions.

She furiously pushed him away.

"I'm not giving her my dress!"

"You are, damn it!" He roughly jerked her back and kept unlacing, lowering his voice. "Be quiet and listen to me, or we'll all be killed." He spoke only loud enough for her to hear. "Do you see that girl with the baby?" More loudly he said, "Keep still or I'll let Ware keep you!" To her again he whispered, "Do you see her?"

Gwendolyn nodded.

"When I tell you to run, you grab her and *run*." He gave the word as much emphasis as he could while striving to look as if he merely continued to chide her. "Get out of the tavern and into the shadows as fast as you can." He spoke quickly, tossing the cloak over his shoulder. "Turn around," he said loudly, forcibly turning her. He leaned closer as he unlaced her dress, speaking into her ear and keeping his eyes on the men surrounding them. "You run, Gwen. Don't stop for any reason. For God's sake, get her and that baby and yourself out of here."

"But—"

"Do as I say. No questions. I'll find you. Believe that. I *will* find you. I hope you have something under this thing." He tugged the sleeves down her arms, exposing the white skin of her shoulders and back.

"My chemise," she murmured, turning about to face him, stepping away to pull the dress off herself. A low murmuring greeted the action, but she ignored it and stepped out of the gown. Holding his gaze, she put the garment in his hands. "I will do just as you say, my lord."

He felt an irrational urge to kiss her, felt in that dangerous moment unutterably proud of her. Nothing on God's earth could have made him desert her, silly and foolish as she'd been this night.

She was left nearly naked by the loss of her gown, a fact made more shameful by the leers and whistles that were gaining strength, and he quickly and deftly took her cloak and covered her again. She smiled shakily and nodded, and Jack, drawing in a breath, said, "Here's your dress, Ware." He turned, tossed the gown on the table. "For your lady, may she enjoy it in good health. Now our business is done."

"Not yet. Yer not leavin' wiv both women."

"Yes, you thieving bastard," Jack said. "I am." He began to move even as he shouted, "Now, Gwen! *Run!*"

Gwendolyn knew she'd made a mistake the moment the driver of the hack she'd hailed outside the Clarendon had pulled to a stop in front of what he'd called "the safest entrance to Saint Bart's."

It hadn't looked safe to Gwendolyn. It had looked, to be perfectly honest, like the entrance to a dark, unwelcoming alleyway. If hell had a gate that was less frightening, she would have been astonished. But she'd come this far and, if Jack Sommerton was somewhere inside that fearsome darkness, she would not turn back.

She'd taken only a few steps into the dank stench of the alleyway before she'd been assailed by two men, who'd first stared at her with complete surprise and then insisted upon escorting her to where " 'is lordship" was. And where his lordship was proved to be a greater shock than the journey it had taken to get to him. Gwendolyn had seen poverty before, and filth and decay, but nothing in her experience had ever compared to St. Bart's. To find the Earl of Rexley—her future husband—in the midst of such a place and engaged in commerce—over another woman!—with the likes of Moses Ware had been almost too much to take in.

She'd realized how much danger she'd stepped into, had heard herself babbling like a complete idiot, had felt a shock of rage that her intended was in the middle of a disgusting hellhole, haggling over a woman with a baby who was most likely his: In short, she'd felt quite angry all the way around. But it had been too late to change her mind or to turn about and leave as if she'd never come. The only choice left to her was to brazen it out, and when Jack had asked her to trust him, she'd felt certain that she could do so. An abominable knave he might be—she'd certainly give him grief over the other woman later—but he was trustworthy. That, she believed fully, was true.

He wanted her to run, he'd said, and, swallowing down her fear, she had said that she would do as he wished. He had covered her quickly with her cloak, yet she felt naked and vulnerable beneath it. And very afraid. He turned away with her dress in one hand.

"Here's your dress, Ware." He tossed the gown on the table. Gwendolyn wondered at how he could sound so perfectly calm and easy. Her own heart was pounding violently in her chest, as it had never before had cause to do, yet he acted as if they were merely in Hyde Park and not in a den of thieves where their very lives were so precariously held. "For your lady, may she enjoy it in good health. Now our business is done."

"Not yet," Moses Ware replied tightly, leaning forward. He was a big man, dark and fearsome to gaze upon. The way he looked at Gwendolyn, with such obvious intent, caused her to shudder. To even think of being touched by him made her stomach churn. "Yer not leavin' wiv both women."

"Yes, you thieving bastard," Jack Sommerton replied with a confidence that Gwendolyn wished she felt. There seemed to be a great many men standing threateningly about them. "I am."

Gwendolyn felt the tension gathering and pulled her cloak more tightly about herself. She looked at the young woman standing beside her, the fretting child clutched in her arms, and tried to think of what she would do when Jack told her to run. The girl seemed even more frightened, which was not, Gwendolyn decided, a very promising prospect.

And then she heard the shout.

"Now, Gwen! *Run*!"

She stood frozen where she was and watched as Jack

lunged at the table that stood between him and Moses Ware. It was all a blur. The table flew up into the air, knocking everyone behind it to the ground. Jack swung back to her and roared again, *''Run!''*

It set her into motion. She grabbed the other girl by the arm and dragged her toward the heavy darkness beyond the tavern's opening. There were men there with pistols aimed into the room, but she made her legs move and wouldn't let herself think of what might happen. The girl behind her felt as heavy as lead, a tremendous weight to be forcibly pulled along, slowing her to an unbearable gait.

Noise exploded all around her. Shouts, pistols, chairs and tables screeching as they were shoved across the wooden floor. And the baby, who at the loud commotion had begun to wail.

''The women!'' Moses Ware shouted over the din. ''Get the women!''

''Oh, God!'' Gwendolyn cried, her heart in her throat. They were so close to the entrance, so close to being quit of the place. It seemed to take an eternity to move even an inch, and yet she knew that she was racing, shoving everything and everyone aside in her panic. Hands clawed at her, men shouted, and yet she found the strength to push past them toward the darkness beyond the open wall.

She saw, with a flash of understanding as she ran headlong, that the men pointing their pistols into the tavern were not pointing those same pistols at *her*. They were shooting anyone who tried to grab her. They were *helping* her. The knowledge gave her a shock of courage.

''Come on!'' she shouted at the girl behind her.

The men shooting into the tavern had cleared a path for them, but once Gwendolyn was across the wooden plank that served as a bridge across the river of sewage, she was on her own. She stopped only a moment to gather her bearings. Shouts echoed everywhere in the maze of alleyways, along with gunfire and the baby's wailing cries.

"Which way?" She looked wildly about. "Which way?"

She couldn't remember from which direction she'd been escorted to the tavern. The darkest alleyway seemed the most inviting, and she gripped the girl's arm with renewed strength and pulled her along.

They ran, filled with panic, for a full minute before the sounds of men made them stop and press up against a wet, slippery wall. The entire rookery had come alive within the same space of time, and the shouts of the citizens filled the air. Dim, flickering lights sputtered to life behind the windows of the rickety dwellings, providing the only light, and doors began to open. The longer they stayed in one spot, Gwendolyn knew, the more surely they'd be hunted down. The baby's cries made them even more vulnerable.

"Can't you quiet her?" Gwendolyn whispered fiercely.

"She's 'ungry," the girl replied, desperation and fear equal in her voice.

"Well, there's little to be done about that, I suppose," Gwendolyn murmured. "But never fear. We'll get the child—and you—out of here. Do you know anything of these alleyways?"

The girl shook her head and held the fussing baby more tightly. "I came in the night, just as you did, and 'aven't been out since."

"Very well. We shall find our way as we can. Come along."

They moved forward more slowly, touching the wall to find their way in the blackness that was illumined only by the dim candles and lanterns, avoiding those alleyways where bonfires showed men lying in wait. They moved more deeply into the maze of St. Bart's, crouching and hiding when voices alerted them to danger, the girl smothering the baby's cries with her shawl until Gwendolyn was afraid that she'd suffocate the child. The smells of the place were beyond imagination, and the women grew wetter and wetter from the slime that clung to the walls and streets. It was only by pure determination that Gwendolyn held on to the contents of her stomach, when every corner that they turned revealed a new stench that made her whole body want to revolt.

She had no notion of how long they crept onward in such stealth before they were discovered. All she knew was that they were no nearer to being out of the blasted hellhole than they'd been at the start.

"There! See 'em!"

A group of young boys shouted, pointing, and were followed by several men bearing torches.

"Run!" Gwendolyn shouted, shoving the girl ahead of her into the darkness. They ran headlong through every opening they came to, fear and pursuit driving them forward. They stumbled into a better-lit alley and found themselves pelted from open windows, cursed and yelled at. The young boys who'd first discovered them picked up stones or bricks or whatever they could find and threw them. Something sharp struck Gwendolyn on her shoulder, driving her against a wall. She shoved herself away and kept running, her cloak flapping wildly about her ill-clad body as she followed the figure of the girl ahead.

They came to an opening where three alleyways converged, and the girl stopped and looked from one to the other.

"Don't stop!" Gwendolyn cried, pushing her into the darkest of the three. They ran until her lungs ached with a white-hot pain. At last, hearing the roar behind them dim, they stopped, collapsing against a wall to gain breath.

"Here." The girl's voice was harsh from their running.

"You take 'er." She shoved the wet, screeching bundle into Gwendolyn's arms. "You take 'er, and I'll draw 'em away."

"No!"

" 'Er name is Kitty," the girl said, sobbing. "Take care of 'er." Leaning to give the baby the flash of a kiss, she pushed away and ran back toward where the crowd had pursued them.

"No!" Gwendolyn cried after her, but the slender figure was lost in the darkness. She could hear the shouts of the crowd and knew that the girl had led them down another alley.

The baby in her arms screamed out her unhappiness and squirmed until the wet blankets around her fell loose, revealing the child. She was so tiny! Just the size of a doll, with flailing arms and legs, her baby skin shining white in the darkness, unadorned save for a sopping diaper. Her eyes were shut in small, tight slits, and her round bird's mouth was hungrily open and demanding. Gwendolyn gathered her close as best she could and continued on, moving quickly but no longer running for fear of dropping the strange, living bundle.

The shouting receded as she made her way, further proof that the girl had led their pursuers away. But with each step she took, Gwendolyn became more convinced that she was only going in circles. She could see no opening leading out of St. Bart's; there was only the never-ending darkness, stench, and dampness, the echoing of shouts and pistols, and alleyways that led to nothing more. At last she came to a fork with one choice showing a small fire. It wasn't one of the bonfires that promised sure capture . . . perhaps, she prayed, it was built for no more complicated purpose than to warm one or two cold individuals.

The child had quieted into exhausted sobs, and her

movements had stilled, as if she had no recourse after her futile exertions save to sleep. Gathering her closer, Gwendolyn slowly moved toward the fire. She saw no one as she neared it, though every shadow promised to hide a stealthy figure. If she could only get past the fire, whose small flames licked upward against one slick wall, without being detected.

She pressed against the other wall, creeping along it, her gaze darting everywhere, at every sound, seeking danger. All at once a figure loomed up from out of the farthest shadow and spoke.

"Are you Gwendolyn Wells?"

He was tall, dark, and dressed all in black, staring down at her from what seemed a towering height. Gwendolyn looked up at him and gasped. The fire lit his features—exposing a harsh, evil face. Black eyes stared out of that face, a devil's face with a devil's eyes. Gwendolyn's mouth opened, but she found that she couldn't speak.

"You *are* Gwendolyn Wells," he stated, and took a step nearer, holding out a hand.

She cried and leapt away, slipping on the slick stones and falling backward. She heard an exclamation and then the baby was snatched out of her arms. Her fingers gripped at the blankets without purchase, and she continued to fall until her head struck the stones and she slid into utter blackness.

Chapter Ten

❧

Gwennie?''

''Here, try this. I apologize that it's not water.''

A cold cloth smelling distinctly of brandy was pressed against her forehead—hurting more than it helped—and Gwendolyn moaned and tried to push it away.

''Gwennie, can you open your eyes?''

Even through the mists of confusion, she recognized the voice. That Tennessean drawl was purely distinct.

''Lad?'' Her head ached as if a hammer were banging on it, and her throat was parched.

''It's me, sweetheart. You've had a bad fall and hit your head, but you're going to be fine.''

She was cold and wet and lying on a hard and equally cold surface. Somewhere in the distance she heard a commotion of shouts and gunfire, while much closer was the murmuring of men's voices.

''Lad?'' she murmured again, struggling to sit and open her eyes. ''I had the most awful dream.''

Warm, strong hands helped her push upward.

''You're all right now, Gwennie.'' He patted her back and pressed her forward to rest against his shoulder.

''But it seemed so real. I was running through the streets of hell, and I saw the devil. The actual *devil*. He reached out to grab me. It was horrible!''

Amused laughter followed this, and Gwendolyn's eyes flew open. The place they were in was dark, but the light of a small fire flickered nearby. She was disoriented, but memory quickly returned.

"I don't see what there is to laugh about," Lad muttered irately over his shoulder. "You scared her out of her wits."

"I've been called any number of things before," said the man who'd laughed. "Boorish, ice-hearted, and—my favorite—colicky, but I've yet to be confused with the devil. At least not within my hearing. It's probably quite apt." He laughed again.

"Yes," Lad agreed dryly. "Exceedingly."

Gwendolyn had pushed away to look beyond his shoulder and found herself staring at a dark, well-dressed, rather handsome gentleman who was sitting beside Lad and grinning at her.

"Oh, dear me," she murmured, remembering everything now. "You're the devil. I mean—oh, heavens! I do apologize, sir! What I mean to say is . . . well, I . . . I'm afraid I don't know *what* I mean."

He was still chuckling but held out a hand.

"I think my wife would agree with whatever it is. Please don't apologize. Indeed, I fear I'm the one who should do so, for taking you so much by surprise. Please forgive me for such thoughtlessness." He took her fingers in his and bowed over them with a nod of his head. "I'm Lucien Bryland, Miss Wells. At your service."

"He's the same Viscount Callan," Lad told her, "of whom I've written you. And I now regret all the favorable remarks I made in those letters. The man's a scoundrel through and through and never to be trusted." He turned to the man in question. "What were you about, giving her such a scare?"

Viscount Callan smiled at him mildly. "It was she

whom we were looking for, was it not? Other than Jack, of course. When a fair young woman matching the description you gave me should appear in these alleyways, what else could I do but inquire as to who she was?''

''He speaks the complete truth, Lad,'' Gwendolyn said, touching the back of her head gingerly and wincing at the tender lump she found there. ''It was my own idiocy that did me in. I'd been running, quite panicked, and—oh, God.'' She straightened, her heart dropping into her belly. *''Where's the baby?''*

''Calm yourself,'' the viscount said at once, ''and have no fears on that count. She's here. Just there, do you see? I managed to snatch her up before you fell, and no harm came to her. She's hungry, wet, and exhausted, but otherwise well enough. I have a child nearly the same age.''

He pointed, and Gwendolyn peered through the dim light to see Lloyd, her cousin's servant, sitting in the corner near a small fire, cradling the sleeping child in his arms.

''Thank heavens,'' she murmured. ''Her name is Kitty. Her mother left her with me and begged me to keep her safe. Then she ran off to draw away our pursuers. What is this place? How did we come to be here?''

They were in what appeared to be a small, ill-constructed animal shed with filthy straw covering the ground and several small windows, out of which four other men were keeping watch. The only doorway was latched by a half-gate that barely held to its hinges. Small protection indeed. The continuing sound of gunfire assured Gwendolyn that they were still in St. Bart's, a thoroughly dismal thought.

''These men work for Jack,'' her cousin answered, nodding toward the men standing at the windows. ''There are many more back at the tavern, lending him their aid. These four came after you and the other girl at Jack's command, to keep you safe, but were unable to find you until they came upon Lucky standing over what appeared to be, to them, your lifeless body."

"I have seldom found myself at such a disadvantage," said the viscount. "If I hadn't been holding the child, I fear they might not have waited to discover whether I was friend or foe."

"They brought you here to this shed," Kerlain went on, "which had been made ready earlier as their point of carrying out the plan Jack had devised to rescue Nancy and her baby. Then they searched Lloyd and myself out— we'd taken a separate path in order to investigate the sound of a woman screaming. The child's mother, one presumes, although one hopes it is not so."

"Nancy is her name," Gwendolyn said. "She sacrificed her own safety for that of her babe. Oh, Lad"—she looked pleadingly at her cousin—"we must find her and bring her out of this place. Lord Rexley came here for that very purpose."

"I know," he replied. "He told me something of this young woman and her child, also of his intent toward them. But, tell me, Gwennie, how did you come to be involved in it? And why the devil are you running about half-clothed?"

With more than a little embarrassment, she told them of how she'd found the note and decided to follow Lord Rexley to make certain of his safety; she also related the adventures that had followed. The two men listened in silence until she was done and then exchanged meaningful glances.

"You'll be making another wager soon, I have no doubt," Viscount Callan told her cousin, who shook his head.

"I promised Jack I'd have nothing to do with it." He

sighed. "A pity. I could have made a small fortune from it."

Gwendolyn had no notion of what they meant, and she pressed her cousin's arm.

"But how do you come to be here, Lad? And Viscount Callan?" She looked from one to the other.

"I returned from Kerlain this evening," Lad said, "having ridden hard to arrive in London as soon as possible so that I might escort you to Almack's. It was a vain attempt, as you know, for you had already gone by the time I managed to make it through the assembly doors. I regret more than I can tell you that I wasn't there to partner you in your first waltz, sweetheart."

"My fault, I fear," Viscount Callan put in. "He had stopped at my country estate briefly to rest and to congratulate me and my wife on the birth of our daughter. I had business in London that could no longer be put aside and asked if I might accompany Lad back to Town. It was a purely selfish request on my part, as I desired his company. But my preparations, no matter how swift, caused a rather longer delay than your cousin had planned, else he would not have missed your first waltz in London. Again, I owe you my apologies."

"A footman at Almack's informed me that you'd already left in the company of Lord and Lady Manning," Lad went on. "I assumed you safe abed at the Clarendon and made my way home in order to keep a later appointment I'd made with Lucky for supper and an hour of cards. Imagine my surprise to arrive at my rooms and find Lloyd busy loading my pistols with the intention of going to Saint Bart's to bring you back out."

"But how could he have known—"

"He's been keeping an eye on you since I left town," her cousin told her. "At my request."

"Lad," Gwendolyn said chidingly.

He looked only slightly abashed. "I know very well the trouble you get yourself into, Gwendolyn Wells, and from what I hear, Jack's had his hands full getting you out of scrapes since I've been gone."

"Only a few," she muttered. "And Lloyd, if he was watching, certainly never stepped in to help." She thought most specifically of the scene in Hyde Park with Lord Astley's dog and wished the manservant had come to her aid before Lord Rexley became involved.

"Be that as it may, it was a very good thing he *was* watching, else Lucky and I might never have found you."

Gwendolyn looked at Lord Callan with a measure of confusion.

"And how did you come to be involved in this, my lord?"

"Oh, I insisted upon coming along to lend aid when Lad was good enough to first meet me and give his excuses," he explained with casual ease. "Jack's my nearest and dearest, and I couldn't very well leave him to languish in such a spot. Aside from that, my wife never would have forgiven me for leaving a lady unrescued, especially one she's eager to meet. Like the rest of the ton, she's heard a great deal about the Earl of Kerlain's famous American uncle and cousin."

"Well, I daresay you shall have even more to tell her after this," Gwendolyn said dryly. "And so you came to Saint Bart's to find me, and did find me, but what of Lord Rexley? He's still out there." She waved a hand toward a window. "And that poor young woman as well. Shouldn't someone be alerting the authorities?"

"Uh, no," her cousin replied. "This is a matter best taken care of privately. I have some knowledge of what it concerns and believe Jack would prefer that it be handled with care. To that end, I'm going now with Lloyd to hunt him out and bring him here. Hopefully we'll find the young woman as well.''

"You'd better do so," Lord Callan advised. "That baby needs feeding."

Gwendolyn clutched Lad's arm as he tried to stand. "You can't go into those alleys, Lad! They're filled with complete madness, and I know whereof I speak. You'll be killed!''

He patted her hand gently. "I'll be fine. Lloyd was born and raised in Saint Bart's and could walk its alleyways blindfolded. It can't be any worse than hunting for game in the Smokies back home. Or fighting in the war, for that matter. Here, take this." He reached down and, to Gwendolyn's great astonishment, picked a musket off the ground. "Jack's men came well prepared for every possibility. Many of them served under his command in the Peninsula, and they prefer these muskets to pistols. You remember how I taught you to load and shoot one all those summers ago in Tennessee?''

She nodded.

"Good girl." He set the musket in her arms. "You help out if trouble comes." To Lord Callan he said, "She's a fine shot too. Used to whip my little brother, Josh, every time at target practice."

"And you too," Gwendolyn reminded him.

"Yes, me too." He bent to kiss her. "We'll be back. Take care of that little baby, and don't let Lucky do anything foolish. He wanted to go in my place, but he drew the short straw. Accused me of cheating, he did, which may or may not be true, but I didn't particularly cherish the thought of taking him home to Lady Clara on a cart. Aside from that, he hasn't got a lick of military training, and these men want someone who knows how to shout the right orders to keep them from getting killed.'' He slapped the viscount on his shoulder. "I'm trusting you to get Gwennie and that baby safe out of here, Lucky."

"On my honor, I will do so. But you'll not get rid of me quite so easily. Despite my dear friend's insistence on lurking about such interesting places, I can't leave him to languish here indefinitely."

Lloyd had made a bed for the baby out of his own cloak and carefully set her there now. Standing, he handed his master two loaded pistols, which disappeared beneath Lad's jacket. Each man who went shouldered a musket over an arm before making his way out the half-gate, which Lad had nearly broken from its hinges when he swung it open.

"I doubt that will keep them from storming the fortress," Lord Callan said with a nod toward the doorway after they'd gone. He smiled at Gwendolyn. "But I very much doubt that will happen. We'll wait half an hour and then get you out of here. I'm tempted to take you now, but I somehow doubt you'd go."

"No, I wouldn't." Gwendolyn sat back against one wall, sighing. The two men who had stayed behind had repositioned themselves to make a better guard. "I won't go even after half an hour. Not until Lord Rexley and the girl are safe."

"Oh, you'll go," Lord Callan said confidently, though kindly. "I'm a ruthless fellow when need be. My wife could tell you all about that. I'll sling you over my shoulder and take you out if I must. But we'll not worry about that yet. Jack's too clever a fellow to get himself killed in a place like this. He was a war hero, you know. Major Jack Sommerton, before he sold his commission. He still works in the king's service on occasion, albeit far more secretively." Like Gwendolyn, he leaned against a wall to rest and stretched his legs out comfortably before him. "He and his men will have taken every precaution before coming here, though I doubt they counted on you showing up. Probably threw everything off kilter."

"Yes, I'm afraid that's so," Gwendolyn admitted gloomily.

"I'm sorry. I didn't mean to cast aspersions. My wife is ever telling me to think before I speak, but it doesn't take root."

"Lady Clara is rather long-suffering," Gwendolyn said teasingly. "Or so Lad has given me to understand."

He laughed. "Not very closemouthed, is the Earl of Kerlain. But, yes, she is, and all to my benefit."

Gwendolyn smiled. He was a dark and somewhat fearsome man, this lord, but not without a certain charm. Still, she felt sorry for whoever his enemies might be. He looked as if he could be a nasty foe in a fight.

"You are Lord Manning's nephew, are you not?"

"Indeed I am."

"Your uncle and his wife, Lady Anna, have been very kind to me since my arrival in England."

"So I've heard, though it's of no surprise to me. Robby and Anna are kindness itself. You're shivering. And wet. Here." He reached into his coat and pulled out a silver flask. "Drink some of this." He pressed it closer when she shrank away. "Go on. It's only brandy and will help to warm you. I wish I might offer you a handkerchief to dry your face and hands, but I used what I had in drying the child and making her a new nappy."

"Fortunate child," she said, uncapping the container and sipping from it. "I would be very glad of dry clothes just now. Indeed, of any decent clothes at all." She took another drink, rather longer. "I don't know why I always thought gentlemen carried inferior drinks in these things. This is of excellent quality."

"The best of my cellar."

"Perhaps I should take to carrying such an item," she

said with a laugh, capping the flask and returning it to him. "Thank you, my lord."

"You're most welcome."

"And so," she said, as she leaned against the wall again, resting, "you're Lord Rexley's closest friend?"

"Since college," he said, casually taking a pistol from an inner pocket and checking it. "I had known of the Earl of Rexley before, as he's my uncle's godson, and had even seen him a time or two, but we didn't actually meet until we attended Oxford in the same year. It seemed natural that we'd become acquainted, of course, but far more came of it. We've been through a great deal together. I count few beings more dear than I do Jack Sommerton."

"Tell me about him, please," she asked.

He looked at her searchingly for a long moment, then sighed and said, "Very well. I don't suppose it would do any harm to give you an idea of the man. Of course, he'll have my tongue out if he should ever hear of it, please bear that in mind. Now, let me think." He gazed at the shabby roof contemplatively. "He's a good fellow, even-tempered and slow to anger, given to much sport, both gaming and otherwise. He's utterly loyal to those he loves and was an obedient son to his parents, although somewhat stubborn. Patriotism got the better of him in his early twenties, and he went off to war despite the pleas of both family and friends. I was among those who insisted that he'd get himself killed. Instead, he proceeded to distinguish himself in service and rise above the rank he'd purchased."

"And then his brother died, and he was made to return home?" she asked.

He nodded. "As the only heir to Rexley, it was impossible for him to continue a life of such jeopardy. He was unhappy but knew his duty. A perfect member of the nobility, is Jack. Always very right and proper. Except for when he pursues his little hobby among these dark places.''

''His little hobby?''

''Perhaps I should rather have called it his favorite form of charity. He's devoted to rescuing as many of the poor and suffering masses as he possibly can, especially women and children. The young woman he set out to rescue tonight is a typical example. She's a prostitute, no doubt, and has the babe to care for. Her master will not allow her to do so while she remains in his employ and has probably threatened to sell the child or get rid of it in a less kindly manner. Jack will take her to one of his estates and provide her with food and shelter in exchange for labor in one of his factories or mills. She'll be allowed to keep the child and raise it without fear of hunger or cold.''

''I had assumed . . .'' Gwendolyn began. ''But that is neither here nor there. I'm vastly relieved to know that his motives in coming here tonight were born out of charity, rather than for any other, more personal reason.''

''I don't think you need worry about Jack in that direction. He's not a saint, mind you, but he's never fathered any bastards that I'm aware of, if you'll pardon me for speaking so bluntly.''

''No, please, I welcome it,'' she assured him. ''I'm rather given to plain speaking myself.''

''Very well. Let me think. What else should you know? Ah, yes. His women. Have you yet visited Brannard? Jack's London home?''

''No.''

''You should probably be aware then, before you do visit, that he's surrounded himself with—''

''Sir?'' One of the men called. ''Company.''

Viscount Callan rolled to kneel before one of the small windows and looked out.

"None of these are Jack's men?" he asked.

"No, sir. Look like Rickard's men."

"Rickard? Who the devil is he?"

"Oh, dear." Gwendolyn joined him at the window. "He's the gentleman Mr. Ware wants. He meant to keep me or Nancy until Lord Rexley delivered Mr. Rickard to him. I gather he's Nancy's employer."

"Damn," Lord Callan muttered. "What the hell is he doing here? Come to fetch his property, no doubt. Well, we shall have to send him on his way to Mr. Ware. Miss Wells," he said, leveling his pistol out the window, "I would suggest you make your weapon ready. They are nearly upon us. Gentlemen, please feel free to ply us with military advice. We've no experience in such matters."

It had been a long time since Gwendolyn had fired a gun, let alone loaded one, but she managed to do both—repeatedly over the next ten minutes—and was amazed at how calm she remained. It was difficult to take aim in the darkness, but she hoped she'd not actually killed anyone. She aimed low at the legs of the oncoming men whenever they actually dared to leave the safety of their shadows and attempt an approach, and between herself, Lord Callan, and the other two men, the alley was soon littered with moaning, crying figures. There had been no attempt of an attack from behind the shack, which both bewildered and alarmed Gwendolyn. Perhaps they were in a dead end, with no chance of escape unless their attackers either died or gave way.

"Well done, Miss Wells!" Viscount Callan praised when there was a short pause in the onslaught. He turned from the window they shared and sat on the floor, resting. "Very well done. I shall have you out to Pearwood after this is over to have you put the fear of God into the pheasant."

"Sir!" The men at the windows lifted their muskets.

"They're retreating, sir. Shall we allow them to gather their wounded?"

"Is that what you normally do?" Lord Callan asked. "I apologize for having no notion. I didn't serve during the war, although I made the attempt to do so." He glanced at Gwendolyn. "Robby literally had me dragged out of a recruiting center. Never saw him so furious in my life. Thought we'd actually come to blows over it." He returned his attention to the men. "Please," he said, waving a hand at the man nearest him, "proceed in whatever manner you believe Lord Rexley would approve."

The man nodded and shouted out the window, "Get yer wounded and go! You 'ave five minutes! Any tricks and we'll let the lady 'ere take 'er best shot!"

The viscount laughed and Gwendolyn flushed. Five minutes later the alleyway was cleared and fell into silence.

"Now what?" she asked.

"Now," said Lord Callan, "we wait five minutes longer and pray that Jack and your cousin make their appearance. If not, we leave."

"No," she said.

"Dear Miss Wells, I find you to be a most excellent female, especially after all we've just been through together, but please don't become tiresome. I don't want to have to hit you on the head and render you senseless. But I assure you I will."

She didn't doubt it was true.

"Men," she muttered. "Brutes, the lot of you."

"Yes," he admitted, "but who would you females have to reform without us? Listen." He held up a hand to indicate the sound of approaching footsteps, then quickly stood. "It's Jack. He has a very distinct and lazy footfall. I'd call it a swagger, but that wouldn't be polite." He helped her to rise as the two men by the window lowered their weapons and stepped back.

Her cousin Lad was the first through the broken half-door. "Back, Gwennie," he said, taking her in his arms as she ran to him, "safe and sound. What a thrashing you gave Rickard's men! They were running to Moses Ware for safety." He laughed.

She was about to reply when Lord Rexley walked in. He stopped in the doorway and stared at her, then reached out an arm and yanked her toward him, hugging her tight.

"If I wasn't so glad to see you all in one piece," he said into her ear, "I'd turn you over my knee. I may do it yet." He pressed his face into her hair, and she both heard and felt him release a breath.

"I'm glad you're alive too," she whispered, and foolishly felt like crying.

He released her suddenly and turned to clasp the viscount's hand. "Lucky." He sounded amused, but his gaze was full of open relief and gladness. "Came to keep an eye on me, did you, Mother?"

"You've thoroughly ruined my only evening in Town," the viscount told him. "A fight at Mawdry's will seem nothing but tame after this. And to think I always believed charitable works could only be dull. That must be Nancy," he said as the young woman who'd followed Lord Rexley into the shack ran to where her baby lay sleeping. She burst into tears before lifting the child into her arms and hugging it tightly enough to wake it.

"Yes, and we must hurry and get her and the babe out of here before Ware and Rickard put their differences aside and come after us with combined forces. My men are guarding the alley." Lord Rexley took Gwendolyn's arm. "Let's hurry."

He seemed to have a small army at his command. Dozens of men bearing weapons escorted them through St.

Bart's dark alleyways until they reached the same opening that Gwendolyn had earlier entered. Lord Rexley picked her up off the ground and literally put her into the first large carriage waiting there, and just as Gwendolyn had settled, Nancy Randall and her baby were likewise pushed inside. The girl collapsed wearily on the seat next to Gwendolyn and pulled down the top of her blouse to feed her crying child.

"Please, God, I hope I never go through the like of that again," she said, her head falling back against the cushioning. The child fell quiet, save for its hungry sucking.

"Amen," Gwendolyn agreed, but the girl had already closed her eyes and looked as if she'd shortly be sound asleep.

The carriage dipped as Lord Kerlain stepped in. He took one look at Nancy Randall and checked his progress.

"Uh . . ."

"Hurry along, Kerlain," Lord Rexley demanded, prodding him from behind. "This isn't the social hour in Hyde Park."

Her cousin reached down and grasped Gwendolyn's hand. "There's not enough room for us all. You'll have to sit on my lap, Gwennie," he said, suiting action to words and pulling her across the carriage to the opposite seat. He set her on his lap and ducked his head as if to hide behind her.

Lord Rexley stepped in behind him and, seeing Nancy Randall, stopped as well. He cast an irate glance at the still-ducking Lord Kerlain and said, "For pity's sake, don't women ever have to feed their children in the United States?" He removed his cloak and tucked it about Nancy Randall, covering both her and the child warmly and modestly before settling on the seat beside them. Nancy opened her eyes only briefly, sighing with contentment before settling her head on Lord Rexley's shoulder. From across the carriage, his eyes met Gwendolyn's. Neither of them smiled, nor frowned. They simply gazed at each other in silence as Viscount Callan joined them and took his place without pause.

As the carriage began moving, Lord Kerlain spoke.

"You'll be taking Miss Randall home to Brannard, I imagine?"

Lord Rexley nodded curtly. "Of course."

"And what about Gwennie?"

"What do you mean, Lad?" She twisted to look at him. "All I desire is to return to the hotel and retire. I can't remember ever feeling so weary in all my life. I vow I'm going to sleep past noon."

"I'm sure that's true, love, but you can't possibly go back to the Clarendon."

"Why on earth not?" she demanded.

"Because you haven't any decent clothes on, my dear," Viscount Callan explained kindly. "And because the doorman and anyone else who might see you entering the lobby will wonder why any lady would be returning to her rooms so early in the morning, without proper escort, and without a dress on."

"But I must go back!" she insisted. "My father will be sick with worry by morning, if he hasn't already discovered me missing."

"I'll send Uncle Philip a note first thing," Lad promised. "He might still be in company with Lord Hemstead, and I may be able to track him down before he returns to the Clarendon. But first we must determine where you'll be."

"Not at Brannard," Lord Rexley said icily. "Don't even suggest it. Take her home with you, Kerlain. She's your relative, after all."

"I would," Lad said, "but her reputation would never survive, even if I could sneak her in without notice. You know what my neighbors are. Her name would be all over London before tomorrow noon.''

"She's your *cousin*," Lord Rexley said.

"Yes, I'm your cousin," Gwendolyn agreed. "Surely there'd be no question of impropriety."

"My dear Miss Wells," Viscount Callan said, "your naïveté is sweet, but I assure you that such a close relationship means less than nothing when the gossips take up their practice. And you've little idea of what is said of the citizens of the United States."

"She's *not* staying at Brannard," Lord Rexley said again.

"Only think a moment, Jack," Lord Callan said. "Even if the gossips weren't a problem, where on earth would Kerlain put Miss Wells in those ridiculous rooms he rents? There's hardly enough room for himself and Lloyd."

"I'm sure we'd do very well," Gwendolyn began, "I require very little room, and—"

Lord Rexley leaned forward. "If it concerns you so much, Lucky, then take her to Barrington."

Lord Callan shook his head. "If Clara were with me, I'd have not the least hesitation, but after what I put my wife through following our marriage, I'll not allow even the slightest whisper to darken our door. You of all people wouldn't wish such a thing on Clara, would you? Hmm?" He looked thoughtful. "We could take her to Robby and Anna, I suppose."

"No," Jack stated firmly.

"I can't think they'd object," Lord Callan said, regarding his friend with a measure of surprise. "Indeed, they'd be more than pleased to lend Miss Wells their aid."

"You'd drop her on them at this time of night?" Kerlain demanded. "When they've got those babies to take care of?"

"Kerlain's right," Jack agreed. "I don't want Robby and Anna disturbed." And he didn't particularly want Robby knowing about this night's adventures either. At least not with the detail that he could readily envision Gwendolyn telling.

Gwendolyn sat up straighter on her cousin's lap and said, "I am not a child to be discussed in such a manner, as if I could not manage for myself. I *shall* return to the Clarendon, and if there is talk, so be it. I don't care in the least."

"Of course you don't, but you should," Lord Rexley said tightly. "If not for your own sake, at least to keep your father from distress." He let out a breath. "Very well. There's nothing else to be done. You'll come to Brannard for the night."

"No, I will not," she told him, and wearily set a hand over her eyes, rubbing at the burning there. "And I don't wish to discuss the matter further."

"We'll have to hurry her in along with Nancy and the baby. I doubt anyone will be up and about to take notice."

"And none of your servants will say anything," Viscount Callan put in. "You've their complete loyalty."

"I'm going back to my hotel," Gwendolyn stated firmly.

"You're coming to Brannard," Jack countered. "I suppose one of the women will have a dress you can wear until something can be fetched for you. You'll bring something in the morning, Kerlain?"

In the face of her exhaustion, Gwendolyn felt her temper slipping away. "My lord, you seem incapable of understanding me—"

"Now, Gwennie," her cousin said, patting her shoulder consolingly, "you've gotten yourself into this mess and you must take the consequences. One night at Brannard won't be the end of you. I'll take care of everything, including your father and proper clothes for you on the morrow, and a few bribes to whoever may have seen you leaving the Clarendon earlier.''

''But it will be *only* for the one night,'' Lord Rexley stated. ''You'll find other suitable lodgings for her on the morrow, Kerlain, or try to think of a way to get her back into the hotel without scandal. Your word of honor on it.''

''Word of honor,'' Kerlain promised, adding, ''as best I'm able to keep it.''

Viscount Callan gave a low chuckle and said, ''This should prove interesting.'' When Lord Rexley glared at him, he merely smiled out the window and laughed again.

Chapter Eleven

❦

Jack woke the next afternoon in an unusually bleary state, a roiling mass of confused thoughts holding him immobile even after he'd stared, blinking, up at the dark-blue canopy of his bed.

Gwendolyn Wells was in his home. He remembered that quite clearly, along with a variety of other facts. Nancy Randall and her baby girl—Kitty, someone had said her name was—were also safely ensconced within Brannard's walls. He remembered St. Bart's and all that had occurred there, most of it unpleasant, certain parts more than others.

He'd never considered himself to be a particularly vulnerable man, save in one regard—the mystery surrounding his birth. But last night he'd discovered that he possessed another Achilles' heel, one he'd never expected to have: a woman with red-gold hair who was foolish, razor-witted, brave, and utterly beautiful. She'd made him vulnerable last night in a way that still filled him with trembling distress. He'd never felt such a deep fear for another human being, not even during the war. If anything had happened to her . . . God help him, he wouldn't have been able to live with the knowledge. When he'd seen Gwendolyn afterward, in that dismal little shack, his relief had been complete. He'd held her fast and hard to know with absolute surety that she was alive and well. She'd smelled of gunpowder and brandy and St. Bart's filth, and he had thought, in that moment, that he'd never smelled any perfume so sweet. The memory now, however, made him groan aloud. Gad, but he was turning into a disgustingly maudlin creature.

"My lord, are you well?"

It was his valet. Jack felt like groaning again. The prospect of dragging his body out of bed was vastly unpleasant. He ached, everywhere, from last night's fighting. He'd exchanged a number of blows with Moses Ware, who had tried to fend him off by breaking both a chair and a small table on his head. Fortunately, the furnishings, like their surroundings, had been plagued throughout with rot and had crumbled to bits without inflicting too much harm. Moses Ware, on the other hand, had suffered a thoroughly smashed face. Jack recalled with satisfaction the sound of crunching bones when he'd held the man down and taken aim at his nose.

"My lord, did you wish to rise? I have a bath just now prepared and ready for you. Shall I have breakfast brought to you here, or do you wish to join Miss Wells belowstairs? She's only just gone down to break her fast."

Miss Wells, he thought. In his home. Involving herself in his affairs and nearly getting herself killed. She was beyond aggravating. She was . . . maddeningly pestilential.

"I am not her fate," he told himself, then again, even more firmly, "I am *not* her fate."

The bed curtains stirred. "My lord?"

"Yes, I'll join Miss Wells," he said, tossing his covers aside. "Send a message downstairs and ask her to await me. I'll not be above twenty minutes. Get my clothes laid out and my razor ready."

* * *

His home was magnificent. Gwendolyn had expected wealth and finery, but Brannard far exceeded her imaginings. There were beautiful homes in the United States, and she'd been in many of them during her travels with her father, but none compared to the elegance and polish of the Earl of Rexley's home. She felt slightly awed simply by the size of it—and this was only his *Town* home. She wondered what her reaction might be upon seeing one of his country estates, which were certain to be even larger and far more elegant. She had the sinking sensation that she'd probably feel very insignificant, as well as rather lost.

But she was determined not to let such overwhelming feelings get the better of her. Nothing had yet been determined, and if she did find herself living in England, she'd somehow become used to living in such places. It was a trifling consideration compared to other problems currently set before her.

It was dark outside and pouring rain. The comfortable breakfast room to which Gwendolyn had been escorted overlooked a large, walled garden, and she stood by the diamond-paned windows gazing out at the drooping beauty of wet shrubs and trees and flowers. The room itself was a distinct contrast, warm and cozy with a fire dancing in the grate.

The door opened and she turned, but instead of Lord Rexley it was only the housekeeper, Mrs. Young, followed by several female servants bearing covered platters and silver pots that they began arranging on a sideboard to Mrs. Young's satisfaction. Gwendolyn had been up and about for the past two hours and had yet to see one male servant other than Lord Rexley's butler. There weren't even any footmen, only maids who tended the tasks usually reserved for males.

"His lordship will join you in a few moments, miss,"

Mrs. Young informed her. "Will you let me pour you another cup of tea? Or some chocolate?"

"Coffee, please, if there is any."

Mrs. Young bobbed slightly. "Right away, miss."

"I'll pour it for her, Mrs. Young." Lord Rexley appeared in the open doorway. "You may go. Thank you."

"Yes, my lord." Mrs. Young bobbed again and left.

He was dressed casually, in trousers and a fine linen shirt, and he leaned indolently against the door frame, looking both a bit weary and amused, watching her. He had bathed and shaved, and his blond hair was still damp from washing. Gwendolyn was very aware of her own outfit, which had been borrowed from one of the maids whose height neared her own. It was the sort of gown that Gwendolyn had never imagined she'd wear, and it made her pause and wonder about the young woman who owned it. The cloth was pink satin, bright enough to blind a person in the dead of night, and the bodice was not only extremely low-cut but, to make it even more noticeable, also trimmed in frilly lace. She both looked and felt like a member of the demimonde and felt heat rising in her cheeks as Lord Rexley's appreciative gaze moved slowly up and down her figure.

Jack, for his part, had to resist the urge to whistle. Gwendolyn Wells was a sight on this dreary morn. He'd seldom seen even opera dancers so fancily or alluringly clad. He had no illusions as to where the gown she wore had come from, and he knew she was thoroughly embarrassed at having little choice but to wear it, but she had only herself to blame, after all, and, he reasoned, it could have been worse. At least she had the figure to carry such an outfit off—in spades. Her hair had been washed and dried and left unbound. It was the most glorious color, even on this dullest of days, a shade that was somewhere between the gold of the midafternoon sun and the red of early sunset.

He pushed away from the door and moved to pour her coffee. "I bid you good morning, or rather, afternoon, Gwendolyn. You're feeling well, I hope?"

"Very well," she said, adding, "Jack."

He filled two china cups with the hot, black liquid, then poured a large dollop of fresh cream into each.

"You look much refreshed after the vigors of last night. You slept well, I gather?"

"Yes, indeed. And you?"

"Like a babe." He turned with care and set her cup on the table. "May I fill a plate for you?" He moved to pull a chair out for her.

"Thank you." She obediently sat. "I'm famished."

"Then I shall make certain to give you plenty. Let's see what we have." Returning to the sideboard, he began lifting lids on trays. "Ham. Bacon and sausages. Eggs. Mmm . . . warm sweet buns. Egad, here is a dish of boiled oats. What a horrid sight. I'm sure you can't care for that." He glanced back to see her shake her head. "What on earth could Cook have been thinking? Perhaps she has a vague understanding of the American palate, but, then, I imagine that's not unusual. I shall have to speak to her about it. And lastly, here is a very fine tart, which I believe is composed mostly of pears."

He filled a plate, waiting for her to tell him to stop. But she didn't, and when he at last set the mountain of food before her she merely sighed with pleasure and took up her fork.

Filling his own plate, he sat beside her.

"This is a lovely room," she said.

"Thank you. My mother preferred for the family to dine here in the mornings, rather than in the formal dining room. She felt it more congenial and relaxing."

"Very wise, and quite true," she concurred. "A woman after my own heart."

"Perhaps so," he said pleasantly. "And now, Gwendolyn, if you don't mind, there's a little matter I wish to discuss with you."

She smiled at him, as angelic a being as could possibly exist.

"Of course. What is it, Jack dear?"

"I have the distinct feeling that you've been attempting to manage me."

"Have I?" she asked.

"With some help from Lucky and your blasted cousin."

"Are you referring to last night in the carriage?"

"Yes."

"Oh, no." She gave a shake of her head. "You'll not lay the blame for their behavior upon my shoulders. I had nothing to do with their getting you to let me stay in your home. If you will recall, I wished to return to my hotel."

"It seemed that way," he said, "but women are such sneaky creatures that I'm not exactly certain whether you meant what you said or not."

"What I may or may not have meant has nothing to do with it. You played a far larger part in your downfall than I. Lad and Viscount Callan didn't have to argue very long or hard before you changed your mind and began to insist that I stay at Brannard."

"I readily accept my own fault in the matter. If I'd been less weary, however, I doubt I would have been so easily gulled."

"Quite so. And I doubt you'll allow it to happen again in the future. I shouldn't worry over it, were I you."

"I don't intend to," he said. "Especially as I mean to exact a promise from you, Gwendolyn *dear*, never to manage me. Or to lend Lad or Lucky your aid in such an undertaking. I detest being managed.''

"Especially by a woman,'' she said with a smile. "I know. I shall attempt never to do it, if I can possibly avoid doing so.''

"That's not exactly the sort of reassurance that I had in mind. I want your promise, Gwendolyn Wells. Your solemn, complete, and irrevocable promise that you'll never—''

"Where on earth did you get so many scratches and bruises?'' she asked, touching a gentle finger to a particularly severe gash on his hand. "You didn't look like this last night.''

"It takes a few hours for the color to come up. I mean what I say, Gwendolyn. I want your absolute promise—''

"Oh, Jack.'' She pressed her hand lightly over his. "I do wish you'd never gone to meet that awful man, and in such a dreadful place. Surely there was a better way to retrieve Miss Randall and her child. You might have gotten killed.''

He pulled his hand away. "I had everything in perfect control until you arrived. And that's another little matter that I wish to discuss. What in God's name induced you to find your way to such a place as Saint Balthasar's? It was an utterly senseless, foolish thing to do.''

"I thought you might be in danger.'' She shrugged lightly and applied herself to her breakfast once more.

He stared at her. "And you thought you might rescue me? Gwendolyn, you . . . complete idiot. You don't have the least idea of what might have happened to you in such a place.''

She grinned at him impishly. "It turned out well enough, did it not? Come now, don't be angry. I meant it for the best, and there isn't another man alive whom I'd

go to such lengths for, so you might at least allow yourself
to be flattered.''

He turned his hand beneath hers, gripping her fingers.
Hard.

''This isn't a game, Gwendolyn, or a joke. You might
have been killed. You might have gotten a great many
other people killed. Don't laugh this off, for there is no
humor to be had in it.''

She tried to tug her hand free, but he wouldn't let it go.
''I know that,'' she said. ''What I don't know is how to
tell you that I'm sorry for it. I don't know how,'' she said
again, more insistently. ''Jack.'' The single word was uttered with so much distress that he knew she was near to
tears. She wasn't good at being afraid or at revealing how
vulnerable she could be, he suddenly realized. Humor was
the way in which she dealt with such things, and she was
pleading with him to help, because she hadn't yet had the
time to learn to trust him with such precarious feelings.
He could appreciate how she felt. He knew what it was to
be vulnerable, to have to learn to trust before opening oneself to pain.

He lifted the hand he held to his lips and held it there a
long moment, pressing his mouth against the curl of her
fingers in first one kiss, then another.

''I can't have you hurt, Gwendolyn,'' he murmured,
lowering her hand to the table again. ''Promise me you'll
never be so foolish again.''

She nodded, not looking at him. ''Yes. I promise.''

He wished he could see her eyes, see if he'd hurt her
himself, with his words. He rubbed his thumb over the top
of her hand in a gentle caress, then released her. ''I won't
mention it again,'' he said, and applied himself to his
breakfast.

A minute or more passed before she commented, with
a smile, looking up at him at last, ''I saw Miss Randall

and her little one this morning, and they're both very fine. Kitty is the loveliest baby.''

"So I hear from several of my maids," he replied. "It was a rather long journey down the stairs, having to make so many stops in order to be told about the child.''

"Yes, your harem is apparently awash with maternal feelings. I was given to understand by Mrs. Young that the nursery here at Brannard is currently being prepared for Kitty's occupation.'' Gwendolyn took a delicate sip from her coffee cup, then directed a quizzical look at him over the rim. "Perhaps you mean to keep Miss Randall here rather longer than I'd supposed?''

Jack wasn't sure which accusation he should respond to first, and he felt vaguely irate that he should care at all. His life and his home weren't any of Gwendolyn Wells's concern.

"My intention is to get Miss Randall and her child out of London as quickly as possible. And I do not have a *harem*.''

"Well, good heavens, I don't know what else you would call such a surplus of female servants.'' Before he could respond to that, she said, "I take it that Kitty isn't your daughter, then. I must say, I'm relieved. Men will be men, of course, but I'd rather start with a clean slate. Oh, and I meant to tell you,'' she went on before he could so much as make a sound, "Lad sent a note this morning. He's taken care of reassuring my father of my where-abouts and safety and will come to Brannard later this afternoon, presumably to take me away. I thought you'd be glad to know of it.''

She was capable of making him utterly crazed within the space of a few short seconds. The worst part of it was that she smiled throughout the whole thing. Her eyes, Jack could swear, were twinkling with amusement.

"I am not—I do not have a harem," he insisted once

more, certain that she'd accused him of that at least, if he was sure of nothing else. She'd said something about him being Kitty's father? Where in blazes could she have conceived such an absurd notion? But perhaps he should let her think whatever she wished. Let her believe that he'd fathered innumerable bastards, that he was a conscienceless swine who took women without due, impregnating them by the dozen and then abandoning them to their fates. Perhaps then she'd leave him in peace. It was exactly what he wanted, and so it was with immense surprise that he heard the words, "And Nancy's child is not mine," issuing from his own mouth.

She smiled. "I know she is not, but you are very good to reassure me, dear."

"Gwendolyn," he said with pure exasperation, "for mercy's sake, be still a moment and listen to me. I am neither your fate, nor your *dear*, and there is no clean slate for us to begin upon. I wish you would believe me and trust that I cannot be persuaded otherwise. I don't wish to hurt your feelings with stronger words, but I will if you drive me to it. As to children," he said, holding up a hand to halt whatever she opened her mouth to say, "I have none, legitimate, illegitimate, or otherwise—"

She gave a sudden, merry laugh. "Oh, Jack, how silly. There's nothing 'otherwise' that a child might be."

He was flustered beyond redemption. "Yes, I know, and what I'm trying to tell you, *Miss Wells*, is that I haven't got any. Children, that is."

She swallowed a bite of tart and said, "Well I didn't think you meant sense, dear."

He looked at the ceiling. "God help me," he pleaded, then returned his gaze to Gwendolyn. "You could drive the Bishop of Canterbury to commit murder. I shall be counting the minutes—no, the seconds—until your cousin arrives to take you away. Preferably to the closest asylum.

How did you ever get about in Boston without being committed for lunacy?''

"You may choose to be unkind so early in the day," she told him, clearly uninsulted, "but I do not."

"That's because you're not the one being managed."

"Very true." The twinkle was back in her eyes. "Tell me about your harem, then. I can't be managing while you're the one in charge of the conversation."

"It is *not* a—"

She waved a hand dismissively, her attention upon her plate. "Whatever it is, then. Tell me how you come to have a house staffed almost entirely by females."

"It's no concern of yours," he muttered, but decided that perhaps she was right. As long as he was speaking she couldn't drive him half-mad with her unbridled chatter. "The women who serve in my household were at one time employed in a far different manner. They wished for safer work and I was in the fortunate position to provide it."

She looked at him with a measure of disbelief. "You mean to say that they wished for more *honest* employment," she stated.

Nothing was surer to bring Jack's ire to the fore than disparaging comments about his staff. "No," he said tautly, "I mean that they wished for safer employment. They were not thieves, Gwendolyn. These women worked honestly at the trade they plied. If circumstances forced them to take up such employ, it can in no way be their fault or assumed that they were somehow dishonest. You will never find better or finer people than those who serve at Brannard or at any of my other estates. They survived in a harsh world, and I, for one, admire them greatly and, yes, even honor them. I cannot help but wonder if those of us who were more gently reared—you and I among them—could have done so well under such daunting conditions. Or even survived."

She had ceased eating in the midst of this angry speech and given him her full attention. The amusement had gone from her eyes, to be replaced by unmistakable remorse. There was no teasing in her tone when she spoke.

"I apologize," she said quietly. "You're right, of course. I cannot, as you say, begin to imagine what it must to be like to live in such difficult circumstances. Forgive me for speaking so thoughtlessly."

His anger melted away beneath her openly sincere apology, and he felt, of all things, guilty. How was it possible for a single female to bring out the worst in him with but a word or two?

"No, I'm—it's my fault, I think." He shook his head slightly. "I shouldn't have spoken in such a manner. It was entirely uncalled for. My mother, if she were still alive, would wring my ears from my head, I believe."

He was relieved to see her smile, to hear her laugh. "Perhaps we might strive to converse on more-accepted topics until we've finished our meal," he suggested. "Afterward, if you like, I'll take you on a tour of Brannard, and we can argue to your heart's content."

Chapter Twelve

❧

"And this dour fellow was my father's grandfather—the second earl. He was something of a scoundrel. Involved in smuggling and all sorts of dastardly deeds. He used to scare my father with but a look when he was a lad."

"I can understand why," Gwendolyn said, moving closer to scrutinize the portrait before her. "What a frightening aspect he has. And such a scowl. I wonder if the painter wasn't terrified of him."

Jack chuckled. "I've often wondered the same thing. Could you keep from shaking in your shoes while surveying such an unfriendly subject?"

The remainder of their breakfast had passed in a congenial manner, and afterward he led her about his home in an indolent, lazy manner, showing her each room that happened to present itself in the undetermined course that they walked. There was a gallery on the third floor, and although it didn't compare to the formal Sommerton gallery at Rexley Hall, it was a pleasant place to be, especially on rainy days. They had spent half an hour or more walking the length of it, contemplating each portrait of Sommerton ancestry and the particular history that went with it in leisurely detail.

"This is my father at the age of twelve," he said, moving down to the next portrait, "with a particularly well-loved setter named Cooper. He was the fourth Earl of Rexley at the time, having already attained the title as his own father had died some months previously."

"Ah," Gwendolyn said with a knowing nod. "That accounts for the sadness. I had wondered."

Jack turned his head sideways a bit to contemplate the painting. He'd looked at it hundreds of times during his life but had never seen anything more than his father at the age of twelve, his arm looped about the neck of a mottled white and brown dog.

"Sadness?"

"Yes, can't you see it? Because his father has died. It must have been terribly hard on him at such a young age. Poor boy. And only think of how difficult it must have been, as well, to take on the burden of the earldom. He looks like a very pleasant young man, however. Was he? Pleasant, I mean."

"Aside from my mother and brother, the most pleasant person I ever knew," Jack replied. "He was a very fine man, and everything that I most admired."

She smiled at him. "Then you clearly take after him."

He shook his head. "I wish I did. It was my goal during all of my childhood. But we were very different. My brother was a better success. David and my father were two of the same kind. Good, gentle souls."

"You miss them," she said gently.

"Every day. My brother died in the United States, just outside of New Orleans, in '14."

"Lad told me. Or rather, wrote me of it."

"Did he?" That surprised Jack somehow.

"Yes. I'm sorry for your loss, and sorry, as well, that your brother's death occurred in my own country. It was a foolish war all around. My own cousin, Lad's brother, Joshua Walker, died in it as well."

"A great many fine young men did, I imagine. That is

the nature of war, even foolish ones.'' With a sigh, Jack moved on to the next painting. "This is David, here. Well, all of us, really. There's a much better family portrait in my private chambers, done when David and I were older, and a formal one at Rexley Hall. This one I never liked.''

"Why on earth not?" she asked, staring up at the enormous work. "It's wonderful! What a handsome child you were. And your brother also, although I think I can see what you speak of when you say that he was more like your father. They look very alike even in the physical sense and have much the same expression. You have perhaps something of the look of your mother. The same smile." She looked at him thoughtfully. "Perhaps."

"Or," he said, "perhaps not."

"No, perhaps not exactly the same," she agreed with equal quiet. "Jack—"

"My brother was a scholar," he said briskly, cutting her off, "like my father. He loved his books. Poetry and mathematics and Greek classics—and botany, which was his passion. I still have every blessed tome he possessed, but aside from poetry they're foreign to me, a mystery I can't unveil whenever I attempt to read one. But at least I've been able to keep them safe. Those and his beloved plants. He had greenhouses at Rexley Hall. My father had them specially built. David nearly lived in them when he wasn't away at school." He stepped nearer to the portrait, gazing at it. "He was the last man on earth you'd ever expect to join an army. To take up arms and kill another being. He was such a gentle soul." He heard Gwendolyn come up behind him. Her hand fell soft on his arm. "I've often wondered if he was able to bring himself to do so, but I simply can't imagine it. I can only see him being terrified, utterly terrified in the midst of battle, and wanting his books and his greenhouses and his plants—and his

family—knowing that he'd never see any of them again."
He bowed his head.

"Oh, Jack." Her fingers pressed on him. He set his own hand over hers and held tight.

"He was their son, Gwendolyn, and when he died they were so brokenhearted. I can't forget how it changed them. Aged them. I wish to God it had been me instead."

"No," she said firmly. "Never that, Jack. You loved your brother and your parents, but he chose his course and the fault was none of yours, or theirs."

He shook his head. "I don't know. He might have joined up because of me. He always looked up to me, always thought that everything I did was—" He had to swallow and shut his eyes for a silent moment before he could speak calmly again. "My parents were very proud when I bought a commission to go into war. Afraid for me as well, but mostly proud. That was when England was still in a patriotic spirit and few people knew what a real horror war is." He released a breath. "I learned quickly enough. God, just the memory of those first few months in Spain still makes me quake. I was such a coward. I wanted to hide in my tent every moment. I spent half an hour after every battle throwing up, until I got better used to so much blood and killing. I'm sorry, I shouldn't be saying such things to you."

"Yes, you should," she murmured. "To me more than anyone else. I think I should have wanted to do the same after battle. Anyone would."

"I suppose so," he admitted. "But to David I was a hero. All of his letters were filled with admiration of his older brother, and I didn't exactly write back and disabuse him of the notion. I had no idea he'd list on his own. I thought all the while I was serving that he and Mother and Father were all safe and happy at home. I used to think of David in his greenhouses with his plants, or sitting in the evenings with Father and carrying on a heated discussion about their beloved books. Or turning the pages for Mother when she played the piano. Or holding his hands out so that she might use them to sort her yarn. He was so patient to do so. God knows I never was.'' He sighed again. ''It made me happy to remember him so. And my parents as well, doing all that they loved. By the time I got his letter saying that he was going to war, he was already gone. It was too late for me to stop him.''

''You couldn't have done so, even if you'd been here.''

''Maybe not. Though I would have tried. But perhaps he would have gone anyway. I'll never know for certain, will I?''

''No, you'll not. And there's no sense in tormenting yourself because of it. Your parents never blamed you for your brother's war service, did they?''

''Oh, no. Never, by either word or look. My mother and father didn't possess that kind of bitterness. They were the most loving of parents. I was so fortunate to have them, Gwendolyn. So very fortunate. You can see, can't you? Just by looking at them, the kind of people they were. I've always wished . . .''

''What?''

''That I was more like them.''

They stood together in silence for a long moment, gazing at the picture. It was a happy outdoor scene, a family of four, smilingly content. The father stood beside the mother, his arm about her waist, the both of them looking down with love at the two boys before them. David, the younger, somewhere around the age of four, was sitting on the grass, occupied with a ball, while Jack, the elder, was standing in front of his parents, leaning somewhat against his mother, his father's hand on his shoulder. The smile on his boyish face was almost smug, as if he was fully aware of his birthright and knew that he was destined to one day become one of England's most revered nobles. The face of aristocracy was fully evident in him, something that he could only have acquired by birth. And yet he stood out in the happy family portrait like the proverbial sore thumb. Everything about him was different. Everything, from his hair color to his features and build. They were fine-looking people, with the kinds of faces that would encourage people to warm to them, but Jack stood out as purely beautiful, like a swan set in the midst of more ordinary doves. The difference was too avid to ignore.

"Come," he said, taking her hand and placing it on his arm to lead her away. "We'd best go down to have our tea before Mrs. Young comes looking for us. It must be going on three o'clock. I wonder where Kerlain is?"

"Are you so eager to be rid of me, then?" she asked, smiling.

"I should be," he told her with a sideways glance, "but truth to tell, Gwendolyn Wells, I'm not. You're good company, for all that you're a thoroughly troublesome female."

"Thank you," she said dryly.

He laughed and set his fingers over her hand. "I meant it for a compliment. Few females aren't troublesome, after all. Tell me about yourself."

"There's very little to tell," she said with a light shrug, matching his slow steps as they moved down the long staircase. "I've lived an exceedingly dull life, I fear."

"I don't believe that for a moment."

"It's true!"

"Come now. You've been four days in London and not a one of them has passed without some commotion that you've either directly been the cause of or somehow been involved in. Do you mean to say that in Boston you never caused any like trouble at all?"

"Of course not!" she replied with affront. "Or, at least, if I did it wasn't always my fault."

"I see."

"It wasn't!" she insisted. "I never purposefully went out seeking trouble, I assure you. It always just seemed to . . . follow me about. Can I help it if people behave foolishly? And men, most especially?"

"I suppose not," he admitted. "Although I don't think they can be put to the blame so much either. You're the kind of female who tends to make men lose their better senses. That sailor on the *Fair Weather*, for an example, is probably a fine fellow in general."

"Mr. Hanbury? Indeed, he was a perfect gentleman until that last day. I admit that I was growing concerned in regard to his attentions, but it's somewhat difficult to know exactly which men are going to become unpleasant, or when. Although there are *certain* men who one knows right away will in time become effusive and others who most definitely will not."

Jack opened the door to the library, where a fire, he saw with approval, had already been laid out and a low table near the settee had been arranged with settings for tea.

"You sound like an expert in such matters," he said, leading her to the settee before moving to the bellpull. "I hope you won't mind taking tea here in the library. I always do when I'm at home."

"No, indeed," she said, looking about with approval. "It's a lovely room, both warm and inviting. I think I should spend a great deal of time here if the house were mine. The portraits of your parents are especially fine."

"Thank you," he said, sitting beside her on the settee. It was dangerous to be so near to her, as his self-control had already been stretched to the breaking point, but he found that he couldn't help himself. He leaned back and regarded his guest contemplatively, wishing, as he'd wished all day, that she didn't possess quite so fine a figure, also that the fine figure wasn't clad in a dress that had the unusual distinction of at once leaving almost nothing to the imagination and yet also luring a man to remove what there was to see what the imagination had left out. That lace decorating the bodice stood out in a ridiculously stiff manner, making the bosom look as if it were some dish about to be presented. He wasn't sure whether he disliked the gown so much because it made him want to lay Gwendolyn Wells on the floor and make love to her or because it made Gwendolyn Wells look like the sort of woman who'd lay him down on the floor first before throwing herself on top. She wasn't that sort of woman, not in the least, but that was difficult to remember on a day like this, when it was rainy and cold outside and warm and cozy inside, and when the idea of lying on any floor in any position with Gwendolyn Wells seemed heavenly.

"So, tell me," he said, forcing a merely conversational tone into his voice, "what sort of man is unlikely to become effusive? I hope I'm counted among them, for I should hate to find myself babbling like good Mr. Hanbury."

"Certain men, and you are indeed among them," she assured him pleasantly, "would never allow their baser natures to rule them, even when much pressed. They are always in complete control of themselves. Lad is such a man, as is Viscount Callan. I'd not expect anything but the direst of circumstances to send any of you into a panic."

Ha! he thought with silent irony. If she only knew how near to panicking he'd been the night before at the idea of Moses Ware putting his hands on her.

"Well you've nothing to fear from me," he told her

casually, "and certainly nothing from Lucky. I've never seen any man more devoted to his wife. As for your cousin—he's a loose cannon, but in principle I agree with you. Enter!" he called when a scratch came at the door.

Mrs. Young delivered a tray laden with tea and cakes, then left at once. Gwendolyn poured without being asked to do so. When they had both settled with a cup, he said, "Tell me about your life in the United States. You were born and raised in Boston, I understand?"

"Yes. My father met my mother there while attending university, and they were married almost as soon as he graduated. He hadn't thought to remain in Boston, as all of his family was in Tennessee, but Mother couldn't be persuaded to live in what she considered to be an uncivilized wilderness. She could seldom be persuaded even to visit when Papa and I went."

"A thoroughly sensible woman," Jack said.

"A thoroughly stubborn one," Gwendolyn countered. "Tennessee is as civilized as any state or country on God's earth can be. And possessed of some of the most beautiful land as well. My aunts and uncles and cousins live near the Smoky Mountains, and you've never seen anything to compare. But," she said with a sigh, "my mother was a true Bostonian, and in her opinion, even the finest families in lauded New York couldn't begin to compare to those in Massachusetts, let alone those in Tennessee. She wasn't even impressed that Uncle Charles was the son of an earl. *Her* family, you see, can date itself to Boston's earliest colonial days, all the way back to a great-great-grandfather who was brother to the Duke of Alborn."

Jack nearly choked on his tea. "You're related to the *Duke of Alborn*? In the Hennerson line?"

She shook her head. "No, through the Jilcott side. My mother was a Jilcott before she married Papa. And her grandmother, my great-grandmother, was a Hays of Cambury, sister to *that* duke. So, you see, Mother tended to think well of herself, except that she felt she had rather lowered the family standard to have married Papa. Not that she ever said so, for she loved him devotedly, but her relatives weren't precisely pleased with the match. It was something of a burden to her over the years, as you might imagine, and made her a bit higher in the instep than necessary—as a way of making up for her marriage, you understand. That was mainly why she couldn't let herself be impressed with Uncle Charles, but as he didn't take his own breeding very seriously, there was never any fuss over it. Despite that particular failing, Mother was the most wonderful person. You would have liked her a great deal, I believe. She always despaired of me too."

He still hadn't gotten past the revelation of her familial connections. "Have you met any of them? Your relatives here?"

Her forehead furrowed slightly. "No. And I hadn't planned on doing so. Should I, do you think? I've always thought them to be a rather stuffy lot, and I've personally had no contact with any of them, despite my mother's pleas. She carried on a faithful correspondence with my great-uncle, the late duke, but I always found his letters to be somewhat tedious and seldom even read them. His son is the duke now. Edmond, I think his name is, although you might know better than I. More tea, Jack? Did you know that Boston is a great deal like London?"

He held his cup out, still dazed. "No. Is it?"

"Very much like, although rather cleaner and far less odorous, if you'll pardon me saying so. We get a great deal of fog, but when the weather is clear it's the most beautiful, delightful place. Everything grows there very easily—flowers and grasses. By the sea or the Charles River, especially, it's quite lovely." She smiled at the thought. "On warm days there is nothing better than to walk down to the shore, or the harbor, and look out at the ships and the sea or to have a picnic near the water. You would find it very pleasant, I think."

"I imagine I would," he said. "You make it sound a most inviting prospect."

"Do I? I'm glad you think so. Perhaps one day you'll travel to America to see it for yourself. There are places there so fantastic that the human mind can scarce conceive of them. Papa says that's why God gave man the sciences, to allow him a sphere where his mind might make some progress, for in nature God alone reigns supreme. I'm sorry," she said suddenly, with a self-conscious laugh. "I'm chattering, am I not?"

"Yes," he said, smiling, "but please don't stop. I like it. Tell me more about Boston. Did you enjoy living there as a girl?"

"Oh, yes," she replied warmly. "It's a wonderful place to be a child, although I think my parents used to wish it were not quite so. I spent a great deal of time outdoors, especially by the Charles River, which we lived very close to. And my friends and I were often down by the sea too, fishing or playing on the shoreline, getting wet and muddy and having a wonderful time. You can imagine how much that pleased my mother."

"I believe I can," he said, grinning. "My own had strong opinions about coming indoors in such a state. And what did you do the rest of the year? It snows in Boston during the winter, does it not?"

She nodded. "And rains too. We enjoy every manner of weather, but, as here, it can bring as much delight as misery. In the winter my friends and I would build snowmen and have snowball fights and ice skate. In the fall, when it was too cold to go near the sea, we'd go yondering."

"Yondering?"

"That's an expression I learned in Tennessee. I think it's a combination of *wandering* and *yonder*."

Jack laughed. "Is it? I shall have to tease Kerlain about that. Do you know, Gwendolyn, I can't envision you as a scrubby little urchin of a girl, running about in fields and the snow. I think you must have always been what you are. Exceedingly beautiful and elegant. A troublemaker, to be sure, but very lovely all the while."

She blushed and smiled with obvious pleasure. "Thank you for such a fine compliment, my lord, but I assure you that I was a complete tomboy. *Urchin*, in fact, is a very good word for it. My parents used to wonder whether I'd ever grow out of it. And I could fight too." She looked him straight in the eye and nodded. "I could. Anyone who's grown up with red hair learns early on to defend herself against the teasing that inevitably results."

"Your hair," he said, lifting a hand to finger a few soft strands, "is perfect. I've never seen anything to compare, and every female must burn with envy because they can't lay claim to such. Surely you couldn't have been teased for it."

"Ha! Spoken like one who's never had a red hair upon his person. It wasn't until I reached the age of sixteen that I ceased cursing this mop upon my head."

"What happened at the age of sixteen? Although I imagine I already know."

"Well, for one thing," she said, sipping her tea primly, "my freckles began to fade, and for another, a young man whom I thought particularly nice asked my parents if he might take me for a walk in the park after church on Sunday."

"Ah." Jack nodded knowingly. "A walk in the park. He must have been a very serious young man."

"Terribly," she said with a sigh. "Afterward, we sat on the porch for half an hour, drinking lemonade, and then he bowed over my hand, bid my parents good evening, and left.''

''And you?''

''Me? I was walking on air. I floated up to my bedroom and started kissing my pillow.''

He laughed and set his teacup aside. ''I can just imagine it! Did the young man ever discover that he was held so dearly in your affections?''

''Heavens, no! I would rather have died than let him discover it. And it was all for the best, for as it turned out he wasn't any fun at all. A complete stick in the mud.''

''Poor fellow,'' Jack said. ''I feel sorry for him. The first of your many conquests, and so roundly rejected.''

''My many conquests?'' she said, her smile dying away. ''I admit to having a ridiculous number of men pursue me, all for foolish reasons, but I've never made conquests of them.''

He sobered too. ''I'm sorry, Gwendolyn. I've touched a raw nerve, I perceive. I meant it for a jest, not to hurt you.''

''There's no need to apologize, my lord. I'm well used to it. My father refers to my many suitors as my 'little hobby.' But it's not that. I find their unwanted attentions quite unpleasant. I've learned a great many useful ways of dealing with men, but it seems impossible to make them stop altogether.''

''Them,'' he repeated. ''Out of so many admirers, you've never found one or two who strike your fancy? In a more permanent manner, I mean.''

''No,'' she said softly. ''Not among them.'' She held his gaze.

''Gwendolyn,'' he said after a moment's silence. ''I find you to be a very beautiful, very desirable, very interesting young woman—but I must tell you plainly that there is not and never will be any relationship between us.

Save, I hope, that of friends. It isn't because of you. Please believe that. I have no plans to make a permanent relationship with any woman. If matters were otherwise, I should find your interest in me exceedingly flattering. But it's impossible.''

There, he thought. He'd told her outright, although as gently as possible, and she'd have no excuse for misinterpreting his words. Bracing himself for tears, he set his teacup aside.

But she only lowered her lashes and smiled.

"Perhaps," she murmured. "But perhaps not. But I, like you, pray we may always be friends, regardless of what may come. I like you very well, Jack Sommerton.''

"And I like you, Gwendolyn, when I'm not wanting to put my hands around your pretty neck and throttle you.''

She laughed, and he did as well, knowing a warmth and contentment that had been absent for a long time in his life. It was good to have someone in his home, someone to sit and talk with, to relax and be comfortable with. He had missed having people in his house—although that wasn't really accurate. He had a house filled with people, most of them women, all of them servants. And aside from that he often had his friends to Brannard for a night of cards and drinking. And from time to time far-flung family members even descended upon him while they were making a visit to London. Only last year he'd played host to one of his mother's cousins who had an eligible daughter to marry off. But despite the pleasure of such company, he hadn't felt with them—not even with Lucky—what he was feeling at the moment with Gwendolyn. He couldn't begin to define what the difference was; in fact, he didn't particularly *want* to think on it. But while she was here, he would let himself enjoy her company and the absence of the loneliness that had dogged him for so long.

Smiling down at her, he stroked her cheek with a sweep

of his fingers, meaning only to impart through the innocent caress something of what he felt, but the touch unnerved him, and her too, for her smile died away and she gazed up at him, wide-eyed. His own gaze fell to her lips, which had parted slightly, and he leaned closer as if drawn by an irresistible magnet.

"Gwendolyn," he murmured, wishing she would push him back. She did raise a hand, but rather than repel him, she set it upon his chest, over the place where his heart felt as if it must explode from pounding so fiercely. The tip of her tongue slipped between her teeth to wet her lips, and that simple, unwitting action was the undoing of him. It took only another inch to bring their mouths together. He kissed her gently, his hand yet stroking her cheek. She made a murmuring sound—not at all a protest—and slid her own hand about his neck.

His fingertips drifted downward to caress her warm skin even as he deepened the kiss. Then he pulled away slightly and cupped her chin in a gentle grip to hold her as he wished, turning her this way and that, moving his mouth over hers in soft, lingering kisses that seemed to steal all her strength away, for she let him do as he pleased. With his tongue he traced the line of her lips, following the path her own tongue had earlier gone, and murmured, "Sweet."

A scratch fell on the door, not loudly, but enough so that Jack came to his senses. He opened his eyes and lifted his head. Gwendolyn's face was tilted up to him, her lips pink and softened from his kisses. The hand that had held her chin, he discovered as his brain cleared, had somehow settled on the bare patch of flesh that her dress left exposed—just above her breasts. He hastily lifted it away and sat back. To his dismay, a reddened imprint showed clearly against her soft, white skin.

"Gwendolyn," he said.

Her eyes fluttered open and she smiled at him dreamily. "Mmmm?"

"There's someone at the door."

"Is there?"

"Yes, confound you." He scooted away and ran fingers through his hair. "The devil! It was not my intent to kiss you. Or anything like it. I apologize."

"I don't know why you should," she said. "I liked it."

"That's the trouble," he told her, moving to the chair opposite her as another scratch fell at the door. "So did I. Now, behave yourself." The imprint on her chest, he saw with some relief, had begun to fade.

"Of course, Jack dear. I always do." The smile she gave him was so filled with lingering intent that Jack's voice came out in an unnaturally high squeak when he called out, "Enter!"

Barton opened the door and crossed the room bearing a small silver tray, upon which a small white card reposed.

"Show him in, Barton," Jack said, rising to his feet and reaching down for Gwendolyn. "Your dear cousin has arrived."

Chapter Thirteen

Gwendolyn had only just gained her feet when the Earl of Kerlain was announced.

"Jack," he greeted, walking briskly into the room, his hair and face yet damp from the rain. "Gwennie, love. I hope the day finds the both of you—land sakes, Gwennie!" He stopped midstride and gaped at her. "What the devil have you got on?"

"Good day, Lad," Gwendolyn said, making a curtsy. "It's good to see you well after last night's excitement. As to what I have on, I believe it's usually called a gown."

"That's not what *I* call it." He began digging about in a pocket while looking accusingly at Jack. "You let her wear that?"

"One of the maids lent it to her," Jack replied. "It was preferable to having her spend the day wrapped up in her chemise and cloak."

"One of your maids," Lad sputtered. "I can indeed imagine what her use for such a dress is."

"You'll be careful, Kerlain," Jack warned in a low voice, "of what you say regarding any of my maids or servants, or you'll find yourself being thrown out of doors. By me."

"Damn you, Jack, I don't mean any disrespect to anyone in your household, but you know the truth better than

I about where that dress has been and what it's been used for. And yet here stands my own *cousin* in it. And what's that?'' He pointed to the still-visible handprint.

"Uh . . .'' Jack's facile brain deserted him utterly.

"Lad, don't be silly,'' Gwendolyn said, setting her own hand over the spot in question. "It's my own hand, you see? How foolish you are. And you've insulted Lord Rexley, when he's been nothing but kind.''

"It won't fadge, Gwennie,'' her cousin told her. "Your fingers aren't that big.'' He glared at Jack, who said intelligently, "Ahem, well—''

"For pity's sake, don't say anthing, you rogue,'' Kerlain growled, "or I'll break your damned neck. Gwennie''—he grabbed her by the arm—"come here.''

"But, Lad—''

He didn't give her a chance to argue, but dragged her across the room.

"And you,'' he addressed Jack, "turn around.''

"I can't see what good that will do. I've already been looking at her all day.''

"Yes, I can just imagine you have, among other things,'' Kerlain said tartly. "Turn *around*, Jack.''

With a sigh, Jack turned. A few moments passed while he listened to Gwendolyn and Kerlain arguing, until at last he was allowed to turn again.

"There,'' Kerlain said with satisfaction, bringing Gwendolyn back to the settee. "Much better.''

Jack surveyed what was clearly supposed to be the improvement: a large white handkerchief that was tucked into the dress, covering Gwendolyn's chest from the neck down.

"You look as if you're about to eat a large meal,'' he commented.

"And an obviously messy one,'' Gwendolyn said, looking down at herself. "It's ridiculous, is it not? But to view the matter in a positive light, at least I feel a bit warmer."

"Aye, there's definitely no fear of your catching a chill," Jack agreed, grinning.

"But I'm sure *you're* feeling much cooler now, my lord," Kerlain remarked.

Jack cleared his throat and said, "If you mean to say that I've been plotting some fiendish evil against Miss Wells's person, then please be reassured. I haven't harmed a hair upon her lovely head." Which was no more than the simple truth, he thought. "And I'd remind you, you're the one who insisted she stay at Brannard."

"Come now, Lad, don't be foolish," Gwendolyn chided. "You know very well how I deal with unwanted attentions. Lord Rexley would have been on the floor by now, on his knees and begging for mercy, if he'd been making a pest of himself, which I assure you he was not." She set an approving gaze on Jack, who smiled with both gratitude and no little discomfort.

"Yes, well, let's hope he can continue on in the same vein," Kerlain said, "because you'll be staying another day or two before I can move you elsewhere."

He stood looking at the two of them, clearly expecting some reaction, but was met by mere silence.

"However, if it's that much of an inconvenience—"

"Not at all," Jack said. "If it can't be helped, then it can't be helped. You weren't able to devise a method of getting her back into the Clarendon without remark?"

Kerlain shook his head. "I was successful in bribing the lone footman who saw her departing last night, but as far as the rest of the hotel staff is concerned, Gwennie's still in her rooms."

"And since Gwendolyn must necessarily leave Brannard at night to avoid notice," Jack said, "it would seem rather odd to have her make a sudden appearance at the

Clarendon—in the middle of the night—when she was not seen to leave. I understand. It would be far easier to sneak her into a private residence under cover of darkness and try to convince the various employees at the Clarendon that they simply missed her departure.''

"Something like that," Kerlain told him.

"I assume you have some other place in mind, then?" Jack asked.

Kerlain nodded. "Barrington. We had nearly decided upon Manning House, knowing that Robby and Lady Anna would have insisted upon playing host to Gwennie and Uncle Philip, but Lady Anna is so busy with her young sons that Lucky finally agreed it would be better not to add to her present duties. Although I must admit I'm tempted to at least ask them."

"No, I think Lucky has the right of it," Jack said quickly. Robby would eventually learn about the debacle at St. Bart's and that Gwendolyn had been there, but Jack would be damned if he'd let his godfather find out that he was looking for Mrs. Toby. At least not until he absolutely had to. So long as Gwendolyn was at Brannard, Robby wouldn't be able to interrogate her. "Anna's far too busy to play hostess at the moment. Barrington's a far better choice."

"I suppose that's true," Kerlain agreed. "And as Lady Clara has been so eager to meet Gwennie and would never forgive him for missing such a chance, Lucky's decided to fetch her back. Once she and the children are installed at Barrington, all will be well. Uncle Philip's to be moved there as well," he assured Gwendolyn. "For now he's remaining at the Clarendon, fully apprised of the situation, and the most-excellent Lydia is putting off visitors by telling them you're ill."

"Oh, dear," Gwendolyn murmured. "I pray she's not

making this fictitious illness too serious. Or at least nothing that involves spots.''

''No, no. A slight chill and nothing more. She's also packing up a number of your belongings, which I'll have delivered sometime later this evening. Once Lord and Lady Callan are in residence, we'll slip you and Uncle Philip over to Barrington in the middle of the night, and no one, hopefully, will ever be the wiser. It will be put about that you've gone there to recover from the illness that was plaguing you, and that will be that.''

''I don't wish to put Lord and Lady Callan to any trouble though, Lad,'' Gwendolyn said. ''She's only just had a baby, hasn't she? And to drag her and her children away from their country estate seems most unkind.''

''If I know Clara,'' Jack said, ''she'll be thrilled. And Lucky's right. If she finds out that she missed the opportunity to have you and your father as her guests at Barrington, she'll be put out. Or as put out as a sweet woman such as Clara can be, which isn't much. You'll like her,'' he told Gwendolyn. ''She's nothing like Lucky.''

''As he's a very kind gentleman, despite looking like the devil,'' she said, ''then I'm sure I shall like Lady Clara very well.''

The library door opened and Barton entered carrying the silver tray again, which he presented to his lord. ''I'm sorry to interrupt Lord Rexley, but Viscount Walsh was most insistent.''

Jack read the card and threw it back on the tray. ''Take him to the Blue Parlor. I'll attend to him shortly.''

''And I thought I was the only person foolish enough to venture out in this weather,'' Kerlain said.

''Walsh,'' Jack muttered. ''What the deuce can he be wanting?''

''You know very well what it is,'' Kerlain told him. ''You'll have to pretend mightily, however, that you don't and get rid of the fellow as quick as you can. The girl is tucked away somewhere with her child?''

''Yes. My staff will have made them safe at his arrival and will keep them safe.''

''Very true,'' Kerlain said with a nod. ''God knows I'd never want to take on the women in this household. You're by far the safest man in London, Jack.''

''I don't understand,'' Gwendolyn said with confusion. ''Why on earth would Lord Walsh have any interest in Nancy?''

''I'll have to talk to him, Lad,'' Jack said. ''There's nothing for it. If he's bold enough to come to me so plainly, he'll not go away without some measure of satisfaction.''

''Don't let it come to that,'' Kerlain advised. ''But if it does, a shout will bring me running. I'll be more than happy to help you get rid of the body.''

''Lad!''

''Calm down, Gwennie, love.'' He patted her shoulder. ''I but jest.'' To Jack he said, ''I'll keep Gwennie here unless you need me.''

''Make certain that you do,'' Jack warned as he made his way to the door. ''If he should divine that she's here or conceive even a hint of it, it will be all over London. Especially about that dress she's wearing.'' This last he added with a smile and a wink at Gwendolyn, then walked out the door.

Gwendolyn turned to her cousin. ''What was that about?''

''Not what, but whom, my dear. And the answer is Lord Walsh. A nasty fellow is Walsh, and I understand that you've taken to dancing with him at Almack's.''

''A minuet,'' she told him. ''I won't say he was the most delightful partner I've ever had, but he was, at least, a perfect gentleman. Indeed, I can't believe there would be any trouble if he knew I was here.''

"Yes, there would be. No one's to know you're here, and aside from that, I'll be damned if I let anyone else see you in that dress.''

"I'll admit that it's not the sort of gown I'd normally wear.'' Gwendolyn sighed and sat down on the settee. "It's rather bold.''

"That's a nice way of putting it. If you were a working girl, Gwennie, you and that dress could make a fortune.'' He sat across from her. "Pour me some tea, will you, sweet?''

She did as he asked, handing him a steaming cup.

"Tell me about Lord Walsh, Lad.''

"I don't know if I should or not. It might be best if you continue to think him nothing more than a perfect gentleman. You're less likely to get into trouble that way.''

"If I promise not to do anything foolish, will you?''

"I don't think so, Gwennie. You can't seem to help doing foolish things—all for the best reasons, I know,'' he added, holding up a hand to silence her, "but foolish nonetheless. What if I were to tell you just how nasty a fellow Walsh is? Eh? You'd go off after the man on your own, and don't tell me you wouldn't, because you would, just as you did last night, and then Jack or I or someone else would have to get you out of trouble again.''

"Really, Lad,'' she said with affront.

"Yes, really, and don't look at me like that, for it won't work. I knew you as a girl, recall, and know the sort of tricks you use to get your own way. So let's forget all about Walsh and talk about Jack instead. You appear to be making a great deal of headway with him. Not exactly what I had in mind, you understand, but I don't suppose I can argue about it now. You're all in one piece at any rate.''

She flushed. "I'm sure I don't know what you mean."

"Gwennie," he said with a laugh, "it won't wash, love. You're after the man, and I mean for you to have him. Or for him to have you. Either way, I intend to help. I rather like the idea of being related to Jack by marriage. It would be better if he was an American, of course, but we can't have everything. And he's not all that bad for a Brit."

"You're worse than I am, Lad," she said, shaking her head at him woefully. "This business of managing people must be in our blood."

"Don't make it sound so dismal, my girl. The art of manipulation is a blessing as well as a curse, and we can both think of others in the family who do it far better than our meager selves."

She sat back with a sigh. "I suppose you're right. As to Lord Rexley, we've had a good start. He liked the dress, although it took all my courage to actually wear the thing downstairs." She grinned at her cousin. "His eyes nearly popped out of his face at breakfast. And this afternoon, before you arrived, he kissed me. That's all, I swear it," she added when he began to look suspicious. "Now, tell me about your visit to Kerlain. Is all well there?"

"Not perfectly well, no, but getting better." He sat forward and reached out to take her hand. "Which is why I'm eager to get this matter between you and Jack quickly settled. I'll be going back to Kerlain soon. For good."

"Oh, Lad," she said, squeezing his hand, "I'm so glad. After all these years and all your hard work."

"Three years it's been," he said. "Three years, more like serving time in hell than living, but I deserved it, and far worse. It was my penance for all my crimes." He smiled grimly. "But it's nearly over and I'll be going home."

"It will all work out, Lad. Everything will be different this time."

"I hope so. I pray so."

"You've all the money you need now to make the repairs to the castle?"

"Almost," he said, releasing her and moving to refill both her teacup and his. "Almost, Gwennie. One more wager would suit me. A large one, as I had with Callan when I wagered on his wife rather than on him. Of course that turned out well for both of us, and he didn't mind the money, but it isn't always so."

"That wager was for ten thousand pounds," she murmured. "It would be difficult to find anyone else to wager you such a sum, wouldn't it?"

"True. Not that it matters. I can't seem to scare up a decent wager to begin with. I'd fix something about you and Jack tying the knot, but I promised him I'd not, so I'll have to dig up something else."

"Perhaps not," Gwendolyn said thoughtfully. "Did you promise you'd not make any wagers involving him? Or involving me?"

"Involving either of you, I suppose. I don't precisely recall. But it doesn't matter, for I hold Jack's friendship dear—despite the fact that he's English—and I wouldn't shade any promises I'd given him."

"Of course you wouldn't, dear," she said with a gentle pat on his hand, "but you've made no such promises to me. Why don't you wager on my behalf? Not your own wager, but mine. Jack's name needn't be mentioned at all."

Kerlain shook his head. "No, I don't like it, Gwennie. And what's more, Uncle Philip won't like it. Your name in the betting books at some men's club? It would be ruinous. Scandalous. Just what you don't need after the fuss you've caused about Town already."

"Oh, very well," she said irately, "just enter my initials, then, which will easily identify who I am once I've won. Enter the wager for me and name any sum you like. Rumors should make it profitable enough."

"Rumors would help Jack to hear about it. Do you know what he would assume?"

"You'd simply deny it," she said. "It would be the truth. Surely he'd believe you."

"Ah, Gwennie," he said with a shake of his head, "I'm glad you're still so trusting and naive. Myself, I think I'd be fortunate to come away with my head still attached to my body. But let me think on the matter for a night or two. How, precisely, would you want the wager worded, if I should decide to place it for you?"

She pondered that for a moment. "Write, if the club you choose will allow it, *A lady's wager, that G.W., an American miss, will wed J.S., an English lord, before the summer is out.* Or *the end of August*, if that's better. I have no notion of how these things are usually worded, but that should be enough to do the trick. And J.S. could be any number of men, really."

Kerlain laughed. "Gwennie, you little idiot. It couldn't possibly be anyone else but Jack."

"Yes, it could."

"Who, pray tell?"

"Why, Lad, you should have thought of it yourself."

She was serious, he realized, and his laughter died away.

"Who do you mean, Gwennie? There can't be another lord in England who goes by the initials of J.S."

"But there is," she said, smiling. "Jere Saxon. Viscount Walsh. He invited me to call him by his Christian name while we were dancing the minuet."

He gaped at her.

"No. Absolutely not." He stood, towering above her.

"You'll not have me putting such a wager as that in White's betting books. Absolutely not, Gwennie. Do you understand me?"

She sipped her tea demurely. "Perhaps, Lad," she said softly. "Or perhaps not."

It had been years since Jack and Lord Walsh had made any attempt to be civil to each other, even in public, though they did on occasion strive to ignore the other's presence for the benefit of other members of the ton. There were few men whom Jack despised as much as he did Viscount Walsh, and he knew for certain that the feeling was mutual. This being the case, Walsh evinced little surprise when Jack stalked into the Blue Parlor where he was waiting and demanded, "What do you want?"

"Good day to you as well, my lord," Walsh replied mockingly, leaning against a bookcase.

Jack moved across the room to where a decanter and glasses were set out and poured himself a brandy. Taking a swallow, he turned to look at Walsh.

"I was busy with my steward. Don't make me keep him waiting, for I'd rather stick my head in a chamber pot than spend any amount of time with you. Is this about last night?"

Walsh sneered at him. "You haven't even got the manners of a pig, you gutter-born bastard. Yes, it's about last night. You've been poaching on my territory again, Rexley. I warned you the last time that I'd not tolerate you cutting in on my profits."

"What a disgusting piece of horse manure," Jack told him, moving slowly closer, the glass clutched in his hand. "That was a *baby* you wanted to sell, you bloody, stinking whoremonger, not a *profit*."

"Don't argue the facts, Rexley. You know what it was. You interfered in my business, *again*. This is the last warning you get. Don't trouble me anymore with your sainted designs. I'll destroy you if you stick your nose in where it's not wanted, and believe me, my friend, I can do what I say.''

"Oh, dear me,'' Jack said in dramatic, fainting tones, setting the back of one hand to his forehead. "I'm quaking in my very boots. Help. Someone save me.'' He drained his glass, then set it aside. "You broke the rules, Walsh, when you sent Gwendolyn Wells in after me.'' He dangled that particular carrot on purpose, to see if Walsh would react. Surely he knew that she'd been there the night before. Rickard would have told him. Or even, perhaps, Ware.

"That deceiving bitch?'' Walsh laughed. "She certainly had me fooled. Your whore, is she? That's what you told Ware.''

It was what Jack had been afraid of. If Walsh discovered why Gwendolyn had been in St. Bart's, not only would her reputation be completely decimated, but she might very well be in danger. Walsh wasn't above hurting anyone, even a gentlewoman, if he thought she might destroy his lucrative source of income.

"Oh, no, that won't wash, my lord,'' Jack said in a warning tone, moving closer. "You sent her in to ruin the bargaining, to spy on me, to throw me into a complete spin, and, by gad, it worked. Very well indeed. She nearly ruined everything.''

Walsh looked befuddled. "I did not send her,'' he said. "I assumed that you had . . . that she had . . .''

"Oh, did you?'' Jack made a snarling sound, and Walsh pushed from the wall to put some distance between them. "It was clever, Walsh, I give you that. I begin to think that the two of you had it planned from the first, from the very day I met her. You knew I'd not be able to abandon a lady—even such a dubious one—to a man like

Ware. Oh, she told me it was for another reason entirely,"
he said when the expression on Walsh's face filled with
surprise, "but I knew that you'd sent her. Well, I got her
out, which is just what you expected, but if you want the
divine Miss Wells to stay in one piece, then keep the lying
chit out of my sight or the both of you will be the sorrier
for it." He shoved a chair aside that stood between himself and Walsh. "Send her tagging after me again, swine,
and I'll leave her to rot, no matter where it may be."

"I didn't send her," Walsh repeated in a low voice.
"You took her with you afterward. You forced her into
your carriage with your foul companions, and now she's
receiving no visitors at her hotel. What did you do to her,
Rexley?"

Jack gave him an evil grin. "What did I do? What do
you think? I put the fear of God into her, that's what. It'll
take her days to recover, I vow."

"She was an innocent!" Walsh told him hotly. "I did
not send her. Oh, God. Poor woman. She must have been
terrified."

"She was," Jack assured him, still in slow, measured
pursuit. "I made her beg for mercy before I finally let her
go."

Walsh began backing toward the door. "I'll see you
suffer for this, Rexley. I don't know how Miss Wells came
to be in Saint Balthasar's, but you may be certain that I
shall repay you tenfold for what you've done to her."

"Impossible." Jack laughed. "Now it's my turn to give
you warning." He saw Walsh fumbling for something beneath his coat—a pistol, probably—but that didn't check
Jack from closing on his prey. "You keep away from the
girls I'm helping, Walsh, or I'll make a bullock of you."
With a swift leap he grabbed the other man by the collar
and slammed him against the door. "Understand it, you
thieving jackal," he said between clenched teeth. "Noth-

ing would give me greater pleasure than carving you to pieces. Give me a reason, and I swear by God I'll do it. You know I can. It's in my blood." He lifted Walsh and slammed him against the door again, so hard the wood creaked and threatened to shatter. "Don't come into my house again, you filthy whoremonger. I'll kill you if you do. And if you value your dear, virginal Miss Wells, then keep her out of my sight. I don't have time to play with such innocents as she is."

He opened the doors and tossed Walsh onto the carpeted floor in the hall, then slammed the doors shut again and leaned on them, holding his breath until he heard Walsh pick himself up and walk away.

Then, and only then, did Jack breathe.

"May God forgive me," he murmured, sliding down the door until he rested upon the floor, "for whatever falsehoods I may have just said, despite them being uttered under complete and total duress. Bloody damned Walsh," he said with more fever. "He could drive a saint to madness."

He rubbed his face with both hands and let out a long breath, praying that the entire household, especially Gwendolyn, hadn't overheard his heated exchange with Walsh. Even more did he pray that Walsh would leave Gwendolyn, when she at last emerged from her supposed illness, in peace. The man had clearly formed a passion for her—understandable, Jack admitted, though he personally found it disgusting—and that might be a problem. For Gwendolyn foremost, and, because of her, for him. It was the last thing any of them needed just now. The very last thing.

Chapter Fourteen

The rain continued for the next three days and nights, almost as if in answer to Gwendolyn's prayers. She did not go outdoors in all that time, but she didn't care. Living inside Brannard with Jack Sommerton for four days in a row was the sort of fate any woman might wish for.

"Thank you, Lydia." She smiled into the mirror at the maid. "What a lovely job you've done with my hair."

Lydia had arrived two days ago with most of Gwendolyn's clothes. The many items she'd ordered, which had not yet been fitted, could wait until the move to Barrington. Lydia herself came to and from Brannard in a discreet manner and kept up the farce at the Clarendon of turning away would-be visitors. She was patient and uncomplaining but clearly more than ready to return to her regular work at Brannard. And that would be soon. Gwendolyn didn't think the girl could be convinced to accompany her to Barrington. Lydia still looked at her, on occasion, as if Gwendolyn were a rather strange and undependable being.

"Thank you, miss," Lydia said, making a slight curtsy. "You look very beautiful, if I may say so."

She was in good looks, Gwendolyn thought critically, mostly due to Lydia's skillful touch.

"All because of you," she told the girl. "I shall miss you when I've gone to Lord and Lady Callan's home."

"Oh, I'm sure that's not so, miss." Lydia made herself busy rearranging the few items on the dressing table. "Barrington's a grand manor, so it is, and the servants there are the talk of the rest of us, I vow. Lord Callan is very rich, although I suppose I shouldn't say so. But he is fussy about his help, if you understand what I mean."

"Of course I do," Gwendolyn said with a reassuring smile. It was clear that, regardless of what Lydia might think of her personally, she wouldn't be comfortable at Barrington. "Tell me, do you think Nancy will be happy at Lord Rexley's estate in the country? Working in one of his mills?"

"I'm sure I don't know, miss, but anything is better than what she was doing. Working the docks and streets is an awful hard life. When Lord Rexley took me away from it and brought me here, I was so glad I wanted to get on my knees and kiss his very feet."

"You, Lydia?" Gwendolyn asked in astonishment. "I didn't know that you had—I'm sorry. I didn't realize. You are such an excellent maid that I just assumed . . ."

Lydia blushed hotly and picked up a strand of pearls to fix about Gwendolyn's neck.

"I'm from Yorkshire, miss. My da is a tenant on a farm, and he and my ma have ten children—my brothers and sisters—not counting me. They're humble folk, my parents, but they made sure each of us was well fed and properly dressed and educated. I was sent early to one of the big, fine houses nearby to be trained as a proper maid—as a lady's maid, miss, because I can read and write. It was a grand opportunity, my parents said, but the master of the house had an eye for some of us younger girls, and he didn't take kindly to being told no. I wasn't there six months before he turned his attentions on me."

"Oh, no," Gwendolyn murmured. "Lydia."

Lydia patted the necklace into place and leaned forward to pick up a soft-bristled brush. "I came up pregnant after another four months and was stupid enough to beg the lady of the house for help. She cuffed me and called me a slut, all sorts of names, and then had the master throw me out. I had but a few coins in my pocket and nowhere to go. My parents couldn't have taken me back, not with another baby to feed, and it was a terrible shameful thing as well."

"But none of your fault!"

"Aye, but they're good, honest people, miss, and it would have grieved them so. And how the villagers would have talked too, especially after my parents had been so proud because their children were educated. I couldn't place such a burden on them or set their neighbors to pointing at them and whispering. I just couldn't."

"And so you came to London?"

Lydia nodded, her attention given to pulling a few tendrils from Gwendolyn's arrangement to curl them about her neck. "With the few coins I had I bought passage on a mail coach for as far as Kingsbury and then walked the rest of the way. I had thought to find work as a maid—I thought it would be so easy, what with all the big houses and fine lords and ladies here—and I had so many plans for me and the baby. But no one would have me. Not without a letter or some kind of reference. Even the agencies turned me away. I don't blame them much. My clothes were ragged and dirty, and I wasn't any better to look at. It had been days since I'd eaten, and I was fainting with hunger, unsteady on my feet, and growing more desperate each hour. It's not to wonder that nobody wanted such a maid in their house."

"Oh, Lydia," Gwendolyn murmured. "How awful. What did you do?"

"What I had to do, when I got so hungry that I'd have

done anything to eat. There was no place else to go but the docks, and that's where Rickard found me.''

Gwendolyn turned in her chair to stare at the girl. ''Rickard? You worked for him?''

''Aye, me and many of the other girls who work for Lord Rexley now. Rickard's not like some of the other rookery lords. He mainly deals in whores, and that's why he hates Lord Rexley so much and wants to kill him, for my lord's taken away so many of his girls and so much of his profits.''

''What happened to your baby, Lydia?''

Lydia was silent for a moment and at last set the brush down. ''He died, just after he was born. He was too small and came too early.'' She bowed her head. ''Probably because of his mother's working as she did. Rickard wouldn't let me quit, even when my time drew near. But it was a mercy, really. If he'd lived, Rickard would have given him to Mrs. Toby, just as he wanted to do with Nan's Kitty, and I never could have lived with myself if that had happened.''

She turned away and drew in a shaking breath. Gwendolyn stood and put a gentle hand on her shoulder.

''I'm so very sorry, Lydia,'' she said softly. ''It must have been the worst moment of your life.''

''Aye, miss.'' She wiped a hand across her eyes. ''It surely was. I wish to God that Lord Rexley had found me before then. He saved my life, though, when he did find me. I shall be thankful to him for that, and for many kindnesses, for the rest of my days.''

''Saved your life, Lydia?''

The girl turned at last, her face wet with tears. ''Yes, miss. Rickard had beaten me near to death for turning away a customer who had a nasty way with women.'' She accepted the handkerchief that Gwendolyn handed her and wiped her cheeks. ''He was such an awful man, miss, and took his pleasure from hurting the girls he had. I wouldn't have him and told him so. But then Rickard beat me for it, which was just as bad. One of my lord's men saw it and went to fetch Lord Rexley. Next thing I know I'm here, at Brannard, in a soft bed and with a doctor to care for me. And then Lord Rexley offered me safe and decent work and a life away from Rickard—as I told you, I nearly wanted to kiss his feet.''

Gwendolyn smiled. "I think I should have too. Now I understand why Lord Rexley's staff is so devoted to him. Were all of you rescued in such a way?"

Lydia nodded. "Nearly all, miss. But it isn't just that, although that's more than enough. My lord has been good to us in other ways as well. After I'd recovered from Rickard's beating, Lord Rexley sent me home for a visit with my family. In his own carriage, mind you, and with an escort, which made me feel grand as a duchess. And he gave me strict instructions that I was to tell them I worked for him, in a proper house and as a proper maid, and to say nothing of the time I'd spent with Rickard or of the babe. You can't know, miss, what that meant to me, to keep my people from grief.''

"I think I can know," Gwendolyn said, "and appreciate. But you, Lydia . . . you have amazed me, for I don't know that I ever could have survived through such as you have. You have all my admiration."

A shy smile lifted the corners of Lydia's mouth. "Thank you, miss. But it's Lord Rexley who deserves your admiration."

"Him too," Gwendolyn admitted readily, "but you more so. And all the women in this household, I now perceive. How soft and foolish I feel compared to them, and to you, Lydia."

"Oh, no, miss!" The girl looked at her, fully astonished. "You're a fine lady, so you are."

Gwendolyn shook her head. "Not in the least, my dear. Not in the very least. I think you much finer than many ladies I've met, and that is God's truth."

Lydia blushed hotly. "No, miss."

"Lydia, will you tell me who Mrs. Toby is? I've heard her name on several occasions but can't place her significance in all that's occurred."

Lydia's gaze fell, and she moved away a few steps. "I'm not certain if I should, miss. Lord Rexley mightn't like it."

"I shall take all accountability if he should ask. Please tell me. I mean to be of service to him, if I can, for I know he seeks the woman."

"Aye, he seeks her," Lydia admitted, nervously folding and unfolding her hands, "but I pray he'll not find her. She's no good. Not to him or anyone."

"But *who* is she, Lydia?"

"She sells babies," Lydia replied, her voice raw and filled with pain. "Mine she would have sold, if he'd lived, and sweet Kitty as well. She's a devil, is Mrs. Toby, and can only mean my lord terrible harm."

Gwendolyn moved nearer to the girl.

"How can she hurt him?"

Lydia shook her head. "I can't tell you that, miss. Please . . . I can't tell you."

"Very well. Can you tell me what it is that she does with the babies? And who she sells them to?"

"That I can do," Lydia said bitterly, "though you'll not wish to hear it. Fine folk seldom do."

"I wish to hear it," Gwendolyn murmured.

Lydia wiped her face with the handkerchief once more, then turned about to look at Gwendolyn.

"She sells them to certain houses, miss, where they're raised to serve as whores. Young whores, mind you. They start their service almost as early as they can know their own names. Five- and six-year-olds—for gents who want young ones who've been trained just so, and there's plenty of them who do. You understand what I'm saying, miss?''

Gwendolyn understood. Perfectly. She felt as if she was going to be sick, and she put a hand to her mouth. A long, silent moment passed as she and Lydia stared at each other.

''Mrs. Toby,'' Lydia went on at last, ''is the one who finds the babies for those houses. Finds them when whores like me has them, and gets them from pimps like Rickard, who takes them from their mamas whether they want to give them up or not.''

''Oh, Lydia,'' Gwendolyn whispered. ''Oh, dear God.''

''There's plenty of money in that particular trade. Healthy babies like Kitty go dear. My little boy, if he'd lived, wouldn't have brought very much. They have to be strong enough to survive a very harsh sort of mothering once they're taken to those houses. They're put in tiny cribs—more like little wooden boxes—and raised like farm stock. Fed and kept warm but never held or loved.''

''Please,'' Gwendolyn said in a choking voice. ''Please, no more. Oh, God.'' She moved to the nearest chair and dropped into it.

''I'm sorry, miss, if I've upset you. It's the simple truth.''

''I'm the one who's sorry, Lydia. You warned me, but I wanted to hear it. And I'm glad you told me, awful as it is. Now I understand why Jack—why Lord Rexley is searching for the woman. He clearly wishes to shut such an evil trade down, and I pray that he will.''

''That's a part of it, aye,'' Lydia said. ''He is a very fine gentleman, is Lord Rexley. There isn't anyone here at Brannard or at any of his other properties who wouldn't do whatever they must for him.''

''That I believe. You needn't fear that any harm shall

ever come to him from me, Lydia, if that's your worry. I mean him only good, I promise."

"Oh, I know that, miss. We all do, for he's been so much happier these few days since you've been here."

Gwendolyn looked at her. "Do you think so?"

"Oh, yes, miss. You couldn't know it, of course, but it's true. He's been gladder to be here at Brannard, when he was never here for a full day and night before, least not that I can remember, and he's been smiling more. We've all of us been happy to see him so. It would be lovely if you could stay rather than go to Barrington."

Gwendolyn smiled warmly. "You have no idea how much I wish I could do so, but it's impossible. And, in a way, helpful. My final intention is to be with Lord Rexley always, here or wherever he may be, but doing so will require some exertion on my part, I'm afraid."

Lydia's face lit with pleasure. "Oh, miss! That would be grand! We've all hoped these many years that our lord would find a good, proper lady to care for him. He's been very lonely, although he'd never say so."

"No, he'd not," Gwendolyn agreed. "And therein lies the problem. Like most men, Lord Rexley requires some convincing before he'll realize just how greatly he desires the married state. And the most troublesome part is that, when he does at last realize it, he must be made to think it his own idea."

"They can be quite tiresome creatures, miss," Lydia said with sympathy, "but very charming and nice as well. And, if you don't mind me saying it, Lord Rexley is nicer than most."

"Yes, he is. Lydia"—Gwendolyn rose from her chair—"can you tell me one last thing, please?"

"If I can, miss."

"What is Lord Walsh's place in all that has occurred recently? Is he somehow involved in this matter regarding

Nancy and her child?" Gwendolyn had tried every trick she knew of to get Jack to tell her about his meeting with Lord Walsh, to no avail. She only knew that he'd returned to the library in an ill-concealed fury, and that he and Lad had spoken privately for some time before her cousin had at last taken his leave.

Lydia frowned. "I really shouldn't be speaking about any of this to you, not even what I told you about Mrs. Toby. Lord Rexley would be full angry if he were to find out."

"But he'll not," Gwendolyn promised. "I'll say nothing to him, I give you my word. And if Lord Rexley is in trouble, how can I help him if I don't know everything?"

Lydia sighed and moved to straighten the set of Gwendolyn's collar. "I suppose you should know, for your own sake more than my lord's. Lord Walsh is a very bad man, miss, and you'd do best to stay far, far away from him. Which I hope you shall do once you know just how wicked he is, for Lord Rexley has told me to let him know if you should receive Lord Walsh ever again."

Gwendolyn made a *hmph*ing sound. "I suppose you'll tell me that Lord Walsh is in league with Mister Rickard?"

Lydia shook her head. "No, miss. Not with Rickard. With Mrs. Toby."

Gwendolyn's mouth fell open at this, but Lydia seemed not to notice. She picked up a small diamond flower and began to fix it in Gwendolyn's hair.

"She works for Lord Walsh, Mrs. Toby does, getting those babies. She finds them and pays the pimp, but the money comes from Lord Walsh. And he's the one who sells them, miss, and takes his profit. That's how he lives so rich and fine, from taking babies away from their mothers and buying and selling them as if they were naught but cattle."

* * *

Jack looked about the parlor to make certain that it was as he wanted it. Fresh roses scented the room, filling several vases, while a fire burned merrily in the hearth, keeping out the chill from the ever-pouring rain. He had been glad of the rain and the excuse it gave him for staying indoors at Brannard in the company of Gwendolyn Wells. He'd not have been able to bring himself to do so without a valid reason; it would have seemed too . . . vulnerable, he supposed. It must have seemed strange to his servants, regardless, for he'd never before let the weather keep him at home. His friends and acquaintances and those various places that he frequented—White's, Mawdry's, and especially Mrs. May's—probably thought he had either fallen ill or died. They'd not have to wonder for much longer, however, for late tonight Gwendolyn would be moved to Barrington, and as soon as she was gone, Jack would resume his life.

He had enjoyed the few days while she'd been at Brannard, perhaps too much. It made him uncomfortable to think of it, but to deny the truth would have been senseless. He had been happy and contented during the last four days. He'd even *awakened* happy each morning, which made him feel both embarrassed and foolish. Spending so much time alone with Gwendolyn had been decidedly improper, at least as far as society was concerned, but he'd not have given up one moment that he'd spent in her company, even under the threat of having to keep her reputation safe by offering her marriage.

He hadn't realized there was so much that two unrelated people could do in his home, with so much pleasure—except for making love, and despite the fantasies Miss Wells engendered, they'd done nothing that even the most exacting of society's matrons wouldn't have approved of. He'd not even allowed himself to kiss her again, despite the many opportunities he'd had and her evident willingness. Because a kiss wasn't where it would end with Gwendolyn; it certainly wasn't where he *wanted* it to end. He was a man of great control, especially in his dealings with women, but he knew that with her he'd be fortunate simply to come away with his wits intact.

What had surprised him the most during their time together was not his sexual desire for her, because that wasn't such an unusual condition for him, especially when in the presence of a beautiful woman. It was that he'd been so utterly contented to be alone with her. He'd always enjoyed the company of women, but he couldn't remember ever spending so much time with a single female without beginning to wish for other sport, or at least the conversation of someone else. Yet his usual restlessness deserted him when he was with Gwendolyn. He felt, from moment to moment, as if he were discovering something new about himself, or perhaps something that he'd simply lost and forgotten, and the sensation was far from unpleasant.

They'd spent hours walking Brannard from its length to its height. She'd told him more about Boston and her life there, about long summer visits to Tennessee, where her father's relatives lived, and about those relatives—a strange lot, it seemed, from the humorous stories she'd recounted. She'd held him fascinated, made him laugh, and somehow managed to make him talk openly about himself, which was no small feat. He doubted even Lucky would have been able to wheedle so many personal facts out of him. He supposed the reason he'd been so open with her was because she hadn't strayed toward the topic of his birth. She was far too intelligent not to have her suspicions—the *perhaps* she'd given him in the gallery while gazing at his family's portrait, and the meaning behind the word, hadn't escaped him—but since that time she'd not so much as made a sideways reference to his origins. And that, somehow, had disarmed him. He didn't regret the vulnerability, for Gwendolyn had proved to be an open and gentle listener. She'd made him forget about Mrs. Toby, Rickard, Lord Walsh, and his search for the truth, for hours at a stretch.

They had found other ways to pass the time too. After a light meal in the afternoons, they had retired to the library, where he'd taught her how to play the sorts of games that correct young ladies generally didn't speak of, let alone learn. Gwendolyn, assuring him that she wasn't a correct young lady—at which pronouncement he'd merely smiled—had taken to gambling with enthusiasm and no little talent. Over the course of three days he'd become increasingly thankful that they were playing for hairpins rather than money.

There had been games of billiards as well, although at this Gwendolyn was less successful. She'd spent more time knocking balls off the table than sending them into pockets and had laughed so much over each mistake that he'd been unable to do anything but laugh too. And one early evening she'd talked him into teaching her the basics of fencing. Gwendolyn Wells possessed of a rapier—pointed at him—had been a sight to behold. She'd undertaken the lesson with a rare seriousness and had impressed him with her lack of fear, even at his attacks. But it was a sport for the quick-minded, and Gwendolyn's facile mind was tailor-made for just such a challenge.

They had also entertained a few select visitors. Kerlain had come twice, spending an hour or so each time and regaling with his cousin old memories, and Professor Wells had arrived after the first day to make certain that his only child was well and not giving her host any trouble. Jack had assured him that he was delighted to have Miss Wells's company, but Professor Wells had given him a long and knowing look. "Gwennie's a good girl," he'd told Jack. "I don't believe she means to cause trouble, but it does have a strange way of occurring when she's about. And that, I can tell you from long experience," he'd insisted above Gwendolyn's loud denials, "is the simple truth of the matter. I advise you to keep your wits about you at all times, my lord, whenever you're with Gwennie." By the time the visit had ended, Jack found himself quite liking the man. He had a great deal of common sense, for a scientist.

In the evenings he and Gwendolyn dined together at a leisurely pace, conversing with as much interest as if they'd not already spent the previous many hours doing the same, and afterward they'd retire to the same parlor where he now waited and talk even more. He should have felt as if words were leaking out of his ears by now, but he didn't. What he felt, and knew, was that when she was gone he was going to miss her and that his home would once again become the lonely place that sent him out into London searching for warmth and companionship.

But that was foolish, he told himself sternly, pouring a small glass of brandy from a table lined with various decanters. He went out so often because that was what young, single men did, because he would be considered odd if he did not, and because he wanted to. Indeed, as soon as Gwendolyn was gone he would take himself off as well—to Mrs. May's house. It had been so long since he'd had a woman that he could hardly sleep at night for the lack. At least he hoped that was why he wasn't sleeping. The alternative didn't bear contemplation.

A scratch on the door notified him that it was about to open, and he turned to find Barton ushering in a vision of beauty.

"Miss Wells, my lord," Barton announced, then bowed and left, closing the door behind him.

"I don't know why he always does that," Gwendolyn said with a laugh. "I'm sure you're not surprised to discover that it's only me again."

He moved toward her slowly, taking her in from top to toe.

"I think I am," he murmured, lifting her hand to place a gentle kiss upon it. "I think I always shall be. Gwendolyn, you're beautiful."

She smiled up at him. "Thank you, Jack. You look very well tonight also."

"Not as well as you." He held her slightly away from him. "This dress is wonderful."

"Do you think so?" She turned about so that he could see all of it. "You may thank Lady Anna, then, for giving me the name and direction of her modiste. Madame Elise bullied me into this color, for I had never liked wearing peach before, but this is quite pretty, even with my hair."

"It is extraordinarily pretty," he agreed. "The color of a new dawn. And your hair is always extraordinarily pretty, with any and every color. I feel rather guilty to have you all to myself tonight. If we were at a party or ball, you would draw every eye."

"Rather like a freak at the circus," she said teasingly. "I believe it's just as well, then, that we're not at a party or ball. Are we to dine here tonight, Jack?" Looking past him, she nodded toward the small table he'd ordered to be set out for them.

"Yes, I thought you might find it pleasant. Relaxing." Now that he looked at it, it seemed merely intimate. He wondered what she would think of him, if she'd believe he was trying to seduce her. Perhaps, he thought with a mental shake, he was. "And warmer. Much warmer than the formal dining room. I thought we might be more comfortable. You might be, I mean. More comfortable." He decided to stop while he was ahead.

"Why, so it is, and so we shall be," she concurred, moving about the room. Stopping at a vase filled with roses, she breathed deeply. "How lovely. Such beautiful blooms." She touched one soft petal with a fingertip. "I do love roses. They make one forget the rain." From across the room, she smiled at him.

And her smile, he thought, did something altogether different to him.

"Ahem." He cleared his throat. "Let me pour you something to drink. Barton iced some champagne earlier at my request. Or sherry, perhaps?"

"You remembered how much I enjoyed the champagne the other night?" she asked, setting her hands together lightly. "How very kind. I should love some. Thank you."

They drank champagne throughout the quite delicious meal that his chef had prepared. Jack had noticed that the food served in his home had become somewhat more pho]elaborate since Gwendolyn's arrival—an effort on the part of the kitchen staff, no doubt, to encourage a romance between himself and his guest. His staff in general seemed to be hoping for something more permanent to occur. His female servants had taken to Gwendolyn with particular enthusiasm, and it had been pointed out to him more than once that Miss Wells was a "right fine lady." Her triumph with them was no small feat. They'd thoroughly disliked every other woman he'd shown even the slightest interest in.

After the plates had been cleared away, Gwendolyn, with a nod, gave Barton leave to fill her glass once more. When he had bowed and left the room, she leaned forward slightly, folding her forearms on the table's edge. They had been talking pleasantly and laughing during their meal, but now she grew serious.

"I haven't yet thanked you for all you've done for me, Jack. For letting me stay in your home."

"It's been my great pleasure, Gwendolyn. There's no need to speak of thanks."

"There is. You didn't want a houseguest, most especially me."

He shifted uncomfortably in his chair. "I wish that I could take back those unfortunate words. They were spoken thoughtlessly, in a moment of exhaustion and anger. But that is no excuse for them, or for such ill manners. I beg that you'll forgive me."

She shook her head slightly. "If there is no need for me to speak of thanks, there is certainly no need for you to make any apologies. You've been very kind to me, Jack, and these last few days have been wonderful. I've enjoyed them so much. I've enjoyed being with you."

He was quiet, contemplating the glass in his hand.

"I suppose I should lie to you. It would be kindest and certainly wisest. But I won't." He looked at her. "I've enjoyed being with you as well, Gwendolyn. Very much."

She smiled. "That wasn't so hard, was it? Thank you. I promise not to make you suffer for such an admission."

He chuckled. "You'd best not, else I shall deny ever making such a maudlin statement. Now, with what activity shall we fill the rest of the evening? Would you like to play a game of cards? Or perhaps a game of chess?"

"Chess?" she repeated, sitting up straight. "I'm quite good at the game. Do you think you dare match me?"

He gave her a look of pure pity. "I shall annihilate you on the board, my dear."

"There won't be enough left of you to accomplish such a feat," she replied. "I'll have you begging for mercy."

"Never," he declared, rising.

"We shall see." She let him help her out of her own chair.

He conceded defeat less than an hour later.

"Gad," he said with a groan. "I can't even claim drunkenness. How humiliating."

Sitting back with a look of pure satisfaction, Gwendolyn grinned at him. "Most gentlemen who play me usually say that my beauty distracted them. I'll allow you the same excuse, if you like."

"You see fit to tease me, you heartless female, while I sit here utterly emasculated. Beaten by a woman! If Lucky ever finds out, he'll never let me hear the end of it."

"Don't feel so badly, dear," she said more soothingly. "I understand just how it is to be beaten by a member of the opposite sex. My father always beats me roundly at chess. Of course, he's the only one who can." She grinned again.

"Heartless and *wicked*," Jack declared. "I don't suppose you'd care to try your hand at billiards again? It's the only thing I've roundly beaten *you* at since you've been at Brannard."

"I would," she said with a sigh, "but you've worn me almost to naught with so much conversation and chess. And champagne." She leaned forward, folded her fingers together, and rested her chin upon them. "Besides, now you must pay your forfeit for losing."

He blinked at her. "My forfeit for losing? Were we playing for some kind of wager? I fear I missed that bit before we started."

"Jack," she said chidingly, "surely you're not afraid of paying a forfeit? A very little one?"

"Where you're concerned, Gwendolyn, I'm afraid of simply breathing."

"Silly." She got to her feet and moved around the table toward him. "Come along. It won't hurt."

He stood when she tugged at his arm, but looked at her warily. "Gwendolyn . . ."

"Here, in the middle of the room, where we'll not be

impeded by furniture.'' She led him to the spot and turned
to face him.

''Impeded for *what*?''

''For this,'' she replied, taking one of his hands and
setting it at her waist, then holding the other in her own
hand. ''Shall I hum?''

Jack stood stiffly in his place, feeling the warmth of her
body pressed closely against his own. Neither of them was
wearing gloves. He could feel beneath the skin of his hand
that she wasn't wearing a corset under her dress. It was
just *her*, and she might as well have been naked for the
effect she was having on him. If she couldn't feel it, the
wanting and need that he pressed against the layers of her
skirt, then she was dead to all senses.

''I don't think this is a good idea, Gwendolyn.''

''Don't you?''

''I retract that last statement. I *know* this isn't a good
idea.''

''Why not? We danced at Almack's.''

''It was different then.''

''How so?''

''Because at Almack's,'' he said, pulling her flush
against his body, against his need, ''I couldn't do this.''
He lowered his head and kissed her. And kept kissing her.
She gave no resistance; indeed, when he released her hand
to pull her even closer, she made only a murmuring sound
and then set her arms about his neck.

He broke contact with her only momentarily, saying her
name and burying his fingers in the soft arrangement of
her hair. When he opened his mouth over hers she readily
answered, and Jack felt his control slipping away. He
kissed her face, her neck, and his free hand moved over
her body, finding the curve of her waist and hip, pressing
against the small of her back to hold her against him more
intimately, and finally cradling her as he lowered her to

the carpet. Lying there before the fire, he found the way to gentle his wants enough to pull away.

"Gwendolyn," he muttered, his eyes closed as he pressed his forehead against her own, "this isn't what you want."

She gently stroked his hair. "I want you."

"Not like this."

"Yes, like this too."

He kissed her again, deeply. His breathing was unsteady when he pulled away, a fact made bearable only by the fact that she was breathing unsteadily too.

"Gad, how will I ever get rid of you now, Gwendolyn Wells?"

She laughed quietly, a low and husky sound, and brushed his cheek with the backs of her fingers in a soft caress.

"It's very easy. You need only tell me that you feel nothing for me. Nothing in the very least. And if you truly mean it, I'll leave you in perfect peace."

He gazed at her in silence.

"Is it so hard, Jack?" she murmured.

"It's impossible for us to be together." He wasn't sure whether he was striving to convince himself or her. "I've told you that before."

She searched his face intently. "Is that as you want it to be?"

He released a breath.

"No."

She smiled so sweetly that he couldn't keep from kissing the corner of her upturned lips. "What I want changes nothing, Gwendolyn. There cannot be anything between us."

"I understand, Jack."

"Do you?" He sat up slowly, pulling her with him

until they both were sitting and facing each other. Before them, the fire briefly popped and flared.

"More than you think. You believe you're illegitimate, don't you? Oh, Jack"—she touched his chin with her fingertips when he looked away—"it means less than nothing to me, even if it should be true."

"I had thought, perhaps, that you'd not realized," he said. "But that has always been too much for me to hope whenever I'm seen standing beside Robby. The resemblance has ever been striking, since I was a boy. You hadn't said anything though, and I had hoped you'd missed it." He smiled at her. "Which was foolish of me, I admit. You're far more clever than most women, Gwendolyn Wells."

"It doesn't matter to me," she said again.

"It should. It matters to me. I don't expect any woman of decent birth to ally herself with me. And regardless of how she or I might feel, I would not ask it of her."

"I can't think marriage to you would be anything but perfectly acceptable in every way. You're the Earl of Rexley, after all. It's rather different than being a gutter sweeper."

He lumbered to his feet and pulled her up as well. Still holding her hands, he said, "I'm a fraud, Gwendolyn. I bear the title of Rexley, but I have no honest claim to it. I don't even know exactly who or what I am."

She frowned. "You don't know for certain that you're Lord Manning's son? He's never told you?"

He shook his head. "I tried to ask him, once, when I was very young, but he turned to stone—deaf, dumb and blind, and then quickly changed the topic. I determined never again to speak of it until I had proof that he couldn't deny. Although you'd hardly think he would, as the truth seems rather obvious. Don't you think?"

She gazed at him in a stunned silence until he at last

moved away, moving aimlessly before coming to a stop by the fire.

"Jack," she said, her voice hushed. "Is that why? Is that the reason you're seeking out Mrs. Toby? To find some kind of proof that you're illegitimate? Because you believe you were one of those babies that she sells?"

He turned around. "How do you know about Mrs. Toby? Kerlain told you?"

"I heard her name during the night of Saint Bart's. How I learned about what she does doesn't matter. I know and—oh, Jack." Her eyes widened and she set a hand to her mouth. "Lord Walsh. Your dislike of him goes beyond his connection to Mrs. Toby. It's personal, isn't it?"

"Who told you about this?" he demanded angrily, striding toward her.

She shook her head. "It doesn't matter. Jack, please"—she set a hand on his arm and looked at him intently—"you must let me help you. Lord Walsh will never lead you to Mrs. Toby, but he might be less guarded with me."

"No." He took hold of her with both hands and gave her a sharp shake. "*No*, Gwendolyn. You stay away from Walsh. He's a dangerous man and I won't have you near him."

"But I can help you to discover the truth! Isn't that what you want?"

"Damn you, Gwen, I said no. I'll have a constant watch put over you if I must, but one way or another, you *will* stay away from Walsh."

"I'll come to no harm," she promised. "I'll be very careful. I know how to handle men far better than you think."

"Not men like Walsh. Never men like him."

"If I were your wife," she said, "I would obey you in this matter. At least," she amended with a tiny smile, "I

think I would. I shouldn't want you to think me unbid-
dable, for I assure you I'm not. Generally.''

"You'll obey me in this matter, Gwendolyn, or I'll find
a way to make certain you do so.''

"Jack, dear.'' She lifted her hands to place them
against his chest. "I'm delighted, of course, to know that
you care for me—despite your reluctance to prove it otherwise—but as I say, you've no authority over me, and I
shall do as I please.''

"Gwendolyn—''

"It won't do any good to argue, Jack,'' she said, sliding her hands upward to circle the back of his neck, "for I
won't listen, and you'll only become that much more overset. I think we should spend the remainder of our time in a
more profitable manner.''

"Oh? I should try spanking you to bring you to your
senses, do you mean?''

"No. I had kissing in mind.'' She lifted her face to him
in an inviting manner.

"The spanking would do you more good,'' he muttered, but gave up the fight as a lost one. She would no
doubt drive him insane, especially if she attempted to lend
him her aid—the very idea of which made him shudder
inwardly. But he wasn't such a fool as to spend their last
hour alone together arguing, and to that end he sighed, set
his arms about her to pull her near, and lowered his head
to kiss her.

Chapter Fifteen

❧❧❧

Lady Clara, Viscountess Callan, wasn't at all what Gwendolyn had expected. Lucien Bryland might look like the very devil, but at least he looked like an extremely handsome devil. Lady Clara, on the other hand, looked like a little gray bird. Her hair was brown and nondescript, her eyes were gray, and her features—well, perhaps the nicest thing that might be said was that she looked very kind.

And indeed she was kind. Lord Callan barely had a moment to make an introduction before Lady Callan took Gwendolyn by the hand and declared herself perfectly delighted to make the acquaintance. The next moment Gwendolyn was being drawn into an inviting, firelit parlor where Lady Clara proceeded to charm Gwendolyn so utterly that she forgot her shock over discovering that Viscount Callan's wife wasn't a diamond of the first water.

She was rather ashamed of herself for expecting a beautiful woman—she, who knew from personal experience that beauty was a poor determination of who or what a person was. Within moments of meeting her, Gwendolyn had discovered the true beauty of Lady Clara. It was the kind that would never dim, the kind that couldn't be taken away by accident or illness. It was the kind, Gwendolyn thought with envy, that held a man's interest from the first day of marriage through the last, so that even in old age Lady Clara would be as beautiful as she had been in her youth.

Lord Callan obviously found it so. The way in which he looked at his wife was testament to the fact. He didn't bother to hide his love or desire but gazed at Lady Clara whenever he was with her as if she were a perfect vision. Gwendolyn had never seen the like, and it made her blush. Her experience with men was rather greater than that of most unmarried females, but in all her days she'd never seen a husband look at his wife the way Lucien Bryland looked at his. If Jack was ever going to look at her in such a way, she thought, then he'd better wait until they were fully alone, because otherwise she'd never be able to keep up a normal conversation with whoever else they happened to be with.

"We're so delighted that you and Professor Wells are to stay with us, Gwendolyn," Lady Clara said, smiling warmly. They had quickly gotten past the use of formal names. "I feel as if I've been granted a marvelous boon. Tomorrow afternoon, when it becomes known that you're here at Barrington, I shall be the most envied hostess in all of England."

Gwendolyn grinned. "I can't think why," she said. "We're so very ordinary, save that you do run the risk of having Papa set this grand house on fire with his chemistry. Perhaps that's the interest?"

Lady Clara laughed with delight. "Oh, dear, I hadn't thought of that, although with Wulf so constantly about you'd think I'd have done so. He did put Cook in a swoon once, now that I think of it, by performing some odd experiment with vinegar and bicarbonate powder that he insisted couldn't wait until he got to his own home. I don't mean to sound inhospitable, but I do hope the professor will confine his chemistry to the Royal Academy, for I should hate to lose Barrington even for the sake of science."

"I shall do everything in my power to make certain he behaves, Clara, but you know how it is with men."

"Indeed, I do. Impossible creatures, the lot of them."

"What's that, my dear?" Lord Callan stood at the door of the parlor with Gwendolyn's father beside him. They had just returned from a short tour of Barrington. "Are you ladies discussing the failings of men behind our backs?"

"Yes, but please do come and join us, Lucien. We've only just gotten started."

Her husband raised his eyebrows, then turned to look at the professor. "Do we dare enter, sir, and take our chances? From previous experience I believe the conversation may not be altogether pleasing to masculine ears."

"I but jest, my lord," said Lady Callan. "Come in and be at ease. Gwendolyn and I shall reserve our conversation on that particular topic until a later date, when we'll have far more time to explore it in depth, as it deserves. Please come and sit, Professor Wells, and let me pour you a cup of tea." She indicated the tray on the table before her, laden with cakes and tarts and china cups waiting to be filled.

He did so, and when he had accepted a cup from her hands, he said, "Gwendolyn and I are so grateful to you, Lady Callan, and to you, Lord Callan, for your kindness and hospitality. Especially in rescuing Gwennie from such a scrape as might have ruined her reputation here in England. I can't include the United States as mattering, for she's already ruined herself quite thoroughly back home."

"Papa!" Gwendolyn protested. "You exaggerate entirely. What will Lord and Lady Callan think of me?"

"That you are delightful in every way," Lord Callan assured her as he seated himself beside his wife and accepted a cup of tea. "I couldn't ask for a better comrade in arms, especially in a place like Saint Balthasar's. If every man in Wellington's army could have shot a gun with your accuracy and speed, Napoleon would have been routed far sooner."

"As I was just telling Gwendolyn, Professor," Lady Clara said, sitting forward, "we're the ones who are grateful that you should see fit to bless us with your presence in our home. I hope you'll not find it amiss if we arrange a small gathering to introduce you to society?"

"A small gathering?" Professor Wells repeated.

"A rather large, formal ball, is what I believe my wife means," Lord Callan said, smiling over the rim of his teacup.

Professor Wells looked rather bewildered, but Gwendolyn beamed. "How lovely! And how kind, although I assure you it's not necessary. We should love nothing better, of course, but it would be so much trouble for you."

"Not at all," Lady Clara assured her. "I can think of nothing more pleasant. My aunt, Lady Anna, was at first quite angry that I should lay claim to the honor, especially after having you here at Barrington, when she and Robby wanted you to reside with them at Manning House, but we've worked the matter out between us. There is first to be a more informal dinner held at Manning House, with many of your fellow scientists from the Royal Academy in attendance, Professor."

At this, Professor Wells straightened his spectacles and looked very pleased.

"And the following evening," Lady Clara went on, "a ball, here at Barrington, to introduce you and Gwendolyn to the ton in a proper manner. It's long past time that it should have been done. You've been in London nearly a fortnight now, and the town is awash with gossip concerning the both of you."

"Not the bad sort of gossip, mind you," Lord Callan assured them. "There's only been talk of how unfortunate it is that you should have fallen ill after your debut at Almack's, Miss Wells. Nothing more serious than that, thankfully."

"And because of your rumored illness," Lady Clara said, "there is an even greater mystery surrounding you, and therefore an even greater desire to make your acquaintance. A ball would be the perfect manner in which to introduce you."

"It sounds wonderful!" Gwendolyn declared. "Does it not, Papa?"

"Most assuredly," her father concurred, "but are you certain, my lord and lady, that you truly wish to do so much on our behalf? It isn't at all necessary, and we don't wish to be a burden."

Lord Callan uttered a laugh. "Professor Wells, you don't know how deprived my wife would feel if you should spurn her suggestion of a ball. She is a social creature of the highest order."

"My husband speaks the truth," Lady Callan concurred, smiling as Lord Callan lifted her hand to kiss it with gentle affection. "He knows me perfectly well. I love nothing better than arranging an event. He spoils me terribly by allowing me to do so whenever I wish, as I so wish to do now. Please say you'll humor me as well."

"Oh, Papa, please, do say yes," Gwendolyn pleaded.

Her father nodded. "It sounds wonderful, so long as Gwennie doesn't make a scandal in the midst of the festivities."

"Papa!"

He laughed and lifted his cup of tea in a gesture of salute. "Lord and Lady Callan, we would be delighted."

* * *

The news of their move into Barrington trickled slowly throughout the ton. Flowers began to arrive the very morning after their arrival, along with cards expressing hopes for Gwendolyn's complete recovery. Visitors arrived too, sending their cards into the drawing room where Clara and Gwendolyn sat chatting and playing with Clara's young children, Jack and newborn Katharine, both of whom were under one year old.

"Jack was born a bit early," Clara explained, smiling down at her daughter as the baby sucked on the knuckle of one of her fingers, "and I became pregnant with Katharine less than two months after he was born. It was more than a little upsetting, I must admit, having two babies so close together, although I wouldn't give up my sweet darling for the world." She kissed her daughter's forehead. "However," she went on, glancing at Gwendolyn, "I've put Lucien on strict notice that I want at least a year before considering another child. I simply don't have the energy for any more babies at the moment."

Gwendolyn, who held young Jack in her lap as the child played with the gold locket she wore, said, "When I marry, I think I'll want to have as many children as possible, as often as possible. What lovely darlings your babies are. They're so beautiful."

Clara turned away each visitor and gave the butler, Hayes, the same excuse each time, that Gwendolyn wasn't yet fully recovered to receive company. "We must be quite cautious for a few days," she told Gwendolyn after turning away several cards, "or people will begin to whisper about the actuality of your illness. A lady must always be several days recovering, you see."

Gwendolyn found the whole matter to be fully amusing, at least until Hayes interrupted and brought in Lord Walsh's card.

"Do please invite him in, Clara," she begged. "I need to speak with him."

"I'm sorry, Gwendolyn." Clara shook her head. "Lucien told me this morning that I mustn't allow anyone to see you who isn't aware of the circumstances regarding your stay at Brannard. To invite Lord Walsh in would only be disastrous. Surely you must agree?"

She did, but reluctantly. Jack had told her, at last, of what had transpired between himself and Lord Walsh a few days earlier. Walsh knew that she'd been in St. Balthasar's, but not why. Jack had told her to pretend a disgust for himself if Walsh should ever nose around about the matter, for the sake of her reputation. But Gwendolyn meant to do far more. If she could get the man to trust her, she might be able to discover something useful about Mrs. Toby, and, regardless how canny or dangerous Lord Walsh might be, Gwendolyn was determined to do whatever she could to lend Jack her aid. The time for convincing Lord Walsh was growing short, however. Soon she must not only speak to him, but also charm him witless.

"I do hope your father is comfortable at Barrington?" Clara asked after the children had been retrieved by their nurses for their morning naps. Hayes had only just delivered a tea tray, and she poured Gwendolyn a steaming hot cup. "He seemed somewhat distracted at breakfast, before Wulf and Lord Hemstead came to collect him."

"You mustn't mind him," Gwendolyn told her, accepting the cup and saucer. "Papa is always muddled before he delivers a speech, and going before the Royal Academy this afternoon has rather amazed him. He's been nervous about it ever since Lad sent us his letter informing us of the invitation. But Papa's experiments with Lord Hemstead and Viscount Severn during this last week have proved so successful that he's most enthused and means to incorporate them into the results he's recorded during his work this past year in Boston. And Viscount Severn is to assist with the demonstrations today, which eases his mind as well.''

''Ah,'' said Clara knowingly. ''That accounts for Wulf's excited behavior, then. Lord Hemstead was his usual calm self, but dear Wulf can never seem to contain his nerves, especially when it comes to the Royal Academy.''

''But I had thought he was already well established in the scientific community,'' Gwendolyn remarked. ''Jack told me that Viscount Severn has made quite a name for himself by modernizing several woolen mills and factories with the new steam-driven machinery. Lord Rexley's among them.''

''Indeed, he has,'' Clara said readily. ''But many of Wulf's more truly scientific endeavors haven't landed quite so well, at least not with the Royal Academy. His early experiments with hydrogen were disastrous, to say the least. I fear he's seen as something of a bumbler, despite his brilliance.''

Gwendolyn, envisioning the large and clumsy viscount, didn't have the least difficulty in understanding this perception.

''This recent connection with your father,'' Clara said, ''and being allowed to assist both him and Lord Hemstead in their experiments is very important to his standing among his colleagues.''

Hayes scratched at the door and opened it at Clara's call.

''The Earl of Manning and Miss Sarah Huntington, my lady.''

''Oh, how delightful,'' Gwendolyn said. ''How very delightful.'' She looked hopefully at Clara. ''We may see them, may we not?'' She'd promised Jack that, if his god-father should ask her about her adventures in St. Bart's, she'd say nothing regarding his quest for Mrs. Toby. His search for the truth would remain a private one until he was ready to make it otherwise.

"Of course," Clara replied, setting her teacup aside. "Lucien could never keep anything from Robby, even if he dared make the attempt. His uncle can usually see right through him, and most of the rest of us as well. I gave up trying to hide anything from Robby long ago. Please bring them in at once, Hayes."

"And so," Lord Manning said as he walked into the parlor a few moments later, "you preferred lodging in this dubious comfort rather than come to Manning House, where my good lady wife is yet railing at me for allowing such a thing to happen."

Gwendolyn moved across the room toward him with outstretched hands. "My lord, how very good it is to see you. I must apologize for any worry I've given you and Lady Anna. Is this Sarah, of whom you've spoken so often? She's even more beautiful than I had imagined!"

Lord Manning beamed with obvious pride and brought forward the girl at his side, who was a younger, smaller image of her lovely mother.

"This is indeed my stepdaughter, Miss Sarah Huntington. Sarah, this is Miss Gwendolyn Wells."

Sarah Huntington made a charming curtsy. "Miss Wells."

"It's good to meet you at last, Sarah, after all I've heard of you. Lady Clara has told me of what a great help you've been to her and Lord Callan during your recent stay with them."

This statement led to Sarah's avowal that she missed helping with the newborn Katharine, and once she had greeted Lady Clara she asked if she might go upstairs to the nursery.

"Anna was unhappy not to accompany us on this

visit,'' Lord Manning said as soon as the little girl had gone, ''but the boys are teething and want her attention. My turn to care for them comes tonight,'' he added in a daunting tone, then took the seat Clara offered him and gave his attention to Gwendolyn. ''Jack came to see me this morning, my dear, before he and Lucien went off to the Royal Academy to make certain that Viscount Severn doesn't faint dead away from nerves this afternoon. We had rather a long talk. About you.''

''Did you?'' Gwendolyn didn't know whether to be pleased or offended.

''We did. Thank you, Clara, sweet.'' He accepted a cup of tea. ''No, I shan't have any cakes. Monsieur Dellard outdid himself at breakfast. Another bite of anything remotely spongy and I shall burst.'' He sat back and regarded Gwendolyn soberly. ''Jack didn't want to talk, mind you. I dragged it out of him.''

''Oh, Lord Manning. That was unkind of you.''

''Yes, but I fear I haven't much of a conscience, which, as my nephew will tell you, has always been a terrible burden for him to bear. My dear, what else was I to do? He exposed you to the vilest sort of dangers, and in Saint Balthasar's, of all places. I stand as something of a father to Jack Sommerton, his own parents having unfortunately passed away, and I had no choice but to take the boy to task.''

Gwendolyn nearly choked on her tea at the mention of the word *father*. It amazed her that Lord Manning could speak as he did in relation to Jack without the least blush or hint of discomfort. He was far too canny a gentleman not to have noticed the striking resemblance between them or to have heard the rumors. Yet he spoke of being a father figure to his bastard son in the blithest possible manner.

''Well he . . . it wasn't exactly his fault that I went to Saint Balthasar's,'' she said.

"I understand that well enough," he conceded readily, "and I've certainly no intention of releasing you of all responsibility. But what in the name of heaven does the boy mean by going to such a place at all?"

"There was a woman," Gwendolyn explained. "A girl, really, and she had a baby who was in danger of being—"

Lord Manning held up his hand. "I understand the full of it, my dear, and can't think it a proper topic of discussion for feminine ears." He nodded meaningfully at Clara, who laughed and made a face at him. "No, I mean what I say. I don't wish to discuss such a tawdry subject in the presence of ladies. I only want you to promise me, Gwendolyn, that you'll not do anything so foolish ever again. If Jack must go about playing hero, then let him, but you're not to become involved."

Gwendolyn attempted to look sorry. "Yes, my lord."

"And if you absolutely feel you must become involved," he went on, "then you're to come to me first, as you should have done that night after Almack's. Anna was in a perfect taking when she discovered that you'd gone out again—alone—after we'd thought you long safe at the Clarendon."

"I do apologize, Lord Manning, to both you and Lady Anna. I would have confided in you that night, but I didn't really know what I'd be getting into myself. And aside from that," she added with an impish smile, "you never would have let me go."

"How very true," he said dryly, and gave Clara a mockingly stern look when she laughed.

There was something of a celebration that night at Barrington when Professor Wells returned triumphant from his speech at the Royal Academy. He arrived with Lord Hemstead and Viscount Severn fast on his heels, each of them already a bit tipsy from toasting their success with other members of the Royal Academy. They were followed by Viscount Callan and the Earl of Rexley, both of whom looked rather relieved to be quit of the company of scientists.

Professor Wells picked his daughter up off the floor and hugged her, declaring, "If you'd only been there, Gwennie! Such an assembly as I've never before seen!" Then he set her down and introduced her to Lord Hemstead, who bowed over her hand and murmured his gladness at finding her so well recovered from her recent illness.

"Oh, yes, indeed, Miss Wells," Lord Severn added, taking Gwendolyn's hand in his and shaking it fervently. He looked slightly pink around the cheeks and even more muddled than usual, as if he couldn't quite grasp that the speech and demonstrations had gone so well. "Bella's been terribly worried. We tried to visit you several times at the Clarendon, as I'm sure your maid informed you. Bella was most distressed. Most terribly distressed."

"Wulf," Lord Callan said as he turned from greeting his wife. "That's enough."

"Oh. I'm sorry, Lucky. I mean"—Viscount Severn blushed beet red and stopped shaking Gwendolyn's hand, releasing her—"I do beg your pardon, Miss Wells."

Gwendolyn refrained from sighing with relief and massaging her tingling fingers. Behind Lord Severn's massive person, she saw Jack lounging against the open doorway. He was a sight to behold, rakish and handsome, smiling at her with a warmth that made her heart turn over. "There's no need to do so, my lord," she told Viscount Severn. "Oh, please, I wish you wouldn't . . ." He'd begun bowing in an obvious effort to convince her of his sincerity.

"Wulf, old chap," Jack said as he sauntered toward them. "Have you taken a moment to send Bella a note, informing her of your success? She'll be waiting to hear from you or Lord Hemstead.''

Wulf stopped bowing and riveted to Jack with sudden intensity. ''Bella! Oh, gad. Told her I'd go straight there after we'd finished. Promised her, I did.''

''She'll be waiting, then,'' Jack said, ''and wondering what's become of you. Poor Bella.''

''She'll be worried,'' Wulf said with complete dismay. He looked at Gwendolyn. ''Can't stand for Bella to be unhappy.''

''Then perhaps you should excuse yourself and go to her,'' Gwendolyn suggested gently.

''An excellent idea,'' Viscount Callan put in. He clapped Wulf on the shoulder. ''You go and fetch Bella, Wulf, and bring her back here to Barrington. We'll make a dinner party to celebrate your victory today.''

''Yes, indeed,'' Lady Clara agreed. ''Do go and collect Bella, Wulf. It wouldn't be the same without her.''

Viscount Severn didn't require further prodding. He turned about with determination, walking past Hayes as he held out his lordship's hat and gloves, and left Barrington completely unaware of his bareheaded, bare-handed state.

Chapter Sixteen

Jack didn't watch Wulf leave. He watched Gwendolyn watching Wulf, and at the expression on her face he said, "Regardless of how it may sometimes appear, he loves Bella. Deeply."

"So I've been told."

"You disbelieve it?"

She looked at him. "No. I'm merely wondering why Bella puts up with such behavior. I think I should find it quite distressing to be so often overlooked by the man I mean to wed."

"I can't think you need worry about that," he said, lifting her fingers to his lips and kissing them. "You'll not allow him to overlook you, whoever the poor fellow may be."

She smiled impishly. "No, indeed, I'll not. You would do well to remember it."

The others had gone into the parlor, leaving them standing alone in the hall.

"No, I won't. Someone will need to warn your future husband of what he's in for." He still held her hand and covered it lightly with his other one. "You're looking very beautiful, Gwendolyn," he told her. It was the simple truth, a mere statement of fact, no matter what she might think of him for saying it.

"You look quite well too, Jack," she replied in an equally friendly, casual tone, as if they were discussing the weather. "Have you missed me?"

He had. Horribly. It had shocked him how much. Brannard, teeming as it ever was with people, had felt even more vacuous and lonely. He'd gone to Mrs. May's to find peace and had discovered, as he'd been in the midst of undressing Georgie, that the loneliness had followed like a specter. Georgie's innocent chattering had only made the feeling press upon him more severely, and he'd suddenly found himself downstairs in Mrs. May's parlor, asking for his hat and gloves. None of Mrs. May's pleading could prevail upon him to change his mind, and he'd spent the remainder of the evening gambling at Mawdry's, losing a great deal and listening halfheartedly to Wulf's nervous predictions of doom regarding the upcoming demonstrations at the Royal Academy. Jack had been exceedingly grateful when Wulf's tiny French mistress, Yvette, had mercifully taken her lover away.

He released her hand and straightened. "Missed you? I've hardly had time to do so. It hasn't yet been twenty-four hours since I saw you last. And I won't believe you if you say you've missed me, for I know very well that you haven't."

"Then, if you're so determined, I suppose it would do no good to tell you that I have." She set her hand through his arm, leading him in the opposite direction of the parlor. "How did you fare this afternoon in the company of so many great minds? Was it quite boring?"

"Now, how am I to answer such a question," he said with a laugh, "without agreeing that I don't possess a great mind? However, to be completely honest, I nearly nodded off a time or two. Not that your father isn't a fascinating speaker, of course."

"Goodness, don't fear that you'll insult me by saying

that he is. I've snored my way through dozens of his presentations. When I was a child, my mother used to say that it was perhaps not polite, but very sensible.'' She glanced at him. "She snored her way through one or two as well.''

"I begin to think I'm in good company. Perhaps I shouldn't mention this, Gwendolyn, but we're heading away from the parlor.''

"Yes, I know.''

"You don't seem to think that Lucky and Clara, not to mention your father, might find it rather odd that we've disappeared?''

"They might,'' she admitted, "but I'm sure they'll reason that if we'd come to any harm, we would have screamed by now. Or rather,'' she amended with a smile, "I would have screamed, and you would have shouted in a brave and manly manner.''

"Thank you,'' he said dryly.

"As we've not,'' she went on, "then they'll mostly likely realize that we're simply engaged in conversation.'' She brought him to a stop before a hallway table on which an ornate clock was set. "Here. We shall strive to look interested in this clock. It's far prettier than the one at the Clarendon, don't you think?''

"I perceive you wish to speak to me regarding some particular topic, Gwendolyn?''

"Well, it's not *precisely* what I wish to do with you,'' she told him, eyeing him in what he could only term a lascivious manner. "But I don't want to shock the servants. That being the case, I think we'd best confine ourselves to speaking.''

Jack didn't care in the least about shocking the servants, but his hosts were another matter. He wished Gwendolyn were better behaved, as her obvious desire to lead him astray so clearly matched his own and didn't inspire him in the least to be good.

"If we must," he said, sighing. "Speak, Gwendolyn."

She turned to face him, her eyes alight with excitement. "I have a plan regarding Lord Walsh—"

"No," he stated, "you don't."

"But I do! He called at Barrington this morning, and—"

"Oh, my God." Walsh was far too desperate to discover why Gwendolyn had been in St. Bart's. The intensity of the man's hunt both bewildered and alerted Jack. "Clara let him in?"

"No, of course not, although I asked her to. Lord Callan had expressly forbidden it, and—"

"You *asked* her to let him in?" Jack could hardly believe his ears. He grabbed Gwendolyn by the forearms. "After I told you to stay away from the man? Gwendolyn, you little idiot!"

"Jack, please, will you let me finish speaking? And if you don't release me, I shall kiss you, right here in the hall, and you'll probably be forced to marry me long before you're ready."

He released her and stepped back.

"There." She brushed at the material he'd wrinkled. "See what you've done. Now, calm yourself and strive to control your unfortunate tendency to be domineering. I don't appreciate being treated as if I were a child who must be told what to do."

"Ahem." Lord Callan spoke from the parlor door. Both Gwendolyn and Jack turned to him. "I'm sorry to interrupt. Were you going to join us anytime soon?"

"Not yet," Jack told him.

"We were just admiring this lovely clock," Gwendolyn said with a bright smile.

Lord Callan looked first at the clock behind them—a

long, assessing look—then turned his gaze to Gwendolyn's. "I see. I suppose that's what has Jack raising his voice. Clara thought perhaps you might be having an argument regarding a serious matter, but I shall tell her it merely involves . . . a clock."

"Lucky, we need a few moments of privacy. May we use the study?"

"By all means," Lord Callan said with a lift of his hand. "There are two clocks in there. Take as long as you like in discussing them. Join us when you're finished. I'll make some appropriate excuses for your prolonged absence."

"Thank you." Jack took Gwendolyn by the elbow and escorted her past the viscount in the direction of the study. "I appreciate it."

"Not at all," Lord Callan said, winking at Gwendolyn as they passed.

"Now," Jack said as he escorted Gwendolyn into a handsome, well-lit room lined with books and paintings and filled with comfortable furniture. "We'll talk. And not about clocks."

"My, what a pretty room." Gwendolyn looked about her. "I haven't seen it before. Clara took me on a tour this morning, but she didn't bring me in here."

"It's Lucky's private study. His sanctuary. She keeps it that way for him."

"Very wise. A husband should have his own private place to get away. You needn't worry that I'll ever resent your own personal retreat, Jack."

"Gwendolyn—"

"Who are these people?" She crossed the room to gaze up at two large portraits hung side by side above the fireplace. "Such a handsome pair."

With a sigh of resignation, Jack went to stand beside her. "Lucky's parents. Edward and Letitia Bryland."

"Lord Manning's brother?" She sounded surprised. "They don't look much alike, do they? Not a very strong family resemblance."

"Not between them perhaps," Jack said with a touch of sarcasm.

"And Viscount Callan clearly takes after his mother. She's very dark, as he is."

"Yes, he looks far more like her than his father. He inherited a great deal from his mother. His title, his money, and his temper. Lord Edward was a great deal more mild-mannered, or so Robby tells me, despite the fact that he eventually murdered his wife and her lover. I'm sure you've heard the whole sordid tale from Kerlain."

"Yes, some of it. Just enough to explain why Viscount Callan once had such a distrust of women, before he married Lady Clara."

"Not before. *While* he was married to her," he corrected. "She broke him of the habit, thank God, though he gave her enough misery before coming to his senses."

"You'd think he would have developed a distrust of men instead," Gwendolyn said. "His father was the one who committed a horrid crime."

"His mother drove his father to it."

"Nonsense," she scoffed. "Men always seem to want to attribute their mistakes to the influence of women, rather than to their own weaknesses, but I fear you give us far too much credit. We're not to blame for every stupidity you fellows choose to embrace."

"Don't fly up into the boughs with me, pray. I'm fully aware of the many superiorities of the female sex. In a household such as mine, it would be deadly not to be."

"Ah, yes. Your harem."

"My staff," he corrected. "Truly, Gwendolyn, I've never believed in ascribing to women anything more powerful than the ability to drive a man completely out of his mind. Also to his knees. And occasionally to drink. Other than that, you're a harmless breed.''

She smiled and set her hands lightly on his chest. "I'm so glad you feel that way, Jack, dear. Then you've nothing at all to fear from my helping you."

He covered her hands with his own. "Now, there you're wrong, Gwendolyn, dear. I value my mind, have no desire to fall on my knees, and I've never particularly enjoyed being drunk."

"Robby came to see me today," she said. "He seems to think I need watching."

"He had a few words with me as well. He's horribly interfering, in a charming sort of way."

"He said he stands as something of a father figure to you and felt it his duty to keep you in line."

Jack's eyes widened, and he pulled away. "He said that to you?" He strove to manage the shock of her words.

She nodded. "He did. Jack, are you certain that he's your father? I know the resemblance between you is strong, but there might be another explanation. I can't believe he'd say something like that if he really was your father. He's not that cruel, to speak so casually of such a relationship."

"I've grasped at those straws before, Gwendolyn. It's nothing new." He pushed a hand through his hair and paced away from her. "Robby's confused me since I was a child, and age hasn't brought the matter any clearer. You'd think he would never have wanted to know me or put himself so much in the face of society's rumors. But since my earliest days he's always been there. One of my father's closest friends. And my mother's. They named him as my godfather, when surely they knew—" He turned to look at her. "Do you know how Lucky and I came to be friends?"

She folded her hands together and rested them on her skirt. ''No.''

''I made his acquaintance at Oxford. On purpose. I had planned it for years, with pure hatred in my heart. Hatred because Robby had treated Lucien Bryland as his son after his parents died but never acknowledged me. I was jealous, you see. Despite every goodness Robby had shown me, I was jealous.''

''But surely you meant Lord Callan no harm,'' Gwendolyn said. ''You're his closest friend now.''

''Yes, now,'' Jack admitted. ''But I certainly didn't plan for that to happen. I meant to use him in order to discover the truth, but it didn't come to pass. Lucky and I—our friendship took me by surprise. We each needed someone to trust, I suppose, and to confide in. The death of his parents had left him very vulnerable, and Clara's betrayal as well—or what he'd seen as Clara's betrayal. I could have destroyed him so easily if I'd wished it, by murmuring my suspicions about Robby. But Robby was all he had.'' Jack moved back toward Gwendolyn, slowly. ''In the end I couldn't destroy that, despite my jealousy. Because I had so much more than Lucky had. A mother and father who loved me, a brother who worshiped me.''

''Then why can't you leave this alone?'' she asked gently. ''Jack, you might be throwing away all you cherish if you go on searching. You can't want that.''

He stood close to her. ''I don't. God knows. But I have to know who I am, Gwendolyn. I *must* know. Beyond that, I haven't planned.''

''And that's foolish,'' she told him.

''Yes,'' he agreed quietly, lowering his head to kiss her. ''Foolish beyond measure.''

He had no idea how long the embrace continued, only that he would have been glad to let it continue on for a great deal longer. His tongue had teased past her parted

lips, and once he'd gentled her surprised protests, he took
a great deal of pleasure in showing her how this sort of
kissing was done. She was an apt student, though shy with
her own tongue at first. In a minute or less, however, she
began to explore more boldly, and he gladly gave himself
up to the delectation of her innocent, ardent caresses.
When she at last pulled away he was disinclined to let her
go and tried to recapture her lips.

"Jack," she murmured, "we have to stop."

"Why?" One of his hands, he discovered, was curved
about her delightfully soft bottom. "We'll tell Lucky that
his clocks held us enraptured for far longer than anticipated. That's all." He pressed kisses on the side of her
face, lingering there a moment before trailing downward
to her neck.

She laughed and pushed at him. "You won't even be
able to tell him what they looked like if you don't stop."

"What they look like? Hmm?" He ignored her attempts to shove him away. "I'll be very happy to have a
look."

"The clocks, Jack. Not me." She laughed again and
stopped his other hand as it fingered her bodice. "Stop,
now. Come and sit down. Behave."

"You're a merciless tease," he complained, letting her
tug him to a nearby settee. "Merciless. But I'd wager
none of your many beaux kissed you like that, eh?"

She flushed darkly and made a face at him. "One or
two may have attempted it," she told him primly, "but
I'm sure you'll be glad to know that neither of them possessed your . . . skill."

He was glad to know it. Very glad indeed. The thought
of her kissing anyone else so intimately was vastly unsettling. He scooted nearer to her and smoothly slid an arm
about her shoulders. "Perhaps you need a better sample to

judge by, Gwen, dear. I should be happy to further demonstrate my . . . skill.''

She scooted away. ''Perhaps, but not at the moment. I already feel as if I need to stick my head in a bucket of ice water, thank you. Lord and Lady Callan will take one look at us and know, I vow. How mortifying. It's bad enough to have those two up there watching us.''

Jack looked about. ''Those two where?''

''Him and her.'' She nodded to the portraits above, which did, indeed, look as if they were staring down at them.

''I don't think you need worry about them, sweetheart,'' Jack told her. ''I strongly doubt they'll say anything.''

''He would be your uncle,'' Gwendolyn said, looking at the portrait of Edward Bryland. ''If what you suspect is true.''

Jack looked at the portrait as well, then shook his head. ''No, not him. I have three uncles, two living and one passed on. And two great-uncles. At least, I've always called them my uncles. And loved them as if they truly were. Edward Bryland is nothing but a face in a painting to me and someone who hurt my dearest friend and my— well, Robby.'' He let out a breath, his pleasant, earlier mood flown. ''What a damnable mess this whole thing is.''

''And I'm going to help you straighten it out.''

''No.'' He touched her cheek. ''I'm growing weary of saying that word to you, Gwendolyn.''

''Then stop saying it. All I ask is that you listen to my idea. Please, Jack?''

''All right.'' He dropped his hand. ''I'll listen. And then I suppose we should return to the parlor.''

''The main trouble,'' Gwendolyn said, ''is that Lord Walsh doesn't trust you. But he trusts me, or, rather, he used to, before what happened at Saint Balthasar's. Now, of course, he doesn't know what to think, but I can easily take care of that with but a few well-chosen words.''

"And smiles, I would imagine," Jack said. "Gwendolyn, my dear, the man *wants* you. He doesn't give a damn about trusting you."

At this, she looked affronted. "Of course he does. He can't take a chance on wanting a woman he can't trust, can he? Would you?"

He very nearly said that since he wanted her and didn't particularly trust her, then, yes, he would, but sagely refrained.

"I know that I can make him trust me again. He'll want to believe that I merely stumbled into Saint Balthasar's by accident and that I know nothing of his involvement with Mrs. Toby and Mr. Rickard. Once I've reassured him, I can easily find a way to get into his house—"

"Over my dead body," he said fiercely.

She rolled her eyes and threw her hands out. "I don't mean I'd go there with him *alone*, for pity's sake. Only think a moment, Jack. I'll talk him into putting on a small event—a dinner, or better yet, a card party. And once I'm in, I can take a look about—"

"God save me," he muttered. "Or you, rather, from such foolishness. You'll get yourself killed sneaking about other people's homes."

"But I can find information about Mrs. Toby!" she insisted. "I know I can, and it's what you want, isn't it? To find her?"

"Not at the cost of your being hurt, Gwendolyn." His tone softened. "I appreciate that you want to lend me aid in the matter, but if you truly wish to help, then you'll stay out of it. You'll only make it that much more difficult for me if you become involved with Walsh. This isn't a game he's playing. This is his livelihood, his only means of floating highly in the ton, and to some members of the aristocracy that's deadly serious. Walsh wouldn't waste a moment's thought in getting rid of anyone—*anyone*, Gwendolyn—who threatens either his good name or his enterprise.'' He touched her chin gently, lifting her eyes to his. ''You understand, don't you, sweetheart?''

''Hmph.'' She looked fully disgruntled.

''Gwendolyn.''

''He'll not know. That I promise.'' Reaching up, she cradled his hand with hers. ''I only want to help,'' she murmured. ''Who else could possibly get near Walsh without rousing suspicions? I'm the only one.''

She was right. He knew it, and hated the knowledge.

''I don't want you getting hurt.''

''I'll not,'' she promised. ''You'll be fully in charge, and I'll follow your instructions to the letter.''

That, somehow, he doubted, but Gwendolyn was who she was. She might drive him insane, but he didn't think he'd want her to change.

''To the letter,'' he repeated. ''You'll take no chances.''

''Absolutely not.'' She smiled reassuringly. ''You'll have no reason at all to be sorry for trusting me.''

Chapter Seventeen

✿

Less than twenty-four hours had passed, and already Jack regretted trusting her.

The day was clear and warm, the rain having vanished completely, and Hyde Park was filled with members of the ton making their daily afternoon parade. Jack had arrived early in order to await the arrival of Gwendolyn and Lord Walsh. She had assured him that she'd have no difficulty in getting the man to take her for a drive in his carriage— she'd been so certain of the fact that Jack had been hard put to argue with her.

He hadn't liked anything about the plan Gwendolyn had put before him, but she had an aggravating way of always sounding so *right* that in the end he'd thrown up his hands and given way. They'd returned to the parlor at Barrington with little remark, save that Lucky had winked in passing at Gwendolyn and Clara had teased Jack that, as he had already claimed more than his fair share of her prize guest's company, he must pay the price by relinquishing her to the rest of them. He'd done so, gladly, needing time and space to think over what he'd just agreed to do. Gwendolyn had spent the remainder of the evening looking as pleased as a cat who'd caught a canary, while Jack had spent the remainder of the evening

convinced that they were both going to end up in the worst
sort of trouble by hatching such foolish, dangerous plots.

To play his part in the coming farce, he had risen
early—after a sleepless night—bathed, dressed, and read-
ied himself with particular care. He'd had his favorite
mount saddled long before it was truly necessary and had
taken the animal for a gallop in the park to settle the
beast's nerves. His own nerves didn't bear speaking of.
They were a mess. And so he sat on his horse, in the
shade of the particular stand of trees he'd chosen to hide
in, and waited for Gwendolyn and Lord Walsh to make
their appearance and give him his cue.

There were any number of acquaintances in the park at
this hour. Few of them saw him in the trees, but those who
did gave him long, questioning looks before nodding politely and turning away. Jack had no doubt that his aloof
behavior would earn him a great deal of gossip before the
day was out. What was Lord Rexley doing hiding in the
trees? it would be pondered aloud. And just before accosting that delightful Miss Wells? He must be fixated on her,
perhaps even in love. Jack could hear the chatter now, and
muttered, "Damn."

At long last Gwendolyn and Lord Walsh came into
view, riding in Walsh's fancy high-perched phaeton. She
was wearing pale yellow, just as she'd said she would be,
twirling a matching frilled parasol over one shoulder and
laughing with what Jack knew was feigned delight at
something her companion had said. She looked, as she
always did, stunningly beautiful, but he was growing used
to that. There was far more to the woman than her out-
ward perfection. He hadn't spent so much time alone with
her without learning that she possessed an inner beauty as
well. What he wasn't used to, and perhaps never would be,
was the amount of attention she drew from whatever men
were in her vicinity. Women paid her attention too, al-

though it was of a far less friendly sort. But men stared, whether they wanted to or not. Looking at the men who were gawking at her now, Jack could perfectly envision their exact thoughts. Gwendolyn Wells was beautiful, feminine, and had a voice and manner like sweet honey—it wasn't hard to understand why her father was beset by so many offers for her hand. But none of these poor, much-deceived fellows who sought her for a mate could manage a woman like Gwendolyn. She needed a strong and cunning hand to guide her safely through the messes she'd get herself into during the course of her life, of which he had no doubt there would be many. Only a man who loved and wanted her exactly as she was could accomplish such a feat.

He heard her soft laughter over the din of other voices and carriages, and Lord Walsh's more masculine laugh in turn. The man was clearly besotted with the woman at his side. Walsh was watching her, instead of the lane ahead of him, and nearly ran into a carriage moving opposite him before taking notice and righting his horses. That made Gwendolyn laugh the harder, but in a manner so charming that Walsh merely looked pleased. She had managed, just as she'd told Jack she would, to talk Walsh out of suspecting her as any source of danger. But that, he reminded himself, didn't make the man any less of a danger to her.

They were to argue, Gwendolyn and himself. That was to be the final part in her plan to convince Walsh that she believed the Earl of Rexley to be a completely loathsome fellow. It was his own fault, Jack told himself irately. He'd been the one to first give Walsh the impression that he held Gwendolyn in contempt. Now Gwendolyn wanted to further the notion.

Publicly.

She would have already explained away her visit to St. Bart's as being Jack's fault, telling Walsh that he'd lured her into following him there under false pretenses, because she believed he'd meant to trade her to Moses Ware in exchange for a prostitute. Why any sane man would trade the likes of Gwendolyn Wells for a prostitute was beyond comprehension, but she had insisted that the story must be told that way.

For his part, Jack was to put himself in front of their carriage and address Gwendolyn with leering incivility, ignoring all of her attempts to pretend that he didn't exist and all of Walsh's attempts to get rid of him. He was to be nasty and contemptible and play his part to the full in order to engender in Walsh a strong urge to protect Miss Gwendolyn Wells from any more of the Earl of Rexley's late-night adventuring.

Lord Walsh was just as slick and smooth as Gwendolyn had expected he would be, and he appeared only too ready to believe the nonsense she was feeding him about her presence in St. Balthasar's dark alleys. Whether he truly believed her or not would become clear in time. He was either something of a fool who could be easily led or, if Jack was correct, a crafty fellow who was merely biding his time, waiting for a chance to spring.

She'd sent him a missive early in the morning, inviting him to visit her at Barrington at his earliest convenience. He had arrived two short hours later, handsomely dressed, bowing over her hand and declaring himself relieved at finding her so well recovered from her mysterious illness. Gwendolyn had been appropriately frail and grateful and with one single hint had set Lord Walsh to pleading for the honor of taking her driving in the park—for the sake of her still-recovering health, of course.

She'd let him lead the course of their conversation as they drove to the park in his fancy high-perch phaeton, the better to gauge the level of his curiosity about the events of what had occurred at St. Bart's. He spoke for some time of his concern regarding her health and of his surprise at the suddenness of her illness. He had attempted to visit her at the Clarendon several times, he told her, and at Barrington, as well, once he'd learned of her move to that establishment. But surely she must know of that, for he'd left both messages and flowers with her maid each time.

Gwendolyn decided that it was time to admit the truth—or, at least, the truth that she wanted him to believe. She pulled the handkerchief she'd tucked into her sleeve out a bit, readying it, and cast her gaze down at her lap.

"Indeed, I've been aware of your steadfast kindness, my lord, and so grateful for it. I've longed before now to confide in you. I feel that I can trust you, Lord Walsh. I *can* trust you, can I not?"

"Of course, Miss Wells," he replied at once, with great feeling. "I give you my solemn word that you may do so. I should be honored to be of any and every service to you and stand ready to prove the truth of this. But you sound terribly distressed, my dear. Please be assured that you may speak freely and safely to me. I wish to help you, if I may."

She sniffed delicately and dabbed at her eyes. "Oh, Jere—may I be so bold as to call you by your given name, my lord?"

"Please do. I should like nothing better." He touched her hand and bent nearer. "Gwendolyn, you're not weeping, are you? My dear, what can distress you so? Is it your recent illness? Perhaps I should return you to Barrington?"

"No, please." She dabbed at her eyes once more. "I must tell you the truth, Jere. I've longed to tell you, to speak of it to someone. I've been so very unhappy. You see, I've not been truly ill, only overset because of what's happened. Oh, my lord. It's so difficult to tell.''

"Gwendolyn, my dear, sweet girl.'' He turned the horses abruptly off the path and into the shade and privacy of a small group of trees, bringing them to a halt. "You mustn't be so unhappy. I'll let no harm come to you. Only tell me what troubles you so.''

And so she told him, haltingly and between tears, a somewhat altered version of the events that had occurred at St. Balthasar's and of how she had come to be there. Surely he'd heard a far different version from Rickard; she knew for a fact he'd heard a different one from Jack. But the varying accounts could only work in her favor, for she was the one he wanted to believe, and he would tell himself that the other men—both contemptible rogues to his mind, she was sure—had merely viewed the adventure through their own ill-colored visions. They were far less to be believed than a gently bred young lady.

It was difficult to judge what his reaction to her revelation was. He seemed relieved, somewhat less taut, and certainly both kind and gentle in striving to assure her that he'd keep her safe from Lord Rexley's lecherous advances and evil designs.

"But I'm so terribly afraid of him,'' she murmured, letting her companion set his arm about her to draw her near. "He was going to l-leave me there! In that awful p-place.''

"I would have found you, I swear it,'' he assured her soothingly. "I would have sought you out and brought you to safety.''

Gwendolyn rested her head upon his shoulder and, with a tremendous effort, allowed him the impertinence of petting her neck with his fingertips.

"He seemed to be such a fine gentleman,'' she said. "I thought I could trust him. How could he have done such a thing? I realize that the child must have been his own and perhaps he even loved the girl—but to have suggested such a trade! Oh, Jere, I just don't understand how he could have done it. Him, the Earl of Rexley. A nobleman!''

"He's not a nobleman, Gwendolyn. Or at least not one born on the right side of the blanket. He's an animal, born in the gutter, which is just where he should have stayed.''

She sat upright and stared at him.

"I don't understand you. He *is* the Earl of Rexley, is he not? You can't mean to say he's merely masquerading.''

"That's exactly what I mean,'' he said. "You've met the Earl of Manning. Haven't you noticed the striking resemblance between himself and Rexley?''

Feigning shock, she blinked at him. "I had assumed that they were distantly related.''

He smiled and patted her hand. "That's because you're a sweet and very kind lady, Gwendolyn. The truth of the matter is that they're very closely related, as closely as father and son. I don't wish to shock you by stating the matter more bluntly.''

"Oh, my goodness. You mean that the Earl of Rexley is Lord Manning's—'' She set a gloved hand to her lips.

He nodded. "He is. And Rexley's mother was a common whore, which is why he embraces the cause of such wretched females so closely.''

"But if that's so, how has he come to be what he is? Has no one contested his right to the title?''

"He was adopted, right and tight, by Lord and Lady Rexley. Manning took his bastard son to them shortly after he'd been born, and they took him in. Nothing was said about it, of course. Bad ton to speak of such things aloud, you know.'' He took up the reins and gave them a snap, setting his horses into motion once more. "Everyone behaved as if Lady Rexley had given birth to the brat, as if he were their actual child. Or that's how the story is told, anywise. I was but a child myself at the time." His tone grew bitter. "Rexley may have been raised to inherit the title, but breeding will out, as the saying goes, and he's little better than an animal. You've experienced first-hand his complete lack of suitability to fulfill such a noble role. He was born in the gutter and he belongs in the gutter. The unfortunate fact, however, is that he can't be got rid of, no matter how it may be wished."

"But if no one knows of the adoption," she ventured, "or speaks of it, then how can you be so certain it's true?"

He smiled at her. "My dear, I've seen the proof with my own eyes. Papers that tell the story well. Not papers of adoption, mind you, but something far better and more compelling."

She gazed at him with widened eyes. "What kind of papers? I fear I don't understand you, my lord."

"I shouldn't think you would, Gwendolyn." His tone was filled with approval. "How lovely and innocent you are. I deeply admire such qualities in a woman. I shouldn't be speaking of such subjects in your hearing, sordid as they are and as confusing as you must find them. I apologize for having done so. Especially after the upsetting events that so recently occurred."

"Yes, you're quite right," she said, pushing away the aggravation she felt at his blatant condescension. But if he liked stupid women, she would readily give him one. "I really don't wish to think upon that dreadful night or of the Earl of Rexley. During my confinement I kept such awful memories at bay by thinking of our dance—at Almack's. It made me feel safe again, just to think of being with you." She had to look away to keep him from seeing the sickened expression on her face. Gad, had she just said such mawkish words? Lad would laugh his head off if he could only hear them.

Lord Walsh appeared to be much moved by them, however, and touched the hands she held folded on her lap with his fingertips.

"You may always feel safe with me, Gwendolyn. I'll not allow Rexley to importune you again. Ever. You may trust that I mean what I say."

"You do reassure me so very greatly, my lord." She smiled up at him with what she hoped was adoration. Whatever it was, it did the trick. He looked fully pleased, and Gwendolyn embarked upon her next task—that of enticing Lord Walsh into giving a dinner party in order to introduce her to some of his more particular friends.

Disaster fell so rapidly that Jack could only sit where he was and stare in shock. One moment he was preparing to leave his hiding place and accost Gwendolyn and Lord Walsh, and the next he was watching, gape-mouthed, as an unthinkable spectacle unfolded. In all his days he didn't think he could have dreamed up a scene so ill-fated.

Lord Walsh's carriage had come to a halt due to the sudden traffic. Another phaeton had drawn opposite them, and Walsh was introducing the couple in it to Gwendolyn. They all appeared to be chatting amiably, waiting for the traffic to clear, when Gwendolyn's attention was drawn away by the sudden appearance of her cousin, who had hailed her on the phaeton's opposite side. Kerlain, Jack saw to his dismay, had a female companion on his arm. Bella. That in and of itself was unfortunate, but not a disaster, so long as Wulf never found out that his fiancée had gone out walking with his rival.

Walsh appeared to be on good speaking terms with Kerlain—which bewildered Jack somewhat, given Kerlain's involvement with the debacle at St. Bart's—and the couple in the other carriage obviously already knew both Kerlain and Bella. They all conversed together happily enough for the space of perhaps two minutes before a loud, angry, and familiar voice made itself known.

Wulf.

Jack dropped his head into his hand and groaned. But when he lifted his head, he saw that Wulf's mere presence wasn't the worst of it. The worst was that Wulf wasn't walking through Hyde Park alone. He had his mistress, Yvette, with him. And in the midst of his outrage and brainlessness, he was dragging Yvette, who was dressed in an outfit consisting mainly of bright red, straight toward Kerlain and Bella.

"Idiot!" Jack muttered furiously, watching the whole disaster unfold. His horse moved restlessly at his angry tone. "You great, gawking idiot!" If he'd had a pistol he would have gladly shot Wulf in the leg, just to distract the fool from his course.

Even from his distance he could hear Wulf's outraged roar, could see the shock on the faces of everyone in the happy little group and Bella's sudden, rigid step away. Kerlain set an arm about her and shouted something at the huge man bearing down upon him, and Yvette, to her credit, tried desperately to find some way of escape. But Wulf, oblivious to all save the fact that his fiancée was in the company of another man, wouldn't let go of her arm.

Jack put his horse into motion with the vague idea of grabbing Bella and getting her out of the park and away from so many curious gazes. Traffic made his progress slow at best, impossible at worst, and he felt trapped and helpless as the debacle continued to unfold.

"Wulf!" he shouted, praying that his huge friend would hear him and come to his senses. "Damn you! *Wulf*!"

But nothing could stop him. Kerlain tried. He managed

to push Bella to safety and tackle Wulf before Wulf could tackle him—a tactic that had worked a time or two before when Viscount Severn and the Earl of Kerlain had come to blows over Bella. But Wulf knocked Kerlain aside almost as if he were invisible—probably not even realizing that he'd done the other man any harm—and with a horrified Yvette still clutched in one hand, confronted Bella.

Jack couldn't see Bella's face for her back was to him, but he could imagine it, and he cursed aloud as he tried to steer his horse around a barouche in his way.

"Rexley!" cried Lady Lynd, whose barouche it was. "What's going on over there? What's Severn about?"

Jack ignored the elderly woman's question but politely touched the rim of his hat and nodded at her and her companions. Then he shouted at her coachman to get out of his way.

Kerlain had crumpled to the ground amid a great many shouts, the loudest of which was Gwendolyn's. She started hitting Wulf with her parasol as he passed the phaeton, whacking him soundly about the head and crying wrathfully as he moved past her cousin's inert body in pursuit of his fiancée.

Wulf wouldn't harm Bella, of course. He would never harm her. Jack understood perfectly well how his massive friend's brilliant but strange mind worked when it came to the woman he loved. In his own bumbling way, Wulf probably believed that he was protecting Bella. And when he realized that he'd actually knocked Kerlain down—a man whom he considered a friend, despite Bella—he'd be horrified. He always was, after it was too late to be of any good.

Bella's hands were covering her face, and at the sight of her distress, Wulf finally paused. He released Yvette as if he'd only just realized he still held her, and then, with understanding dawning upon his craggy features, he looked about him at the havoc he'd caused—at Kerlain and Yvette and all the people who were watching them, then finally at Bella. He held his hands out to her, pleadingly, but she stumbled away, weeping.

"You great, stupid *fool*," Jack muttered, forcing his horse forward between two carriages. "I'll kill you with my own hands, I will, if I can get them around your thick neck."

Yvette had disappeared as expediently as she could, but the damage had been done. Kerlain was yet lying on the ground, Bella was hopelessly distraught, Wulf was helpless in the face of the mess he'd caused, and Gwendolyn was climbing down from Lord Walsh's carriage, parasol in hand.

Jack was close enough to hear her as she began again to beat Wulf with her tiny umbrella. Everybody in the park could probably hear her. She was shouting at the top of her lungs and putting every ounce of strength she possessed into the whacks she landed on Wulf's unaffected and uncaring person.

"Beast!" The parasol landed on Wulf's skull with a dull *thud*. "You great, stupid, horrid beast!" It thudded again on his chest and again on his shoulder. The last whack bent the tip of the delicate screen.

Wulf paid her no heed but continued pleading with Bella, who wept into her hands and shook her head against his words. She pointed once toward the direction in which Yvette had disappeared and then turned and fled the opposite way, across the grass. Wulf shouted Bella's name in a voice filled with despair and started to follow after her.

But Gwendolyn, oblivious to anything but the intention of beating Wulf to death with her tiny parasol, stood in his way.

"Oh, God. Gwendolyn," Jack whispered with horror.

"Get away from him." Then, praying he'd somehow gain his notice, he shouted again, "*Wulf*!"

But Wulf saw only Bella running away, and Gwendolyn was merely an obstacle in his path to reaching her. An obstacle such as Kerlain had been—one that needed moving, just as Kerlain had. Jack watched in helplessness, trapped in a circle of carriages, as his huge friend reached down and picked Gwendolyn up.

Jack didn't recognize the sound of his own voice, dark and murderous as it roared out of him. But something in it caught Wulf's attention, for he stopped in the midst of tossing Gwendolyn aside and looked at Jack, who, having jumped down from his horse, was shoving his way through the stopped carriages.

"Put her down gently, Wulf," Jack commanded loudly, striding toward him. "Gently."

Wulf blinked at him in bewilderment before seeming to realize that he held a screeching, struggling female in his arms.

"Miss Wells!" he said with open surprise.

She whacked him with what was left of her parasol. "Don't you speak to me, you great lout! Put me down!" She kneed him in the stomach—a blow that would certainly have doubled over a lesser man. Wulf merely grunted. He did, however, do as Jack told him and carefully set Gwendolyn down.

Walsh had at last climbed down from his phaeton and attempted to take her into his arms. She pushed him aside and turned on Jack, who was only steps away.

"I'll *kill* him!" she declared, shaking her parasol at Wulf.

"Not before I do," he muttered under his breath. He suffered a shockingly strong urge to take her into his arms and hug the breath out of her, to reassure both himself and her that everything would be all right. Instead, and for

Walsh's benefit, he addressed her icily. "Miss Wells. Causing another scene, are we? Can't you keep her out of trouble either, Walsh?"

"Rexley," Walsh said tightly, setting a protective arm about Gwendolyn despite her stiffening at the touch, "I cannot allow you to speak to a lady in such a manner."

"Save it," Jack told him savagely. "I don't have the time or the desire to discuss this particular *lady*." He gave the last word a nasty twist and turned away. He didn't want to see Walsh touching her. It made him itch to smash the man's face in. "Wulf. Stop that. You're going to smother him."

Wulf was on his knees beside Kerlain, who was sitting up and rubbing his head. With his usual good humor Kerlain was assuring his assailant that he was perfectly well and had only had the breath knocked out of him from Wulf's ungentle handling, which he was growing used to and therefore Wulf could stop apologizing.

"Glad you didn't harm Gwennie though," Kerlain said with a chuckle. "I wouldn't have taken kindly to that at all, I fear."

"Jack." Wulf lumbered to his feet, pulling Kerlain up with him. "Jack, I've got to find Bella. She saw Yvette. Oh, God. What shall I do?"

"Let me go, for one," Kerlain said, trying to push free of Wulf's iron grip. "Gwennie, I'm all right. Don't make such a fuss. Leave Wulf alone."

She had pushed Wulf away from her cousin with both hands and was fairly snarling at him.

"I don't care so much for what he did to you, Lad. But he should be shot for humiliating Bella. Shot!" She shoved Wulf again. It didn't budge him an inch.

"Bella," Wulf murmured, running a hand through his shaggy black hair. "I've got to find Bella. Jack," he said pleadingly, "you've got to help me find her. I don't know where she's gone off to." He began looking frantically in all directions. "Bella!" he shouted, moving toward the trees where she'd disappeared. "Bella!"

"Wulf! You damned—" Jack gave up. Wulf couldn't be stopped. He sounded like some kind of wounded animal as he started running across the park, shouting out Bella's name.

Kerlain touched his arm. "I'll go after him and make sure nothing happens. You'll take care of all this?" He nodded toward the assembled masses, present in various carriages and on horses, all of them watching the scene with avid interest.

Tomorrow morning this would be a featured article in all the papers. Wulf had well and truly embarrassed Bella this time, Jack thought. And Gwendolyn's name would be listed with relish, along with his, and now Walsh's. What an awful mess the thing had turned out to be. What a horrible idea it had been from the first. He'd wring Gwendolyn's pretty little neck at the very first opportunity and then shoot himself for being such an idiot as to go along with her nonsense.

"It's too late for taking care of." He glanced at Gwendolyn, who was still fuming. At least she wasn't letting Walsh put his hands on her again. "Go on," he told Kerlain, jerking his head toward where Wulf had gone. "Don't let him upset Bella any further." He held him back briefly with a hand on his arm. "But don't make it any worse, Lad. For pity's sake, don't get him angry all over again."

"Never fear, Jack," Kerlain said, dusting himself off. "This thing may appear to be a disaster, but it's the best thing that could have happened for Bella and her loving fiancé. Trust me."

Jack leaned closer to him and spoke in a low voice. "Your American cousin has a bad habit of using those same words," he said. "Truth to tell, Kerlain, I'm getting damned well sick of hearing them."

Chapter Eighteen

❧❀❧

*O*nce, a few years before, one of Gwendolyn's suitors had climbed the rose trellis to her bedroom window and sneaked inside to prove his great devotion to her. Or so he had afterward claimed. She'd been more than a little irate to be woken from a sound sleep by a passionate young man and had left him crawling on her bedroom floor in groaning agony while she'd gone to fetch her father and a few servants to escort him out of the house.

What she remembered most about the entire unpleasant event was that she'd at first believed the man's voice and touch were part of her dreams. It had given her an unusual fright to come blearily awake and discover that they were real, that *he* was real, and a few awful moments of confusion and panic had followed before her senses cleared enough for her to repel the man's advances.

This time, when she felt the hand on her shoulder and heard someone whispering her name, she reacted without pause and flung up into a sitting position with her fists flying before her. Her right connected soundly with somebody's face and, uttering an exclamation, he went flying back to land on the carpeted floor. Gwendolyn tossed the covers aside and leapt down after him.

"Gwen—" was all he could get out before she landed

on his prone body. All the air whooshed out of him and he choked on the rest of the word.

"How *dare* you!" she shouted, her fists raised and ready to finish the job. "Lord Callan will murder what's left of you!"

He managed to knock her first two blows away, so she reached down to grab his hair and pound his head into the floor. Just as she'd gotten a good grip he drew in a gasping breath and hissed, "Gwen!"

She froze. "Jack?" She peered at him in the darkness. "Jack?"

"Keep your voice down!"

She released his head. It fell to the floor with a thud and, from Jack, a sound of great relief.

"What on earth are you doing here? It's the middle of the night."

"I had the foolish notion that we needed to talk," he whispered fiercely. "Especially after everything that happened this afternoon." More calmly he added, "I'm sorry if I gave you a start. I didn't mean to frighten you."

"And I don't mean to complain," she said, "but as it happens, you *did* frighten me."

"I'm sorry," he said again.

"What was I to think?" she demanded, setting her hands on his chest and leaning closer to his face. "You might have been some awful thief, intent upon doing me bodily harm."

"I do apologize." Her gown had ridden up around her thighs when she'd straddled him, and he touched her calf with warm, gentle fingers. "As it was, you nearly did me a bodily harm. I think I'm going to have a bruise."

"Oh, Jack. I hope not. Did I truly hurt you?"

His fingers stroked up and down, softly.

"A little."

"Where?" She leaned even closer, examining him in

the small light from the fire in the hearth. "I don't see any swellings."

"Swellings." He shifted beneath her uncomfortably. "I don't think we'd better talk about them. Ahem." He cleared his throat. "Gwen, dear, this is a delightful position and, as you are probably aware, I'm enjoying it immensely, but I do think you'd better get off me."

"Let me kiss your swelling first."

He groaned aloud and tried to lift her off him; she laughed and held on tight.

"Gwen."

"Kiss me first, Jack," she said, between dropping swift, tiny pecks on his face. "A proper kiss, to show me how you missed me."

"Missed you?" He tried to catch her elusive lips with his own, but it was like chasing a butterfly. "It's only been a few hours since I saw you last."

"Yes, but it's been ages since you kissed me."

He took her head between his hands, guided her mouth down to his, and gave her what she'd asked for. A proper kiss. A very long, thorough, proper kiss. By the time she lifted her head he'd forgotten all of his good intentions. His hands had wandered up under her nightgown, discovering the warm curves of her legs and the soft skin of her thighs. She didn't seem to mind the improprieties he was taking. She certainly didn't seem to be frightened of what they might lead to. Even in the darkness he could see her smiling down at him in the impish, teasing manner that he found endlessly enchanting.

"How are your swellings now, Jack, dear?"

"Healthy," he said, sliding one hand farther up her thigh to her hip, which he discovered, to his delight, was bare. "If you were sitting in my lap, rather than on my belly, you'd know that for yourself. What do you have under this thing, Gwen?"

"Nothing. It's far more comfortable, I find. Are you going to make love to me, Jack?"

"Yes." He reached up and kissed her again, then let her go with a sigh of regret. "But not tonight."

"Why not?" The disappointment in her tone almost made him change his mind.

"Because it isn't what I came for. And I have the sneaking suspicion that with the way things have been happening when I'm with you, Lucky would walk in on us, followed by Clara and your father and God alone knows who else. Will you please get off me, dear, before I stop caring about such trivialities?"

"Oh, very well." She slid off him and stood. "There really is a great deal to discuss. How did you get into Barrington without notice?"

"There are all sorts of ways." He stood as well and dusted himself off. "I've broken in a number of times since Lucky and Clara took up residence, to see if he had anything among his private papers that might be of use. He didn't, which relieved me, rather. Gwendolyn, your hair is beautiful beyond belief." He reached out a hand to stroke the length of her unbound hair.

She captured his hand and held it. "You've broken into Barrington before? Without detection?"

He shrugged. "It's a simple matter. I've acquired a great many skills over the years from my associates in London's darker alleys. I have no doubt that if Robby hadn't fostered me off on my parents, I'd have grown up to be a thief of great note. It's in my blood."

"So is nobility," she told him. "Lord Manning's blood is blue, if not bluer than most. *If* he's your father." She leaned against the bedpost and regarded him levelly. "Lord Walsh seems to think he is."

"Does he?" Jack asked with false surprise. "I'm all amazed. Did he say anything in particular about it?"

Gwendolyn recited her conversation with Lord Walsh and watched, with sinking heart, as Jack's countenance became increasingly grave. When she was finished he nodded in silence, then wandered toward the fire and gazed at the hearth in a thoughtful manner.

"I suppose you were right, then. I'll need to have a look through Walsh's house and see if I can't discover a thing or two about my mystery, as well as about Mrs. Toby." He looked at her. "A legal adoption? Are you certain that's what he said?"

"He said it was done all 'right and tight.' "

"Hmmm." He turned back to the fire. "I had never thought of that before, that it had been legally done. But it makes sense. My parents wouldn't have wanted the connection contested. They never even appeared to notice the rumors that were flung about. And with Robby they were always perfectly comfortable. I've always found that so bewildering."

"Which is probably what drives you to discover the truth," Gwendolyn said, strolling slowly toward him. "If your parents had been uncomfortable around Lord Manning, or if he'd made a point of avoiding them, then all of your suspicions would have been confirmed." She stopped in front of him. "And then you'd be able to hate him, or them, or someone. You did hate Lord Callan for a time."

"Yes."

"I can't help but wonder what will happen to your friendship with him, and with Lord Manning as well, when you finally know what happened."

He stared at the fire. "I've thought of that until I'm sick from it. Heartsick. I suppose that sounds maudlin and foolish."

"No." She set a hand on his arm. "No, my dear. None of this sounds maudlin. Only very sad. You were wonderful this afternoon in the park. I'm sorry I lost my temper and made such a fuss. I've tried to do better of late, but Lord Severn behaved so horribly that I couldn't seem to control myself. Poor Bella.''

"I met Lucky at White's earlier this evening, and he told me that Clara was able to calm her. He was curious to know why you and I aren't on speaking terms, suddenly. I'm not certain that he believed my tale of being jealous about Lord Walsh. He said that next I'd be telling him we'd had a disagreement over a clock.'' He uttered a laugh.

"Lord Callan gave me a talking-to as well,'' Gwendolyn confided unhappily. "Over supper. He's as canny as his uncle. I can't believe he doesn't know that you've been searching out the truth of your birth all these years. Surely he's heard the rumors and seen the likeness between yourself and Lord Manning.''

"Oh, he's seen it. In our salad days, when he used to get drunk regularly and discuss the failings of women, Lucky would occasionally ramble on about how Robby and I look so much alike. He'd say that there were times when he couldn't tell us apart. It was distressing, to say the least. I was always thankful that he was drunk and didn't remember the next day what had passed. He never spoke of such things when he was sober.''

"What happened to Lord Severn? Clara said that Bella wouldn't come out of her room to speak to him, even at her father's insistence, and Lord Callan said that by the time he got to White's, the viscount was ranting and raving.''

"True to form, as Wulf ever is when it comes to Bella. He was torn between what he wanted to do—kill Kerlain or apologize to him, run to Bella or run to Yvette. Kerlain and I were hard-pressed to keep him in his chair. We were glad to see Lucky, I vow. It took the three of us an hour to keep him from jumping up and returning to Lord Hemstead's. Once, when Bella had nearly broken their engagement over something he'd done, Wulf stood beneath her bedroom window all night long—in the pouring rain, no less—and begged her to just talk to him. She finally took pity on him and Lord Hemstead's neighbors at three o'clock the next morning.''

''Why on earth doesn't he just marry her? Not that I think it's a particularly good match for Bella, of course, but you'd think he'd at least want to make certain of her.''

''Marrying Bella is one of those things Wulf is always intending to get around to, rather like making the grand tour that he's put off since leaving Oxford. Or getting his hair trimmed. You've probably noticed that it's rather overlong?''

''It looks like an abandoned bird's nest,'' Gwendolyn said.

''He's fortunate not to have a beard to match,'' Jack told her. ''His valet shaves him while he's still sleeping; otherwise it doesn't bear contemplating what he'd look like.''

''I fail to see why Bella puts up with his nonsense,'' Gwendolyn remarked angrily.

Jack held up his hands. ''She loves him,'' he stated simply.

''Love,'' she replied, ''is not a fit excuse for allowing oneself to be walked upon like a carpet. I hope this last episode will bring her to her senses.''

''Who, Bella?'' He looked at her with amazement. ''Never. She may give Wulf a few days to suffer in misery, but she loves him far too dearly to cut things with him forever.''

Gwendolyn crossed her arms over her chest in a defiant stance. ''Not when he parades his mistress under her nose, I'd wager. And in public, no less. If you'd visited such a humiliation upon me, I'd have your manhood on a platter.''

He laughed. ''You would too, I have no doubt.'' With his fingertips he tilted her face up to his, gazing at her with a tender affection that he couldn't hide. ''I think the man who wins you will be fortunate to have such a jealous wife as you will make, Gwendolyn Wells. But you needn't worry, for a man would have to be entirely out of his wits to take a mistress when he has a beautiful, enchanting woman like you waiting at home.''

''Would you, Jack?'' She looked at him intently. ''Ever take a mistress?''

His fingers slipped up to cup her cheek in a gentle caress, and then he dropped his hand. ''No. I would never subject you to such a humiliation. Not today, not tomorrow, not ever—regardless of what may happen between us.'' Before she could speak, he pressed on. ''As to Bella, she needn't worry about Yvette any longer. She's given Wulf her notice.''

Gwendolyn gaped. ''She gave *him* notice?''

''After we left White's, I dragged Wulf to Yvette's house to make his apologies.''

''His apologies? Why on earth should he apologize to that little strumpet?'' Gwendolyn demanded. ''After she had the very nerve to parade about Hyde Park on the man's arm, as if she had a right to do so, and knowing full well that a great many of his acquaintances—and Bella's—would see them together. And dressed as she was,'' Gwendolyn said, moving angrily to one of the chairs before the fire and plopping down in it. ''Bright red. Who could fail to notice her? She probably had the whole thing planned.''

''Gwendolyn,'' Jack said patiently, sitting in the opposite chair and leaning toward her, ''I understand how the thing looked to you, because you've made a great many assumptions about women like Yvette, but you are far mistaken. There was no scheming on Yvette's part. Wulf had been kept busy for several days because of your father's presentation at the Royal Academy, and he'd not been to see her all that time. She wanted to go for a walk in the park, just as you wished to do after being kept indoors at Brannard for so many days. Surely you can understand that.''

Grudgingly, she said, ''I suppose so. Although she might have taken a walk with her maid.''

''She might have,'' he admitted, ''and I know for a fact that she has, on many previous occasions. But, my dear, strive to put yourself in her place for a few moments. Yvette is a man's mistress—his servant, if you wish to name her so—but that doesn't make her an animal, devoid of feeling, who simply performs for his pleasure. She's a person, and a very good person too. I like her a great deal, and much as I value you, Gwendolyn, far above any other woman, none of your frowning will change that.'' Jack sat back more comfortably in his chair. ''You'd like Yvette, little though you may credit that thought. She's an honorable woman.''

Gwendolyn rolled her eyes at this.

''She is exceedingly honorable,'' Jack repeated. ''And she's put up with Wulf and his numerous eccentricities for a number of years, to my great admiration. Almost since he was a boy fresh out of college, and you can only imagine what he was like in those days. In her own way, I think she loves the fellow.''

''She must,'' Gwendolyn muttered, ''for I can't think money alone would make any woman stay with such a fool. Why did she give him her notice? Because he embarrassed her?''

''No. Because he embarrassed Bella. Yvette knows that Wulf loves Bella, and despite the fact that their marriage would be the end of her own relationship with her employer, she's always held to the notion of true love as being terribly romantic. Well, she's French," he said by way of explanation, "so that's hardly surprising. That he should have so openly and thoughtlessly humiliated Bella offended this sense of romance deeply."

"And she's finished with him?" Gwendolyn asked.

"Completely. She told him to make things right with Bella and marry her at once."

"You're right," Gwendolyn stated. "I do like her."

He chuckled. "She likes you too. She very much admired your way with a parasol and told me that if she'd had such a weapon handy, she would have helped you in striving to beat some sense into poor Wulf. She did the best thing, however, in disappearing as quickly as she did. Only imagine how much worse the ruckus would have been if she'd stayed."

"What will she do now that she no longer has a . . . protector?"

"Go back to France most likely, with the settlement Wulf will make on her. She's never particularly admired the English. In France she can retire and live out her life in ease. Wulf's disgustingly wealthy, you know. He'll make certain that she's well taken care of."

"And what of Lord Severn? Will he find himself another mistress?"

"I can't think he will. He's distressed over the loss of Yvette, naturally, but he's not really much of a womanizer. If he hadn't been so comfortable with her he would have given Yvette up long ago. No, I think he'll finally marry Bella and be a faithful, devoted, somewhat bumble-headed husband."

"And they'll live happily ever after," Gwendolyn said with a sigh, lifting her arms over her head and stretching lazily. Her hands came to rest on the top of her head and she gazed at Jack with a tired smile. "Lord Walsh was very kind after the embarrassing spectacle. He apologized prodigiously for exposing me to anything so awful."

"Did he really?" Jack asked with raised eyebrows. "And what did he make of your skill with the parasol?"

"Why, that I'm a brave and courageous woman, of course. He admires me more than he can say."

"Gad," Jack muttered, "how did you stomach it?"

She laughed and stood, crossing to him. "With difficulty. But I reminded myself that I was suffering for a good cause." She dropped into his lap and snuggled close.

Jack slid his arms about her. "I don't know that the effort is worth it. I hate seeing you with Walsh. Laughing with him. Smiling at him. When Wulf picked you up Walsh didn't do anything to stop him." His arms tightened. "You might have been hurt. Or killed. Wulf didn't even know he'd picked you up. God alone knows what might have happened if he'd tossed you aside without care as he did to Kerlain."

She traced the curve of his cheek with a fingertip. "Lad was all right. Once he regained his senses, I mean."

Jack gripped her hand and held it still. "You told me at Almack's that you knew I was your fate from the moment you set sight on me on the *Fair Weather*."

"Yes. That's so."

He gazed at her, trying to find the right words to say what he wished.

"I scoffed at the idea, because—to be perfectly truthful, it frightened me. But when I saw you in Wulf's hands and knew what he might do to you . . . I've never felt anything like that before. I felt that if anything happened to you my own life would be . . . finished."

"I understand, Jack," she murmured gently.

"Do you?" He gazed at her. "I wish I did. It still frightens me. I've been trying not to think about it."

She laughed and whispered, ''Coward,'' before pulling him toward her.

She opened her mouth to him at once this time, and teased him with her own tongue, deepening the kiss as if she were well used to such intimacy. She trusted him, he knew, and that was why she offered herself so freely. It was a gift, and one he would not take lightly. Not with her. Never with her. Just to touch her made his soul light as with a hot flame, so hot and needy—only for her.

He stood, lifting her in his arms, not breaking the union of their mouths until he laid her down on the bed and followed.

''Jack,'' she murmured nervously, pushing at him before he could touch her. ''Take your coat and your . . . shirt off.'' She stared up at him in the dark, her eyes large. ''Please.''

He wanted her to do it—the words were on his lips to beg her—but she was new to this, so innocent, and it was a small thing, if it gave her comfort.

He nearly tore the garments away, his heat rising as he watched her watching him. At last he knelt on the bed, moving toward her, over her.

''Gwendolyn,'' he said, meaning to calm her, but she lifted a hand and touched him before he could say any more.

''Jack,'' she whispered, wonder filling her voice, ''how warm you are. And so . . .'' She left the thought unfinished as her hand smoothed over his chest. ''I've never—''

''I know,'' he said, lowering himself slowly. ''I know, love.''

He kissed her, and let her touch him until her shy, sweet caresses grew bold enough to make him feel as if he was about to go up in flames. His own hands had made discoveries too, touching her breasts lightly over the cloth of her nightgown, but with great care, stopping when she stiffened, waiting until she pressed against him with fervent consent.

The buttons came undone with ease, and then he slipped his hand beneath to find warm, silky skin.

"Oh," she said as his fingers feathered over a nipple, already hard with desire.

"Is it all right?" he asked against her mouth. "I won't—Gwendolyn . . . only tell me . . ."

"No, please, it feels so . . ." Her mouth found his again, giving him her answer.

He was painfully taut with need, and she had reached the place where he knew he could have her. Moving restlessly against him, pressing her breasts, her body, into his hands, told him that he could go much further. But he wouldn't. Not tonight. Not until he knew that he had the right to make her his forever. On this he was resolved, but the temptation to be as close to her as possible was one he couldn't deny. Pushing the cloth of her nightgown down to her waist, he bared her, just as he was bare, and held her, skin to skin, his arms wrapped about her.

"Hold me, Gwendolyn," he murmured, wanting her to know how it felt, just them, like this. "Tightly." Her arms, so feminine and soft, slipped about his waist. He buried his face in her hair and lay on top of her, breathing deep, pressing his arousal against her so that she knew this was what he craved, to be inside of her, loving her as a man loved a woman.

He tamed the embrace, kissing her face, her neck, and lower, to touch and caress her breasts with gentle care, slowly, and then kissed her mouth again, pressing their bodies close even as he rolled to his side and pulled her up against him.

She was quiet, letting him pet a hand through her hair, and over her shoulder, down her back, over and again, calming them both in a warm, comfortable silence, cradled against the other. It occurred to him again, in his contented happiness, how much she trusted him. The knowledge was the only thing that made him rise up and away from her.

"You're going to sleep," he said.

"Mmmm." She yawned and stretched. "You're too comfortable."

"I'm not sure if that's a compliment," he said, leaning to kiss her, "but I think you're right." He began to pull her nightgown back up. "I'd better leave."

"Stay," she whispered, reaching out to set a hand on his chest.

He smiled gently and said, "Not tonight, Gwen."

She lay still and let him cover her, staring up at him the while. He tied her nightgown primly and then kissed her again. "There's going to come a time, soon, I pray," he said, "when I'll not leave. Not unless you make me."

She touched his face with her fingertips, reached up, and kissed him, touching his lips with her tongue.

"When that time comes," she murmured, "you'll be staying."

He took her hand and pulled it to his mouth. "The next time I see you I suppose we'll have to snarl and fuss to keep Walsh convinced. I hate the idea."

"I suppose we will," she said, letting him tug her up to a sitting position. "He's giving a dinner party for me in a few weeks," she went on as he searched for his shirt and coat. "I'll have a look through his papers, then, and see what I can find."

"No." He turned to face her in the midst of pulling his shirt on. "*I'll* have a look through his papers. You'll keep him occupied so I can do so undisturbed."

She blinked up at him. "I hardly think you'll receive an

invitation, my dear. You can't mean to break into his house as you've done here.''

"Of course I do.''

"But you can't!''

"Of course I can.'' He began to tuck his shirt into his pants. "It will be especially simple during a party. Even the servants will be busy.'' He shrugged into his coat with ease. "Come and kiss me good night, sweetheart.'' He led her toward the door.

"You came through the door?'' she asked with bewilderment.

"You thought I climbed in the window?'' He grinned. "Silly. Only second-rate thieves resort to such nonsense.''

Stroking her hair, he kissed her gently before setting her away.

"Sweet dreams, Gwendolyn.''

"Be careful, Jack.''

He opened the door with so much care that it made no noise, then peeked out the slight crack to make certain the hall was clear. He turned and smiled at her before slipping out, blowing her a kiss before he silently disappeared.

Chapter Nineteen

❦

The formal ball that Viscount and Viscountess Callan held in honor of Professor Wells and his daughter, Miss Gwendolyn Wells, was an unqualified success before the first hour of the event had passed. Gwendolyn, standing in the receiving line, felt as if her hand was about to fall off from being so often shaken and saluted. That Lady Clara bore the whole thing with such easy grace didn't go without notice. Gwendolyn at last leaned toward her and demanded, "How do you stand it so well? You seem to enjoy this!"

"Not in the least," Lady Clara replied, her smile fixed upon her face and her gloved hand reaching out to clasp that of their next guest. "I merely keep in mind that if I don't forbear, my dear Lucien never will."

At this, Gwendolyn chanced a glance further down the line to where her handsome host stood. He looked as if he'd rather be anywhere else on God's earth than he presently was and bore each new arrival with ill-concealed aggravation. He must have felt Gwendolyn's gaze upon him, for he looked at her and made a face of complete long-suffering that almost made her laugh. Straightening, she said to Lady Clara, "I see what you mean."

Professor Wells excused himself from the receiving line as soon as a sufficient number of Royal Academy members had made themselves known. Lady Clara, shortly after this, excused herself on account of having to nurse her young babe. This left Lord Callan and Gwendolyn to greet the stragglers, among whom was the Earl of Rexley.

"Jack, well met!" Lord Callan greeted. "About time you showed up. Egad, but you're fit to dazzle the ladies." He looked admiringly at his friend's elegant outfit, comprised almost entirely of black, which served to set his white-blond features that much more starkly in contrast.

"Yes," Lord Rexley said, casting a dismissive glance at Gwendolyn. "So I am. I hope you've a good number of pretty ones here, or I shall wish I'd not come."

Lord Callan seemed amazed by this tart response and let go of his hand. "You know Miss . . . ah . . . Gwendolyn."

"Indeed." He took the step that brought him in front of her. "Quite sufficiently. Miss Wells."

It was perfect, she thought, lifting her chin. He sounded entirely hateful. Each time she'd met him in public during the last week, he'd sounded exactly the same.

"Sir," she said in an equally quelling tone. "How good of you to come."

She made no offer of her hand, and he gave no indication of wishing it. He walked away without another word, leaving Gwendolyn to deal with Lord Callan's stunned exclamations.

"What the devil's going on?" he demanded of her. "Jack's never behaved in such a boorish manner before this. Good gad. It's not in the least like him."

"Why, Lord Severn," Gwendolyn said, leaning past him as the shaggy viscount bore down upon them, grateful for a reason to turn Lord Callan's attention to other matters. "I'm so glad you came. I must beg your pardon for my horrid behavior when last we met." She took the hand he held out to her.

"No, no, Miss Wells," he said with great intensity. "My fault entirely, I promise. You should have hit me harder to bring me to my senses, and I wish to God you had, for I hurt my darling Bella, and she's never going to forgive me. Hope one of the parasols I had sent over was able to make your loss right."

"Indeed, they're all lovely," she assured, trying to get her hand free from his increasingly avid grip. "Perfectly lovely, all seventeen of them. I shall enjoy them exceedingly."

"Good, good. That's grand. I'll have my man of business stop buying them, then, so long as you're satisfied." He at last released her and turned to his friend. "Lucky, is she here? Has she come?"

"Bella is indeed here," Lord Callan told him, "and I want you to calm down, Wulf, and behave yourself. You may as well know that she's in company with Kerlain tonight—"

"Kerlain!"

"Yes, and I'll tolerate no scenes," Lord Callan advised sternly. "Regardless of whether they dance, stroll in the gardens—whatever. I don't want you losing your temper or I'll ask you to leave. Bella's my guest, and I'll not allow you to embarrass her here."

Wulf's demeanor became pleading. He took hold of his host's coat and dragged him nearer. "But, Lucky, you've got to arrange something. A meeting. Please? You must, for she won't talk to me, and she won't answer my letters." In his desperation he began to pull Viscount Callan off the floor. "You've got to get her to talk to me or I swear I'll lose my mind. I haven't been able to think clearly for days, let alone perform experiments. If Bella won't see me I might as well dig a hole in the ground and give up the ghost right now."

"I'll do my best," Lord Callan promised, covering his

friend's hands and bending his fingers to exert a release. "Wulf, old chap, do let go of me. Yes, that's a good fellow. Now, don't start pulling at your hair or you'll look more of a fright than you already do." Lord Callan brushed at his elegant coat to smooth the cloth Wulf had wrinkled. "Go along inside and find Jack, and I promise I'll speak with Bella at the very first opportunity. Until I give you leave, stay away from her. Your word of honor on it."

"Yes, of course." Wulf took Lord Callan's hand and shook it. "Of course. Word of honor. Won't so much as look at her until you say it's all right, Lucky. Promise you."

"Good man. Along with you now. Jack's just inside. Very good."

When he was gone Lord Callan gave Gwendolyn an apologetic look. "I'm sorry for Wulf's behavior. I realize how odd it must appear to you."

"To anyone," she said, "but please don't apologize, my lord. I find I quite like Viscount Severn, better and better, indeed. Bella told me all about their betrothal, and how it came to be, and why she's put up with waiting for him so many years."

"He was in love with her the moment he set eyes on her," Lord Callan said. "He'd come to London straight out of Oxford to begin his apprenticeship with Lord Hemstead. Jack and I came along to lend him company and to—well, for the usual reasons young men come to London. Neither Robby nor Jack's parents were in Town at the time, and we set out to wear ourselves right down to the nubbin. Jack and I did, I mean. Wulf could only think of meeting his hero, Lord Hemstead. The morning he was to go and introduce himself he was a wretched mass of nerves, not fit for anything but the worst sort of teasing, which Jack and I readily dealt out. We promised him that

when he returned that night, we'd take him out and celebrate. But later, when he came back to Manning House,
where we awaited him, he was in a complete daze. He'd
met Viscount Hemstead's daughter, Miss Christabella
Howell, and fallen completely, hopelessly in love. She was
the most beautiful creature on God's earth, the most wonderful, sweet, darling, et cetera, et cetera. You know how
he goes on. Bella evidently felt the same way—though
God alone knows why, as she could have had her pick of
any man in England—for less than a month later they
were engaged.''

''But why haven't they wed? That's what puzzles me
so deeply.''

Viscount Callan looked about him to see who was near.
A few servants stood not far away, ready to receive any
additional guests, of which, at the moment, there were
none.

''The truth is, my dear,'' said Lord Callan, leaning
toward her confidentially, ''Wulf's not very . . . to be
polite . . . I think it might best be said, learned about
women.''

''My lord,'' Gwendolyn said, looking at him closely,
''surely I don't understand you aright. The man had a mistress for eight years or more. If he hasn't learned anything
about women in all that time, he may never.''

''Clara would ring my ears from my head for even discussing such a delicate topic with you,'' he replied, and
lowered his voice even more, ''but the fact of the matter
is, Yvette was more companion than mistress. He rescued
her from a . . . damnation, how shall I put it? Clara will
have my head, I vow. Just say that it was a violent attack.
We were all of us coming home from one of our drunken
revels, walking in an alleyway—this was shortly after
we'd arrived in London—and came upon a rather brutish
fellow who was . . . uh . . .''

"Yes, yes, I understand," she said, fully aware of his discomfort in describing the matter. "Lord Severn rescued Yvette, I take it?"

"He nearly broke the bastard's—pardon me, the villain's—head. Bashed him against the nearest wall. Knocked him out cold. Just as well, of course, as Jack was ready to commit murder upon the fellow's person. Yvette was unharmed, thankfully. She'd only just arrived from France, poor girl, and couldn't speak but a bit of English. She threw herself at Wulf and burst into tears, and he bumbled about in his usual way, trying to get rid of her. Gave her all the money he had, made me and Jack give her our money as well, and the three of us escorted her to a proper inn where she could get lodgings. But she followed us back to Manning House—or followed Wulf, rather."

"Poor girl," Gwendolyn murmured. "She must have been all alone and so very frightened. He was clearly her only hope for safety."

"That's what we thought as well. It was Jack who suggested that, as she seemed determined to stay with her rescuer—and as she was a deuced pretty girl—Wulf might as well set her up in her own house and take care of her. You have to realize that Wulf was half-seas over at the time. We all were, truth to tell. I don't think he even realized what Jack meant, but he said it sounded like a devilish good idea and he'd be glad to do it, et cetera, et cetera. He went on in his usual Wulf-like way until we told him to stop. But damned if the fellow didn't take Yvette home with him and the next morning went out and rented a house for her."

"And she became his mistress?"

"I always supposed she did, but of late, I've had reason to doubt. The thing is, she came to see me three months after Wulf had set her up, her having remembered where

Manning House was—not that it would have done any good to try to find Jack, as he'd already gone off to war by then. We had quite a time trying to understand each other. My French is abominable, and her English, then, still limited. But we managed well enough. She was looking for Wulf. Hadn't seen him since he'd rented her the house, despite the fact that he'd had his man of business send her a handsome allowance every month.

"I promised her I'd look into the matter and sent her on her way, but when I later saw Wulf and told him about Yvette's visit, he looked at me with complete bewilderment. I mean to say, more than his usual bewilderment, you understand."

Gwendolyn choked back a laugh and nodded. Lord Callan smiled and looked about to see if any guests were approaching. None were, and he turned back to finish the tale.

"He had completely forgotten about Yvette, you see. His every waking moment was consumed by his love for Bella and his chemistry. When he did at last remember the girl he'd rescued, he seemed amazed to discover that he was supposed to look in on her from time to time. I can't recall exactly what it was that he said, but it was something to do with his opinion that she was already taken care of and what did she want to see him for?"

"Oh, my heavens," Gwendolyn said. "What a dunderhead the man is. Poor Yvette. She must have assumed that he didn't find her pleasing."

"I'm sure she did, but Yvette's a smart girl. When Wulf finally did go to see her, after I told him to, she must have found some way to bring him back, for he began to see her regularly after that. But although they've always been affectionate whenever I've seen them together, I've sensed that all may not be what it appears. Wulf finds her to be very sensible and has often gone to Yvette for advice regarding Bella. I've begun to wonder if she hasn't stood more in the way of friend and adviser than anything else. A companion, just as I've told you." He nodded at Gwendolyn's shocked expression. "It would explain a great deal."

Gwendolyn blinked several times before saying, "Do you mean to say that Lord Severn is . . . that he's . . . and *that's* why he doesn't wish to marry Bella? Because he doesn't know what to . . . to do?" Just saying that much made her face hot.

He shrugged lightly. "I can only say that it seems a reasonable judgment, given Wulf's passionate love for Bella, set against his fear of marrying her. And he certainly never had anything to do with women while we were at Oxford, that I can assure you. He'd sit and wait for Jack and me while we were—well, I'd best not go into all that. But he'd sit belowstairs and fiddle away with his chemistry, and could not be lured from it by any wiles. Not even when he was precious drunk, I vow. Until he met Bella, he seemed not to have an interest in the fairer sex and, to be blunt, certainly had no experience of them."

"Oh, my," Gwendolyn said, and opened the fan at her wrist to ply it. "My heavens."

"Can you think of any more plausible reason why a man that desperately in love wouldn't marry the woman he's so utterly devoted to?" Viscount Callan asked. "He's probably afraid he'll hurt her, knowing Wulf. He's got this desperate fear of ever bringing her harm. But as he is, it's understandable."

"He's never kissed her."

"What?"

"Bella," Gwendolyn said. "He's never really kissed her. Not in eight years. Not once. Just a peck here and there on holidays and such. She confided it to me—and if you breathe a word of it, Lady Clara won't be the only one to wring your ears off."

Lord Callan held a hand to his heart. "You'll never hear it from me, I vow. On my honor." He leaned closer. "What did she say, exactly?"

"My lord, for all that you're a devil," Gwendolyn declared, "you're also a horrid gossip. But, then," she added, smiling, "so am I." She snapped her fan shut. "He's saluted her hand, once or twice, as is commonly accepted, but nothing more. And she's tried so hard to enflame him to a greater passion—poor girl!"

"Gad, and poor Wulf." Lord Callan set a hand to his forehead. "They've been going about all in a circle, I perceive, and all these years. Is it any wonder he's so jealous of your cousin, whose experience with women is clearly much more refined. But there's no time to ponder the difficulty now," he said when she began to protest, "for here comes Walsh. Smile your prettiest, Gwendolyn, dear, and get the dratted fellow away from me as soon as possible. I can't abide him."

The ball held at Barrington served not only to introduce Professor Wells and his daughter to society but also marked the affecting reunion of Miss Wells with her maternal relatives, the Duke of Alborn and the Duke of Cambury and their wives and children. Society was taken by great surprise to discover that the beautiful American was so well and nobly connected, and her standing among the ton—despite her unfortunate propensity for getting into scrapes—rose considerably, especially among the mothers of eligible, unmarried sons. Unfortunately, the young lady seemed to have developed a preference for Viscount Walsh, a gentleman who, though well-born, was possessed of an extremely dubious reputation. But as he moved only on the fringes of accepted society, Miss Wells would doubtless come to her senses and be persuaded to consider another, far more eligible match. A great many gentlemen hoped it would be so and decided to throw their hats into the ring. Miss Wells was surrounded by a thick circle of admirers the moment Lord Callan escorted her into the ballroom to begin the dancing.

The Duke of Alborn, being the highest-ranking nobleman present, opened the ball by leading Miss Wells to the floor and partnering her in a minuet. When this was over she danced a waltz with her father, while her cousin, the much admired Earl of Kerlain, chose Miss Christabella Howell to be his partner for the same dance. During this, it was readily noted that the lady's betrothed, Viscount Severn, paced about the periphery of the dancing area, wringing his burly hands until his particular friend, the Earl of Rexley, grabbed him by the collar and dragged him to the punch table.

The evening, much of the ton perceived, was filled with the promise of rumor and gossip.

Far more arresting than the enlightening circumstances regarding Viscount Severn and Miss Christabella Howell, however, were those that circled the Earl of Rexley and Miss Wells. They had been seen arguing throughout much of London for the past many days, whenever they happened to meet—which was strangely often, given their intense mutual dislike. The London gossips were on notice: this feud was one to keep an eye on. Tonight they did, and when later in the evening Miss Wells and Lord Rexley happened to meet in the middle of the room, their open disdain held all those present enrapt. Miss Wells, standing upon the arm of Lord Walsh, her latest beau, looked upon Lord Rexley as if he were a lowly maggot, and Lord Rexley, handsome and fine to the thinking of the other single young ladies in the room, gave the usurping American her just due, which was to say, he snubbed her as if she didn't exist.

Gwendolyn was never so grateful for her cousin's intervention as when he claimed her hand for the next waltz, taking her out of Lord Walsh's constant care.

"If you marry that disgusting oaf simply because of your wager," Lad said as soon as the music began and he'd pulled her into the dance, "I'll save you the trouble of a divorce and kill the swine at the first opportunity that presents itself. Gwennie," he said more reasonably, "why in the name of all that's holy are you going about with that man? Especially after I told you to keep away. Surely you can't be trying to force Jack to the altar by making him jealous?"

"I might ask you the same of Christabella Howell. After Lord Severn nearly killed you simply for walking in the park with her, you must be mad to pursue the acquaintance."

"My girl," he said in a warning tone, "you'll not fob me off so easily. Bella isn't anything even approaching Walsh, and well you know it. I stand as her friend, and nothing more, but you and Walsh . . . I can't begin to fathom why you're so often in his company, save that you've brought my worst nightmares to truth and decided to bring the man to justice for his wicked deeds. Tell me, I beg you fervently, my sweet, that I'm not right."

She smiled at him with angelic innocence. "Lad, my dearest, most beloved cousin," she said, "how very handsome you look tonight."

"Gwennie—"

"And how, indeed, is my wager coming along? I've heard nothing of it and had assumed you'd not placed it in the betting books."

"I've not, and if you don't behave yourself, I won't."

She shrugged. "It was for your benefit alone that I gave you leave to place it, not my own. I'll have Lord Rexley whether you profit from it or not."

"Will you?" He looked at her with exaggerated surprise. "After you've just consigned the fellow to the very devil with but a look, in front of God and the world? What game are you playing, Gwennie? Tell me, or I'll find a way to discover it alone."

She laughed. "I should like to see you do so, dearest Lad. We might make a wager on that alone. Now, come, don't be so foolish," she said in an appeasing tone, "and don't be cross. Would I ever do anything to overset you, dear?"

"Yes," he replied frankly. "You would. And I won't have it, Gwennie."

"Of course you'll not," she said. "But do think of putting my wager into the betting books, will you? You need the money, and only think of how the odds will improve, now that Jack and I are no longer speaking."

He sighed heavily. "Very well. I'll put the wager into the betting books, but when Jack hears about it, which he will unless he suddenly leaves Town and stays gone, he'll be in a rage. I only want you to be prepared."

"Don't worry." She smiled up at him. "I've had years to prepare myself for that particular man. There's very little he could do, I vow, that would surprise me."

Another hour passed before Gwendolyn was able to sneak away for a moment of peace. Lady Clara had earlier shared the location of her own secret hideaway—the garden room, easily accessed by sneaking down the short, dark (and handily curtained) hallway just off the music room—and had encouraged Gwendolyn to make use of it when she wanted a brief retreat from the crush of her many admirers. The door, just as Lady Clara had promised, was unlocked, and Gwendolyn quickly slipped inside, shutting the door and leaning on it with a sigh of relief.

The room was dark, but pale moonlight filtered in through the French doors that ran the length of the garden side of the room, casting a dim glow throughout. Outside, on the wide veranda, Gwendolyn could see guests lounging in the cool night air and, further away, in the garden, strolling along Barrington's lamplit pathways. Aware of the whiteness of her gown, she stayed in the room's shadows, sinking into a chair near the cold fireplace and lifting first one foot, then the other, to pull off her satin slippers and drop them to the floor.

"Oh, that's better," she murmured, leaning into the comfortable chair with her eyes closed. "Mmmm," she intoned happily, to which a masculine voice replied, "This sounds promising. She's clearly in a good mood."

Gwendolyn sat bolt upright. "Jack?"

"Shhh." He was at the door, closing it even more softly than he'd opened it.

She jumped up from the chair and hurried across the room and into his open arms.

"Oh, Jack," she murmured, turning her face into the kisses he pressed on her hair and cheek. "I've missed you so."

"Show me how much," he whispered, finding her mouth. She fitted herself to him and opened herself to his searching tongue, replying with an equal and fierce desire. His hands moved over her body without care for the delicacy of her gown, pressing her hard against him, into him, lifting her feet off the floor in his needy grip.

"Gwen," he whispered harshly at last, his mouth pressing into her neck, nuzzling, kissing. "I want to kill Walsh every time I see him touching you. If he's dared to do anything more than kiss your hand, I'll—"

"That's all he's dared, I swear it," she said, touching his lips with gloved fingertips to quiet him. "Please, Jack. It's bad enough I'm so often in his company, I don't want to talk about him, of all things, right now."

"Neither do I," he said, pulling her farther into the shadows and kissing her again. His hands were on her breasts before she made him stop.

"Jack, my dress—good heavens," she laughed when he tried to kiss her again. "You're going to leave me— Jack!—you're going to leave me wrinkled in the worst possible place."

"Places," he corrected, obediently sliding his hands down to her waist and kissing her nose. "It's a devilish pretty gown, I must say." He looked down at her and ran a finger softly over the rim of the low-cut bodice. "Rather revealing, however. Every man in the room is drooling over you. I've been ready to commit murder any number of times in the past few hours."

"I've felt the same way," she told him. "It should be some sort of sin for a man to look as you do, and to-night"—she ran her hands down the front of his elegant black coat—"you're in especially good looks. So many women have been following you about it's a wonder you can walk at all without falling over them."

He chuckled. "Jealous?"

"Yes," she admitted, "but I mean to put an end to such foolishness soon enough. Who do you have the sup-per dance with? If it's that silly, clinging Miss Boon I shall be quite put out, I warn you."

"You *are* jealous," he said, pleased. "As it happens, I've claimed Bella for my partner, so you've no need to fear that I'll be having supper with anyone else. She wants to talk to me, she says. About you."

"Does she?" Gwendolyn asked, fingering the fine, white linen shirt beneath his coat. "She must want to tell you the same things she's been telling me these past many days—when she hasn't been crying over Viscount Severn, mind you. Bella, like Lad, Lord Manning, Lady Anna, Lord and Lady Callan, and most especially my poor father, is determined that you and I shall make up whatever we've been arguing about and cry friends. I tell you, Jack, I'm hard-pressed to come up with any more excuses.''

"I'm tired of it too. One more week," he said, cradling her close. "After Walsh's party we won't have to sneak about anymore. I should have just broken into his house on my own weeks ago to save us all this misery.''

"He's too well guarded," she said. "You need the distraction of the many guests who'll be there. He was quite surprised that so many members of the ton accepted his invitation. He's never given a successful dinner before now, I understand.''

"No, not Walsh. He's barely accepted by society, despite his title. It's why he wants you so badly, I think.''

She lifted her head and looked up at him. "You told me before that it was because of my irresistible person," she said teasingly.

"That too," he replied with a grin, "but who can blame him?" He pressed his hands on her hips, pulling her hard against him. "A man would have to be dead not to want you that way. Or possessed of a different nature. But you've something Walsh wants even more badly, I think.''

"And that would be? . . .''

"A noble bloodline, and the respect of the ton. If he should marry you, his standing in accepted society would rise considerably.''

"Noble bloodline." She looked at him with disbelief. "Really, Jack. Come, now.''

"I don't know of any other young lady in London who can lay claim to not one but two dukes for relatives and have them fighting for the honor of leading her out for the first dance during the ball held in her honor, as well as an earl—however dubiously titled—for a cousin.''

"Jack, this is me you're talking about. Gwendolyn Wells, of the United States, who you've been praying will never disgrace you by scratching herself on the hindquarters or spitting in public. Why, you begin to sound almost fond of me.'' She batted her eyelashes with great exaggeration.

"Fond,'' he repeated tonelessly. "If you only knew how I've suffered these past many days—because of you, who has done everything to bewitch and confound me— you'd never make light of such a thing.''

"Poor Jack,'' she said, kissing his chin, then his neck. "How shall I make it up to you?''

"I doubt you can,'' he said, sniffing. "My wounds are much aggrieved.''

"But I should try,'' she said, trailing kisses along his cheekbone. "Shouldn't I?''

He tilted his head to give her better access to his ear, which her clever tongue had begun to caress.

"I'm sure you should,'' he murmured, his hands tightening their grip on her. "I have a very good idea of what might be the best—''

He lifted his head at the sound of voices approaching. Gwendolyn lifted hers too, but before she could say a word Jack had lifted her in his arms to carry her across the room.

"Jack!''

"Hush!''

"My slippers! They're on the floor!''

"Grand,'' he muttered, pausing to look about. "Where the deuce are they?''

The search was immediately abandoned as the voices drew ever closer, and Jack dove toward a dark space between a bookcase and a huge Italian desk cabinet. He squeezed into the small opening and sat on the floor, cradling Gwendolyn on his lap. Together, they peered out to where one of the French doors was being opened from the garden.

"Here we are. Lady Clara said it would be open. Come and sit, my dear."

It was Lad. Jack's hand covered Gwendolyn's lips just as she made a noise of exclamation, successfully muffling the sound.

"It's so dark." The voice was clearly Bella's. Gwendolyn murmured a protest behind Jack's determined hand.

"Quiet," he whispered into her ear. When she nodded he took his hand away, and their two heads slowly peeked out to see what the intruders were doing.

"We'll only take a moment until you've composed yourself," Lad said in a reassuring tone, leading Bella into the room. "We'll leave the door open, you see? Anyone could come in and be welcomed. Sit here, where the breeze will cool you, my dear." He led her to a chair near the open door and, when she was seated, moved to the chair Gwendolyn had earlier occupied. "I'll sit over here, and we'll have nothing to fear in the way of propriety. You must know I would never allow any hint of scandal to touch you, Bella."

"Very smooth," Jack whispered into Gwendolyn's ear. She shoved an elbow into his chest, producing an "Oof!" before he subsided.

"I do know it," Bella replied in heartfelt tones, pressing a handkerchief to her eyes. "You've been so very good to me, Lad. You've been the only one to understand."

"My dear, please don't weep anymore," he said gently. "You know that Wulf loves you, and you alone.

I've been telling you that since long before you knew about Yvette, and I promise you it's the truth. Why won't you believe me?''

''Aha,'' Gwendolyn murmured, turning to Jack with a look of great satisfaction.

Bella's weeping could be heard across the room, and then she said in a muffled tone, ''He's had a mistress, all these years. While I've been *devoted* to him, and *waiting.*'' She sobbed. ''Waiting, for *eight* years. And thinking the fault was with me, while he's just been perfectly . . . content . . . because of *her*.'' Another sob. ''He—he just doesn't want me. I never wanted to th-think it, but it's true. He doesn't l-love me at all.''

''Bella, my dear, sweet girl,'' Lad said gently, moving toward her, going down on his haunches to take her hands. ''You mustn't try a man by what you merely perceive as true of him. It's well said that a man should be judged by what he does, rather than what he says, but it's equally true that men have a troublesome time with revealing what they feel within. More often than not, they strive to hide it with great desperation. God alone knows how I've hurt those I care for by hiding what's in my heart. But Wulf has never been such a fellow. He's readily told the world how dearly he loves you, without shame or hesitation. I can't count the number of times I've heard him declare it. And he's told you as well. Hasn't he, Bella? I know he must have done so.''

She sniffed. ''Yes, but—''

''My dear, there's nothing to doubt about such a thing. It's a rare measure of love that causes a man to speak of it so happily. Sweet Bella''—he gathered her hands up and kissed them—''you and I are two of a kind. The love we so desperately crave has been just out of our reach, and nothing we could have ever imagined could be so cruel. But here at last is your chance to grasp the wonderful love that awaits you. Wulf wants so desperately to make things right. He longs to make you his wife, especially now, when the matter seems so hopeless. You must trust me and do as I've told you."

"Oh, Lad, I don't think I can," Bella said with desperation.

"I know, sweet. How very well I know," Lad assured her. "Only see him, will you? Give him a chance to reveal what's in his heart. Please, Bella. I can't bear to return to Kerlain without knowing that all is well with you, for I hold you as dearly as any friend can."

Bella sniffled again, then nodded. "Yes. Of course, I'll see him. I do want you to be happy, Lad."

"Hmph," Jack intoned sarcastically, to be elbowed by Gwendolyn again.

Lad made his departure, and Bella sat where she was, sniffling quietly into her handkerchief. The sounds of music, talk, and laughter filtered into the room from the open French door, evidence of the ball's healthy life. A few very brief moments later, Wulf's tall, muscular person shadowed the doorway.

"Bella?" He sounded very forlorn and timid.

"I'm here," she said, sniffling.

"This should be good," Jack muttered, to which Gwendolyn said, so softly that it was more of a noise than a word, "Hush!"

"Lad said I could come and . . . and speak to you." He stood in the doorway as if he'd bolt at any moment.

"Yes. He convinced me to see you," Bella said. "To give you the chance to explain, although I doubt very much, sir, having seen your mistress with my own eyes"—here she gave a sob—"that it can be done."

The sound of her weeping set Wulf into motion. He flung himself on his knees before her and began pleading with her to stop.

"Here we go," Jack said with a weary sigh.

"Shhh." Gwendolyn set a finger to her lips. "I want to hear this."

"Oh, Bella," Wulf said despairingly, "please don't cry. I can't bear it—you know I can't. I'm sorry you saw Yvette—oh, don't—" At the sound of the other woman's name, Bella wailed all the louder. "Bella, please, I swear I won't see her ever again. I promise you, on all that's holy. On my honor. I'd swear it on my mother's grave, but, you know, she ain't dead yet. I could swear on my great-aunt Sophy's grave, if that'd make you feel better. Anything you like, Bella, only please don't cry anymore."

Bella wept quietly into her handkerchief. "What do you want me to do, Wulf?"

"Forgive me," he said in a small voice.

"And then what?"

"And then . . . go on as we were before."

She broke into fresh tears. "I t-trusted you, Wulffrith Lane. I l-loved you. I w-waited all these years, believing all the excuses you g-gave for delaying our marriage, which I now perceive were n-nothing but *lies*. You d-didn't wish to m-marry me because you already l-loved another!"

"Oh, Bella," Wulf groaned, dropping his head into his hands.

"And now," she said, sobbing, "when I'm p-practically on the shelf because of you, you w-want me to f-forgive you? Very well. You're f-forgiven." She drew in a shaking breath and rose. "But I won't go on as before."

"Bella." He reached out to touch her skirt, still kneeling before her. "I can't lose you." He sounded as if he'd start weeping too. "I love you. I can't go on without you."

"Then make me your wife," she said in a trembling

voice, "and swear that you'll never again be unf-faithful."
A teary hiccup followed this.

Wulf was silent a moment, then murmured, "All right,
Bella. We'll get married."

She hesitated. "We will?"

"I could never love anybody but you. I can't lose you.
And no matter what it seemed like, I never was unfaithful.
I never—what I mean to say is—not with Yvette or with
anyone." The words tumbled out in a desperate jumble.
"I swear it, Bella. Please believe me." Still fingering her
skirt, he inched forward on his knees, so tall even kneeling
that his head was nearly level with hers. "Please, Bella."

"Oh, Wulf!" Bella threw her arms about his massive
neck and hugged him tightly. "I do love you so." She
took his face between her hands and, without giving him a
chance to protest, kissed him on the lips.

"Good girl, Bella!" Gwendolyn cheered softly.

The kiss ended with a loud smack, and despite their
distance and the darkness, Jack and Gwendolyn could see
Wulf's dazed response. He wobbled back and forth and
finally said, "Bella!" as if she were the eighth wonder of
the world and he'd been the one to discover her. He
dragged her close again and kissed her a second time.

"Gad, we'll be here all night," Jack murmured into
Gwendolyn's ear. "After eight years they've got some
catching up to do."

It was rather embarrassing, Gwendolyn admitted, and
she felt rather like a Peeping Tom, watching the other
couple engaged in an ardent, though admittedly clumsy,
embrace. At last Bella pulled away and said, rather breath-
lessly, "Oh, my spectacles are all fogged."

Jack choked back a laugh, and Gwendolyn covered his
mouth with her hand, giving him a warning look.

Bella removed her eyeglasses and began to wipe them.

Wulf didn't help. He had his face buried in her neck and was making sounds of great, muffled contentment.

"When will we be married, my dearest?" Bella asked, perching her spectacles on her nose again.

"Mmm? Married?" Wulf seemed disinclined to discuss anything at the moment. Bella pushed at his rocklike shoulders until he looked at her.

"Yes. Married. When?"

He smiled at her in the darkness. "As soon as possible," he said. "I'll have to finish up my experiments with Professor Wells first, of course, and then there's the conference at Oxford this next October—I'll have a great deal to prepare for that. We might plan it for next May, but I did promise your father I'd lend him my aid on the—"

"Oh!" Bella pushed him away with such force that he nearly toppled over. "You—horrid—beastly—*wretch*! You'll never change!" She burst into tears.

"Bella!" He tried to reach for her again.

"Here!" She pulled the glove off her left hand and tugged at the engagement ring on her finger. "Go and f-find some other g-girl who'll w-wait forever! I w-want n-nothing more to do with you," she cried, pressing the ring into his hand. "*Ever* again!"

"Bella!" Wulf cried with horror. "Love! I only meant that—"

Weeping, she pushed away from him and ran out the French doors onto the veranda. Wulf stumbled to his feet and ran after her, shouting out her name.

Gwendolyn dropped her hand from Jack's mouth and sighed. "That poor dolt will never get it right."

"I'd better go see if I can find him," Jack said. "I hate to ask you to get off me, sweetheart, as this is an immensely pleasurable position but, truth to tell, my legs have gone numb."

"Oh, dear." Gwendolyn squirmed her way off his lap

and out of their hiding place. "I'm sorry. Let me help you, Jack."

With the use of her shoulder beneath his left arm, he slid up the wall until he was standing. "Now," he said, resting there until the feeling in his legs returned completely. "Let me hold you a moment before I go out. You'll try to find Bella?"

"Of course. I'll make certain she's all right."

"Good." He hugged her tightly. "Don't be surprised if half the household is wondering where you've got off to. You're the guest of honor, after all. Or one of them."

"I'll tell them I was resting. Oh—I've got to find my shoes."

"Kiss me, then," he murmured, "and then find them and get back to the ball. And don't let Walsh dance with you again or I'll rip his head off."

He slipped out the hallway door after checking to see that it was clear, and Gwendolyn crept across the carpeted floor, looking for her slippers. They should have been just near the chair where she'd dropped them, but they weren't. She had just gotten to her hands and feet to feel about for them when she was interrupted by a low, masculine voice.

"Looking for these, Gwennie, sweet?"

She looked up to find Lad, lounging against the open French doors. Fortunately, behind him the veranda was empty of guests. He was holding out his hand, upon which, on two fingers, her slippers dangled.

"Yes!" She stood and crossed to him, snatching the dainty shoes away. "What do you mean by taking them?"

"You'd rather I left them for Wulf and Bella to see? Or Jack, perhaps? Strange that the two of you should have disappeared at the same time. Walsh is looking everywhere for you."

"Lad—"

''Oh, don't worry, my girl.'' He lifted her chin with a fingertip. ''My lips are shut tight. Come, put your slippers on and we'll stroll out as two cousins can do without comment.''

''Thank you,'' she said with relief, bending to do as he said.

''I won't even ask what you were doing in here,'' he said magnanimously, offering her his arm when she straightened. ''But I do believe I'll put that wager into the betting books very soon. Yes indeed.'' He led her toward the French doors. ''Tomorrow morning it will be the very first thing I'll do.''

Chapter Twenty

꧁ ꧂

There was nothing to be found in Lord Walsh's study. Jack had already searched the man's library, drawing room, and bedchamber to no avail. This was his second visit to the study, which he had started with, and yet nothing he'd found appeared to be related to anything more sinister than Walsh's numerous unpaid debts. Not that he'd expected Walsh to be such a saphead as to leave documents bearing Mrs. Toby's name lying about, but he had thought to find something relating to the baby-selling scheme. A list of collected moneys without source, perhaps, or false accounts, or even names and delivery dates. It wasn't inconceivable that Walsh would have such documents in his own home; indeed, it was more than likely that he did. But where?

Music and laughter, mingled with various voices engaged in animated conversation, drifted up the flight of stairs, seeping through the closed door and into the darkness. Jack had listened for Gwendolyn's particular voice all night, sometimes hearing a snatch or two of her distinct, alluringly feminine laughter. The sound was both a balm to his longing and a salt to his jealousy. He couldn't help but wonder which man, or men, she was presently enchanting with her pretty self.

He missed her, wanted her. Spent his restless nights

thinking of her, whether he was lying in his bed striving to sleep or walking London's alleyways trying to maintain his sanity. And every time he saw her—which was rather often given that they were both invited to many of the same events—she treated him as if he were the lowliest worm on God's earth. A despicable man not even worthy of an effort at contempt. It made him crazy. Of course, he behaved in the same manner in return, as if she were a silly, stupid female so far beneath his notice that she hardly existed. They were clearly doing a good job of their playacting. All of London was awash with talk of the mutual hatred that had so suddenly sprung up between the Earl of Rexley and Miss Gwendolyn Wells. No one knew quite what to make of it, but there was plenty of speculation.

Jack had been talked to so many times that he was becoming sick of it. Lucky had pulled him aside more than once to try to bring him to his senses, as had Clara, Lady Anna and, worst of all, Robby. But, then, few people could match Robby in sarcasm and direct, meaningful stares, a combination certain to drive the most innocent sinner to his knees in abject apology. Jack considered himself fortunate to have come out of each encounter as yet unscathed.

The most ironic thing about the entire situation was that he longed to share it with Gwendolyn, to sit with her in peace and quiet and compare their experiences in the matter. He wanted to regale her with tales of the talks he'd been given, to hear her own, and to laugh together about the insanity of it all. How pleasant that would be, he thought now as he felt his way through the darkness of Walsh's study, looking carefully at each wall to see if it might reveal a hiding place. Just to see her in private, to have her smile at him again instead of snarl, and to hold and kiss her—to feel her response—gad, it would be like a bit of heaven. And even if he couldn't do that, just to speak to her without the pretense that surrounded them would be enough.

"There's got to be a hiding place in here somewhere," he murmured, fingering the edge of an ornate picture frame. "Somewhere."

The knob to one of the room's double doors turned, and a man's voice came around the edge as the door opened. "Gwendolyn?"

Lord Walsh stepped into the room, a candle in one hand.

"Gwendolyn? Are you hiding in here, my sweet? I've come to claim my prize."

Hiding behind the window curtains, Jack stood utterly still.

"Gwennie?" He took a few steps into the center of the room. "I'll find you yet, you little minx."

Little minx? Jack thought furiously. How could Gwendolyn bear such stupid nonsense?

Walsh stood in silence for a few seconds longer before turning and leaving, closing the door carefully behind him. Jack stayed where he was, waiting until fading footsteps signaled Walsh's complete departure. He had just pulled the curtain aside when the doorknob turned once more. Letting the curtain fall, he was still again, listening as a much softer step entered the room. This time there wasn't any candle to accompany it.

"Jack?" It was Gwendolyn. "Are you here?"

He pulled the curtain aside. "What are you doing in here?" he demanded in a harsh whisper. "Walsh is looking for you."

Her dress was a luminous white, and she looked like a ghostly spirit as she moved toward him through the room's darkness. "I know. We're playing hide-and-seek."

"Hide-and—"

"Shhh." She set a gloved finger to her lips. "It's a lot of foolishness, I know, but he's one of these fellows who thinks childish women are wonderful. He's always wanting to play these horrid games." She set both hands on his arm, pleading. "Tell me you've found something. Please. I don't think I can suffer that idiot much longer. He's perfectly disgusting. Why, Jack." She blinked at him in the darkness. "What a dashing outfit. You look just like Mr. Ware."

It was, he thought, a kind way of saying that he looked like a dockworker at best and a common thief at worst.

"Dark clothing comes in handy when one is breaking into homes with the intention of stealing something. Maybe we should play a game on Walsh. Why don't I kidnap you and we'll go play hide-and-seek on the other side of the island? God, I've missed you." He pulled her behind the curtain with him and lowered his head to kiss her. With a sigh she slid her arms about his neck and readily acquiesced.

"I've missed you too," she murmured some time later, resting her cheek against his chest. "I'll be so glad when this is over. Every night I lie awake and wait for you to come. But you never do."

He slid a hand gently to the back of her neck, caressing. "The next time I come to your room, I might not leave. And then you'd be stuck with me for the rest of your life, because Lucky would get Robby, and Robby would get a special license and a pistol, and we'd be man and wife before the next day was through."

She chuckled and pressed closer. "It sounds lovely. Have you found anything yet?"

"Not yet." He pulled the curtain aside and looked into the darkened room. "I've looked in the most obvious spots, but there's got to be a hiding place in here somewhere. Help me look."

"How grand!" she said, pushing away and gazing up at him excitedly. "I've always wanted to play at cloak-and-dagger."

"You would, Gwendolyn, dear." He kissed her nose. "I can only pray you'll find it more enjoyable than hide-and-seek, for I should hate it if you suddenly found me an idiot. You take that half of the room and I'll search over here. Look behind things. Plants, paintings, furniture."

Five minutes passed in frantic searching before Jack heard her low cry of triumph. He crossed the room to where she was kneeling at the bottom row of a large book-case.

"Look! Is it a safe?"

"It is," he murmured, bending to inspect the place where Gwendolyn had removed a number of books. "An inconvenient spot for one, but clever enough. It would have taken me a good while to find it without your help, love." He grinned at her. "You've the makings of a first-rate thief, Miss Wells." Then he added, in a mimicry of Walsh, "You little minx."

She laughed. "Does this mean I get to accompany you on your next break-in?"

"Absolutely not." He jiggled the safe's padlock experimentally. "I need light for this. Can you find a candle, Gwen? Quickly, now. Walsh must be wondering where you've got to."

"He determined that his prize for finding me will be a kiss," she said, standing. "It's been bad enough having to let him slobber on my hands. If he puts his lips on my face, I vow I'll be violently ill."

"That should dampen his ardor. What is your prize to be if you find him first?"

"A jewelry box."

Jack stopped fiddling with the lock and looked at

Walsh's desk, where Gwendolyn was expertly lighting a candle.

"A jewelry box?"

She glanced at him before setting the tinderbox aside. "A small silver jewelry box that I admired in Rundell and Bridges." Picking up the candle holder, she moved back to where he knelt, carrying the small circle of light with her. "Lined with velvet. It's very pretty."

"What on earth were you doing in Rundell and Bridges?" he demanded. "With Walsh?"

She knelt beside him in a single graceful movement, setting the candle on the floor near the bookcase. Lifting innocent eyes to his, she replied, "Looking at rings, of course. He wants to marry me."

Jack had never given much credence to the idea that a heart could feel as if it had been hit by a hammer—despite Wulf's and Lucky's avid descriptions about how susceptible they'd been to such dreadful feelings after they'd fallen in love with their women. But it happened to him just as they'd described it, and it *hurt*.

"Marry?" he repeated dumbly. "You?" The idea of it grew inside him with awful force. "To *Walsh*?"

"It's what he wants, you fool, not me. For pity's sake, I waited years and crossed an entire ocean to find you; I certainly have no plan to let you off the hook that easily. I'll simply tell him that I'm already spoken for," she said primly. "Are you going to open the safe or not? I need to get back to the party before anyone else comes in search of me."

He reached out and gripped her hand. "You tell that lecherous bastard that if he proposes marriage to you I'll bash his bloody head in. Do you understand me, Gwendolyn?"

"Yes, Jack, dear," she replied. "I'll tell him, word for

word, that you're going to bash his bloody head in. I promise.''

"And if he buys you any boxes, or rings, I'll—"

"Jack, you really must get on with this.''

"—beat him to a pulp. You aren't to take any gifts from him, Gwendolyn. Not so much as a hair ribbon.''

"I don't *want* any gifts from Lord Walsh. All I want is to have a reason to refuse his company, so if you'd please get on with it, I can stop seeing the man.''

Grumbling, Jack pulled a slender, needlelike pick from an inner pocket and bent to toy with the lock. It gave way in seconds, and he swung the safe's small metal door open.

"I think we have it." He handed several folded papers back to Gwendolyn. "And what's this?" he asked, still peering into the depths of the safe. "Money, jewelry . . . his debtors would be interested to know about all this, I'd wager. Hmmm. Dueling pistols. My, my. I wonder what they're hidden away for? Usually a man mounts such items on his wall, like a trophy of sorts.''

"Jack? What's this? It has Mrs. Toby's name on it. Nora Toby. And—look!—there's an address!''

He sat up and looked at the paper she held unfolded in her lap.

"It's some sort of contract." He took it from her. "Robby's name is on it too," he murmured, just as they heard Walsh's voice calling out again.

"Gwendolyn?''

The doorknob turned. Jack reached back for one of the pistols in the safe.

"Gwendolyn? Have you sneaked in here while I was looking elsewhere, you naughty—girl." He stopped in the doorway, staring at the sight before him.

"Good evening, Walsh," Jack said civilly, pointing the pistol at the intruder from where he yet sat on the floor.

"Be quiet. Close the door behind you and move to that chair by the desk."

Lord Walsh's face filled with rigid fury. "Deceiving slut," he said to Gwendolyn, the candle shaking in his hand. "Lying, deceiving bitch! I meant to *marry* you."

"Hold your tongue," Jack ordered. "Close the door and keep quiet. I'd hate to ruin your little party by killing you."

"Those guns aren't loaded, you fool," Walsh said, sneering. "I'll see you hang in Newgate for this. A proper death for a proper bastard, wouldn't you say, Rexley?"

"You'll see yourself hang," Jack told him, tossing the pistol aside. "These papers should prove more than a little interesting to some of my friends in Parliament."

"What? For selling babies born off prostitutes? No one will care about that." He took a step farther into the room. "Least of all your friends in Parliament. They might mind if I was making a profit off stolen goods, but not from bastards born in alleyways."

"They'll care," Jack told him. "And your reputation will be ruined. Try finding a bride who'll have you after that, Walsh. Or a friend. You'll be a pariah."

"And so will you, Rexley." Walsh set the candle he held on his desk. "You've been on the edge of ruin for years, ever since the resemblance between yourself and Manning became clear. This will push you over for good. And your whore with you." He looked at Gwendolyn with contempt. "I should have had you when I had the chance. Maybe I will yet." He reached into a drawer and pulled out a small pistol. "This one," he said, training the gun on Gwendolyn, "is loaded. Now, give the papers to Miss Wells. I want her to bring them to me."

"I'll not do it," she said, pushing the one paper on her lap to the floor. "You might as well shoot me, my lord. I vow it would be worth it just to be out of your company.

And if you truly think I would ever wed a man with manners like yours, you're far wrong. And aside from that—''

"Gwen," Jack warned.

"—your breath smells," she finished in daunting tones, as if that would somehow cow the man.

Jack had to choke back his laughter. Walsh tightened his grip on the gun.

"The papers," he said. "Bring them to me or I'll kill her."

"In your own home?" Jack said, still laughing. "How do you think you'll explain it away? 'She insulted me because my breath smells, so I shot her'?" He laughed harder. "And only think of what the American government will say."

"They'll be outraged," Gwendolyn stated primly, folding her hands in her lap. "President Monroe will demand your immediate execution. I met him once, you know," she told Jack, who was still laughing, "when Papa went to Washington to receive an award." She looked back to the outraged Walsh. "He's a very nice man, and if you kill me he'll have you drawn and quartered. On Pennsylvania Avenue, no doubt. Not that we've ever done that sort of thing in the United States, mind you, for we're exceedingly civilized, but—"

Jack put his hand over hers. "You're chattering, dear."

"Oh. I am sorry. I'll be quiet."

"Thank you."

"Just so long as you take care of this horrid man. I've had my fill of him."

"I will." He patted her hand. "Don't worry over it."

"The papers," Walsh demanded, shaking now with his rage. "One of you get up and bring them to me. *Now*. I don't care which of you I kill, damn you."

"Bella?"

The sound of a forlorn voice drifted into the room.

"Bella? Sweetheart?"

Wulf pushed the study door wide.

"Are you in here? Bella?"

Walsh swung about to face him.

"Wulf!" Jack shouted. "Get out!"

"Jack?"

"Oh, gad," Jack muttered, pressing his hand to his forehead. "Could this get any worse?"

"Jack, are you in here? Have you seen Bella? I tried to talk with her, but she started to cry, and I—"

"What do you want, Lord Severn?" Gwendolyn asked politely.

Walsh turned the gun on her again. "You keep quiet, bitch!"

"Miss Wells?" Wulf stepped into the room. When he saw that it was she whom Lord Walsh had addressed, he lost his temper. "You—" He started toward Walsh. "How could you possibly—and to Miss Wells! She's a very nice lady!"

He picked Walsh up as if he were a chair and cast him to the floor. The gun went off. Jack threw himself on top of Gwendolyn, who squawked at the sudden trampling.

"Jack, for heaven's sake!"

He held her down and lifted his head.

"Wulf! Are you all right?"

Shouting started up from below. Jack sat up, pulling Gwendolyn with him.

"Wulf! Are you all right?"

Wulf staggered into the light of the small candle.

"I'm all right, Jack," he said numbly, holding his shoulder. "But I think I . . . hurt Walsh." Then he fell facedown on the carpet.

"Wulf!"

Jack crawled the few inches to reach him, gripped and

turned the huge man over. "You damned idiot." He cradled him. "Wulf."

"He's not dead," Gwendolyn said, pushing at him. "He's only fainted. I wouldn't be surprised if he's done Walsh a greater injury. Jack, you must go. *Now!*"

The voices drew closer. Footsteps sounded loudly as they raced up the stairs.

"The contract." She pressed it into his hands. "Take it. I'll manage everything here. Go!"

He felt as if he couldn't move. Or think. His mind refused to work. "Wulf," he murmured, his hands moving over his friend in a desperate attempt to find life.

"He's not dead, I promise you. Lord Callan will take care of him. Please, Jack!"

She shoved at him until he went, stumbling backward toward the nearest window. The last thing he saw was her face turned toward him, beautiful in the candlelight, and worried for him, even as her hands pressed against Wulf's bleeding wound. "I'll take care of everything," she said. "Go, Jack. Find Mrs. Toby. And don't worry for me or for him. I won't let Wulf die. Bella would never forgive me if I did."

He knew she wouldn't let him die. Gwendolyn understood what Wulf meant to him. She'd make him live. She would. And Lucky would too. Jack told himself that over and over as he slipped out the study window, and only thought to himself later of what he'd told her—that only second-rate thieves went in and out of windows.

Chapter Twenty-One

❦

The first person through the study door, luckily enough for Gwendolyn, was her cousin, the Earl of Kerlain.

"Gwennie!"

"Thank God," she murmured, scrambling to pick up the papers on the floor. "Come and take these, Lad." She folded them in a disorganized bulk. "Quickly! Stuff them somewhere under your jacket."

"But Wulf"—he knelt beside his insensate friend—"and Walsh. What in blazes is going on here, Gwennie?"

"Take these!" She demanded, shoving the papers at him with one hand and scooping up books off the floor with the other. "Don't let anyone see them. Don't say anything about them. Or about Jack. No matter what Walsh or Severn may say."

"*Jack*!" He thrust the papers down the front of his vest. "What's he got to do with this?"

"Hurry!" Turning on her knees, she hastily shoved as many books as she could in front of the still-open safe. "And don't let that rat sneak out either!" she pointed at Walsh, who was starting to moan.

"Kerlain?" Lord Manning strode into the room just as Gwendolyn shoved the last book into its place. She swung about and sat down on the floor with a *thump*. "What on earth—Gwendolyn?'' Lord Manning looked at her questioningly.

She smiled up at him. "My lord, how good to see you. I'm sorry if we've ruined the party. Lord Severn isn't dead, so please don't worry about that." She felt herself starting to babble, and stopped.

"Wulf!" Lord Callan shouted from the door, and forcibly pushed past a number of gawkers who stood there. "Wulf! My God!"

"He's alive, Lucky," Kerlain assured that man as he joined him at Lord Severn's side. "The bullet's in his shoulder. Bleeding like the very devil though. We'll need to have a look at it, see what we can do. Help me."

"Gwendolyn"—Lord Manning reached down a hand to help her up—"are you all right?"

"Oh, yes," she assured him, standing and brushing at her skirts. "Thank you, my lord. Can you do something about having Lord Walsh arrested at once, please?" She glanced at the ever-increasing crowd at the door. "I shouldn't want him to escape."

Lord Manning patted her hand. "That's unlikely, my dear, as he's yet unconscious. Is he the one who shot Wulf?"

"Indeed he is. Viscount Severn was bravely attempting to rescue me from Lord Walsh's unwanted attentions. I don't know what might have happened if he'd not come in upon us so suddenly, for Lord Walsh had threatened me with the weapon first."

"I told you to keep away from that bastard, Gwennie," Kerlain said as he and Lord Callan unbuttoned Viscount Severn's vest and shirt. "What were you doing up here with him, anyway?"

"Rejecting an offer of marriage," she said, lifting her chin. "I declined as politely as I could, but he became violent in his behavior and repulsive in his advances. He brought the gun out when I refused to do as he demanded. Fortunately, Lord Severn heard my cries and came to my rescue. He's a hero, and Miss Howell may be rightfully proud of her brave fiancé.''

There was a loud murmuring at the door about Miss Howell, who was yet belowstairs, and a general decision that she should be fetched at once, despite Lord Severn's distressing and bloody condition.

''Don't get Bella!'' Lord Callan shouted back at them, too late. ''Idiots. That's the last thing we need. Get a doctor, for God's sake. And towels. Where's Walsh's housekeeper? I want something to stop this bleeding.''

''My dear,'' Lord Manning said to Gwendolyn, taking her elbow and leading her toward a chair. ''You'll want to sit down and calm your nerves before the constable arrives.''

''Yes, I'm sure I will,'' she said in faint tones, striving to look frail—always something of a difficulty for her. ''It all happened so quickly. I'm not sure just how much I can recall, except, of course, for Lord Severn's brave rescue.''

She'd only just sat down when Lord Walsh started to moan more loudly. Lord Manning went to peer down at him. ''I believe he's coming to,'' he said, bending over to pick up the gun from the floor. ''Now, how did he come to be insensible, do you think?''

''Excuse me, my lord.'' Gwendolyn pushed past him. ''There's something I must do.''

Kneeling, she took Lord Walsh's head in her hands, lifted it up, and brought her own near. ''Can you hear me?'' she whispered fiercely, shaking him. Blearily, his eyes opened. ''Listen very carefully,'' she went on, only for him to hear, ''the room is filled with witnesses, and I've told them that you merely made a pig of yourself in your advances toward me. I've hidden the papers. Do you understand that?'' She shook him again, and he mumbled a yes. Gwendolyn tightened her grip. "Say one word about Lord Rexley, and I'll give those papers to Lord Manning. You'll not only be tried for shooting a peer of the realm, but for a great many other crimes. And you," she said, shaking him again, "know better than I what they'll be."

"He'll talk," Walsh whispered, wincing at the effort to speak. "Rexley."

"He won't, you fool. He'll take care of Mrs. Toby without making the matter public. You know I speak the truth."

His eyes opened a bit wider, and his features hardened. With a thin smile, he murmured, "Then I'll talk. How will Rexley like that?"

Gwendolyn dropped his head on the floor and straightened.

"Lord Manning?" she said loudly. "There's something I'd like to tell you about Viscount Walsh—"

"All right!" Walsh said fervently, gripping her arm. "All right. It will be as you say." He groaned and closed his eyes.

"What is it, my dear?" Lord Manning asked from where he stood above her.

"Only that Lord Walsh," Gwendolyn said, pushing the man's hand off her arm, "would like a cold cloth to press against his aching head."

Lord Manning looked dissatisfied at this and began to say more but was distracted as Bella entered the room, screaming hysterically and diving between both Lord Kerlain and Lord Callan to throw herself against Viscount Severn's bleeding chest.

Viscount Severn, having waked to a stuporous state, murmured, "Don't cry, Bella. Can't stand to make you cry."

"Easy, old boy," Lord Callan said, pulling Bella away.

"You'll be all right." To Kerlain he said, "We've got to get this bleeding stopped."

"Bleeding?" Wulf repeated, disoriented, his voice slurring. "Is Bella all right?" He suddenly tried to sit up. "Bella!"

With a Herculean effort against the viscount's great strength, Kerlain pushed him back down. "She's fine. She's right here. You just rest easy."

"Oh, Wulf," Bella cried, and threw herself on his chest all over again.

"Jack?" Wulf murmured, lifting a hand to touch Bella's hair. "Where's Jack?" Panic filled his voice and he tried to sit up again. "Jack! Walsh was going to—"

"He's unharmed," Kerlain assured him rapidly, pushing him down once more. "Steady, Wulf. Don't upset Bella any more than you have. Just keep quiet." He cast a glance at Gwendolyn.

"Jack's not here," Lord Callan told his injured friend, pressing a cloth against his wound. "You've only imagined it, old boy. This may hurt a bit. Hold still."

Lord Severn grunted and petted Bella. "He *was* here," he murmured blearily. "I saw him. I think. Dressed like a dockhand."

Lord Callan chuckled. "Then you most assuredly conjured him up. The Earl of Rexley, as you very well know, is the last man on earth whom you'd see dressed in anything less than perfection. Hold him still, Lad. I'm going to press hard now to stop this bleeding."

"Wait," Wulf said faintly. "Wait, Lucky . . . got to get . . . out of m' pocket. For Bella. Show her."

"What is it, Wulf?" Lad asked.

"Here." Wulf patted at his coat, closing his eyes. "For Bella. Got to . . . give it to her."

Lad dug in the pocket Wulf yet held his hand over and pulled out a piece of paper.

Wulf forced his eyes open and took the paper. "For Bella." With an effort he grasped her hand and pressed the document into it. "Special license," he murmured. "Marry me, Bella? Tomorrow? Please?"

"Yes, Wulf," Bella managed against her tears. "Oh, yes, I will." She started wailing again.

"Congratulations," Lord Callan said. "Bella, sweet, if you could stop hugging him a moment, please, before he bleeds to death? You'll never get to marry him if he does." To the crowd still standing at the door, he turned and shouted, "Will one of you stop gaping like a lackwit and go to fetch a bloody doctor!" To Kerlain, he said, "Hold him tight, Lad."

Gwendolyn bit her lip as Lord Callan bore down, causing Viscount Severn to cry out in pain. Bella, sitting beside her fiancé, pressed her hands hard against her mouth, and tears streamed down her cheeks.

"Poor Wulf," Gwendolyn murmured. "And poor, dear Bella."

Beside her, the Earl of Manning nodded. "Indeed. But his suffering, though a sorrow for Bella and vastly unpleasant for him, is, I think"—he paused, and she could feel him looking at her—"a blessing for Jack."

"My lord," she protested, "I fear I don't comprehend what you mean. How could Lord Rexley possibly benefit from the injury of one of his dearest friends? And such a criminal injury as this?"

"That," he said, taking her elbow, "is what I would like to find out. I think you should come downstairs to the parlor and find a quiet spot in which to rest until the constable arrives."

Gwendolyn faltered beneath his steady gaze. "You do?"

"Yes, my dear young lady, I do. And while you're resting," he said, leading her toward the crowded doorway, "you and I will have a nice little chat. Shall we?"

"I know you're not quite up to an interrogation this morning, Gwennie," the Earl of Kerlain said as he closed the door to the parlor he'd escorted her to, "certainly not after last night's exertions, but I fear you're about to get one."

Gwendolyn sank into a chair near the fire. She'd been expecting this, knowing very well that Lad would read the papers he'd concealed as soon as he could. He'd been a tremendous source of help to her the night before, especially in rescuing her from Lord Manning and in keeping Viscount Severn quiet about Jack, but now was the time of reckoning.

"Do you think Lord Callan is starting to suspect that there's more to what happened last night than appears?" she asked. "He seemed happy enough to let us speak privately just now, but he had a strange expression on his face."

"What I think," Lad replied, helping himself to a glass of Lord Callan's best brandy, "is that Lucky Bryland has better manners than I ever knew. Of course he suspects something. He'd be a fool not to. And Robby—I'm surprised he didn't beat me over here this morning. Never seen you look so cornered as you did when he got you alone last night." He grinned as he sat opposite her. "The good earl looked none too pleased when I interrupted. But you did."

"I was thoroughly relieved," she admitted, "and most grateful to you. I've always had a great deal of confidence when dealing with men, as you know, but Lord Manning is more than I can manage. He has this way of compelling people to speak, whether they wish it or not. I don't know how Lady Anna can bear it."

"Easily. He knows better than to try that sort of thing on her. She doesn't put up with his nonsense."

"Clever woman," Gwendolyn murmured. "Thank you for sticking by me last night until the constable arrived."

He gave a casual wave of his hand. "Don't speak of it. Of course I'd stick by you. We're family, after all." He sipped at his brandy before asking, "You seemed to manage him well enough. Not Lord Manning. The constable."

"Oh, him." Gwendolyn rested her head on the chair and briefly closed her eyes. "He's the sort who thinks— rather like Lord Walsh—that a woman hasn't got a brain in her head, and I was perfectly happy to give him what he expected."

"He did appear to be gentle and solicitous," Lad commented. "Even to Walsh. I imagine he'll be treated well until Parliament gets around to judging him. Robby, fortunately, will be able to sway the members toward justice. He speaks and they listen."

"How is Viscount Severn?" she asked. "Lord Callan said he'd be perfectly fine, but I thought perhaps he was only trying to reassure Clara and me."

"Wulf? He's stout as an ox. The doctor dug the bullet out and put the fellow to bed. Bella's nursing him now, which, as you may imagine, he's enjoying quite a lot."

"They've fully reconciled, then?"

"Oh, yes, quite fully. Wulf held her hand all the while the doctor was digging out the bullet, and rather than scream, as I would have done"—Lad gave a dismal shake of his head—"he spent the while apologizing to her and begging her not to cry and telling her they'd get married right away."

"I'm so glad," she said. "They'll be happy together, despite Lord Severn's rather strange manners. Are you brokenhearted, Lad? You cared for her a great deal."

"You know better than that, Gwennie. I've simply been

a friend to Bella, someone who could commiserate with her circumstances regarding Wulf. But I do admit to finding her more than a little attractive. I've always had this thing about women who wear spectacles."

"Oh, Lad. How foolish."

"It's true!" he insisted. "They give a woman such a knowing look. Makes a man wonder exactly what sorts of thoughts are lurking within that intelligent gaze and just how likely he is to discover them. A real challenge, that. It's very alluring."

"Men," she said. "I swear you're demented, the whole lot of you. Very alluring indeed. It's just one more article for a woman to take off, or for you to take off for her. *That's* what you find so blasted intriguing."

"Gwennie, you wound me," he said, placing a hand over his heart. "As if I should contemplate dear, sweet Bella with such evil intent. She's only ever been a friend, I swear it. Wulf's had nothing to fear in that quarter."

"Good," she said, and rubbed a weary hand over her forehead. "I'll be glad when this is over. I didn't sleep at all last night. I can't remember when I've felt so exhausted."

"You do look pale, my girl. But we hardly finished with the constable before three in the morning, so perhaps that's to be expected. Was Uncle Philip very upset?"

She nodded. "This morning. Or this afternoon, rather. Clara was good enough to demand that they let me sleep late. But he was waiting for me when I did at last come down. He even missed several hours of experimenting with Lord Hemstead just to speak to me."

"That sounds dire."

"It was. He insists that we return to Boston as soon as he's finished his work with the Royal Academy. The other scandals have been bad enough, but this—I've never had a suitor who's gone about shooting people before. Especially one who nearly killed Viscount Severn, whom he holds not only as a respected colleague but also as a friend. I think he was angrier about that than any danger I might have been in.''

"Don't be foolish," Lad chided. "Uncle Philip may have spoken about his distress over Wulf, but he was without a doubt more concerned with you and your safety.''

"That may be," she admitted. "I've never professed to understand the workings of the male mind, not even my own father's. What I do know is that he's given me strict instructions not to cause any more trouble. Which is vastly unfair, really. How on earth could I have known Lord Walsh would become so unhinged?''

"How indeed?" Lad pondered, reaching into his jacket and pulling out the papers she'd given him the night before. Unlike the last time she'd seen them, they were now carefully and neatly folded. "Would you like to explain what you were doing with these, Gwennie? Or how you came to know that Walsh would have them? And while you're at it, don't forget to include Jack's part in the matter. I want every detail.''

"I'll tell you," she promised. "At least as much as I know of it. There's still a great deal that I don't understand. But you must swear to me, Lad, on your very honor, that you'll speak of it to no one. Not to Lord Callan, certainly not to Papa. To no one.''

"Everything that you say to me will stay between us alone," he said, "until you give me leave to speak of it. I give you my word of honor on it.''

"Very well," she said. "First off, I really don't even know what's in those papers. There wasn't any time to look at them before Walsh came upon us.''

"You and Jack?''

"Yes. I don't suppose that you've seen him today?'' She worked hard at keeping the hopefulness out of her voice. "I truly imagined that you'd go to him first with those papers."

"You thought right, Gwennie, but he wasn't at Brannard. His servants didn't say so, but I had the feeling that he'd not been home at all during the night. It's not unusual for Jack, but after what happened at Walsh's home, they're a bit nervous. Now," he said, sitting forward and handing her the papers, "have a look at these, and tell me what happened. Afterward we'll speak of what's to be done."

Days passed after Lad's visit. Three days, to be exact. Gwendolyn spent each of them waiting for Jack. Visitors came and went, and a note from the House of Lords arrived informing her that her testimony would be required in the matter concerning Lord Walsh, but there was neither word nor sign from Jack. None of their guests had seen him, though Gwendolyn had thrown every caution to the wind and asked. Lord Manning had come on the second day and put the same question to her: Where was the Earl of Rexley? She'd truthfully answered that she didn't know, but fervently wished that she did. When he pressed her about what had occurred in Lord Walsh's study, she only shook her head. He was, amazingly, too dispirited to try to force the truth out of her and afterward left her in peace regarding the matter.

Even Lord Callan, who seldom left Barrington without the company of his wife, had gone out in the evenings, searching those places that he and Jack and Lord Severn used to frequent. On the third day he asked Gwendolyn if he might speak to her in private.

"If you know where he is, Gwendolyn, you must tell me," he said, pacing about his study, where he'd taken her. "Jack's gone off before, of course, and he's a grown man—I'm certainly not his parent by any stretch. In truth, it's usually been him who's kept me out of trouble. But this business with Walsh has me unsettled. And there's been no sign of Jack anywhere. He's not been to Brannard since the night of Walsh's gathering. If you have any idea where he's gone off to,'' he stopped pacing to turn to her, "tell me. I promise, on my honor, that Jack will never know you did so."

The pain and worry in his tone was evident, but Gwendolyn could only look away. She might have told him that Jack had been at Barrington the night before, in her room, but she had only the flimsiest evidence to provide. She hadn't actually seen him, she had only found, that very morning, on the pillow next to her own, the silver jewelry box that she had so admired at Rundell and Bridges. She was yet feeling her own measure of disbelief at its appearance. Surely Jack had been the one to leave it, but why hadn't he woken her? Spoken to her? How could he have simply come and gone without so much as letting her know that he was all right?

Lord Callan dropped into a chair. "God, I'm so tired. You are too, I know. Everyone is. Robby's been shuttered off like a lamp suddenly blown out. Kerlain and I go out searching every night in different directions, but every time we speak it's as if we're circling each other in a boxing ring, trying to figure out who'll make the first move. My sweet Clara tries to make things better, but she's as bewildered as the rest of us."

"I'm so sorry, my lord," Gwendolyn murmured. "I wish I could do something to help. Say something."

"I know you do." He lifted a hand to the bridge of his nose and rubbed. "I think I've been expecting this to happen almost since I've known Jack, but somehow days and weeks and months would go by and I'd try to pretend that it would come to nothing. Robby's never said anything about his relationship to Jack, though heaven alone knows how many hints I've dropped in that direction. And Jack's been just as bad.'' He lowered his hand and looked at her. ''Seeing them together over the years, laughing and easy with each other, has been very strange.''

She nodded sympathetically. ''You know then, about the rumors?''

''Everyone knows about the rumors. But I've known *them,* Robby and Jack, and my head's been spinning for years about what the truth is. The worst part is that neither of them will ever confide in me, as if they think I'm some complete idiot who hasn't got eyes in his head. Or perhaps they have the idea that if we simply don't admit the truth, it will go away.'' He threw his hands up. ''I've given up trying to understand what either of them thinks.''

''I'm sure it hasn't been their intention to insult or hurt you, my lord.''

''Not insult, no. Or hurt, I suppose. But I've known for years that Jack's been searching for some kind of proof about Robby being his father.''

Gwendolyn shifted uncomfortably. ''You have?''

''He doesn't realize that I know,'' Lord Callan said, ''but it's been pretty obvious that most of his catting about London's darker alleys has been a search for his origins. We've never spoken of it. I've always let him assume that I think it's simply been because of his charitable works. He's my dearest friend,'' he said, ''and I wouldn't hurt him by revealing that I know what he's been about. But I did hope, I suppose, that in time he would give it up.''

''Would you?'' she asked. ''If you were him?''

''I don't know. Perhaps not. But, then, my parents weren't as decent as Jack's were. I always envied him his mother and father, and his brother, David, as well. They were magnificent people. And they loved him so well.'' He gave a sigh and shook his head. ''If I'd been that fortunate in my family, I wouldn't make any attempt to dig up another set of relatives. It would seem ungrateful, somehow.''

"But you're his friend," she murmured, "and perhaps even closer than that—a blood relation. Surely you must understand.''

"Of course I understand," he replied unevenly. "I just don't know what good it will do for him to know the full truth of his birth. Indeed, I fear it may do far more harm than good—for him, for Robby—for everyone concerned. Gad.'' He sounded as weary as he looked. "Why the devil won't he give up and be content with the way things are?''

She had no answer for him. Jack had told her of his need to know the truth about himself, but she still wasn't certain that she understood it perfectly either. Lord Callan had summed the dangers up well. Jack had so little to gain from pursuing the course he was set upon, and everything to lose.

Chapter Twenty-Two

❦

She came awake with a start, knowing even before she opened her eyes that he was there.

"Jack."

Blinking away her bleary stupor, she looked about in the darkness until she saw him sitting in a chair near the fire, his long legs stretched out before him, his blond head leaned into one hand, his face turned away.

"Jack!" She threw her covers aside and slipped barefooted out of her bed. Padding across the carpeted floor, she went to him. "Are you all right?"

He looked up slowly, and at the sight of his face she stopped. He was haggard, full-weary. The lines on his handsome face were deepened, aging him, and his eyes were rimmed with red, filled with exhaustion. He'd neither shaved nor changed his clothes since she'd last seen him, and he looked as if he were too miserable to care. He also smelled heavily of liquor, and she could see that he was more than halfway drunk. She wondered if she should be angry or insulted that he had to come to her in such a state, but all she could feel was love and relief and a deep gladness that he was with her at all.

"Oh, Jack." She knelt beside him, reaching out to gently touch his stubbly cheek. "Where have you been, dear?"

He set his own hand over hers, pressing his cheek into her palm and murmuring, "I didn't mean to wake you."

"It doesn't matter. I'm just so glad that you're here."

"I lied," he muttered. "I did mean to wake you. And then I changed my mind. You look very happy when you sleep."

"Is that what made you change your mind?"

He smiled. She could feel the muscles in his cheek beneath her hand, which he yet held fast against him. "No, beautiful Gwendolyn. I changed my mind because I'm drunk."

"I see. That was thoughtful of you."

"Well, it *was*," he told her, turning his face to kiss her fingers. "I had this plan, you see. A grand, great, glorious plan. Thought it out for days now. I was going to make love to you and then tell your father all about it, and then you'd have to marry me. You'd have to, because you'd be ruined. And I'd be ruined. So we could get married and be ruined together. Don't you think that clever, my beautiful Gwendolyn, dear?"

"Very clever."

"But not terribly original," he admitted with a sigh. "I meant to do it, God knows. But you were lying there so clean and contented, and I'm so"—he looked down at himself and wrinkled his nose—"drunk. And filthy. I thought it must be awfully disgusting for a woman to have a man make love to her when he's so . . . so . . ."

"Drunk," she finished, rising up to sit in his lap. His arms readily enfolded her as she pressed close to him. "And filthy. I wouldn't find it disgusting, Jack. I love you."

"Don't," he muttered, rubbing his cheek against her hair. "For pity's sake, don't love me. I can't have you. And you don't want a man like me."

"Yes, I do."

"That doesn't matter," he said grumpily, although he kissed the top of her head, "because you can't have me either. Won't have you married to a . . . drunk, filthy, base-born . . . bastard."

"I shall marry whom I please," she said, "and you'll have little say in the matter, I fear."

"We'll see about that." He lifted a hand to curl his fingers lightly about her neck, tucking her against him. "I came last night too. Wasn't drunk then."

"I found the jewelry box. It's lovely, dear. Thank you."

"Did you like it?" He sounded pleased. "I didn't want that oaf Walsh buying it for you—although I suppose he wouldn't, now—but it seemed like you wanted it." His hand drifted down to her hip. "Victor had to go in and buy it, can you imagine?" He was suddenly amused. "The great Earl of Rexley couldn't go into a store because he was dressed like a thief, so he sent in a thief dressed like a gentleman to make his purchase." He chuckled. "Victor thought it grand to make the transaction on the other side of the table for once."

"Why didn't you wake me last night?" she asked. "We've all been terribly worried about you."

"I was going to wake you, but you looked so happy."

"I think that was your excuse for not waking me to-night. Also that I was clean and content."

"Well, for all those reasons. I can't recall the rest, exactly. I left the jewelry box and went directly out and started drinking."

She pushed away and looked at him. "You've been drinking since last night?"

He nodded. "Steadily." Then he added, with self-derision in his tone, "I hate being drunk. Disgusting thing to do, isn't it? Don't you find me disgusting, Gwendolyn?"

''No,'' she said, ''although I do find you rather bother-some at the moment. As well as a bit stupid. But I've years to grow used to the occasional peculiarity. Did you see Mrs. Toby? Is that's what made you start drinking?''

''Not her,'' he said with a solemn shake of his head. ''You're the one got me drinking. Mrs. Toby helped. I did see her. Talked with her. She wasn't all that I'd expected, I must say.''

She set a hand against his chest and gazed into his eyes. ''Tell me what happened, Jack.''

''I tracked her down at that address on the contract. Bell's Crossing. Not Queen's Crossing, as old Annie thought. Bell's Crossing. Took me hours to ride there. Got lost a time or two in the dark. Good thing Victor has such a good sense of direction. He was the damnedest fellow in Spain. Could always find our way for us, come rain, snow, whatever. And without a map!''

''And how did Mrs. Toby receive you?'' Gwendolyn prompted patiently.

''Not very happily.'' He ran a hand over his face, then leaned his head against the chair and gazed at her. ''She lived in a big, fine home near the sea, which is probably why I could never find her before. Didn't expect a woman like that to be living like a queen, after all. And there were babies there. Sweet, tiny babies.'' He fumbled for her hand, found and squeezed it hard, and closed his eyes. ''Nurses to take care of them, just as if it were some kind of hospital. Can you imagine, Gwen? Just as if they weren't—'' he faltered, and turned his face away toward the fire. ''God.''

She leaned to look into his face, making him meet her eyes.

''You've taken care of them, Jack? They're safe now, aren't they?''

''Yes,'' he whispered. ''They're safe. Five infants, all

safe. I paid the nurses to stay with them until some of my people came from Rexley Hall to take them there. It hardly matters. Mrs. Toby may be out of business, but others will take her place. Where there's a demand for goods, someone always rises up to fill it."

"It does matter," she murmured, "to those five children. And to the others who you'll rescue in the future, for I have no doubt you'll never stop doing so, certainly not now. What did Mrs. Toby have to say about the contract? Did she answer all of your questions?"

He was silent for a moment, lifting his hand to touch her face with his fingertips. "I love you," he whispered. "I've never loved a woman before, not like this. It's so strange. It hurts dreadfully. But it can't be helped. I've tried, but you've gotten wedged in my heart like some kind of prickly thorn. Can't remove the damned thing, even though I want to."

"Very romantic," she said dryly. "You may try again when you're sober. And I love you too." Leaning forward, she softly kissed his lips. "Now," she murmured, "tell me the full of it."

He kept touching her face, his fingers delicately tracing her eyebrows and cheekbones, her lips.

"My mother's name was Lara. Did I ever tell you that? Not my real mother, who raised me. The one who had me. Lara. I've known about her for years now, but I couldn't be certain that she was the one—she just seemed to be the one who fit best into the puzzle. But now I know. She was the one. Lara. Isn't that a pretty name?" His long forefinger drifted caressingly down the line of Gwendolyn's nose.

"You don't know the rest of it?"

He shook his head, seemingly occupied with the tiny hollow in her chin. "That's all anybody ever knew of her, not the rest of her name or where she was from or who her people were. She showed up in Drury Lane one day, pregnant and looking for work. There was only one sort of work to be had there, and she was pretty enough and young enough that, despite the pregnancy, she had plenty of customers. She lived in a house that Mrs. Toby owned. A whorehouse. Mrs. Toby wasn't a proper madam, you understand. She only rented rooms to whores and took a share of their wages to keep the constable at bay. This was long before she'd hooked up with Walsh, but she wasn't above selling a child in those days, if she could find a buyer. Lara was sickly toward the end of her pregnancy and couldn't work, but Mrs. Toby let her stay in the house with the expectation of profits from the child . . . which she felt certain she'd make because there was word on the streets about a gentleman who was seeking a young, pregnant girl by the name of Lara.''

She took hold of his wandering fingers. "Was it Lord Manning?"

"The very man." Gwendolyn both felt and heard the struggle he made to keep from letting the words betray his emotions. "Robert Bryland," he went on huskily but steadily. "The Earl of Manning. He had half a legion of detectives out trying to find her, searching the city, everywhere. There was a reward in a ridiculous sum. He wanted to find her before the child was born. Perhaps he meant to . . . do something for her. For me. I don't know.''

"Oh, Jack." Tears burned in her eyes at the pain in his tone. "You know he'd not abandon a young woman whom he'd gotten with child. Not even a . . .''

"Whore?" Jack finished for her. "Perhaps not. I don't suppose he would. Good, conscientious Robby that he is. But his efforts ran a bit late. Not his fault, really. Lara swore she'd leave Mrs. Toby's establishment if any fine gentleman showed up looking for her, and she must have meant it, for Mrs. Toby didn't send for Robby until the girl was almost dead. They spoke before she died—Lara and Robby. Mrs. Toby wasn't able to eavesdrop as she'd wished, but very loverlike they were, she said. Robby stayed with her until she died and wept like a child when she was gone. Very dramatic,'' he said bitterly.

"Your mother must have loved you very much," Gwendolyn said. "Can you imagine how frightened she was? To know that she was dying, that she was leaving you without a mother to care for you? At least—thank God—she had the comfort of knowing that she was leaving you with Robby. She must have known that he would take care of you. And he did, Jack. No matter how it came about. He made certain you were placed in a good and loving family."

"Yes," he whispered, swallowing heavily, lowering his gaze. "I suppose that's true. And he had to pay to take me away too, as it turns out. Mrs. Toby threatened to tell the world about his bastard son, gotten off a sixteen-year-old whore, unless he paid. He gave her what she asked for, but made her sign the contract in turn. There were two copies, one for him, one for her, so that she'd remember her part of the bargain and what would befall her if she went back on her word. Years later, when she wanted to quit selling babies for Walsh, it was what he held over her to make her go on. It's amazing that he never thought to blackmail Robby, or me for that matter. I probably would have paid him a fortune to keep his mouth shut."

"But then you would have known the truth as well," she said gently, lifting his chin until he looked at her. "Walsh wanted to keep you wondering and hurting with doubt. But now you know. Or at least part of it." She gave him a tender smile. "And nothing has changed, dear. Not really."

"You're wrong, Gwen. It's all changed. All of it." He held her gaze for a solemn moment, then with a deep groan pitched forward, gripping her hard and burying his face against her neck. "God. *God.*"

Gwendolyn couldn't hold her tears back any longer. His pain was like her own and hurt deeply, sharply. She held on to him as tightly as he was holding her, until her fingers ached, and she said fiercely, "You're the Earl of Rexley. You are, Jack."

He shook his head against her neck, uttering a sound of despair and misery.

"Yes," she insisted. "Nothing can change it. Your parents gave you that. Knowing whose son you were."

"Gwen." His fingers dug into her so that she arched against him. He seemed to want to bind them together with the effort. "I wish to God I'd never met you." His voice was hard and grating. "I don't give a bloody damn about being an earl. Don't you understand? It's *you.* I let myself hope, and now I have to—" He lifted his head and looked into her face, searching. "You understand, Gwen. My beautiful Gwendolyn." He petted her hair with his hands, his movements clumsy and drunken, desperate. "How am I to let you go? Is there some secret to it? Some magic to undo this spell you've cast on me?"

She shook her head, tears wetting her cheeks.

"I've spent the day trying to think of how to get my life back to the way it once was," he said, "but it's impossible. I used to think of how awful it would be to know the truth, to know that everything I am is a lie—but now . . . I'd have given up my earldom, my title, everything, to have you. Gladly, I swear it. But I can't . . . can't ask you to wed yourself to such a man." He closed his eyes and, holding her face between the palms of his hands, brought her nearer, so that his lips spoke against hers. "I never knew love would be more of a madness than anything else. All of my life I've been so sane, so calm.

You've upended me completely, Gwendolyn. Just to be near you, to watch you sleeping—it makes me happy in a way I've never known. I'll love you forever, be maddened for you—want you like this.'' He touched her lips with his tongue, caressing, compelling her to open, and then kissed her, joining their mouths together with fervent desire. His hands held her just so, his fingers warm on her face, directing the sway and give of her to better fit them, and then they drifted lower, to her neck, to softly touch and stroke, and lower still, to untie the laces of her night garment. But there he stopped, his fingers tickling the bare skin above her breasts, and he pulled away, gentling her as she tried to follow, finally lowering his face and pressing against the curve of her neck. He sobbed once, then fell silent. She felt his tears wetting her skin, but he made no sound of grief, only movements of it, his hands clutching fistfuls of her gown at her waist, pulling her nearer as he pressed ever closer, seeking.

''Jack,'' she murmured against her own tears, holding him. ''I'll never leave you. How could you think it? I've found you at last, after waiting for you so long. My whole life, since I knew anything of men, I've looked for you. Nothing on earth could make me leave you now. Certainly for nothing so foolish as your birth.''

They sat in a long silence, until they had both calmed. He fell so quiet and relaxed that she began to think he'd fallen asleep, until he murmured, ''Why do Lad and your father call you Gwennie?'' His fingers began exploring the skin of her shoulders again, the touch so soft it sent shivers down her spine. ''It's the stupidest thing. You're not a Gwennie in the least. A Gwen, yes. A Gwendolyn, better. Never a Gwennie.'' He drew the word out as if it were the sort of insult one child might taunt another with.

She smiled and stroked her hand against his temple,

through his soft blond hair. "I've always hated my name in any form. A thoroughly stupid name, it is."

"Thoroughly lovely, as you are," he countered.

"Are you going to speak with Lord Manning?" she asked.

"In the morning."

"Then you must sleep." Pushing from his lap, she stood and took his hand. "Come. On your feet, my lord."

"No, Gwendolyn—"

"Yes, Jack." She tugged until he stood. "I won't take advantage of you, I promise. Much as I should like to." She purposefully waggled her eyebrows at him, with the intended result. He laughed. "Come and lie down, you foolish, drunk, filthy, and silly man. What fun I shall have in years to come telling our grandchildren about this."

She led him to the bed and pushed until he sat, whereupon she helped him out of his jacket and, with greater effort, his boots. He lay down on top of the covers without much coaxing and sighed loudly as he made his head comfortable on the pillow.

"Gad, I'm weary."

Gwendolyn lay beside him, beneath the covers, so as not to offend his modesty.

"Then sleep, dear."

"Let me hold you. Just that." He slid an arm beneath the covers, beneath her waist, and turned her until her head rested on his shoulder. "Like that, Gwendolyn."

"Go to sleep," she said again, whispering. "I'll keep you safe."

Eyes closed, he smiled.

"Let me dream, then," he murmured, "and hear your voice. Tell me about Boston. About your picnics by the river and how you played by the shore. I long to see you there."

"One day you will," she promised, stroking his stubbly cheek. In a soft, gentle voice she began to speak of things she'd already told him but told him again, gladly, even after he'd fallen deeply asleep.

Chapter Twenty-Three

The Earl of Manning was a patient man. Normally. He'd bided his time over the past three days as calmly as he possibly could, although his wife, who, if not particularly patient, was certainly far more long-suffering than he, might have argued over the exactness of this. But to his mind he'd been patient—indeed, more than patient—and after three days that was the most that could be asked of him. On the morning of the fourth day he directed his valet to dress him for travel, for he intended to collect his nephew, Lord Callan, and drag him off, whether he wished it or not, in any direction that presented itself as useful in the start of a search for Jack.

It was a relief, therefore, when his butler, Hemmet, announced to his lordship that the Earl of Rexley waited below and wished to see him. There was a measure of trepidation, too, accompanying the relief, but Lord Manning had been expecting that—and what he believed was to come—for some time now.

"Bring Lord Rexley to my private study, Hemmet, if you please," he directed, rising from the breakfast table to kiss his wife.

"Your study, my lord?" Hemmet repeated with unconcealed surprise. Lord Manning always received his guests in either the library or the parlor, but rarely in his study.

"Yes, Hemmet," his lordship repeated. "To my study."

Jack, waiting belowstairs in the entryway, gazed at his reflection in a large wall mirror. The common thief was gone, washed and shaved and polished away, and in his place stood the image of the Earl of Rexley, an elegant and refined nobleman. Jack had spent his entire life, since his earliest days, learning how to be the Earl of Rexley. It was not *who* he was, but it was certainly *what* he was. He had always been a little jealous of David, who had been allowed so much more freedom in following his own inclinations regarding the course of his life. When he'd been very young, Jack remembered, he'd been something of a brat about having to behave just so, having to learn so many things, having to remember that he'd one day be the earl. Not that his parents had been taskmasters—if anything, quite the opposite—but there had been no avoiding the fact that he was The Heir. It was only later, when he'd begun to realize that he might lose it all, that he'd been stricken by how much being the Earl of Rexley meant to him. It was more than simple identity or security—although the idea of suddenly finding himself a known bastard without a home or name to call his own was certainly daunting. Being an earl was all he was really good at. Well, perhaps that wasn't entirely true. He was good at the basics of thieving, and he'd been a good officer in the army. Unfortunately, he didn't fancy making a living as a thief—Gwendolyn certainly wouldn't want to be wed to such a fellow—and he passionately hated the bowing and scraping and hypocrisy required of career officers. He'd been fairly successful at being an earl, he believed . . . hoped. And he liked being a member of the aristocracy. It had its certain unpleasant bits, but what occupation didn't?

The trouble was that when he looked in the mirror, he

saw the Earl of Rexley but didn't see himself. He was a pretender, an impostor, dressed for the part and playing it to perfection but holding no right claim to be this man.

"My lord?" It was Hemmet. "His lordship will see you. Please follow me."

Jack was surprised to find himself escorted to Robby's private study. He'd only been in the room a time or two—although he'd once broken into Manning House with the intention of searching the room for papers but had given up the idea before he reached the study door. He'd been seized by the suspicion, mid-hallway, that Robby in his omniscience would somehow divine that he'd been there and would give him a knowing look upon their next public meeting that would send Jack directly to his knees in confession.

Years he had waited for this moment. Almost from the age of ten. He'd envisioned it over and again, sometimes with anger, often with pain, but usually with immense dread. He had spent hundreds of hours minutely dissecting each word he would say and then refining them even more. He'd anticipated every conceivable response Robby could make and planned his own cunning replies. So prepared was he that he might have sworn he could carry the thing off in his sleep. But now, stepping across the study threshold to find Robby waiting for him, Jack felt every bit of his long-practiced speech evaporate. He couldn't even remember how it began.

Robby made it easier. Good, reliable Robby, who stretched out a hand to take one of Jack's and hold it in his strong grip.

"Jack, we've been worried about you," he said in the same voice that had sometimes chided, sometimes lectured, and sometimes carried Jack through his most difficult moments. Robby had always been there, if not a father in name, at least one in duty. The sight of his smiling face made Jack feel stupidly like weeping.

"I'm sorry," he said, striving to collect himself. "It was not my intention to cause any unpleasantness."

"Of course not," Robby said kindly, releasing him and inviting him toward the fire with the lift of a hand. "I know very well that you did not. And, of course, you're a man full-grown and don't need to tell anyone where you're going or how long you'll be absent. It was merely the circumstances surrounding your disappearance that had us rattled. Come and sit. I'll pour you a drink."

Jack didn't take a seat but stood near the flames, feeling in need of their warmth, and looked about him.

"This room is very like you," he said. "I've not been in it often."

Robby was bent over a cart, pouring brandy into glasses. "No, I suppose not. I like to keep it for myself, I fear. Don't even let Anna in much, although Sarah has the run of it when she likes. I often find myself in company with her dolls. Here you go, Jack. You don't wish to sit?"

"No."

"Very well. So long as you're comfortable. Have you seen this portrait?" He lifted his glass toward a spot just above the fireplace, where a large painting resided. "That's my father, the fifth Earl of Manning. I believe you've seen a far better portrait of him at Bryland Park."

"Yes, in the portrait gallery." Jack set his glass aside. "Robby, I—there's something I've come to speak with you about." He found that he couldn't look at the man; his gaze flicked restlessly about the room. "I can't think it will come as a very great shock—although we've never said a word about the matter before—for surely you can't have ignored the great resemblance between us or not heard the rumors that have been floating about the ton since I can remember."

He finally made himself look at Robby and held his gaze.

"Yes, of course I've seen the resemblance and heard the rumors," Robby said at last, very gently, "but—"

"I have proof of it," Jack blurted out recklessly, wanting it all out in the open before he fell apart. "That you're my father. I've been looking for the truth all these years. In stinking alleyways and whorehouses, by breaking into other people's houses. You've probably known about that too—God alone knows why you never said a word to me."

"Jack," Robby tried again.

"I even stole into Manning House once," Jack said, uttering a laugh, shaking his head and running a hand through his hair all in one nervous moment. "I meant to go through everything in this very room to see if you had some kind of papers. I lost my nerve at the last moment, although if I'd gone ahead I doubtless would have found the other copy of this." He pulled the folded contract from beneath his jacket and thrust it at the other man.

"Doubtless," Robby said calmly, taking the paper and setting his own drink aside to unfold it. He looked it over briefly. "Yes indeed. You most certainly would have found the other copy." He lowered the paper. "You've spent years searching for the truth, when you already suspected what it might be. Jack, why didn't you simply ask me? Did you think I'd lie to you?"

"Why didn't I ask?" Jack repeated angrily. "I tried, that one time when I was eleven, and you changed the subject to horses, of all things, and afterward behaved as if I'd never mentioned the matter."

"I meant," Robby said with a shake of his head, "later, when you were older. How could I have explained it to you when you were so very young? And when I hadn't your parents' permission to say anything? None of us ever imagined that you'd see our resemblance when you were yet a child. But all these years, since you've become a man, you've never come to me with your suspicions."

"And you never came to me," Jack retorted. "Why didn't you *tell* me, Robby, rather than wait for me to ask? Why didn't anyone tell me? My parents, and you—why the hell didn't any of you give me the truth when you knew I must have wanted it?"

Robby sighed. "Sit down and calm yourself, Jack."

"No, damn you. You're a few years too late to be exerting a parent's authority over me." He felt childish, foolish. Hot tears needled at his eyes. "God," he muttered, rubbing a hand over his face. "I'm sorry." He turned away, striving to master himself. "Sorry, Robby."

"It's all right." Robby's voice was gentle, soothing. "I understand. Truly. You feel betrayed, and rightly so, because your mother and father and I kept the truth from you. I always wanted to tell you, especially when you grew older and the resemblance between us became so much greater. But your parents made me promise I'd say nothing unless you directly asked, and even then only if neither of them was alive to do the teliing themselves." He set a comforting hand on Jack's shoulder. "What you're feeling now is understandable, but I assure you we had the best of motives. None of us wanted to bring you pain."

"Did you know that I was searching for the truth?"

"I did," Robby admitted. "I had hoped you'd eventually come to your senses and give it up. It does little good for you to know who your actual father is, not when you had Miles and Dorothy Sommerton for parents. Do you think they loved you any less because you weren't born of them? Can you possibly think that they loved David better because he was?"

The tears came then, seeping out beneath his lids despite his desperate efforts to hold them back. Even with the proof of the contract in his hands, he'd yet hoped for some explanation, some miracle, to make him what he wanted to be. Their son, and not his. He had no claim to Miles and Dorothy now, or to David, just as he had no claim to his name and title. He felt as if they had died again, and he knew the pain of their loss so deeply that his heart ached with it.

Robby's hand squeezed hard on his shoulder. "Jack, you were their greatest delight. What further proof can you ask than that they were so fiercely determined you should never know the truth? Do you know what your father told me when I submitted that we should tell you? He grew angry—if you can believe such a thing, for I certainly could not. Miles was always the gentlest and sweetest of men. But he grew truly angry when I spoke of the matter and told me that *he* was your father and no other man would claim you as such."

Jack squeezed his eyes shut tightly against the tide of emotion the words wrought. "Did he say that?" he murmured thickly.

"That and a great deal more. And your mother with him. She was even angrier than he was."

Jack shook his head. "Not Mother." It was impossible. "She never once raised her voice in my hearing, not even when I was at my worst."

"She raised it that night, I assure you. They were both fully irate at the thought that anyone else might lay a claim to you or that the rumors surrounding you should be given any credence. In the face of all that, how could I go against their wishes? They were dear to me too, and I had given them my promise to follow their bidding in the matter. At least insofar as my approaching you about it. If you should be the one to ask me, however, then they allowed that I could speak freely. Do you want the truth, Jack?"

Jack wiped his face with the palm of one hand, then drew in a deep, settling breath and turned to face him.

"Yes."

"I want you to know this one thing, and believe it," Robby said solemnly. "I have always loved you dearly and should have been glad above all things to be able to call you my son. But I cannot claim that honor. I'm not your father."

Jack stared at him in stunned silence. After a stilted moment he reached out and fingered the contract that Robby yet held.

"It is proof only that I took you from Mrs. Toby and bought her silence," Robby said. "That's all. The actual truth is much harder. For me, still, it's hard. Will you sit with me and listen to it?"

Numb, Jack nodded, and followed Robby to the chairs to sit.

"I wanted you to come here to my study so that you could see the portrait of my father," Robby said. "So that you might see the very strong resemblance between him and yourself—"

"Merciful God, Robby," Jack said, his voice filled with horror, "you're not going to tell me that *he's* my father." He actually felt faint at the idea.

"Oh, no, my heavens. Goodness, no." Robby chuckled with pure amusement. "He was dead two years before you were even conceived, my boy. Goodness me." He laughed again. "I only wanted you to see that the family resemblance is quite strong, also that it leaps about a bit. My brother, Edward, for instance, didn't look at all like either myself or our father. He took after our mother."

"What's that got to do with it?" Jack asked.

Robby shifted uncomfortably and seemed to be seeking the right words. "I suppose what I'm trying to say is that you may have inherited your features through your father but that they go somewhat further back—to your grandfather, of whom you're the spitting image.''

Jack shook his head in incomprehension. "The fifth earl is my grandfather then, but if you're not my father, then how—''

"Edward," Robby said bluntly. "My brother Edward is—was—your father. Or your sire, I should say, as he never behaved as a father on your behalf."

Jack's mouth gaped, and he stared at Robby in complete shock.

"Lucky didn't take after Edward either," Robby went on, "from which you might derive some small consolation."

"But it's . . . *impossible.*"

"I know," Robby said sympathetically. "However, it's true."

"But he was a murderer," Jack murmured. "He killed his own wife. Lucky's mother. And I don't look anything at all like him."

"No, but neither does Lucky, and as I said, you do look like him." Robby nodded at the painting above them.

"Oh, dear God," Jack said with dawning understanding. "If it's true, then Lucky and I are—''

"Brothers." Robby nodded. "You are, although Lucky doesn't know it. I didn't tell you the truth because your parents wouldn't let me, and I didn't tell him the truth because he didn't need to know any more evil about his father. It was more than enough that he'd killed his mother, don't you think?"

Jack felt as if he'd been dropped off an extraordinarily high cliff. "I don't know what to think."

"I'll tell you the full of it, and you'll understand perfectly well. I suppose it's best to start with that gentleman there." He looked at the portrait again. "My father. He died when I was but eighteen, leaving me in charge of my unruly brother, who was only a year younger. My father could hardly control Edward when he was alive, and I did little better after he was dead. Edward had been betrothed to Lucky's mother since he was a lad, but had not yet met her. He was convinced that he'd formed a lasting passion for the daughter of one of our neighbors, Squire Reventry. You know him well. And his family.''

"Yes, of course," Jack said, his thoughts tumbling. "You always made certain that Lucky and I went to visit at Reventry Hall when we were at Bryland. You mean to say that Squire Reventry is my grandfather? That Lara was one of his daughters?''

Robby set a very direct, level gaze upon him. "You must promise me, on your honor, Jack, that you'll never reveal to him or his family what I'm telling you now. You'll understand when I've told you about Lara. I made the contract with Mrs. Toby because of her. Lara made me promise, you see, and I'll tell you nothing more without yours.''

"You have it.''

Robby smiled at him. "You'll not regret it. She was a lovely girl, your mother. Lara Reventry. I'm glad to speak to you of her at last. A beautiful, perfectly lovely girl, she was. I was half in love with her myself, although she was some years younger than me. If I'd had any idea that Edward was bedding her I'd most likely have beaten him senseless. But he was in love with her, or so he swore, and meant to marry her. He went to break the betrothal between himself and Letitia Barrington, and that was the fatal mistake.''

"He fell in love with her instead," Jack said.

Robby sighed and stood to fetch their drinks. "Unfortunately for himself and Letitia and Lara, yes." He put Jack's drink in his hand and took his seat again. "Madly, desperately in love, which was a condition that would lead him in later years to kill not only his unfaithful wife and her lover, but also himself. But I get ahead of myself. Edward met Letitia and determined that not only would he wed her, he would do it as soon as he possibly could, despite the fact that he was only nineteen and she only seventeen. He returned to Bryland Park to await her father's decision and consoled his loneliness for her by continuing his attentions to your mother.''

"Lara Reventry," Jack said.

"Yes. And Lara, poor girl, yet believed that they were to be married. How could she know any differently," Robby asked, "when he never told her otherwise?" He gave a dismal shake of his head. "Edward was my brother, and a good man in his way—which I don't expect you to believe, as you never knew him—but he was, in all truth, a tremendous coward. He couldn't bring himself to tell Lara that he was going to be wed until the very day that it happened. And by then she was already pregnant with you.''

Jack sat back in his chair.

"Lucky is four months younger than me," he said at last.

"Yes. He was conceived a few months after his parents' marriage, and you just before it. Lara came to Bryland after the wedding, looking for Edward. She said nothing to me of her condition, but I knew something was far amiss, for she was terribly distraught. She left a note for Edward, poor girl, and begged me to forward it to him. I did as she asked, sending the note on its way to Italy, where Edward had taken Letitia for a honeymoon. By this time she was nearly two months gone with child and must have lived in daily dread of beginning to show. Lara came to me several times after that, desperate for word from Edward, but there had been none.''

"Her family didn't know that she was pregnant?"

"No," Robby said, "and there was the great sadness of it. The Reventrys are a proud family, with a long and noble history. A finer lineage you'd be hard put to find in all of Great Britain. That being so, Lara couldn't have wanted them to know about her predicament. When I think of it now, how she must have suffered, how she must have prayed that Edward would at least lend her some manner of assistance, my heart aches dearly for her. That she chose to leave her home, her family, and make her way to London to support herself and her child speaks more than words can of how desperate she was to keep the truth from them."

At this, Jack sat forward. "I know something of what she suffered after arriving in London. She was half-starved when she at last turned to prostitution. It must have been her last choice."

"It always is for such girls, is it not?" Robby sipped at his drink. "I've long admired your care of such women, Jack. You've done it for her sake, have you not? She would have been very pleased, I think."

"How did you discover that she was pregnant?"

"Edward wrote me, at last, from Italy. You may rightfully accuse him of being a selfish bastard, but he did write at once upon receiving the missive I'd forwarded from Lara, and he begged me to take care of her, to do everything that I might for both her and the child. By then, however, Lara had disappeared. Her family had no idea where she'd gone—they were terribly distraught simply by that alone, and I couldn't add to it by exposing her reason for leaving. So I set out in search of her myself.

"Now, you must understand, Jack, that I was very young and scared to death of the entire situation. I had no idea of where to look for Lara, or what to do with her when I did find her. That being the case, the moment I arrived in London I sought help. Your father's help, to be precise. The Earl of Rexley had been my own father's closest friend, despite the difference in their ages, and had helped me through a great deal after Father's death. It was natural that I should seek his aid, and he and Dorothy were more than glad to give it. They told me that when I found Lara I should bring her to them, and they would make certain that she and her child had every care. They had no children of their own and thought that they would never be blessed with any. To help a young mother in trouble would have given them great joy, as you surely know."

"It was their favorite form of charity," Jack murmured, gazing at his folded hands. "Mother always told me, from my earliest memories, that we must help those less fortunate, especially children and their mothers. You said that I've done what I have for such women because of Lara, and that's partly true, but in all truth I did it more for Mother. Because she would have wanted me—and David, too, if he'd lived—to follow her own example." He frowned thoughtfully. "How did you finally manage to find Lara?"

"Mrs. Toby," Robby said. "She'd heard of the award I was offering for word of Lara and sent me a missive at nearly the last moment, telling me where I could find her. I arrived only hours before your mother died, Jack. It was the worst moment of my life, to see Lara lying so near to death, so pale and weak, and to know that Edward was the cause of it. Edward and my own stupidity in not reining him in as I should have done. She could hardly speak, so little was her strength. She asked only two things of me: to take care of you for all of your life, and to never let her family know of her shame. She made me swear on my very honor to fulfill these promises, and I gave her my word. I stayed with her until her last moments, and all her thoughts, Jack, were of you. Her beautiful baby, she called you. Over and again she said it. It grieved her deeply to leave you, even in my care. I have often wished that I could have eased her fears by telling her that you were to have such a fine mother in Dorothy. Lara would have been so glad to know it, but I didn't know myself, in that moment, what I was going to do with you."

"You took me to them, though? My parents?"

"I did indeed, after I'd given Mrs. Toby a sufficient amount of money and obtained her signature on that contract. I must say that I was terrified when she put you into my arms, pretty a baby as you were. You were wet and hungry and squalling as if you'd been grievously harmed and would never get over it. I was frightened just to hold you, and the drive to Brannard was the longest in my life. I could only pray that Miles and Dorothy would help me do something with you, for I hadn't the slightest notion." He laughed at the memory.

"Oh, but Dorothy was wonderful. She took one look at you—poor, pathetic little bundle that you were—and lifted you out of my arms at once and into her own. And you, so hungry and wretched, only screamed the harder. I can't think how it is that she and Miles fell so in love with you, but they seemed to know without any doubts that they wanted you.

"At first I was fairly confused about how the thing could be done, for you were my nephew and Edward's son, and I suppose I had some idea that he or I should have you. But I don't think I could have wrested you away from Dorothy, even if I'd tried. She had latched on and wasn't going to let go. So"—he shrugged and lifted his hands—"what else could I have done that would have been better for you? And for Lara, whose body I yet had to convey back to her family? Leaving you with Miles and Dorothy seemed the only answer to every problem."

Jack raised his eyebrows. "You took Lara back to the

Reventrys? What on earth did you tell them about what had happened to her? They must have been horribly shocked and distressed.''

''To have Lara brought home in a coffin, yes, of course they were. As to what I told them, I lied, and have no shame for it. I told them that Lara had run away to London because of her unhappiness over Edward's marriage and had found work for herself as a lady's companion. She was too ashamed to write her family and tell them of her location, but when she had fallen ill she'd sent a note to me, begging me to come to her. I found her on her deathbed and promised that I'd take her body home to Reventry Hall. They believed every word and never questioned me further, though I imagine they've wondered if there was more to the tale. Especially Squire Reventry, although he's never said as much. But it was better not to probe, I think. They were able to bury Lara with all the reverence and dignity that she deserved.''

Jack ran a hand through his hair. ''It's unbelievable,'' he said. ''Squire Reventry—that whole family. I've known them, spoken with them. As if they were simply acquaintances. And they're my own family. Lara is buried right there, and I've never known.''

''And you'll continue to behave as if you don't,'' Robby cautioned. ''It would devastate the squire and his family to know the truth. Lara wanted to spare them that. And in all truth, Jack, they're not your own kin. Your family consists of Sommertons on your father's side and Balians on your mother's. You have every legal and moral right to claim them, just as they have always claimed you.''

''Have they?'' Jack asked tartly, emptying his glass and setting it aside.

''Yes, they have,'' Robby said with equal measure. ''You know they have.''

"I suppose that's true," Jack admitted, gazing at the fire. "How did my parents manage that? Why haven't any of my numerous cousins tried to claim the title?"

"For the simple reason that nothing could be proved. Miles and Dorothy left Brannard the very night I brought you to them, not even waiting for their things to be packed. They took you back to Rexley Hall at once and put out word that Dorothy was with child. It may seem silly—it certainly seemed that way to me, but strangely enough, it worked. She remained completely out of sight for six months, and they received no visitors during that time. Another year passed before they returned to London, and by then rumors were so confused about your actual date of birth that the whole thing passed off very well. Until you were quite a bit older and began to look very much like a Manning. Then rumors began to fly hither and yon, and no stopping them. Which was especially unfortunate for your dear mother, because people assumed that she and I had—well, you've heard what's been said about some supposed affair that led to your creation. But it was too late for those disgusting lies to create any harm. Miles and Dorothy had legally adopted you and made you their heir, and if anyone in the family wished to contest it, they were to be written out of any inheritance at once. Aside from that, it seems to me that all of your relatives like you very well. I can't imagine that a one of them has ever so much as hinted that you've no right to the earldom, have they?"

Jack thought of his family, of uncles, aunts, cousins. He had always felt well loved by them all.

"No," he said quietly. "They've not. I've been very fortunate." He hated the idea of losing the only family he'd ever known. He would miss them all terribly, just as he would miss Robby and Lucky and even scatterbrained Wulf. "I would have liked to know that Lucky was my brother all these years. It's still so hard to accept. Edward Bryland!'' He made a doleful sound. ''I don't know that I ever met the man while he was still alive. Or even saw him. But you—you've been there since I can remember, Robby. How is that I never met your brother, when you were my godfather?''

''Dorothy and Miles made certain to keep you away from him and him from you, although he never knew you existed. I lied to him, too, when he at last returned from Italy and asked about Lara. I told him exactly what I'd told Squire Reventry and said that there had been no child. He probably assumed she'd made up the entire story of being pregnant in a desperate attempt to ruin his marriage. I don't think he even visited Lara's grave to pay his respects. He was by that time consumed by his sick passion for Letitia.'' Robby lifted his glass and sipped from it, then gazed at Jack reflectively. ''As to Lucky, if you wish to tell him, you may do so. He'll keep the truth to himself, as we both know. But you must ask yourself whether it would do anyone any good, especially to him. He couldn't love you better than he does now, knowing that you're related by blood. You are already as close as any two brothers could be.''

''I suppose I'll have to tell him,'' Jack said, still gazing at the fire. ''He'll wonder why I've stepped down from the title, and I can't lie to him. I'll go away, of course, so as not to be an embarrassment.''

''Step down from the title?'' Robby repeated. ''Go away?''

''I'm not the true Earl of Rexley, Robby. I'm a fraud, despite the fact that circumstances aren't quite so bad as I had believed. My birth is somewhat respectable. I had always assumed Lara was a common prostitute, although there is little consolation in knowing that she was forced by circumstances into such an awful trade. But regardless of the quality of her lineage, and Edward Bryland's, I'm yet a bastard and must accept that and who I truly am.'' He rose and wearily leaned one hand against the mantel. ''If Gwendolyn will have me after all this, we'll go back to her home. To Boston.'' He uttered a bitter laugh. ''The United States is the last place I should have ever thought to live, but I cannot lose her. Which isn't particularly noble of me, I realize, for I've never worked at any useful trade and haven't any way to support her. But I'm just selfish enough to bind her to me forever and do what I must to take care of her.'' He heard Robby getting up and glanced at him. ''Perhaps I'll indenture myself to some kind of smith. Do you fancy me being any good at molding silver? Or iron? What the devil are you doing?''

Robby was searching about his desk, wrathfully scattering papers in his purpose.

''I'm looking for something to beat you with. Something heavy and sharp, which will inflict a great deal of pain.''

''Robby—''

His godfather turned about in a furious motion.

''You stupid, wretched, *ungrateful* boy. I have never in my life been so ashamed of a man. You dare to stand there and insult your parents and all that they did for you and gave you by throwing it away as if it were some kind of . . . of worthless filth!'' He slammed a hand on his table with loud force. ''By God, you will *not* do so, sir. I'll beat you with my bare hands if I must to knock some sense into you.'' He put up two fists and approached Jack with menace.

Jack had never seen him look so angry. He put his hands up to ward him off. ''Robby, for pity's sake, calm yourself.''

''Only after I've set your ears to ringing, Jack Sommerton.'' He took a swing at him, which had Jack stumbling away and knocking his chair aside. "Stand still and take what you've got coming to you," Robby demanded. "You'll not malign your parents in my hearing. Ever!" He took another swing, following as Jack backed away in disbelief.

"I don't malign them!"

"All because your tender feelings have been hurt," Robby said furiously, circling him. "Poor Jack, taken off the streets where he might have starved to death, or worse, and adopted by a loving family. Poor, poor Jack." He struck out quickly, catching Jack in the chin and knocking him sideways against a wall.

The blow stung, but only enough to shock Jack with the fact that Robby had actually hit him. He shook his head to clear it and rubbed his chin to ease the pain.

"You mistake me, Robby," he said insistently. "It's for the love of their memory that I want to make things right. I never should have been the earl."

"You were *always* meant to be the earl!" Robby returned heatedly.

"David should have gained the title," Jack told him. "And he would have done so if he'd lived."

Robby dropped his fists. "What a singularly *stupid* thing to say. What on earth makes you think David would have inherited the title if he'd lived?"

Jack leaned against the wall, fingering his chin. "Because he was the legitimate heir."

"Jack, I think your wits have gone wandering. Perhaps you need another blow or two to straighten you out. Do you recall your parents raising David to be the earl?"

"No, but—"

"If I remember correctly, it was something you used to complain about regularly, that David had so much more freedom than you, as you were the heir and he was not."

"I don't know why they raised me as the heir," Jack

argued. "But it was a mistake. David was the legitimate son."

"Sit down." Robby pointed at the chair. "And be quiet. I'll tell you this once, and once only."

Jack obediently sat. Robby set his hands behind his back and paced toward the fire.

"David was a wonderful young man," he said, "and your parents loved him dearly. But he would have made a dreadful earl. No, don't speak. I'm telling you the truth, and you know it. I don't malign your brother by saying that he was far too placid by nature to desire such a position of responsibility. He would have hated every moment of it and made a great muddle of things, I have no doubt. You, on the other hand, are a marvelous earl. Miles and Dorothy were terribly proud and relieved to know that you would carry on in the tasks set before you with every capability. And you have done so, just as they'd hoped.

"Now. I accept your sense that you have no right to the title. There is some small merit to the argument regarding your birth, but birth, as we both know, is not always the best selector of a man's worth. Especially when it comes to the aristocracy."

"Robert Bryland," Jack said tartly, "*you're* the one who, since I can remember, has always gone on and on about families and lineage and the like."

"Very true," Robby admitted, "but, then, I'm something of a snob. Besides, if it comes to that, we've already ascertained that your lineage is impeccable. My brother may have been a scoundrel at best, but he was well-born, and no denying it. Jack, for pity's sake, put all that aside. Your parents always intended that you would inherit the earldom. It was given to you by something far more honest than birth. It was given to you out of love, and not so much as a gift but as a charge."

He sat down in the chair opposite Jack and spoke more

gently. "They expected you to fulfill all their hopes, to carry on the Sommerton name with honor and pride. You were their son, Jack, in every way that counts. Just as much as David was. They would have gladly died for you. What better proof could a child ask of his parents' love?"

Jack closed his eyes, feeling tears threaten again.

"They gave you all that they could," Robby murmured, "including your very life. In return they asked you to do this for them. To take on the earldom and all that comes with it and to discharge the task to the best of your ability. Will you throw everything back in their faces by running away, Jack? Will you do that to those two people who loved you so well? Could you possibly be so filled with ingratitude?"

"No." Jack shook his head. "No." He opened his eyes and looked at his uncle.

"Well, then, my lord," said Robby, taking one of Jack's hands and squeezing it in his firm grip. "You'd best be the man your parents made of you and get on with fulfilling your duties. You've a great deal more to accomplish for them. And for yourself. And that includes, I think, marrying a particularly pretty American of whom they would have greatly approved and filling your nursery with a variety of the grandchildren that they always wanted."

Jack smiled past the tears that misted his vision.

"Yes," he said, and laughed. "I will."

Chapter Twenty-Four

❧❧❧

$\mathcal{J}$ack left Robby and went directly to Barrington, triumphant in mood and ready to claim his woman. Lucky greeted him in the entryway and, before he could deliver the scold that he'd opened his mouth to speak, found himself taken up in a brisk hug.

"What on earth is that for?" he demanded, straightening his clothes after Jack put him down. "And where have you been? I've been searching every dismal alleyway in London, looking for you."

"Lucky," Jack replied somewhat giddily, setting an arm about his brother and friend and leading him toward the study as if he were in his own home, "you're a grand fellow and a good friend. Better than a brother to me, you are. Or as good as. You've always wanted a brother, haven't you? Just consider me yours."

"Perhaps I'd have done better to want a sister," Lucky said, looking at him suspiciously. "You're in a good mood for a man who's got a lot of explaining to do. What's going on?" He sniffed him. "You're not drunk, are you?"

"Not at all. But you may wish me every happiness." He opened Lucky's study door and ushered him in. "I'm about to become related to the Earl of Kerlain, if you can believe such a thing. Through marriage." He shut the door behind him, closing in Lucky's exclamation.

Professor Wells granted him an interview half an hour later, and ten minutes after that, Gwendolyn was escorted by Lucky's own hand to join them. Professor Wells kissed and congratulated his daughter, told her without hesitation to be good and say yes, and then left them alone.

"Jack?" She looked at him expectantly.

Jack took her into his arms and kissed her, then smiled and said, "Gwendolyn, my dear, I've come to grant your fondest wish and make an honest woman of you."

In retrospect, it probably wasn't the wisest manner in which to propose. Her expression became markedly cool and she disengaged herself from his embrace.

"Have you? Your visit with Lord Manning went well, I gather?"

He supposed she'd want to hear about that before accepting his proposal, and so he told her, briefly, what had transpired between himself and Robby.

"And so you see, Gwendolyn, there are no further impediments to our marrying. You've run me to ground, just as you always said you would, and I've magnanimously decided to concede victory to you."

She eyed him steadily and replied, "Thank you for such a lovely offer, my lord. I shall consider it with all due respect and let you know of my answer sometime in the near future. Now, if you'll excuse me, I must go and sort my stockings."

He was almost too shocked to move. Almost. She didn't make it to the door before he reached her.

"Gwendolyn, what is this?" he demanded, swinging her about to face him. "You've been telling me that we were going to marry almost since the moment we met, and now you're going to go off and *consider* it?"

"Yes," she said, lifting her chin and pulling her arm free of his grasp. "While I sort stockings. Good day, my lord."

She made for the door again. He stopped her again.

"I don't know what mischief's gotten into that facile brain of yours, but I'm not going to put up with it. We're going to be married, damn you. You love me, Gwendolyn Wells."

This time she lifted a hand to lay it carefully on his chest. "I do love you, Jack. I'll never deny it, no matter how angry I may be with you, which, considering your astonishing thickheadedness, will be often."

"Then say yes," he told her, pleading, "and we'll be married, just as you wished."

She sighed and dropped her hand. "Thickheaded you may be, Jack Sommerton, but not stupid. I'll think about your charming proposal, and you think on it as well. One of us will surely come to a sensible conclusion. Good day."

She left him standing there, shaking his head with incomprehension. Lucky and Professor Wells had been standing just outside the door and looked at him questioningly.

"She said she'd think about it," he told them, whereupon Professor Wells sat down in the nearest chair, set his head in his hands, and said woefully, "She'll be the death of me. The very death of me."

Jack left Barrington and went to White's with the intention of drinking until he finally understood women, though he privately believed it would be a futile effort, and was eventually tracked down there by Kerlain.

"Well met, good fellow," he greeted, slapping Jack on the back and taking a seat beside him. "You've come home at last. Thought Lucky and Lord Manning would pull all their hair out before you finally floated to the surface. I have news for you, both good and bad; which do you want first?"

"Things could hardly be worse," Jack told him morosely. "You might as well tell me the bad news."

"Very well. I've just been to see Gwennie, which made me come here to look for you, and she's mad as a bear with a tick in her ear. Says you're a idiotic, thickheaded fool and all other sorts of unpleasant things. I wouldn't try to approach her for a day or two if I were you. She'd probably be glad to break your nose if she could get close enough."

"Thank you," Jack said dryly. "I believe I already knew all that. What's the good news?"

"I went to see Robby before I went to see Gwennie, and he and I have matters regarding Walsh settled. Or at least we will have once he calls in a few parliamentary favors. No one will discover the truth about your private situation. Walsh will be quietly transported to Jamaica, where he will serve an indefinite indenture to a particularly nasty plantation owner, and all of his various enterprises will be shut down. We're attempting to find the whorehouses he's sold children to, but what we'll do with the brats once they're found is impossible to say. I suppose they'll go to workhouses, which is hardly much better, is it?"

"Send them to me," Jack told him. "To Rexley Hall. I've recently decided to build several new children's homes, to be dedicated to the memory of my parents and my brother, David. They'll be good places, I vow, where unwanted children will have every decent care and opportunity available. Regardless of their parentage."

"That sounds promising," Kerlain said. "I should like to support your many good causes, Rexley, when I've at last got my own affairs in order and Castle Kerlain rebuilt. Have you told Gwennie about your plans yet? She'll be thrilled, of course. Loves children, she does. Always has. But I've told you that before, I recall." His tone was good-natured and teasing, but Jack wasn't in the mood for it.

"I'm not even sure she's going to marry me now," he said grumpily, staring into his wineglass. "Although she will, or I swear I'll kidnap her and take her off to Gretna Green. I *will*," he insisted when Kerlain laughed.

"I can't think it will be necessary, Jack. She's madly in love with you and has meant to have you from the very moment she met you."

"She certainly didn't act like it an hour ago. Women," he muttered. "Gad."

"You've just made her angry with your clumsy proposal. That's all."

Jack sat up straight. "Clumsy! It wasn't anything of the kind."

"Here, I'll show you something that will make you feel better. Hello, you, stop a moment." He waved down a passing servant. "Fetch the betting book for Lord Rexley, if you please. He wants it."

"For pity's sake, Kerlain, I don't want the damned betting book."

"Yes, you do." To the servant he said, "Bring it at once."

A few moments later he had the large, leather-bound ledger opened on the table.

"You haven't had a look in here lately, thank God, or I'd have been done for. Every day I've expected you to show up at my meager door and plow Lloyd down in an attempt to murder me. Here it is." Kerlain pointed to a particular passage. "Do you see? *A lady's wager*."

Jack bent to read the entry. Then he looked at Kerlain.

"You did this? After you swore you'd never involve me in your wagering?"

"Not me, old man. Gwennie. She asked me to enter it in the books for her. However, I do admit to putting my money on her." He smiled angelically. "A surer bet I've never run across. Well, other than the one I made with Lucky about him and Lady Clara."

Jack could only stare at him and blink.

"The trouble with you, Jack," Kerlain went on pleasantly, shutting the book, "is that you don't understand women. Now, me, I've had so much trouble with the creatures that I could write a book on the subject. Gwennie means to have you, but not when you make such a daft proposal as you did this afternoon. Come, now, think a moment. Do you believe a woman's going to say yes when you've just finished telling her that she's run you to ground?"

"She's been chasing me," Jack said faintly. "I thought she'd find it amusing to hear me admit defeat."

"Oh, Jack," Kerlain said, groaning. "You poor, demented cretin. I'm sure she will, after you're married. Then you can tease her about it to your heart's content, and if I know Gwennie, she'll laugh her head off. But when you ask a woman to *marry* you, you should at least mention the usual reason."

Jack was flustered. "I'm not going to say *that* to her when I'm asking her to marry me. She already knows I want her."

Now it was Kerlain's turn to stare. Then he laughed, long and hard, going so far as to slap his knee and draw the attention of every other man in the room. By the time he'd gotten himself under control, Jack was ready to kill him.

"I m-meant," Kerlain stammered, chuckling, "that you should tell her you l-love her, you great fool. Oh, gad." He wiped at his eyes and grinned at his companion. "You didn't tell her that you love her."

"Of course I told her that I love her," Jack said indignantly. "It was the first thing out of my mouth. I'm certain of it."

"Well, she didn't hear it, so you'd best go back and try again and make sure to speak more plainly. Heaven knows what it means to a woman to be properly asked for her hand."

"It means something to me too," Jack muttered. "I've only done it the once. And wasn't even given an answer. But I take your meaning. You may be certain that the next time I do it she'll understand completely. You'll collect on this particular wager, Kerlain."

"Good," his companion said, patting the top of the closed ledger. "It will be my last, pray God. I'll stay in London until your wedding, and then I'll be heading home to Kerlain. For good, I hope."

Jack looked at him curiously. "You make it sound as if that were something unusual. It's your familial estate, Lad. Surely you could have gone there any time you pleased."

"No." Kerlain shook his head. "I was banished from paradise three years ago and not allowed to return until I had paid in full for sins committed. Or at least made enough money to pay for them." He smiled down at the ledger, on which his hand yet rested. "I don't believe the one who did the banishing ever thought I'd manage to come up with the necessary funds to redeem myself, but she's in for something of a surprise. One that I shall relish delivering."

Jack heard the word *she* at the unfortunate moment when he was taking a swallow of wine, which he subsequently choked on.

"*She?*" he repeated between fits of coughing.

"Yes," Kerlain replied mildly, standing and patting Jack's shoulder. "Don't strangle on the word, my friend.

Let me know how things go with Gwennie. And remember—I've got a small fortune riding on the outcome.''

Gwendolyn wasn't asleep when she heard Jack enter her room late that night. Her eyes were closed and she was resting, but when she heard him drawing near enough to touch, she said, "If you've come to discuss clocks, I'm not in the mood."

He wasn't smiling when she opened her eyes.

"I haven't," he said, reaching down, "come to discuss clocks."

She gasped as the covers were tossed back and his arms slipped beneath her body to lift her out of the bed.

"I've come," he went on, striding toward the fire, "to give you another chance to listen to my proposal. Now." He put her in a chair and stood back, looking at her. "If there's one thing I've learned about you, Gwendolyn Wells, soon to be Sommerton, also Lady Rexley, as well as the Countess of Rexley, is that you're a damned managing female. Going to give me time to think about my proposal, eh? Going to think about it yourself, were you?"

She folded her hands primly in her lap and regarded him politely. "Yes. You've got it perfectly right, Jack, dear."

"Have I, Gwendolyn, dear?" he said. He shrugged out of his jacket and tossed it on the opposite chair, then began unbuttoning his waistcoat. "I'm going to get *you* right if it's the last thing I accomplish in life. Which, considering the way matters have been proceeding with us, it probably will be. I can see it all now, lying on my deathbed"—the waistcoat joined his jacket and he started to untie his cravat—"I'll gasp my last words, 'I understand her at last!' and then die a happy man. Come and help me take these blasted boots off."

"Jack," she said, kneeling to do as he requested.
"Have you come to make love to me?"

"Yes, and don't give me any argument about it, for I
haven't come to argue any more than I've come to discuss
clocks." He took her by both shoulders suddenly and
dragged her onto his lap, where he proceeded to kiss her
with all the desperation that he'd held within since she'd
walked out on him earlier in the day. "But first," he murmured when he'd at last pulled away, "I'm going to tell
you that you're the most beautiful female I've ever set
sight on, that I've been scared to death of you from the
moment I met you, and that I love you deeply, fully, and
completely. Now there's only one thing that I want to
know in return."

She lovingly cradled his cheek in the palm of one hand.
"What's that, dear?"

"Have you known how I've felt all along? And when I
proposed this afternoon?"

She smiled. "Yes."

"God save me," he muttered before finding her mouth
again, "you'll drive me insane yet."

An hour later Gwendolyn felt as if she was the one
who'd gone insane.

She was nearly twenty-four years old and, she'd assumed, possessed of more than the average experience of
men. But she'd been afraid. Of what Jack was going to do
to her. And no matter how gentle he was, or how slow and
understanding, she'd not been able to relax. When he'd
removed the remainder of his garments, she'd covered her
face like a child and lain on the bed as rigid as a board.

"Come, love." There was humor in his voice as he'd
climbed onto the mattress. Gwendolyn had drawn in a
long breath when she'd felt the heat of his body pressing
against her own. "Surely you're not afraid of me?"

She was. Deathly afraid. But she said, as if he'd

gravely insulted her, "Of course not. Don't be silly. Afraid—ha!"

"Then look at me, darling. You've seen part of me before. And touched too." His voice was warm, coaxing. She felt his fingertips on her chin and couldn't hold back a squeak. "Sweetheart, shall I go away? We can wait until our wedding night."

"No!" she said quickly, afraid he'd truly leave. "Don't you dare go away, Jack Sommerton. You started this, and I want you to"—she swallowed—"finish it. Now. Or I'll never forgive you." Her hands were still over her eyes. "You never mind me. I'll follow your lead. Go ahead with whatever you . . . usually do."

He laughed. "*Usually* isn't a word I think of when you're involved, darling, but very well. Don't look if you don't want to. I'll take care of . . . whatever." He started to untie her nightgown and she squeaked again. It took ten minutes to get the dratted thing off, over her head, and still she kept her hands over her face.

He was ominously silent, not touching her, and at last she parted her fingers to peep through them. He was smiling down at her, so handsome and dear to her that she felt her heart pounding violently beneath her breast—her naked breast, just as the rest of her was naked.

"What's the matter?" she asked. "Is it that bad?"

He chuckled and, one by one, pulled her hands from her face. "Life with you," he said, kissing her, "will never be dull, my beloved. Gwendolyn"—his tone was as gentle as his touch when his hand stroked her, starting at her shoulder and petting softly down her arm—"let me love you."

He loved her tenderly, kissing her with long, slow kisses, touching her breasts with his hands and mouth until she cried out from the pleasure of it, stroking her everywhere with knowing hands, gentling her fears, letting her touch in turn.

"Yes, love.'' He whispered encouragement as she grew bolder. "I'm your fate. Yours. Don't be afraid.''

How beautiful he was, hard and lean, so masculine, silky smooth and hot. Her fears melted away, along with her shyness, when she realized that he would let her do as she pleased, kiss and caress, and he'd neither laugh nor protest.

When he finally came into her she was no longer afraid, not even of the pain, which was brief. He was her fate—just as she'd told him, just as he'd admitted—and she was his. She'd searched for him, him only, all these years, and now at last he was hers.

Lying beside him now, warm and contented, she sighed and toyed with his fingers, which lay upon his chest, as her head did.

"I didn't hurt you, did I?'' she asked.

He smiled against her hair. "I think I'm the one who's supposed to ask that.''

She grinned. "You made more noise than I did. I thought for a moment that you were going to faint.''

"So did I,'' he said, chuckling. "Good thing I put the chair against the door, or Lucky might have burst in upon us at the worst possible moment.''

She sat up. "Oh, heavens. But they're all the way down the hall. Do you think he heard?''

Jack ran a finger down the curve of her waist. "The whole house probably did. Your father doesn't carry a pistol about, do you think?''

She lay down with a groan. "We're ruined.''

"Not at all. Just consider that you've won your wager.''

Gwendolyn sat up again. "You know?''

He nodded. And smiled. "Every last detail. The only

other thing I want to know is if you'll marry me by special license, or if you're going to drag me through days of hell and misery in order to have a large wedding.''

"Do you dislike large weddings, Jack, dear?"

"I dislike being away from you, Gwendolyn, dear. I won't make love to you again if you want a formal fete, not until we're married. It wouldn't be fair to any child we may create, if we haven't already created one." His fingers touched her belly.

"You won't make love to me again?"

"Not until you're Lady Rexley," he said in a determined but wavering tone as one of her hands stroked softly against his chest.

"Then I think," she said, bending to kiss him, "that you'd best get us a special license, Jack, dear."

His arms pulled her downward. "First thing in the morning," he whispered, "my very dear Gwendolyn."

It was difficult to know who cried harder at the wedding, Viscount Severn or the Earl of Manning.

Robby's excuse was that he always cried at weddings, being such a sentimental creature as well as terribly fond of Jack. Wulf's muddled reasons were that he was so happy for Jack, and Miss Wells looked so pretty in her dress, and also that he was put so much in mind of his own recent wedding—which had taken place only two days before, and during which he'd also cried, for many of the same muddled reasons. Bella had borne it gladly, handing him several handkerchiefs, one after the other, until the ceremony was over, much as she was doing now.

Still weak from his recent injury, Viscount Severn had been unable to take his new bride on the honeymoon to Italy that he had always dreamed of. Instead, they were to leave for Lord Severn's immense country estate to spend the remainder of the season and had only delayed their departure in order to attend Jack and Gwendolyn's wedding.

"Ain't you going to take Lady R on a wedding trip, Jack?" Wulf asked when he, Jack, Lucky, and Lad had a chance to speak privately, following the wedding breakfast. "I'm taking Bella to Italy soon as I get this blasted thing off." He indicated the sling that kept his arm pressed against his wounded shoulder. "Always wanted to see Venice and them places with Bella." He blushed, just saying her name, and glanced to where his new wife stood speaking with Gwendolyn and Clara.

"No, Gwendolyn and I are going home to Rexley Hall," Jack said. "She's longing to see Nancy and baby Kitty again, and there are several new infants that she insists she must personally oversee the care of. Loves children, she does."

"Told you," Lad said with a grin and a wink. "Just wait until you have your own." He sighed. "All these happily married men surrounding me. How very strange. It puts me much in mind of a day not so long ago when I sat with the same three men at a table in White's and proposed a certain wager." He smiled at Lucky. "And now look at you all. Especially you, Wulf. Never seen you so pleased. Things must have gone well for you on your wedding night."

Lucky covered his mouth and choked on his laughter, and Jack had to look away and clear his throat.

Wulf blushed up to the roots of his hair. "Well," he said, "Bella's an awfully nice wife. And the nicest, prettiest gel in the whole world besides." He glanced again to where she stood, an adoring expression on his face. "Wish I'd married her ten years ago, so I do."

"She would have been fifteen then," Lucky told him. "I think there's a law against such things."

"Is there?" Wulf asked. "Just as well, I suppose. She's

got me all upended, I declare. Can't even think of chemistry these past two days. Not when Bella's about. Can't think of anything but her.''

''Which is a very good thing for Bella, I daresay,'' Jack murmured, and the other men laughed.

Later, as the guests drank champagne and surrounded the newly married couple, Lad managed to sneak Bella for a walk in Barrington's sunny gardens. When they returned, Bella was smiling and holding his arm, the sight of which caused Wulf's hands to curl into fists and demand that Kerlain release her.

''Gladly,'' Kerlain said, delivering Bella to her husband. He bent to kiss her hand and said, ''I shall miss you terribly, divine Christabella, but will take heart in knowing that I leave you with one who loves you well. Wulf,'' he added quickly, before that man could lose his temper, ''good-bye. Take good care of your sweet lady wife and make certain to let me know when we may expect to congratulate you on the first of your progeny. I imagine that all of your fortunate children will be blessed with Bella's good looks and your massive brain—a set of siblings the likes of which England has never before seen.''

Wulf shook Lad's hand with bewilderment. ''You're leaving, Lad?''

''I'm going home,'' he said, ''to Kerlain. I only stayed to see Bella and Gwennie safely wed. Wish me well, Wulf. And do be good to Bella. If I didn't have other commitments, I swear I'd stay and steal her away from you.'' He winked at Bella, who blushed prettily and smiled behind her hand.

Kerlain shook hands with all those assembled and kissed most of the ladies. He hugged his cousin long and hard.

''You'll come to Kerlain for a visit, won't you, Gwennie?''

"Of course we'll come," she promised. "Jack will want to tease you for having kept him in the dark so long. I'll try to make Papa stay and come as well. You won't mind having a mad chemist in your grand estate, will you?"

"Not so long as he refrains from blowing the place to bits. It's already falling to pieces as it is."

"Kept in the dark about what?" Jack asked, standing with an arm about his wife. He accepted Lad's hand when he offered it. "You might as well tell me now and get it over with."

The Earl of Kerlain smiled charmingly. "Some secrets are best kept as long as possible. I'm glad you took my advice and married Gwennie," he added. "I knew you two would be right for each other, oh, ye of little faith."

"Just as you knew about Lucky and Clara?"

Lad shrugged. "It's a gift. One of my many. I can only pray now that I'll be able to make use of them at Kerlain. Wish me luck, my friend."

Jack did, sincerely, and watched with the others as the Earl of Kerlain took his leave.

"He should find his own woman," Wulf muttered amidst the calls of well-wishing. "And leave mine alone."

"Oh, Wulf," Bella said with a laugh, hugging his arm. "How foolish you are. Lord Kerlain doesn't want me."

"Doesn't he, by gad?"

"No, of course not," she said, sighing after the sight of the handsome earl as he rode away. "He's already married and very much in love."

Everyone standing nearby, save Lady Anna, Clara, and Gwendolyn, turned to stare at her.

"Kerlain's got a *wife*?" Jack demanded.

"Indeed, he does," Lady Clara assured him, which

caused her husband to look at her with a measure of consternation.

"You know about it, Clara?" he demanded.

"Of course she does," Lady Anna answered, to the equal consternation of her own husband. "Doesn't everyone?" She smiled conspiratorially at the other women and said, "Come along, ladies. We must help Lady Rexley to dress for her wedding journey. Quickly now. They'll want to be on their way before long"—she waved them toward the stairs, adding, sotto voce—"if I know anything about men," which set Clara, Gwendolyn, and Bella to laughing as they climbed.

"Women," Lord Callan muttered, watching them go. "Such strange creatures. I think they were laughing at *us*."

"My dear boy," said his uncle. "Don't tire yourself with thinking. They *were* laughing at us."

"Lad's married," Wulf murmured, scratching his shaggy head. "I can't believe it. I thought all these years that he was after Bella."

"He told me that he'd been banished from paradise," Jack put in quietly. "For three years. Poor fellow."

"He must love this secret wife of his," Lucky said.

"He must," Jack agreed. "I wouldn't have understood that sentiment three short months ago, but now," he said, gazing up the stairway to where his lovely American wife had disappeared, "I understand it perfectly."

He was her fate and she was his and together, he thought, longing even now for the moment when she'd walk down those same stairs to join him again, they'd make their own paradise.

His search was over.